"Through vibrant description and well-paced action, Karen Hancock creates a compelling world of both horror and hope. *Arena* gives Christian fantasy lovers something to cheer about."
—Brandilyn Collins, bestselling author of *Eyes of Elisha*

"When other books are long forgotten and out of print, I believe people will still be reading *Arena*. It's destined to be a classic."
—Rene Gutteridge, author of *Ghost Writer*

"An allegory for the third millennium! If you liked *Pilgrim's Progress* and *The Matrix*, then you'll love *Arena*."
—Randall Ingermanson, co-author of *Oxygen*

"*Arena* is a wonderful and clever allegorical tale with all the excitement of good science fiction."
—Judith Pella, author of *Written on the Wind*

"Clever, creative and full of non-stop action, *Arena* is a wonderful introduction to new writer Karen Hancock. Don't miss the opportunity to wrap your mind around this fascinating book."
—Gayle Roper, author of *Summer Shadows* and *Spring Rain*

"Karen Hancock's *Arena* sets a new benchmark for contemporary allegory—thoroughly imagined, intelligently written, and as vivid as last night's unsettling dreams. Well done!"
—Kathy Tyers, author of the FIREBIRD trilogy

KAREN HANCOCK

# ARENA

BETHANY HOUSE
MINNEAPOLIS, MINNESOTA

Published by Bethany House Publishers
A Ministry of Bethany Fellowship International
11400 Hampshire Avenue South
Bloomington, Minnesota 55438
www.bethanyhouse.com

Printed in the United States of America by
Bethany Press International, Bloomington, Minnesota 55438

**Library of Congress Cataloging-in-Publication Data**

Hancock, Karen.
    Arena / by Karen Hancock.
       p.  cm.
    ISBN 0-7642-2631-2 (pbk.)
    1. Psychology, Experimental—Fiction.  I. Title.
    PS3608.A698 A89    2002
    813'.6—dc21                    2002000969

To Kathy Tyers

KAREN HANCOCK graduated in 1975 from the University of Arizona with bachelor's degrees in Biology and Wildlife Biology. Along with writing, she is a semi-professional watercolorist and has exhibited her work in a number of national juried shows. *Arena* is her first novel. She, her husband, and their son, whom Karen homeschooled for eight years, reside in Arizona.

For discussion and further information, Karen invites you to visit her Web site at *www.kmhancock.com.*

# ACKNOWLEDGMENTS

With gratitude and appreciation . . .

To my Lord and Savior, Jesus Christ, in whom we live and move and have our being and for whom all things have been created, who alone is worthy of praise.

To Colonel R. B. Thieme, Jr., my pastor and teacher for twenty years, and to Robert R. McLaughlin, my pastor now, for their tireless devotion to the daily study and teaching of the Word of God and willingness to stand upon the truth regardless of how unpopular such a stand might be. Without their daily teaching, I never would have been able to write this book.

To Nancy Belt, Donna Henley, and Kelli Nolen, those rare and precious true friends who know how to sift the wheat from the chaff, overlook transgressions, and lift up a brother when he has fallen. You are refreshments to my soul.

To my husband, Stuart, who has labored alone for years, allowing me the time and opportunity to write, even when it appeared nothing would come of it.

To my son, Adam, who has been a joy and a privilege to raise, and whose fascination with Super Mario Brothers sparked the germ for this story.

To Kathy Tyers, for critique, encouragement, and steadfast assistance over the years.

To Steve Laube, for kindness, persistence, insightful editing, and most of all, for taking the risk.

To all the other readers and critiquers God provided before He saw fit to grant me the social validation of publication—you will never know how much satisfaction and encouragement you gave: Linda Smith; Edward Willett; Greg and Katie Solewin; Jeanette, Aimee, and Kris Ratzlaff; Lelia Foreman; Travis Langley; and Penny Olsen.

And finally, to God the Father, for His marvelous plan for my life, which includes not only seeing this book in print, but all the years of waiting for His perfect timing.

The Lord is good to those who wait for Him, to the soul who diligently seeks Him.

# CALLED

"IF YOU SEEK HIM,

HE WILL LET YOU FIND HIM..."

1 CHRONICLES 28:9

# CHAPTER

# 1

"They won't be taking blood or anything, will they?" Callie Hayes looked up from the clipboard in her hands to the dimpled youth behind the receptionist's counter.

"Our physical evaluations are noninvasive," he assured her. "Completely painless."

"For goodness' sake, Callie," Meg Riley protested beside her. "It's only a *psychology* experiment. Why are you giving him the third degree?"

"I want to know what I'm getting into this time." Callie pushed slipping wire-rim glasses back up her nose as she flashed an accusing glance at her companion.

Meg was petite, freckled, and green-eyed, her face framed by chin-length black curls. She wore a white spaghetti-strap T-shirt with blue shorts, and she'd been Callie's best friend since fourth grade. Together they'd endured adolescence, the divorce of Meg's parents, a two-year obsession with Zane Grey novels, high school, and college. After graduating from the University of Arizona four years ago, they'd both settled into a holding pattern—Meg waiting for a teaching position at one of the Tucson school districts, and Callie just waiting. It was through Meg's temporary job with the university's Psychology Department that she stumbled onto the world of the paid guinea pig. "Easy money," she dubbed it.

But Callie discovered there were *reasons* guinea pigs got paid.

*"Thirty dollars,"* Meg had promised last time, *"and all we have to do is lie in the sun for a few hours."*

Ha! It was bad enough having strangers smear squares of sunscreen on her bottom and peer at them every fifteen minutes, but when the local news crews showed up, Callie nearly died of embarrassment—and swore she'd never let Meg talk her into any such thing again.

"This isn't like the sunscreen business," Meg assured her. She turned to the receptionist. "We had one bad experience, and now she's paranoid."

The baby-faced youth nodded. His nameplate read *Gabe*, and though he looked like a high schooler, Callie guessed he was a college freshman.

"Ask as many questions as you like," he said. "I'll answer anything that won't affect the integrity of the experiment."

Callie frowned, fingering the end of the thick red braid that hung over her shoulder. "No drugs?"

Gabe's blue eyes widened. "Of course not! As our flyer says, we offer evaluation of and instruction in the decision-making process. There are absolutely no drugs."

"So what do we have to do for the fifty dollars?"

"You'll be negotiating an obstacle course and—"

"Obstacle course?" Callie looked up from the waiver. "That won't involve heights, will it? Rope climbing, that sort of thing?"

"Good grief, Cal," Meg cried. "It's not boot camp."

"Just let the man answer, okay?"

"It *is* on the ninth floor," Gabe said. "Are you acrophobic?"

"Only once I get to the tenth floor." She laughed nervously.

"Maybe we can help with that."

"I was just joking." The last thing she needed was another bout with a shrink.

Gabe shrugged. "Well, we've had good success with phobias—and fear in general, for that matter."

"See?" Meg's short dark curls brushed Callie's shoulder as she leaned close. "It's not like that other thing at all. In fact, it might even give you an excuse to miss your sister's birthday bash tonight. Unless you think the Mr. Right she's got for you this time really *will* be Mr. Right."

Callie snorted. Her sister, Lisa, moved in an alien world—upscale, fashion-fixated, and socially saturated. Lisa's Mr. Rights were inevitably lawyers or MBAs, all acquaintances or co-workers of her husband's. Expecting another version of Lisa, the men were always disappointed when they met her short, dull, tongue-tied little sister.

Callie detested the whole scenario. And the possibility of having an excuse for missing the affair was a powerful incentive. "How long will it take?" she asked Gabe.

"Not more than a few hours if you follow instructions. We do ask that you commit to finishing the experiment, however."

"And we won't have to do anything embarrassing or improper?"

He looked amused. "Only if you choose to."

"Come on, Cal," Meg murmured. "You said you'd do this."

"Oh, all right." Callie signed the waiver and handed it over. *It's only for a couple of hours,* she consoled herself. *And who knows—maybe I will gain new and powerful insights. Maybe I'll learn how to say no to Lisa. Maybe it'll even turn my life around like the flyer promises. There's no denying it could use some turning around.*

Four years out of college, she was still making minimum wage raising rats for biology experiments. She still lived in a rented apartment, still had to endure her mother's lectures about finding a man and getting focused, and still wasn't any closer to doing what she really wanted to do—paint. Unfortunately that was something both her mother and sister considered completely unacceptable. A career in art was too unreliable. Worse, her deadbeat father was an artist—when he wasn't following the horse races or losing his money in Las Vegas—and she didn't want to be like him, did she?

At her mother's insistence, she had gone into pre-med. But she was not accepted at med school after graduation—much to her relief—and thus far the only thing her science degree had turned up was the rat-raising job. A job that somehow spilled from part time into full and consumed all her energy, so that little art got done, and she stayed where she was, trapped, frustrated, and waiting for a miracle to set her free.

Gabe told them to go on up and indicated an elevator panel in the textured beige wall beside the desk. Meg hesitated, looking uncertain, then leaned over the counter. "Alex Chapman was supposed to meet us—"

"Yes. He's waiting upstairs."

As they entered the elevator Meg nudged Callie's arm. "He's waiting for us! Did you hear?" She fluffed her black curls and groped in her purse for a breath mint. "Do I look okay? What am I gonna say?"

"Hello usually works." Callie tried not to think of the dark well of space beneath her feet, pushed away thoughts of cables snapping and cars plummeting. The last thing she wanted was to have an attack here.

"But what about *after* hello?" Meg persisted.

"You never had any problems talking to Jack."

"There's a light-year of difference between Jack and Alex. Wait'll you see him, Cal. He is *so* gorgeous."

"So you've said. Many times."

"Have I?" Meg giggled.

Callie watched the six blink out and the seven appear over the door. Uneasiness churned in her middle. She was okay up to the seventh floor, but after that, things got dicey. Floor-level fear was a fairly common manifestation of acrophobia, but because it didn't match the stereotypical fear of heights, it was harder for others to relate to. You were expected to freak out when you looked out a lofty window or stepped onto a rooftop observation deck, and most people nursed enough of their own latent acrophobia to sympathize. But falling into a full-blown panic just because the numbers changed on an elevator panel? Even she knew it made no sense.

Not that it mattered. Above the sixth floor, she got jittery. And above the ninth . . . *STOP it! Don't think about it!*

"Frankly, I think you were an idiot to return Jack's ring," she said to Meg, desperate to distract herself. "He's a good guy, and he loves you."

Meg gestured dismissively. "Jack's even more predictable than *you* are. He's a stick-in-the-mud. I want some excitement."

"Excitement." The seven gave way to an eight. "You *have* lost your mind."

Meg grinned. "You mean my heart."

"You don't even know the man."

The eight changed to a nine, a chime pinged, and the elevator opened at the end of a gleaming, door-lined corridor. On the ninth floor.

*Don't think about it. Everything's fine.*

She followed Meg into the hallway, smelling the pleasant crayon scent of the floor wax and feeling abruptly disoriented. Hadn't the elevator faced *across* the building's width when they'd boarded it?

The dark-haired youth awaiting them distracted her from further musing. This must be the famous Alex—the handsome-as-a-Greek-god, I-die-a-thousand-deaths-each-time-he-looks-at-me real reason Meg was here. A graduate teaching assistant for Dr. Charis's Psych 101 and a doctoral candidate in the psychology of the paranormal, Alex was set to receive his degree in less than a month. Meg figured she had to make a connection today, or forget him.

Though Meg had billed the guy as movie-star caliber, Callie found him unexceptional. Dressed in a white tunic and slacks, he was of average stature, with glossy black hair and dark, long-lashed eyes. His face was open and friendly, but hardly stunning. Gabe, the receptionist, was better looking.

He did have a nice smile.

"Meg! Great to see you. And you brought a friend!"

As Meg introduced them Callie had to admit he was a likable guy, one of those people who instantly made you feel at ease.

"We really appreciate what you're doing here," he told them. "Without volunteers like you, our project would be nothing. I hope you'll find it worth your while." He motioned down the hall. "Shall we get started?"

"So what is this obstacle course like?" Callie asked as they walked.

"I'm afraid I can't tell you," Alex replied. "The experiment demands that all participants begin with the same level of . . ." He smiled at her sidelong. "Well, ignorance."

"You mean we have to go into this blind?"

"More or less."

Alarms went off in her head. Red lights flashed around images of experimenters hovering over her posterior and TV reporters aiming large-lensed cameras.

"I hope the obstacles aren't tires and ropes," said Meg, "because we're hardly dressed—"

"Oh, we'll provide appropriate apparel."

"You mean it *is* tires and ropes?" Callie asked, aghast.

Alex laughed but wouldn't commit either way.

He led them to an L-shaped room where three people waited in white plastic chairs lined against peach-colored walls. A picture window dressed with vertical blinds—thankfully closed against the morning sun—filled the left wall. Callie took care not to look at the window and concentrated on following Meg and Alex to the counter. There a boyish Asian in a gray-yoked tunic gave them clipboards with medical forms to fill out, after which they were called to the examination room at the back. Callie went first, leaving Meg in happy conversation with Alex.

The exam was decidedly unorthodox. Instead of using blood pressure cuffs, thermometers, and blood vials, the lab tech, a handsome, muscular youth named Angelo, pressed her hand against a jellylike plate and flipped a switch.

"This is pretty fancy equipment," she exclaimed as the plate vibrated beneath her palm.

"Takes fingerprints, temperature, blood pressure, and blood chemistry all at the same time," he boasted with a grin. "State of the art. Now please step up onto this disk."

She complied, looking around curiously. "It must be a pretty physical obstacle course if you have to examine us first."

"Just follow the instructions, and you'll be fine. You need to put your jewelry and such in the bowl there." He gestured to a steel receptacle sliding out of the wall. "Glasses, too."

As Callie deposited watch, earrings, and glasses in the bowl, Angelo stepped into a cubicle across the room. Then a low hum sounded above her and a studded circular plate descended from the ceiling, stopping well above arm's reach. She heard some clicks, and the hum changed pitch. Abruptly, ribbons of multicolored light swirled around her, the incongruous scent of warm taffy tickling her nostrils.

"My goodness! What is this?"

"Organ scan," Angelo called from his booth. "Relax."

Again the ceiling plate clicked and whirred. The taffy scent faded, and now a tingle burred through her body like a tiny whirlwind. It stopped a moment later, and the humming ceased. As the lights faded Angelo emerged from his controls. "You're the picture of health," he said with a grin. "I'd guess you're a jogger."

"I do my share. Would you have disqualified me if I wasn't in good enough shape?"

"Well, if you had a bad heart or something, we'd have to address that," he said, helping her down from the raised disk. "But you don't."

He gave her a cream-colored jumpsuit and sent her off to a changing booth. Stitched with pockets and zippers, the suit was fashioned from a fine, buttery fabric that seemed unlikely to withstand the rigors of an obstacle course. Though she felt silly wearing it, it was very comfortable.

Only one person remained in the waiting room when she returned—a thin man seated by the hall doorway whose open stare made her even more self-conscious about the jumpsuit. Keeping her distance from the window, Callie sat as far as she could from the pointy-chinned stranger. But she'd no sooner settled when, to her chagrin, he got up and sat one chair away from her, regarding her with an almost leer. "You here for the experiment?"

Suddenly aware that even the Asian receptionist had left his post, she nodded and looked around for a magazine. There were none.

"Better reconsider," he said. "Strange things go on around here."

Curiosity made her look at him. His hair was lank and gray, his skin waxy pale, and he had an unpleasantly strong earthy smell. "Like what?"

His black eyes bored into hers, and she thought—absurdly—that they weren't quite human.

The chair squeaked as he leaned close. "Have you noticed . . . that none of the workers here"—he looked around conspiratorially—"have beards?"

Callie blinked. She tore her gaze away, flushing. "No, I hadn't noticed," she said, thinking of going back down the hall to look for Meg. Or even the lab tech, Angelo. And where was the receptionist?

The stranger leaned closer. The earthy odor acquired a taint of decay. "They're aliens," he whispered. "Can't grow beards like regular men. And they're plotting to kidnap you. Better reconsider."

Callie rose, heading for the hall to the examination rooms. Before she reached it, however, the stranger stood and, chuckling softly, left the room.

Breathing a sigh of relief, she sagged into a chair. No beards? Aliens? What nuthouse did *he* escape from?

She was almost giggling when first Meg, then the receptionist, and finally Alex returned. When she told him of the incident, he wasn't surprised.

"Calls himself Hermes. I think he's one of those homeless guys from over on Fourth Avenue. I'll send someone to escort him out."

As they headed for the next station, Callie asked about the project's sponsor, which Alex identified as a private foundation called Aggillon, Inc. When she asked why they were interested in this project, he looked at her askance, one dark brow raised in amusement.

"It just seems like a lot of money's being spent here," she added hastily. "I wondered what the justification was."

"You don't think turning people's lives around is sufficient justification?"

She opened her mouth to contest his overblown claim, but saw Meg glaring at her from Alex's other side and swallowed her words.

He stopped outside a pair of double doors. "I'm afraid these psych profiles are tediously long, but try to answer as honestly as you can."

"Where is the course?" Callie asked suddenly. "Is it on this floor, or will we go somewhere else?"

Alex grinned. "You are the curious one, aren't you?"

"Paranoid is the word," Meg muttered.

Alex laid a hand on the door handle nearest him. "You'll enter on this level." He pulled the door open for them. "While you're completing the profiles, I'll program your starting sequences. One of the techs will take you to an orientation room when you're ready."

Program your starting sequences? Could the course be computer generated? With a virtual reality unit they could set up any sort of obstacle course they wanted, in no space at all. Perfect for a ninth-floor operation like this. It also explained the ritzy jumpsuits. But virtual reality units had to be expensive—just like every other piece of equipment they had in this place.

"Are we not going through together, then?" Meg asked, stepping into the opening.

"You might meet each other once you're inside, but at the beginning, each of you will enter on your own." He paused. "Any more questions?"

They shook their heads. As he walked away Meg leaned against Callie and whispered, "I haven't talked to him this much all year!"

"I didn't think you'd have trouble talking." Callie steered her friend through the doorway. "Have you asked him out yet?"

Meg looked chagrined. "Every time I start, my throat freezes up."

"Meg—"

"Don't worry. I'll do it."

The room beyond the doors held rows of white Formica-topped tables lined with more plastic chairs. About twenty people sat scattered throughout, bent over legal-sized sheets of white paper. Callie was relieved not to find the alien-obsessed weirdo among them.

A table near the door was manned by yet another youth in a gray-and-white uniform who looked as if he hadn't graduated from high school. Perversely Callie found herself studying the smooth skin on his face, realizing the business about the beards was true. Not only did none of the workers sport one, none even looked capable of growing one. From Gabe to Alex to the muscular lab tech, Angelo, to this desk worker, they all looked too young to be doing what they were doing.

She settled with Meg in a corner of the room, skimming the questions as she chewed on the end of her braid. *It's nonsense, surely.* But . . . what about that organ scanner? The jumpsuit's strange fabric? Even Alex's evasiveness about the obstacle course became suspicious.

"All right, what's wrong?" Meg's whisper cut into her thoughts.

"What makes you think something's wrong?"

"You're chewing your hair."

Grimacing, Callie dropped her braid and picked up her pencil.

"So what's the problem?" Meg repeated.

"I don't know. Just . . . well, there *are* things that don't make sense around here."

"Like what?"

"The money. The equipment. Why anyone would be interested in such a dippy project."

"It wouldn't be the first dippy project a private foundation financed. Maybe they're using it as a tax write-off." Meg paused, studying her thoughtfully. "You don't like it that they won't tell you what to expect."

"Not at all."

Meg grinned. "Where's your sense of adventure, girl?" She leaned on both forearms. "So what do you think of Alex?"

"He's cute enough, I guess."

"Cute! Are you blind? He's gorgeous."

"He's attractive, Meg, but no more than anyone else here. Not as much as some, in fact. And that's another thing. There isn't one ugly guy in this whole operation. Not one zit, not one speck of dandruff, not one head of less-than-lustrous hair. No one's too fat or too skinny, or has buckteeth or clunky glasses. Don't you think that's a little weird?"

Meg's green eyes widened. She shook her head. "I think *you're* a little weird."

"I'm serious, Meg—"

"They're probably too old for zits—"

"Too *old?* Some of these guys have barely hit puberty. I doubt even Alex has to shave more than once a week."

A crease formed between Meg's brows. "So what's your point? You think there's something fishy going on because a few guys can't grow beards? That the crazy guy was right, and they *are* a bunch of aliens?"

It did sound absurd, stated flat out like that.

"What do you think they're going to do? Rape us? Kill us? Take us to Mars and perform weirdo examinations on us? Look around, girl. We're in the middle of Psychology East, Room . . . I don't know, 910 or something."

Callie frowned at her.

Meg frowned back. "Your sister's right. You *are* getting paranoid."

That was the word for it, wasn't it? Embarrassed, Callie tossed her braid over her shoulder. "Never mind."

"Callie—"

"No, you're right. I'm being ridiculous. Forget it."

She focused on the questionnaire. Alex hadn't exaggerated—it *was* long. Two hundred multiple-choice questions filled both sides of the two legal sheets, covering all manner of preferences, from food to climate to religion. She found them depressing, for they reminded her of all the ways she was failing at life and what a total wimp she had become.

Meg finished first and left to turn in her sheets. Some time later Callie submitted her own sheets, then followed the attendant to a windowless cubicle that smelled of ozone. A small Formica-topped table, two plastic chairs, and a tall blue locker comprised the room's furnishings. She sat at the table and waited, feeling claustrophobic and fighting off unpleasant notions of alien kidnappers. *Surely*, she reassured herself, *if Alex and his crew really were kidnapping people, they wouldn't let that nutcase wander around warning everyone.*

The door swung open, startling her, and Alex entered with a blue nylon day pack, which he dropped on the table. "So," he said, settling across from her, "Meg tells me you're an artist."

She looked away, embarrassed. "It's just a hobby."

"But one you'd like to see become a career."

"That doesn't look likely."

He smiled. "Life has a way of changing rapidly, often when you least expect it."

She shifted uncomfortably.

He unzipped the day pack's top compartment. "This holds everything you'll need to—"

"What do we need a pack for, if the course is going to be virtual reality?"

He cocked a brow. "Who said anything about virtual reality?"

"If there are different obstacles for each individual, I figure they must be computer generated."

"Oh."

She frowned at him. "You don't have room up here for a limitless array of real obstacles."

"You seem to know more about what we're doing than we do."

Annoyance flared. "Well, if it's not virtual reality, what is it?"

"A course with various obstacles—some decisions to make, instructions to follow. I'm afraid that's all I can tell you."

She frowned at him again, tapping a fingernail on the table. Baby-faced researchers, science-fiction technology, secrecy and evasion. Her fears might be unfounded, even paranoid, but every fiber of Callie's being was screaming at her to beware. And now that it looked like she wouldn't be with Meg anyway, what was the point of staying? Was it really worth the fifty dollars?

She drew a deep breath and stopped tapping. "I think I'd like to withdraw. I just can't go into this blind. I'm sorry for wasting your time, but if you'll return my—"

"Unfortunately that's not possible."

She stared at him.

"Miss Hayes, you didn't come here because of your friend. You came for yourself. Why not give yourself the chance to find the answers you're seeking?"

"What do you mean, 'that's not possible'?"

Alex sighed. "I'm afraid you've already entered the experiment. Your only way out now is through the Arena."

She blinked in confusion.

He drew a slim black book from the pack. "This is your field manual. You'll need it to find the exit."

*He's not going to let me go.*

"I advise you to heed its warnings," he went on, "for there is—"

She stood and strode to the door. Alex made no move to stop her, and in the three steps it took her to reach it, she realized it must be locked. Clenching the unmoving knob, she struggled to control her rising panic and finally turned back to him.

"You can't do this," she whispered.

He regarded her with something like compassion. "You did agree to take part, Miss Hayes."

"I agreed to inkblots and fitting pegs into holes."

"You knew it would be an obstacle course when you signed on."

"No legitimate experimenter ever refuses his participants the right to back out. It's not even legal."

"We operate by a different legal system. Surely you read the waiver you signed?"

She stared at him mutely. Yes, she'd read it, but not that closely, not all the paragraphs of fine print. And shouldn't they have made it plain to her what she was signing?

Continued protest, however, seemed useless. Perhaps if she refused to listen to his instructions, refused to pick up the equipment, refused even to look at him—she shifted her gaze to the blue locker—he would conclude she was too much trouble and let her go.

From the corner of her eye, she saw him frowning.

"Refusal to accept our instruction is itself a decision which our experiment is designed to incorporate," Alex said. "We will not suffer, nor will the project, but you will find the experience disagreeable."

She looked steadfastly at the locker.

"Miss Hayes, if you continue to refuse me, I'll have no choice but to deposit you on-site, utterly unprepared."

She said nothing.

He sighed. "Your initial objective will be to pass through the Benefactor's Gate. A guide will lead you from it to the exit. As long as you follow the instructions, you'll have no trouble."

She maintained silence. He went on, but she tuned him out. The remark about depositing her on-site had unnerved her. Surely, he was bluffing. . . .

Then it hit her—illegal as this was, they could never just let her go. They'd have to kill her, or wipe her memory, or addle her mind.

Suddenly she couldn't breathe. Swallowing hard, she interrupted him. "Why are you doing this?"

His expression was genuinely pained. "You'll understand in time," he said. "The white road will lead you to the Gate. Stay on it and keep moving. That's very important. There is evil in the Arena. But as long as you stay on the road, it cannot harm you."

He stood and stepped toward her, offering the pack. She backed away, and he stopped with a sigh. "We intend this for your benefit, Callie. You've come to us because you don't like where your life is going. You want something better. Don't let fear and stubbornness keep you from finding it."

He held out the pack again. She backed against the door, half angry, wholly terrified. What would he do now? *Make* her take it?

He just stared sadly into her eyes. And vanished.

The pack fell to the floor with a muffled clatter, and she flinched back, gasping. Before understanding could sink in, the table, chairs, and locker followed him into oblivion. Then the cubicle's four white walls pulsed with red light and drew in around her. Just when she thought she would be crushed, they too dissolved, and she fell into nothingness.

# CHAPTER

## 2

The world came back to Callie all at once. She stood in a circular, glass-walled shelter with a slatted wood roof. It was surrounded closely on three sides by the red rock walls of a small grotto. The air smelled damp, and water trickled behind her.

She turned numbly, heart slamming against her breastbone.

*"I'll have no choice but to deposit you on-site, utterly unprepared."*

He'd really done it.

Beyond the glass at the grotto's rear, a dark pool gleamed beneath the moisture-blackened rock and a mat of ferns and grasses. To its left, tucked between the cliff and the glass, stood a ten-foot-tall fountain of long, tough, swordlike leaves resembling the South American pampas grass widely used in Tucson landscaping designs. Except the leaves of this plant were segmented. And appeared to be made of glass. And bristled with golden spines. A raft of them spilled across the roof slats overhead, quivering in the still air, and Callie thought she heard a faint chiming. Needle pricks raced the length of her spine, and she didn't need a botanist's manual to tell her this bizarre cross between a cactus and a grass was not from the world she knew.

*Impossible!*

She turned away and saw the sign—blue letters floating in the glass wall:

DROP-OFF POINT 24
Proceed along path
to your right.

Below this hung a transparent ten-inch cube, marked on the side nearest her with three gold circles arrayed around a central point of light. A path, made of the same white sponge as the shelter floor, led to the grotto's mouth thirty feet away, where it disappeared around the rock.

A trembling began in Callie's fingers, light and fluttery.

She executed another slow spin. The trembling spread to her arms and shoulders, stuttered across her back. Her legs turned to water, and she sagged to the floor, catching her head in her hands. Eyes closed, she forced herself to take a deep breath. Then another.

When she felt solid again, she lifted her head. The plant was still there, along with the sign and the transparent box. Drug-induced hallucinations, perhaps? Computer-generated virtual reality? Maybe she was actually sitting in a lab, encased in electronic hookups. But surely she would have some recollection of being hooked up, some awareness of gloves and helmet. Surely it wouldn't seem so . . . real.

And it couldn't be real. Because if it were—

Her thoughts raced.

*The hall outside the elevator that ran the wrong way, the weird organ scanner, the men who looked too young and had no beards—who vanished into thin air.*

*Who weren't men at all.*

The bright lights were back. She fought them off, forcing herself to face the truth.

They were aliens.

A roil of conflicting emotions swelled—fear, anger, and a sense of helplessness that shook the foundations of her being. Control, organization, and planning—these were the tenets by which she lived. She didn't believe in flitting about impulsively. She made lists of goals and tasks, kept neat and careful calendars, and always considered the consequences of her actions, thereby avoiding dangerous and unpleasant situations.

Yet somehow she'd been ripped from her safe, secure life and transported to this alien place to fulfill some . . . *alien* purpose.

She had read about such things in science-fiction novels. She had even seen a TV show with wild-eyed people talking about being kidnapped by aliens—hokey stuff that belonged on the front page of supermarket tabloids.

Suddenly it was her life.

Even as it terrified her, the notion outraged her. She was no slave to be snatched up at their whim. How dare they! Maybe she'd just sit here and wait them out. If all their subjects did that, they wouldn't have much of an experiment.

But all their subjects wouldn't.

Her stomach churned. Most subjects wouldn't realize what they had gotten into until it was too late. Meg was probably going along right now, following instructions, never realizing she had no choice.

*But I don't have to go along. If I refuse to move, they'll have to release me eventually.*

Alex's words returned. *"Your only way out now is through the Arena."*

Maybe he was bluffing. But could she gamble her life on it? What was to stop them from simply killing uncooperative participants? Or letting their arena do it?

*"There is evil in the Arena. . . ."*

Callie hugged herself, sick and fearful all over again. Her gaze dropped to the blue day pack at her knee. *"This holds everything you'll need. . . ."*

Unfair. Outrageous. Horrid.

She gritted her teeth—hating the direction reason was taking her—and yanked the pack into her lap.

The first thing she drew out was the field manual Alex had shown her earlier. Its black cover was inscribed with three gold interlocking circles and her name. She set it on the rubbery floor and reached into the bag again, pulling out a handful of black rubber donuts, wire half circles, and small turquoise cubes. She also found numerous abstractly shaped ceramic pieces—blue, orange, red, and clear—some only a few centimeters wide, while others filled her palm.

"My equipment, huh?" she muttered, certain Alex was listening. "Everything I'll need, you say. I just have to put it together, right?"

Across from her, the weird plant chimed as if in answer. She glanced up, frowning. Had there been that many arms pressed against the glass before? Probably. She was looking at it from a different angle now.

Returning her attention to the ceramic pieces scattered before her, she immediately found two that fit together—a clear, five-inch-long rod, and a short thick elbow about two inches wide, one leg flattened into a tab, the other pierced with a hole at its end. The hole was just the right diameter for the rod, which seated itself with a click when she inserted it, then refused to come out again.

She held the resulting implement up to the light, noting the slight depressions on the tab, as if to accommodate thumb and forefinger. So what was it, then? A writing stylus? A key of some sort? A temperature probe? Part of some other construction altogether? She had no idea. It did slide nicely into the slim pocket along the seam of her left thigh, though, so that's where she left it.

She fiddled with the rest of the pieces for a few more minutes, then opened the book. It smelled of fresh ink, and the pages stuck together. Turning to the title page, she read:

*Instructions for Participants*

Below the title glowed a holograph of a crystalline arch marked with the same three interlocking circles as the cover.

Several pages of introduction followed, then a list of five rules jumped out in boldface:

1. STAY ON THE WHITE ROAD AT ALL TIMES.
2. PROCEED IMMEDIATELY TO THE NEAREST GATE.
3. AVOID DISTRACTIONS.
4. FOLLOW THE INSTRUCTIONS GIVEN IN THE MANUAL.
5. AUXILIARY SUPPLY BOXES WILL PROVIDE ANY ADDI-TIONAL NEEDS. DO NOT LEAVE THE WHITE ROAD.

"Guess I won't leave the white road."

The next page offered a thicket of text explaining the rules. She skipped it, paging randomly. Tissue-thin pages displayed numerous construction diagrams plus paragraphs of fine print explaining how to use the strange stew of ceramic pieces.

After the diagrams, however, the remaining three-quarters of the book was indecipherable gibberish. "How useful," she muttered. "An instruction manual I can't read. Why would they give me a manual that makes no sense? Why are they doing any of this?" Instead of getting answers, it seemed she was just accumulating more questions.

The pack's lower section held only a plastic liter bottle of water and two foil Snak-Paks whose use was obvious. As she restowed her "supplies," the plant encasing the shelter shivered again, its chiming sounding lower and louder. She frowned at it. Had those filaments been sticking through the wood slats before?

Uneasiness stirred. Maybe it was time to go.

At the corner of her eye, the blue letters suddenly flared fluorescent magenta. She began to gather up the ceramic pieces.

A loud buzz made her look up as another of the plant's glassy arms slipped between the roof slats, bobbing in the air above her head, golden spines sparkling. With a gulp she tossed the manual in her pack and continued fumbling with the rest of her scattered supplies.

The magenta letters began to flash, and the buzz changed pitch and silenced. Then the shelter vanished along with the spongy white circle on which she crouched. Their support gone, the plant's arms slapped the sandy foundation in successive, hissing clinks, spraying her legs with tiny spines.

A rootlike tendril wrapped around her foot. With a cry, Callie jerked back—off-balance, clutching the pack to her chest. The runner clung, winding with startling speed around her ankle. She hopped backward, wrenching at it, but the tentacle stretched and held, as another curled over her toe.

Panicking, she fell backward and, in a burst of wild strength, kicked herself free, then scrambled for the path three yards away. Once she was back on the spongy surface, well out of the plant's reach, she stopped, heart hammering, and watched the tendrils grope over the equipment parts she had been forced to leave behind. New dread tormented her. What if she couldn't get out of this place without those pieces? What if—

The six-inch-thick pavement beneath her vanished as if a light beam had switched off, dropping her onto its sandy foundation with a jolt. She stumbled backward and turned to see the path disappearing section by section. Worse, all the bits of shattered arm that had sprayed the grotto were now taking root, sprouting new arms and runners with impossible swiftness.

Horrified, Callie sprinted for the path, gained it, skidded around the grotto wall, and raced into a wider canyon. When she stopped and turned back, the grotto opening was still there, but the path no longer entered it. Holding the day pack like a shield, she shoved her glasses back up her nose and wheeled slowly, taking in the black-streaked red canyon walls, the blue sky, and the utter stillness. It looked astonishingly real.

Thankfully she spied no more of the cactus grass. Her boots and jumpsuit, though coated with red dust and stained with yellow plant juice, had shielded her legs and feet from the spines. Her hands were another matter. Patches of short golden prickles bristled from the backs of them, and the skin was already burning and reddened. Having no tweezers, she pulled them out with her teeth, hoping they weren't poisonous.

She was about to open her pack for the water bottle when an ear-piercing screech shattered the quiet and froze her in midmotion. The sound bounded back and forth between the cliffs, fading into a growling grunt and then to silence. . . .

Pulse pounding, she bent to pick up the pack she'd dropped. Mountain lions screamed—but that was no mountain lion. That was nothing like anything she'd ever heard in her life. Almost running again, she followed the undulating path downstream, past sheer walls on one side and a crumbling talus slope on the other. The canyon hairpinned frequently, preventing her from seeing more than a few hundred yards ahead, and she was uneasily aware that if anything awaited her, she had no hope of evading it.

As time passed and she encountered no more unpleasant surprises, her pace slowed, and she relaxed, her mind returning to questions of how and where. It was all so convincing. She could almost swear she'd been transported to the Utah canyon lands. She'd backpacked there only a year ago with Meg and Jack, Meg's ex-fiancé, so she knew the area. Rugged and sparsely populated, it was traversed by few roads. The aliens could have easily set up a course there with no one the wiser.

However, that theory didn't explain how they had transported her the length of Arizona in the drawing of a breath. Was their technology so advanced such a feat was no problem for them? The orientation room *had* vanished from around her. . . .

No, that was too farfetched. More likely she was in a carefully constructed set, with complex machinery lurking behind clever façades. Computer-generated imagery could give the impression of the orientation room dissolving. And that *would* explain the rule about staying on the road. Step off and you'd see the wires, cords, and gears that made it all run, just like on those behind-the-scenes tours at Disneyland.

She grimaced. Disneyland did not evoke happy memories. Her father had taken her there for her seventh birthday, a year after he'd divorced her mother. It had been the first time Callie had seen him since he'd left, and she had looked forward to it for weeks. Only to ruin everything.

After their behind-the-scenes tour—her father had insisted she understand it was all a fake—they'd boarded the Skyway. As the little cable car bore them quietly above the crowds she'd at first enjoyed seeing everything from such a lofty vantage. But halfway across, dark demons had fluttered up around her, plucking at her clothing, threatening to wrench her from the car and hurl her to the pavement below. Screaming in terror, she had clutched the railing so desperately the ride operators had had to shut the machine down to get her off.

Patrick Hayes did not take embarrassment well. Furious, he'd brought her home and suggested her mother take her to a shrink. Callie cried herself to sleep that night, and hadn't seen her father since.

The incident precipitated a spate of phobic attacks, and finally her mother dragged her to a doctor, then to a series of disagreeable therapists who smiled too much and asked too many questions. She remembered little of it now, mainly recalling the sickening dread that always preceded her appointments. The attacks had finally ceased on their own, and in retrospect, everyone blamed it on the trauma of her parents' divorce. No one except Meg knew her fear of heights had lately returned—with frightening intensity. What would they say was the cause now? The trauma of a nowhere life?

A shadow flicked across the path in front of her, bringing her up short. Overhead a large, pale flying-something disappeared beyond the canyon's rim. It didn't come back, though, so she moved on.

"Can't say life's boring anymore," she muttered. "Nothing like the last time, huh, Meg? Oh, brother! Just wait till I catch you!"

Memory of her friend's chirpy assurances made her boil. Meg had become such a flake since she'd dumped Jack. All this experience-life-as-an-adventure stuff—hang gliding, dream exploration, yoga, seeking after a higher consciousness. . . . If they hadn't known each other so long, and if Meg wasn't her only real friend, Callie would've dumped her long ago.

How *could* Meg have known Alex all those months—lusted after him, for crying out loud—and not notice he wasn't human?

A fork in the road interrupted Callie's thoughts and brought her to a stop. Angling off what looked to be the main path, a branch headed up a boulder-clogged cleft, looping around the rocks like a casually thrown rope. She pushed up her glasses and frowned. Deeply cut and shadow-swathed, that cleft held promise of gaining altitude swiftly. Which meant she might soon find herself in a place where the exposure would goad her slumbering acrophobia to life.

The branch's very lack of appeal, however, argued for its being the correct choice. Unless there wasn't a "correct" choice. Maybe one route was simply shorter. Or offered different obstacles.

Dared she stop to consult the manual? Whatever had screamed, she hadn't heard it again. Nor had the flying thing returned. She glanced around, rubbing the tender welts on the backs of her hands. No sign of any of those cactus-grass things, either. Surely her captors wouldn't begrudge her a rest and a drink and a handful of trail mix. If they'd supplied the food and water, they must intend her to use it.

She settled cross-legged on a clear stretch of road and pulled out the water bottle and foil Snak-Pak, which turned out to contain a cupful of tan pellets.

"I fed some of this to my rats just this morning!" she muttered, wrinkling her nose. Lifting a handful in mock salute, she tossed a few of the pellets into her mouth—and was surprised to find they tasted like oatmeal cookies. "Okay, so maybe it's not rat food."

She crunched a few more, washed them down with the water, and then got out the manual and turned to the introductory material.

*Welcome to the Arena. We hope you enjoy your stay. As you will discover, we have engineered the playing field to conform to your homeworld parameters—*

Homeworld? Did that mean she was no longer on her homeworld?

*Gravitational forces, day-night cycles, and atmosphere have been tailored to meet your biological needs. In addition to many of your homeworld species, a number of innovative bioforms have been engineered to add excitement and interest to your journey.*

The light, fluttery feeling returned. Innovative bioforms? Like that thing that screamed?

*For your comfort and safety, please stay on the path and follow all instructions.*

She skimmed ahead. The section closed with—*We appreciate your participation in our project and hope you'll have an entertaining adventure.*

"Entertaining adventure?" she squeaked. "Give me a break!"

The next page reiterated the "initial objective" Alex had given her: *Follow the white road to its end, and there pass through the First Gate, pictured on the title page.* The manual said nothing about splits in the road.

She turned the page, reviewed the five rules, and launched into the paragraphs of elaboration that followed. As Alex had said, the white road was a safe zone, undulating through a treacherous countryside whose engineered bioforms could be downright deadly. The plant that attacked her would have eaten her if given the opportunity, and its spines carried a mild poison that would produce discomfort for at least a day. The scream she'd heard was probably the territorial call of a rock dragon—six-foot-long lizards said to frequent canyons such as this. An unarmed woman would make easy pickings for a big female, but the path supposedly repelled them, so she'd be safe as long as she didn't leave it.

The material accompanying rule number two, "Proceed immediately to the nearest gate," was informative but not reassuring.

*To encourage forward momentum, portions of the track have been engineered to disappear after an elapsed interval of time.*

"Which you neglect to specify," she noted sourly.

*It is wise, therefore, not to linger, especially at the beginning. Should the worst happen and you do stray off the road, we have provided fourteen identical gates located at equidistant intervals around the Arena. No matter where you are, there will always be a safe road in the vicinity that will take you to one of them.*

"So long as the 'innovative bioforms' don't get you first," she muttered.

*Safehavens have been provided for your comfort along the roads. You may stay in each up to twenty-four hours. Food, water, energy cubes—* whatever they were—*and first-aid supplies are available there for your convenience.*

She skipped ahead to rule three, "Avoid distractions." *Antagonists within the Arena are at work to prevent you from attaining your—*

Something moved at the corner of her eye, and Callie looked up.

At the mouth of the boulder-choked cleft, a patch of gray weeds quivered in the quiet air. Silence pressed around her, deep and anticipatory, and a sense of being watched crawled up her back. She coughed, but the creepy feeling did not wane.

With one eye on her surroundings, she stuffed the Snak-Pak and water bottle back into her pack. Standing, she reshouldered the bag, then flipped through the manual's thin pages one last time, hoping something might catch her eye. No luck. No index, either. She was on her own.

Pushing her glasses back up, she surveyed her two choices again. Surely most "participants" were not as stubborn as she and had eagerly received the orientation she'd disdained. No doubt the prescribed method of path selection was part of their counsel. Since the lower road looked the more traveled, it seemed the logical choice—and the easiest. There was no point in confronting her fear of heights unless she had no other options.

She slid the manual into the right rear pocket of her jumpsuit and was just starting forward when a sibilant hissing issued from the cleft. She froze, her heart once more pounding against her rib cage.

The silence returned.

Mottled red-brown to blend with their surroundings, rock dragons could supposedly sit motionless for hours awaiting their prey. But several careful inspections of the surrounding rock walls revealed nothing, and when no further sound followed the first, she exhaled deeply. "Wimp," she muttered, her voice grating in the quiet. "It was probably just—"

Something scrabbled among the boulders and burst from the gray weeds—a blood red lizard? Insect? Crustacean? Whatever it was, it scuttled crablike across the sand, zipping by her and back along the road, then darted left into a crack in the rock.

Callie stood very still, struggling to put a name to the creature and failing. Another engineered bioform? Curiosity prodded her to investigate, but caution stood in the way—she'd have to leave the road to do so.

"Curiosity killed the cat," she reminded herself and set off briskly down the lower path. Only when she'd put a curtain of rock between herself and the gloomy cleft did her uneasiness abate.

She soon encountered a second branching where the canyon widened briefly. Again she chose the low option, proceeding along a small stream through a field of pungent yellow wild flowers. Six Ys later, however, she was decidedly uncomfortable. The sheer walls loomed close, and the sun—or whatever was substituting for it—was clearly descending. She'd been prudently staying on the canyon floor, but now impatience flapped its dark wings, demanding more results for the time and effort she'd expended. If she went up, maybe she could see the arched gateway she sought. "Okay," she said. "Next opportunity, I'll do it."

Only now the opportunities stopped.

Worse, her road had acquired an unsettling dinginess. The incoming paths she'd passed earlier had been similarly discolored, which she'd taken as indications of heavy use. Now she wondered if they might have been tricks, side spurs to confuse and distract. What if, at that first juncture, she'd chosen the wrong path?

The thought of backtracking nearly brought her to tears. As far as she'd come, she'd never make it back before dark. And there was that rock dragon to consider as well.

But if she *was* off the path . . .

Maybe she was just being paranoid again. Maybe it was the light reflecting off the surrounding red rock. Or dust. She paused at yet another turn and squatted to rub her fingers across the pavement. Sure enough, they came away coated with a fine red grit. "See?" she told herself. "It's still white underneath. Nothing to worry about."

And then that sense of being watched poured over her again, thick and stifling. Nape hairs erect, she eyed her surroundings—sand, rock, a few weeds. Nothing at all alarming. Yet the feeling persisted. Creepy. Invasive. Almost . . . evil.

Slowly she arose, rubbing her fingers on her thigh.

Then, out of the corner of her eye, she saw it standing twenty feet upstream, half hidden by a boulder. It jumped immediately out of sight, but the afterimage remained—humanoid, hairless, all arms and legs, with luminescent gray skin and two pitlike eyespots.

More alien than the cactus grass or the red crustacean—or even Alex and his vanish-into-thin-air trick—this thing's very aura reeked of otherness. It struck a chord of such primal terror, she had backed ten yards downstream before she knew it.

She stopped and pulled herself together. It hadn't attacked her. Maybe it couldn't. Maybe it was in another dimension. Maybe it wasn't even dangerous.

No. It *was* dangerous. Intuition, perhaps, but definitely as strong a feeling as she'd ever known.

Fighting panic, Callie hurried along the path, desperate now for an escape route. No matter what heights she had to brave, it was better than being down here with that *thing*.

But the canyon snaked on with no new branches—as if the creature had waited until she was trapped before revealing itself. It followed her steadily, and she glimpsed it now and then, peering from behind the rocks, an unnerving hunger in its "eyes."

Finally, in the late afternoon, bone tired and increasingly desperate, she rounded a bend and found deliverance. Her narrow canyon

descended sharply into another, the juncture marked by a stand of
bright green cottonwoods. Stopping at the top of a twenty-foot limestone cliff, she spied the Y she sought. One leg continued down to the
intersecting canyon. The other wound through the trees and switchbacked up the wall behind them.

Laughing with relief, she descended the switchbacks alongside the
cliff and was just starting across the grassy swale toward the beckoning
cottonwoods, when a low voice sounded behind her: "I don't think you
want to go that way, miss."

Callie whirled with a cry. On the rock behind and above her
crouched a brown-skinned, bearded man with glowing blue eyes.

# CHAPTER

## 3

He was not another alien after all, but human, like her. And his eyes didn't really glow—they were just so blue, they contrasted dramatically with his beard and tanned skin. Dirty brown hair curled over his shirt collar, and he wore a scratched leather vest above filthy jeans and sturdy hiking boots. A sheathed knife as long as his forearm hung at one hip, a holstered gun at the other. He carried a rifle with a rubberized stock and a white ceramic barrel encircled with wire rings.

Was he another participant? Or one of the distractions that rule three instructed her to avoid?

"What's down there?" she asked.

"Swarm of harries." His voice was low and pleasant, at odds with his appearance. He dropped lightly to the ground before her. "Believe me," he added, squinting at the trees, "you don't want to stir them up."

She inspected the cottonwoods doubtfully. He pointed past her, sleeve and forearm layered with dirt. The smell confirmed his need for a bath.

"There in the tallest tree," he said. "That blob hanging in the middle."

She finally saw it—a pale mass suspended from a stout, bright-leaved branch. Other smaller shapes hung scattered around it. She shaded her eyes. "Harries, you say?"

"They look like flying manta rays. Paralyze their victims with the venom in their stingers, then suck the blood out of them."

Callie shuddered. Suspicion swirled through her. She turned back
to him. "I thought the white road was a safe zone—a place where things
like that can't hurt you."

"It is." He eyed her appraisingly. "I figure you left it, oh, on the
first or second branching."

"Left it? What—"

"Look back the way you've come." He gestured over his shoulder.
"It isn't white, it's pink. You're on a sucker path."

She was well aware of the road's dinginess, but the manual had said
nothing about sucker paths. "Who are you, anyway?"

"Just another 'participant.' " The man's lips twitched bitterly.

"So why are *you* off the road?"

He shrugged. "After you're here long enough, you realize there's no
point to it."

"But if it's a safe zone—"

"It goes nowhere."

She regarded him with renewed suspicion. *Antagonists within the
Arena work to prevent you from attaining your goal . . . avoid all distractions.*

"So, uh, where do *you* think I ought to go?" Callie asked.

"I'm headed for camp now. You can come with me, or go back and
try to find where you went off. I wouldn't advise that, though."

"Naturally not."

"I beg your pardon?"

"Nothing. You say you have a camp? There are others of you,
then?"

"Yeah, we have a good-sized group." He glanced past her shoulder.
"Look, if you don't mind, I'd like to get going. I've got fresh meat with
me." He pointed up the rock, and Callie saw his backpack leaning
where he'd left it. Twice the size of hers, it had a dog-sized lizard tied
across its top. Rock dragon, perhaps?

"They'll be hunting soon," he added. "I'd rather not be here when
they break."

*The old pressure-sale method,* Callie thought wryly. *Pitch your product*

*and give the customer five minutes to decide. Come on, Alex, do you think
I can't see through that?*

She motioned toward the canyon walls. "By all means. Don't let me
stop you."

He frowned, regarding her with those intensely blue eyes.

She waved him on. "Go ahead. But thanks for the warning."

"Those things will kill you, miss."

"I'll take my chances." Callie headed toward the trees, feeling his
eyes on her back.

Ahead, the pale blob fluttered and rippled.

*Avoid all distractions,* the manual said. *Don't leave the white road.*

Except . . . he was right about the first branching. She'd avoided the
whiter path because of her fear of heights. A fear Alex must have
known about, since she'd mentioned it to the receptionist.

She glanced back, but the stranger was gone.

Surprise gave way to smug assurance. *See? He was a distraction. If
these things were as bad as he said, he wouldn't let me walk right into them.*

She'd nearly reached the grove now, the gray blob differentiating
into pale lavender wings and flat manta-ray bodies. Layered onionlike,
they slid over one another in a writhing mass, a translucent wingtip
occasionally stretching out from the huddle. The sphere began to pulse.
She slowed, staring up at it. Fear needled her extremities. Her intended
route passed directly beneath the throbbing mass.

*So what're you going to do? Go back?* Callie chewed on her lip, waf-
fling again, her stomach quivering. Irritation overwhelmed her fear. *He
was just trying to scare you off. Now get on with it.*

Resolutely she forced herself forward. A comb-and-waxed-paper
trilling danced around her, and the breeze carried a sweet, musty odor.
She walked faster.

The old cottonwood loomed above. As she drew under it the trilling
mounted. Then the quivering blob contracted, throbbed, and burst like
a grenade, flinging pale, purplish manta shapes into the air. They
flapped up through the branches to the open sky, whirling like debris
in a dust devil.

Callie wanted to run for the rocks, fifty feet away now, but that
would take her off the path. Doggedly she followed the pavement as it

curved away from safety. Her scalp prickled, and her hands shook. She broke into a trot, rounding the hollow and coming out into the flat.

The stranger's voice rang out from the rocks across the clearing. "Here they come!"

A pale shape dove by her. She dodged sideways, glimpsing shiny, jointed appendages dangling wasplike from its posterior. A turquoise beam shot from the rocks to the beast, now a yard in front of her. *Thwip, thwip, thwip.* Its body deflated in a puff of purple smoke, fluttering to the path like an empty sack. Two more beams burst from the rocks, downing two more harries as they swooped.

Ahead, the stranger rose from his hiding place and told her to run. Again she was tempted to leave the path. But nothing had touched her yet, and she wasn't convinced anything could.

A series of beams slit the air in a succession of rapid thwips. Callie was aware of more hits, more puffs of purple gas, more falling sacklike bodies. Car-sized boulders loomed ahead on the left. Maybe they would afford some protection.

But then a harry caught her from behind, tentacles slapping along the left side of her back in lines of tingling heat. She staggered, crying out more from shock than pain.

The lavender shape skimmed by and imploded in a puff of purple. She dodged the plume as best she could, coughing on the sickening-sweet smell.

*But I'm on the path*, Callie protested, looking down through watering eyes to be sure. Nausea and dizziness churned in her. The heat on her back gave way to numbness.

More thwips. More beams. Tentacles came at her face. She spun away into another attack, and fire tracked along her upper arm. After that, reality devolved into nightmarish chaos. Shadow shapes whirled around her—malevolent wing flaps, hirsute tentacles, bulbous bodies bursting into purple at the ends of blue-green lines of light. Dead rays littered the ground, tripping her. One burst over her head, dowsing her with the eye-watering, stomach-turning gas. She doubled over, staggering on wobbly knees. Tentacles slapped across her back, and new waves of hot numbness sent her reeling. As she sought to regain her balance, a harry clamped on to her right hip, tentacles winding down her leg like a tetherball round its pole, a thousand burning needles pumping venom into her flesh. The wing flaps clutched her leg. The mouth bit through fabric and skin into her waist.

Panicked, Callie beat at the leathery body, white light spreading in amebic splotches across her vision. Someone was screaming hysterically.

*I'm going to die. I'm going to die here, and I don't even know where I am!*

She saw her mother. Lisa. Daddy . . .

Suddenly the stranger was looming over her, firing the rifle with one arm as he ripped the harry off her leg with the other. He lifted her effortlessly. Her legs and left arm were numb and useless, but she clung to his neck with her right arm as he carried her among the rocks, firing as he ran.

It grew hard to breathe. The white splotches swelled. Something slapped her ear. . . .

The next thing she knew, she lay on her back at the rear of a low-ceilinged cave. The stranger crouched by the entrance, shooting at the harries outside. Beside her lay his pack and the rock dragon, dried blood caking its pointed teeth. A milky eye stared at her alongside a serrated blue face crest. It stank of sour socks.

*Thwip, thwip, thwip.* Turquoise light flared pink and faded.

The man drew back, opened a panel in the rifle's side, and pulled a small pink cube out of it. Tossing the cube aside, he slapped in a replacement and resumed firing, all one-handed. His left arm dangled at his side, his shirt sleeve slit in several places to reveal a bicep scored with red welts. Another welt seared across his cheekbone, and his eyelid drooped above it.

*Thwip. Thwip—thwip.*

Callie knew she should help him, but it felt as if a boulder lay atop her chest. She couldn't feel her left arm or either of her legs. Was the poison spreading? Would the numbness soon creep to her heart? And if it wasn't spreading, would it wear off? Or would it leave her paralyzed for life?

The amebic lights returned to carry her into oblivion.

When she came to, she was alone in full darkness and still unable to move. She thought the dark bulk beside her might be the pack with its smelly burden, but where was the man? Had the harries gotten him?

Panic rattled through her, and she fainted again.

When she awoke for the third time, the man had lit a small three-legged lamp and was laying sticks for a fire. The pile of branches to his right revealed where he'd been earlier—collecting firewood.

Her mouth was cotton dry, her head ached, and her stomach felt as hollow as a dead tree. But at least she could sense her limbs again—cold and tingling unpleasantly. Her pack lay at her feet, but her attempts to reach it only proved she couldn't even roll over, much less sit up. After a brief struggle she sagged back onto the dirt, gasping.

The stranger squatted beside her. "Want some help?"

"A drink," she croaked, shocked at the inhuman sound of her voice.

The smell of him was strong as he lifted her to a sitting position against the wall. His nearness made her uneasy, and she kept her eyes off his face, concentrating on the water pouring over her parched lips and tongue. Seeing she could handle the bottle on her own, he let go and eased back. She drank eagerly until he stopped her, then licked her lips and dropped her head back against the rock.

When she opened her eyes, he had returned to arranging the firewood into a small teepee. Her glance flicked to the scarlet welts on his face, the clumsiness of his left arm. "You saved my life," she rasped.

He didn't look up. "We're not out of this yet."

"Surely the worst is past."

Silence.

"Look, I'm sorry I didn't believe you."

"I'm sure you are."

She frowned, her good feelings toward him evaporating. "Well, it's only my first day—"

"That's obvious."

Callie snapped her lips shut. *All right, forget it.* She let him work in silence for a few moments, then said, "I don't suppose you have a name."

"Pierce." He positioned another stick.

"I'm Callie Hayes."

No reply.

*Great,* Callie thought. *A macho male with a chip on his shoulder.*

*Well, two can play this game.* She drew the manual from her back pocket and started to read. But she'd lost her glasses in the harry attack, and the dim light made the print too fuzzy to see without a struggle. In the end she had too many questions and not enough patience to ignore him, so presently she tried again. "You said there was no point staying on the white road. What did you mean?"

Pierce laid the last stick onto his teepee, then drew a long-barreled handgun from his holster and fired a burst of green light at the wood. Yellow flames licked greedily upward.

"The gates are there," he said, pulling two metal stakes from his pack. "You just can't get to them."

"You know this for a fact?" She pushed a lock of hair out of her face. "You've actually seen one?"

"Of course."

"Well, maybe it was an exception."

"I've been to all fourteen." He began to pound a stake into the hard earth on one side of the fire. "The routes to reach them are different, but the gates are all identical—and all identically unattainable." Rocking back on one knee, he met her gaze. "This place is like a doughnut— the Inner Realm's the hole, the Outer Realm's the cake, with a ring of cliffs between the two. All the gates stand atop those cliffs, and all the roads end at the bottom. So while you can see the gates just fine, you can't get up to 'em. Though believe me, many have tried, long and hard—myself included." Grimly, he finished pounding in the stake.

Callie watched him, frowning. *Maybe he's lying. Maybe he really is a distraction and this was all staged.*

But she couldn't believe that anymore. He seemed too bitter, too frustrated, too much like her—another victim trapped in the same nightmare. A sick feeling settled into her middle. Fourteen gates, but not one was accessible?

"Why give us a task that's impossible?" she wondered aloud. "Why give us a manual—"

"Who knows?" he snapped. "As for the manual, obviously you haven't read it. The thing's about as useful as your boots." He pounded the second stake into the ground opposite the first. "The part you can read is cryptic or flat wrong, and the rest's gibberish."

"Maybe it's some sort of code, and we just need to find the key."

"If there is a key, *I've* never heard of it. And I've been here long enough, I should have."

She frowned. "How long *have* you been here?"

He gave the stake one last blow, then sat back on his heels, staring at the flames as they crackled among the sticks. "Five years this summer."

Not five days, not five months. "Five years?" she whispered.

Bitterness twisted his lips. "Some experiment, huh?"

"But . . . how? They said . . ." She'd long ago stopped believing she'd get out of this mess in a few hours. But five *years*?

"Like I said, it's not for lack of trying," Pierce added. He got up and drew a haunch of meat from a tarp-covered pile near her feet. As he impaled it on a spit, she realized the carcass of the rock dragon had disappeared.

While the meat cooked, he went through the jumble of components in her pack, noticing right off that she was missing some pieces. She told him about the cactus grass. He listened without comment, and she trailed off to a halt, feeling embarrassed and stupid. "I do have this, though." She showed him the key-stylus-pen she'd made.

He took it from her, turning it between his fingers.

"Do you know what it is?" she asked.

"No." He handed it back. "I had one, too, once. Never did figure out what it was for."

"Then maybe it *is* significant."

"I doubt it. They gave us a lot of useless stuff. Probably to confuse us. They're like that."

Pierce surveyed the remaining parts from her pack, then began fitting some of them together. Swiftly, one of the long-barreled hand pistols took shape. She didn't recall seeing instructions for that in the manual.

"It's a SLuB 40," he said, handing the weapon over. "See here?" He pointed a grimy finger to the inscription at the barrel's base.

Callie peered at it. "Those aren't letters."

"No, but it looks like 'SLuB 40,' so that's what we call it."

He started to assemble a rifle similar to his own, but ran out of pieces before he finished.

"Looks like the SLuB's gonna be it. At least you've got plenty of E-cubes." He scooped up four of the blue boxes. "They power everything else. Mind if I take a few?"

"Go ahead."

Balancing two cubes on his thigh, Pierce slid another pair into his rifle's side chamber, then replaced the cubes in his SLuB. By that time their dinner was ready.

The lizard meat had a strong muttony flavor. Callie would never call it tasty, but once she'd tantalized her stomach with the first bite, she all but inhaled the rest, even ate a second slice. As she wiped her greasy fingers on her jumpsuit, the comb-and-waxed-paper trill of a passing harry drew her gaze to the dark opening.

"They won't bother us in here," Pierce said. "Not at night."

"And in the morning?"

"They'll hunt a few hours past dawn, then swarm again for the day. We should be able to move out after that."

They lapsed into silence. After a few minutes, Callie leaned her head against the rock and closed her eyes. "I assume I'll be able to walk in the morning?"

"Should be, yeah."

She sighed. Five years. Were there others who'd been here as long? Longer?

Her thoughts drifted to home. Lisa's party would be well under way, her sister waiting with her latest stockbroker prospect for Callie. Eventually she'd call Callie's apartment, and Mom would begin preparing her lecture on being considerate. By evening's end they'd be miffed. But not worried. They knew Callie disliked the glittering, semiformal bashes. Even aside from the matchmaking, she resisted getting dressed up, had no taste for mingling over cocktails, and loathed the incessant one-upsmanship. Her conversations—if any—were brief, dribbling into awkward silences as she and the other party struggled to find a way of escape.

No, her family wouldn't start worrying until morning, and the police wouldn't start searching for twenty-four hours. By then Dr.

Charis's experiment would have vanished, likely leaving no clues and no one to question. Even if there was, what could the police do against beings who defied the laws of physics and zapped bodies through space in the blink of an eye?

Callie's throat tightened. Tears blurred her vision. What she wouldn't give to be home painting right now—her cockatiel pacing along the bookshelf—to hear Meg's bubbly laugh and endure her latest dumb fad, to be able to clean the rat cages on Monday. Right now, she'd even prefer Lisa's party.

Because deep down she knew there was a real possibility she would never attend another of Lisa's parties again.

# CHAPTER

## 4

"I wish I had a comb," Callie muttered, pulling her fingers through the tangled locks of her waist-length hair the next morning. "They provided all this other stuff—why not that?"

Pierce sat across the ash-filled fire ring, scraping the lizard hide. "What'd you say?"

"Nothing." She tilted her head, and he disappeared behind a curtain of red hair. Her captors hadn't supplied sleeping bags or toiletries; why expect a comb? Besides, they had claimed their obstacle course would take only a few hours. Issuing overnight gear would have made their victims balk.

Pierce's knife rasped across the rough hide, and a fresh wave of sour-sock smell assaulted her. She flicked the curtain of hair over her shoulder. Sleep and the harries' attack had made it a rat's nest. It wouldn't take long before it was greasy, matted and—considering how filthy her companion was—vermin infested.

The thought made her squirm.

*Well, I don't intend to be here that long.* Dividing her hair into three sections, she deftly plaited them together, wincing when she touched the still-tender spots on the backs of her hands.

Pierce continued to scrape the hide, fastened now to a wooden hoop. Once he'd satisfied himself she'd be able to travel this morning, he'd turned to the lizard skin and his own silent thoughts.

His welts had disappeared, and his eye and mouth no longer drooped. In the morning light Callie saw he was only a few years her senior. The brown, scraggly beard obscured his features, but clean-shaven, bathed, and wearing decent clothes, he might not be bad looking.

He looked up then, right at her, and she averted her gaze, face warming. Behind him the harries swooped through the emerald glade, their kazoolike trills rising and falling.

"It'll be about an hour," Pierce said, glancing over his shoulder.

Cautiously Callie drew her legs beneath her to stand and, forced to crouch beneath the sloping roof, walked the four steps to the cave's mouth. Muscles quivering, she sagged onto one of the boulders, blinked away a swirl of dizziness, and peered into the glade. She blinked again. "It's gone."

"The sucker path? Nah. It's still there. It's just not even close to white anymore."

"Yes, but—" She broke off. *I didn't believe you.*

"My friends are camped up on the mesa, like I said. You can come with us."

She twisted round to face him, hissing as the movement pulled the bite in her side. "I'd rather find the road again. I don't suppose you'd help me?"

He snorted. "It's miles out of my way, and I should've been back last night as it is. Besides, I told you—the gate roads are a waste of time."

"I'd like to check that out myself."

"Well, *I'm* not taking you back. The most my friends can wait is one more day." He set aside the knife and picked at a fatty spot on the hide. "And there's no guarantee the section you're headed for even exists anymore."

Callie hugged her legs to her chest, unwilling to admit aloud that he was right.

"Traveling the Outlands alone is a dangerous proposition," he added, picking up the knife again.

"You seem to be doing well enough."

"I don't usually travel alone. And I'm not a rookie."

Chewing her lip, she turned back to the glade. Harries swooped back and forth through the trees. They'd have killed her if not for Pierce, and distraction or not, his course of action did sound the most sensible. If there were as many gate roads out there as the manual indicated, sooner or later she'd cross another one, no matter which way she went.

There was the alien watcher to consider, as well.

An hour later the harries swarmed, their matlike forms turning the sky gray. One by one they glided in ever-tightening circles around the quivering knot of bodies in the middle tree, each finally jerked in to the others like filings to a magnet. In twenty minutes the sky was clear. Pierce waited another ten, and then they picked their way up the boulder-strewn slope to the canyon rim.

As she came over the top Callie staggered to a halt, astonishment sucking her breath away. A range of rugged, snowcapped mountains reared up to the left, presiding over an endless expanse of barren mesas, wind-scoured spires, and terraced sandstone cliffs. A hot breeze whipped her face, tousling tendrils of hair before her eyes. Clearly her Disneyland theory had to be revamped. This was no mere stadium, no "arena" in the usual sense of the word.

"Imagined something a bit smaller, did you?" Pierce stopped beside her and squinted at the vast landscape. The wind pressed back his brown hair, exposing a white wedge of untanned skin on his forehead. "I figure this Arena, as they call it, is about the size of the western half of the U.S."

"And we're supposed to cross it in a couple of hours?"

"If that's what you're thinking, Miss Hayes, you're in for a major disappointment." Slinging his rifle over one shoulder, he started across the sandstone, paralleling the mountains.

*Maybe time's skewed here*, she thought as she hurried after him. *Maybe five years here is only a few hours back home.*

Pierce set a brisk pace, but Callie matched him easily. She had taken pride in being one of the strongest girls in the university hiking club, often outdoing most of the guys. Feeling the need to redeem herself after the bumbling of yesterday, she kept abreast of him and spoke conversationally.

"So if you're not looking for a gate, what are you and your friends doing out here?"

"Hunting. Townspeople will give fifty E-cubes for a dragon horn."

"Townspeople? There are *towns* here?"

"Lots of 'em, once you get past the Outlands."

"And where is that?"

"Couple hundred miles that way." He waved toward the vista on their right. "These mountains are the Arena's outer boundary. Everything's inward from here."

They walked in silence for a bit, and then she said, "What about that Benefactor the manual talks about? The one that's supposed to help you get through the Gate?"

He grunted.

"It plainly says you need his help to get through it."

Pierce kept his eyes on the rumpled terrain. "Too bad it doesn't say what he looks like or where you're supposed to find him."

"Well, I'd think somewhere around the Gate—"

"Like sitting under it?" He flashed her a disgusted glance. "Lotta good that does if you can't get up to it."

"Maybe he's the one who—"

"Besides, how could one guy be in fourteen places at once?"

"Maybe it isn't one guy."

"It specifically states there is only one legitimate Benefactor."

"He wouldn't have to be in fourteen places at once. They probably know when someone's approaching."

"Oh, and they just beam him to the right place, is that the idea?"

"You don't have to be snide about it."

He shook his head. "You're just a rookie. What do you know?"

"At least I'm not choking on cynicism."

"Wait a few years." He paused, then added, "You'd better walk behind me. A person can stumble into lots of nasty things out here if she doesn't know what she's doing."

Stung, Callie dropped back.

They hiked all morning, saying little. Not only did the wind make talking difficult, but Pierce's unflagging pace became a challenge for her, after all. He only stopped to point out potential dangers—and he had not exaggerated the perils of the mesa top. Stretches of apparently solid ground hid holes of "dry quicksand" that could swallow the unwary traveler in less than five minutes. A head-sized rock tossed onto one such deceptive pan vanished in an instant.

Then there was the redclaw—low thickets of thorny, ash-colored branches from which stretched hidden runners. Each ended in a woody, football-sized pod that lay open and ready for action, its jaws snapping shut with enough force to drive their serrated edges into the demonstration branch Pierce used to trigger it. After that the runner slowly retracted, dragging its prize toward the distant thicket to be digested. It presented little threat to a man with a SLuB, but the pods were devilish to pry loose from one's boot.

There were also a number of cacti, from ankle to shoulder high, all equipped with poisonous spines. The plumes of cactus grass, called fountainweed, she had already met.

As for the fauna, the primary predator in this region was the rock dragon. A big female with as many teeth as a crocodile stalked them for an hour before Pierce dispatched it. Callie watched in morbid fascination while he deftly skinned it out.

She learned that the red crustacean-insect things were sand mites, and they flushed tens of them at a time from the grass throughout the morning. Pierce shot every one of them, and finally Callie asked if he was trying to impress her or something.

"They're drawn to your book," he explained, ignoring her jibe. "If I didn't shoot them, they'd be climbing all over us."

They stopped for lunch near a seep in a bank of tiered sandstone. Pierce stomped through the surrounding weeds, flushing out mites and killing them before he settled beside her on a flat stretch of rock. "There's probably a den nearby," he said, portioning out flatbread, lizard jerky, and dried fruit. "There usually is around water."

As Callie poured him a handful of cookie pellets from her second Snak-Pak, she asked why the sand mites wanted the manual.

"To eat it. I think they like the ink."

"So they bite."

"A big one can take off your thumb. They get agitated enough and a den of 'em will clean your bones in half an hour."

They ate in silence after that, Callie nervously eyeing the weeds.

When he finished, Pierce stretched out and fell instantly asleep. She regarded him with amazement. *Surrounded by perils, and he just switches off?* Of course, he had lived five years in this world. Maybe it was safer by day than by night. *Now there's a cheery thought.*

She ate the last of the pellets, then stretched her shoulders and pulled off her soft-soled boots to massage her battered feet. Though the boots showed surprisingly little wear, they provided neither support nor protection against the hard ground, leaving her toes bruised, her heels aching, and the balls of her feet already blistering.

Rubbing the arch of her right foot with both thumbs, she squinted across the down-sloping mesa. In the distance loomed the blue-shadowed face of another canyon wall. Beyond that, the red and ochre plain stretched to infinity. There was no sign of any gate, though without her glasses, she couldn't be sure.

The vista reminded Callie of a family vacation taken before her parents' divorce. It had been desperately hot and the car must have overheated, because they'd stopped in the middle of nowhere. She remembered how the air had danced and jittered over the dark, empty road as it ribboned through a vast white salt pan.

Mom had panicked and blamed Daddy. Why couldn't he think for once? Why couldn't he be responsible? He'd slapped her silent. Callie remembered how red and sweaty Lisa's face had been, her eyes round and wide as she'd watched her parents argue. Mom stomped off to the other side of the car, but Daddy gathered Callie and Lisa on the shaded side of the car and drew them stories in the salt. He often entertained them with his stories, drawn as eloquently with his finger in the soft white sand as with pen and paper. Once the car cooled, they went on. And afterward Daddy had made a painting of that day—white ground under a hot orange sky with a tiny car and four tiny people beside it. He'd called it "Breakdown." Only recently had Callie understood the metaphor he'd intended it to be.

Grimacing, she put away the past and pulled out the manual.

Pierce sat up fifteen minutes later. His eyes flicked to the book, his expression stony. Then he said, "This would be a good time for you to try out the SLuB."

"Try out the—but—"

"Killing and bloodshed don't appeal to you, huh?" Irony laced his voice. "Well, that was home. This is here." He reached across her to snag her pack and pull out the SLuB. "You should know how it works."

He showed her the black ON button beside the trigger. "You line up peg and notch on your target to aim. Fire in short bursts or it'll overheat. The blue E-cube is your power source. When it turns pink, you have to replace it."

He popped the cube out in demonstration, snapped it back in, and offered her the piece.

She eyed it distastefully.

He cocked a brow.

Well, he had a point. Right now she was totally dependent on him. If they ever did see another road, she wanted to be able to go to it with or without him.

Gingerly she took the weapon.

He showed her how to hold it and how to stand, adjusting her hands and shoulders until she had it right. His touch and nearness made her acutely self-conscious, and she was relieved when he stepped back and permitted her to shoot.

She wasn't as bad as she expected to be, and even Pierce seemed impressed. When they finished, he suggested she keep the weapon out, so she slid it dutifully under her belt—

And noticed her manual scuttling across the ground toward the sandstone bank.

As she leapt after it, understanding caught up with perception—a sand mite had it, lofting the slim volume with dark blue pincers. She followed the creature around a bend in the rock and saw it was headed for a large hole in the bank ahead. Pierce yelled something, but her attention was focused on the manual. Without thought of what might lie in that hole, she dove for the manual and caught it on the threshold. The mite released one claw from the prize to snap at her. Sitting down hard, she dodged the snapping pincer and worked to pry the other off the book. Abruptly the creature let go and clamped on to her thumb. Gasping, Callie dropped the manual.

A rapid clicking issued from the den as a second, larger mite burst from the darkness to seize the fallen prize. Suddenly Pierce was at her side, stomping book and bioform with a heavy, booted foot. She heard the crunch of exoskeleton as he jerked her upright and pulled her away.

"The manual!" she cried.

Cursing, he snatched it up and shoved her forward with his free hand. "Get out of here!"

Eyes smarting with the pain of the pincer still clamped to her thumb, Callie hurried around the bank. As she reached their gear on the rock she was panting hard. Pierce was already there, scooping up the packs and his rifle and urging her onward.

Together they scrambled over the tiered bank and up the mesa. Glancing back, Callie was horrified to see a tide of red bodies inundating the flat rock and clambering over the first bank in pursuit of them. With both packs slung over his shoulder, Pierce fired into the advancing tide, spraying the mites with a line of light that left the front edge of the hoard charred and smoking, while those behind recoiled in a rush of clicking claws. Pinning his weapon to his chest with an arm, he drew his knife, grabbed the mite still hanging from Callie's thumb, and severed the insect's body from its pincer. The mite landed on its back, legs writhing. He crushed it.

For what seemed like hours, they raced over hummock and ravine without pause. White light was creeping into the edges of Callie's vision when Pierce finally let her stop. She collapsed against a mound of sun-warmed sandstone, gasping and dizzy, hardly noticing when he seized her wrist and pried off the disembodied claw with his knife tip. She sagged back, nauseated by a renewed rush of pain, while he rustled in her day pack. Through the pain and exhaustion she felt him apply something slick to her thumb, and blessed numbness swept away the fire. Reveling in relief, she slid to the ground.

"What's the matter with you?" Pierce's voice came low and tight. "Didn't you hear me tell you to stop?"

She looked up at him. "It had the manual."

"You should've let it go." His blue eyes flashed. "The stupid thing's not worth dying for—and they would've killed you." He tossed her pack into her lap and walked away.

Callie pressed her lips together, smarting from the reprimand and feeling unjustly accused.

*How was I supposed to know?* she thought at his back as she pulled herself upright. *I'm just a rookie, remember? And I'm not losing the manual, no matter what you say.* I'm *not the one who's spent five years wandering through this nightmare because I didn't follow instructions.*

She followed him up a steep grade, nursing her indignation. Gradually, though, other thoughts intruded—that he was partially right, that she should have used more sense, that he could have hung back and let her pay the consequences of her folly but instead had come to her rescue. Again.

Most curious of all was that he was the one who'd saved the manual.

Some time later, he stopped so suddenly she ran right into him. Recoiling in embarrassment, she started to apologize, then saw he wasn't listening, at least not to her. He stood rigidly, staring over the sunbaked mesa.

She scanned the landscape in sudden alarm. What was it? Rock dragon? Harry? Something else? Something worse?

She glanced at him again. The breeze toyed with his hair and parted his beard, but beyond that he might have been stone, his eyes glazed, as if he searched with an inner sixth sense.

At length he unslung the rifle to hold it before him and started on.

"What?" Callie asked, moving at his side. "What's the matter?"

He regarded her as if he'd forgotten she was there. An expression of—horror?—spasmed across his face.

He shook it off. "Nothing. It's nothing."

"Don't tell me it's nothing."

"It was a false alarm, all right?" Irritation sharpened his voice. "Forget it." He lengthened his stride and drew ahead of her.

They crossed a rocky ridge and dropped into a ravine, heading up its dry bed toward the cloud-wreathed mountains. Callie's abused feet welcomed the smooth sand, and she hoped they might stay on it awhile, but Pierce soon stopped again, crouching over something on the ground. As she peered over his shoulder he touched an apelike footprint in the sand.

Humanoid, but not human. Could a Watcher have left it?

His fingers—long and expressive—moved to a depression beside and behind the first track, then to another farther away. Telling her to stay put, he climbed the hill, occasionally stooping to peer at the ground. He searched the other slope as well, then stood on the ridge, gazing into the distance. She was about to slog up after him when he turned and skidded down the slope to her side.

"They're old," he announced. "Probably a day at least. Looks like they were heading southwest."

"Who?"

Pierce shifted his pack and squinted at the ridges enfolding them. "Good thing we're downwind. Come on."

"Why? What is it?" But he was already striding away, angling up the hillside off the line of tracks.

Callie hurried after him, sensing he had not ignored her out of discourtesy. She had to jog to match his strides but didn't complain. He gripped his rifle tightly, scanning the landscape as if attack were imminent.

They left the ravine to scale an expanse of barren rock. Shadows streamed across the red-lit land as gloom gathered in the hollows. The mountains loomed before them now, and the terrain roughened, rising steeply in tiered sandstone shelves. Limestone teeth jabbed up between sage and juniper. A faint acrid odor rode the capricious breeze.

The shelves ascended to a small flat-topped mesa ringed by stunted junipers and tall red rocks. A stench of urine, so strong it made her eyes water, all but knocked Callie over. As she followed Pierce across the flat, the awareness that something dreadful had happened here hit her hard. Long black lines scored the rock, and pieces of what looked like shattered bone littered the ground. To the right, an old juniper stood charred and skeletal, while its neighbors, still green, were torn and chewed, the earth at their roots churned up as if spaded.

She stopped where four stout wooden pegs protruded from the sun-baked earth in a man-sized rectangle. There were no straps or bindings, but a damp red-brown stain at the rectangle's center hinted of a grim purpose.

Pierce passed the pegs with a cursory glance, stopping at a narrow trench beyond them. Six inches deep and three wide, it carved through the hardpan for a good five feet and linked two deeper postholes. To either side, a fine blue powder dusted the ground.

Something about the scene repelled her, as if an object of great evil had stood at that spot and the fabric of reality had not yet recovered from its presence. With a shudder she gave the site a wide berth and went to investigate a curious scatter of white sticks farther on.

Only they weren't sticks. They were human arm and leg bones, broken and recently stripped of flesh, the bloodied shanks sucked dry of marrow. Trembling, Callie continued along the edge of the flat. She found a broken arrow amid spots and streaks of blood, and then a rose-hued one-inch cube caught at the base of a weed. She found another nearby. And another, splotched with turquoise. Scooping them up, she realized they were spent E-cubes and hurried back to show Pierce.

But when she saw his face her words died in her throat.

He still stood rigidly before the trench, his blue eyes moving over it in weird, shifting jerks. His face was pale and sweat-sheened beneath his beard, his terror unnerving in its baldness.

"This was your friends' camp, wasn't it?"

He didn't answer. His eyes flicked from the trench to her, and then to the rocks, the ruined trees, and the ravaged ground. More E-cubes lay scattered along the rocks where his companions must have taken cover. There was a great deal of blood.

He grabbed her arm, hard enough to hurt, and dragged her back down the way they'd come. By the time they stopped, he was hyper-ventilating. His eyes darted wildly as he gaped around, seemingly unable to decide which way to go.

More unnerved than she'd been since this whole nightmare had started, Callie laid a hand on his arm. "Pierce?"

He didn't respond. She squeezed the muscle, rock hard beneath her fingers. "Come on. Get a grip."

The blue eyes swam around to her.

"Whatever happened, they're gone now," she said quietly. "And you're our only hope of survival. Calm down. Think."

He stared at her, his distress shooting out in ragged spears. Then he closed his eyes and drew a long breath, shuddering beneath her touch. When he opened his eyes, he was himself again—or at least close enough.

"What happened up there?" she asked. "Who attacked your friends?"

He stared across the crimson-dyed mesa. "Trogs," he whispered and shuddered again.

She thought of the arrows and pegs and ravaged bones and swallowed a suddenly sour taste. "Aliens?"

He shook his head. "Humans . . . sort of . . . mutants." He speared fingers through his hair. "We can't stay here."

"But they're gone—"

"They're less than two miles away. I couldn't tell earlier, but—" He swallowed and caught her arm. "They'll smell us the minute the wind changes. Come on."

"Where are we going?"

"To the mountains. That's where my friends will have gone. If any of them survived."

# CHAPTER

## 5

Though the cloud-cloaked peaks loomed higher than ever, by night-fall the mountains' forested lower slopes remained a good ten miles away. As the sun dropped below the distant horizon, Callie and Pierce had only scrub pine and juniper to shield them, and not much of that.

Pierce stopped at the foot of a steep slope and turned to search the land below them. Callie followed the direction of his gaze, the wind enfolding her from behind as it swooped off the mountainside. *"When the wind changes they'll smell us,"* he'd said. Now he loosed a breath of decision, stripped off his pack, and pulled out a small hatchet. They continued up the ragged slope, zigzagging over uneven shelves of rock to a hollow bounded by a juniper-studded ridge. Midway across it, a gnarled old juniper bowed beside a massive sandstone block, and it was there he decided they'd shelter.

"Do you know how to build a lean-to?" he asked her.

"Sort of."

Turning, he hacked and tore a good-sized clump of sage from the ground, then handed Callie the hatchet. "Cut as many branches as you need from the other junipers. Pile 'em around this big one—between it and the rock. Make it look natural."

She stared at him. "We're going to hide?"

"Yes."

"But what if they come?"

"If I do my job right, they won't. Keep your SLuB ready. And watch out for the redclaw over there. I won't be long."

Callie swallowed her protest as Pierce turned and descended the bank, dragging the sage after him. At the bottom he tossed the bush aside, reshouldered the pack, and jogged into the gloom, leaving Callie on her own. From this vantage she could see the pale outcropping where the Trogs had attacked Pierce's friends, steeped now in twilight. On a promontory several miles beyond it, a gleam of light flickered amid a cluster of dark spots. She could not tell if they were moving.

The hatchet's thunking chops echoed across the hollow like gunshots, advertising her presence to anything nearby. Even without it, pulling and twisting the branches free made a horrible racket, and it took nine good-sized limbs to complete a lair under the juniper. By the time she was finished, her hands were cut and scraped, her bitten thumb throbbed, and her legs shook with fatigue.

She climbed onto the rock beside the juniper to await Pierce's return. It might be wiser to hide in the lair, but she couldn't bear the thought of huddling there alone, unable to see what might lurk outside.

Overhead, stars twinkled into view against the rapidly darkening vault of indigo, while out on the distant promontory two fires flickered now, bright pinpoints on a sandstone sea. She turned to the mountains behind her, pulling a strand of windblown hair from her face. Junipers jabbed the skyline to her right—dark, twisted witch forms climbing the ridge. In the hollow below, the gloom had acquired a foglike substance, thick and dark among the darker blots of the trees.

Restlessness simmered within her. Why was Pierce taking so long? Had he surprised something unpleasant? Lost his way? Stumbled off a cliff in the darkness? Doggedly she put her worries aside, assuring herself he knew what he was doing and would be back.

The breeze died to a faint stirring of air perfumed with sage and juniper. She folded her legs yoga style on the rock, which was still warm with its store of the day's heat, and sighed. *If I hadn't left the road, would I be in one of those Safehavens now?* She wished suddenly for Meg. Though this was so much bigger than a simple, airheaded misjudgment, it was hard for Callie to continue being put out with her. And right now, she longed for a friend. Had *Meg* stayed on the road? Had she been dropped off at the same point, or was she hundreds of miles away? It was a depressing thought.

Out in the shadow-clad trees a twig cracked, followed by a rattling of rock. Callie sat forward, adrenaline prickling across her back and arms. Trying to remember Pierce's instructions, she drew the SLuB and turned it on. The immediate fine vibration against her palm comforted her, but her sore thumb made it hard to hold the weapon.

Another rattle and scrape. Closer this time.

Her scalp crawled. Her palms grew damp.

Peering into the twilight, she willed a form to appear in the thickening fabric of night.

*It's probably Pierce*, she told herself. *I should let him know where I am*. But visions of huge, hirsute humanoids stilled her tongue and made her heart pound in her throat.

How long she sat there rigid and trembling she did not know. The last light waned, wrapping her in folds of velvet blackness. Starlight limned the junipers and rocks with silver, washed the ground with a pale glow. The last flippet of breeze died, and stillness settled over the land.

"Miss Hayes?" Pierce's low voice came so unexpectedly—and so close—that she flinched and sucked in an involuntary gasp.

"It's okay," he said. "Don't shoot." A round shadow moved by her knee, and she dangled her legs down the rock face. His hand touched her thigh, moved to her waist, and then to her arm to steady her as she slid down beside him. He didn't let go when she was down, and she didn't pull away.

"Where's the shelter?" he asked. The familiar musky tang of his body odor was unexpectedly comforting.

"Here." She groped for the opening, his hand on her shoulder, and then crawled under the branches. The pungent scent of juniper filled her nostrils, and spiny leaves pricked her palms and knees. Pierce eased in beside her, pulling the last branch across the opening.

His pack and leather vest were gone, but it was a close fit, nonetheless, pressing them shoulder, arm, and thigh against each other. He was hot and sweaty, and she could hear the rush of his breathing, his face only inches from her own. Normally she would have found such closeness intolerable. Now she had to fight to keep from pressing against him like a lost child.

"What if they come?" she whispered. "We'll be trapped."

He shuddered, but his voice was firm. "Trogs' night vision is way better than ours. After dark, we're better off going to ground. I've laid a false track in case they come by."

"And if it doesn't work?"

"That's what the weapons are for. Now we'd best keep quiet. Voices carry a long way out here."

He fell silent, and from the rigidity of his body, Callie guessed he was searching again with that inner sense of his. She sat equally rigid at first, adrenaline surging with each new rustle or crackling twig. But as time passed and nothing happened, exhaustion overpowered her fear, and soon she was dozing off, dream images mingling with reality—Meg pointing a TV camera through the branches, her father standing in her kitchen doorway, backlit by the bright afternoon outside, Pierce shuddering beside her, warning her not to let them smell—

Her body jerked, startling her awake, and the SLuB shifted. Something was pulling it from her grasp. She grabbed for it—

"It's all right, Miss Hayes," Pierce whispered. His fingers had closed around her hand and the SLuB at her first movement. "I'll keep watch."

"But you did it last night." Her voice was slurred. "And don't call me Miss Hayes."

"Okay, Callie." He tugged at the SLuB. "But I'd rather not be shot in the knee, if you don't mind."

As he slipped the weapon free she relaxed against him, her head falling onto his shoulder.

Her sleep was plagued by horrible howlings as unseen monsters chased her down an endless red-walled canyon. She woke once, disturbed when Pierce moved his arm from under her head. Cold air rushed against her, and she shifted closer, seeking his warmth and the comforting contact of his body. He did not pull away and, after a few moments, dropped his arm around her shoulder. The next time she woke, dawn light filtered into their juniper-bough shelter. Pierce was sound asleep with Callie curled securely in his embrace, one arm draped across his chest.

Realization stiffened her, and she pushed away—

Which startled him awake. Mortified, she leaned forward and pretended to listen for sounds from outside the shelter. It was a few moments before she heard anything but the rush of her own blood.

An innocent quiet, punctuated by birdsong and insect whirs, pressed around them. Pierce said nothing and, to her intense relief, presently eased away the bough at the opening and crawled out.

Dismayed by how stiff and sore she was, Callie reached back to brush the prickling leaves from her side and struck the hard carapace of a sand mite clinging to the back of her shirt. With a cry of revulsion, she lurched out of the lair, jittering around as she tried to slap it loose. Pierce jumped down from the rock, seized her shoulders, and spun her around to pluck it off. She heard it crunch beneath his boot.

Feeling foolish now, she turned back to thank him, but he was already walking away. "Watch out when you get your pack," he said over his shoulder. "There'll be more."

Four of them clung to the pack. Shivering as she imagined them crawling over her while she slept, Callie gritted her teeth and pulled them free one by one, crushing each with a rock. After she finished, she went looking for Pierce and found him on the other side of the sandstone block. He had redonned his weapons and the leather vest, but there was no sign of his pack.

"Nothing came by except the usual," he said. "Rabbits, coyotes, a rock dragon—probably a juvenile from the size of its tracks."

"What about those horrible howls? Did I just dream them?"

The thought of dreaming reminded her of how she'd awakened this morning, which brought the blood back to her cheeks. She averted her eyes, studying the distant folds of landscape.

"There were mutants up here, all right, but not close. Like I said, sound carries a long way out here."

He pulled two packages of nuts from his vest pocket and handed one to her. "You filled your water bottles at the seep, didn't you?"

She nodded. "What happened to your stuff?"

"I left the lizard carcass as bait and hid the pack. If I'm lucky, they won't have found it."

Soon they were headed toward the mountains again, angling sharply left from their previous course. Callie was not nearly as energetic as she'd been yesterday. Her legs creaked with stiffness, and her collarbone protested the renewed burden of the pack, light though it was.

Presently they came to a place where something had gouged a great wound in the land. Rocks were upended, sagebrush uprooted and half consumed. A nearby juniper had been ravaged, limbs stripped of leaves or torn off altogether, trunk gored, bark shredded to expose the white cambium beneath. As before, the place reeked of urine.

"Well, they found the carcass," Pierce said, squatting over a dark, scuffed place scattered with chips of bone.

Callie gaped at the spot. "They ate all of it?"

He rose and continued up the drainage. "After they pass through the fire, they eat everything they can get their hands on."

"What do you mean, 'pass through the fire'?" She glanced around uneasily.

"They have a device that generates a curtain of energy. I have no idea what it is—some kind of radioactivity, I'd guess. It gives them a rush of power, a shot of super-strength. If they're injured, it'll heal them—for days afterward their flesh regenerates at a hyperaccelerated rate. If you don't kill them right off with a clean head shot, you usually don't kill them. It also makes them crazy hungry. For food and . . . other things."

A rustle drew the barrel of his weapon, but it was only a sand mite. Surprisingly, he refrained from shooting it. Ascending a gentle rise, they found another mutilated juniper, shoved onto its side, its roots clawing the sky. Branches littered the ground and mingled among them was the frame on which Pierce had strung the lizard hide, now splintered and gnawed. The skin was gone.

Callie stared at the naked frame. "They ate the hide, too?" She was beginning to understand why Pierce was afraid of them.

"Ah!" His cry of satisfaction drew her gaze. Standing in the crown foliage of the downed tree, he bent out of sight and re-emerged with the pack. "I tied it in the middle where they'd have to think to get it," he explained. "The fire curtain makes them irrational, too. Maybe it's the hunger. Anyway, I hoped the hide would distract them and—oh. Look here." He crouched beside a scraped patch of sand and picked up a bloody curl of dragon skin. "This is probably the same youngster that came past our lair. Looks like two or three mutants. You can see where they ate the bloody dirt."

She came up beside him, gripping the shoulder pads of her pack. "I guess they don't take prisoners, then?"

He stood. "Better to be eaten."

His gaze fixed on the light-washed hollow ahead and went briefly blank. Then he said, "They probably rejoined the main group before daybreak. Come on."

As they gained elevation the juniper and sage gave way to oak and pine. Patches of knee-high grass waved in every clearing, hiding a multitude of sand mites. Repeatedly they had to stop and pick the creatures off their legs, yet Pierce continued to refrain from shooting them—to save E-cubes, he said—stomping them to death instead.

Midmorning Pierce found a scuff in the dirt he called a footprint. He pointed out another scuff soon after, then a crumpled weed and a black mark on the shoulder of a rock. But it was the clear, ridged sole print at the base of a young oak that finally convinced Callie. Their pace slowed now, and she welcomed the opportunities to rest. Her feet were killing her, and the harry bite in her side ached. Her thumb, swollen and purple, still throbbed, to say nothing of her stiff shoulders, her tender collarbone, her overworked back, and her head, which was pounding dully.

Gradually, tall straight-trunked evergreens replaced the oaks. The ground grew softer, dustier, matted with pine needles, the air redolent with warm sap. Pierce talked of meeting his friends before nightfall.

They stopped for lunch on a rock overlooking a dry stream bed. Rough-barked pines marched up the opposing slope, and a particularly massive specimen curved out of the rocky bank below them and to the right. A stand of oak blocked Callie's downstream view, but she wasn't about to get closer to the drop-off than the ten feet she already was. Pierce, nearer the edge, could keep watch.

"At least one of them's hurt," he said, portioning out the last of his jerky and hardtack. "That's why we're gaining on them."

Callie glanced at him sidelong. "Your friends?"

He nodded, studying the ravine.

"You're pretty good at this stuff, aren't you?"

"I grew up tracking deer and cattle in country not much different from this."

"You lived on a ranch?"

"Just outside Durango."

Somehow she hadn't taken him for a cowboy. She supposed it fit, though—the tracking, the familiarity with weapons, the ease with outdoor life. "So how'd you end up here?"

His sky-colored eyes glanced at her and quickly shifted away. He bit off a piece of hardtack. "I was riding fence line. Came upon this white panel truck parked in the middle of nowhere. The guys with it said they were doing a survey, and I figured they were Division of Wildlife. They asked for my help." He crunched down the last of his hardtack. "Next thing I knew I was here."

He didn't ask how she'd gotten hooked, so they sat in silence, listening to the birds calling from the trees. A bee droned toward them, inspected a crumb on the rock, and floated off. With a sigh, Pierce stretched out on his back, cradled his head in his hands, and closed his eyes.

Callie watched him surreptitiously, taking in the lean form, the broad shoulders and narrow hips, the corded, muscular forearms. He was a far cry from Lisa's lawyers and MBAs. More like one of the heroes in the cherished Zane Grey novels of her adolescence.

A cowboy.

His breathing deepened. He shifted against the rock's gritty surface and turned his face toward her. Asleep, he looked almost boyish. Perversely her mind snapped back to this morning when she'd awakened in his embrace.

Hers was not a touching family. Expressions of affection were not explicitly discouraged, they just never occurred. She couldn't recall more than a handful of times when her mother had hugged her, and she had no recollection of any such demonstrations from her father. Lisa, the consummate psychologist, had initiated more physical contact in recent years, but it was an uphill battle. And as hard as it was to touch each other, they certainly didn't throw themselves on strangers. The way she was snuggling with a man she hardly knew this morning made her feel almost . . . dirty.

Of course, she'd been desperately afraid last night, and he *was* her only hope of survival. The thought of going it alone in this wretched world was not one she liked to contemplate.

*And yet, I must.* Callie frowned across the sun-dappled ravine. *Because the longer I stay with him, the farther from the Gate I get.*

Downstream a flock of birds took flight in an explosion of wing beats. They wheeled overhead and vanished beyond the spiring trees.

*Maybe one of his friends will help me. . . .*

No. They were *his* friends, out here for the same reason he was. If anything, they'd be less cooperative in a group. But if they meant to trade their lizard parts with the townspeople maybe they'd—

Pierce leapt to his feet, snatching up his rifle as he did, astounding her with his ability to come instantly and thoroughly awake. Now he stared downstream with that eerie not-quite-here expression on his face. "They're after us," he whispered.

A shrill scream split the air, punctuating his words. Whatever made the sound was coming up the draw behind the oaks.

Pierce pulled her off the rock, scrambled around the trees, and flung himself flat on the needled ground. "Get down!" he hissed, inching forward on belly and elbows.

Callie dropped beside him, leaf tips pricking her forearms. Dust tickled her nose, and she fought off the sneeze as she searched the drainage bottom for their pursuers. *There!* Three tall figures with grotesquely overdeveloped brows and jaws stalked into view. Bearded, shaggyhaired, and furry, with their arms dangling to their knees, they looked like protohumans. Trousers covered their lower bodies, each garment a different color—red, orange, brown. All three carried crossbows and quivers of short arrows—*quarrels* she thought they were called—hung across their backs.

Pierce had them in his sights. "You take the one on the right," he said. "On my word."

She looked at the SLuB in her hand—when had she pulled it from her belt?—then at the approaching men. "You mean . . . shoot him?"

"Dead center. Forehead shot if you can."

Though the air was cool, sweat beaded his brow. Below, the ugly trio moved toward them, following the stream bed, gazes on the ground.

"Pierce, they're people, I can't—"

"They're not people," he growled. "If they catch you, they'll kill you. But in their own good time. Now would you aim that thing?"

The leader dropped to all fours, sniffing the ground like a dog. Then he threw back his head, loosed another hair-raising howl, and took off on three legs, carrying the crossbow in one hand. He was leading his companions along the very route she and Pierce had taken less than half an hour before.

Callie thumbed on the SLuB and braced her elbows against the ground, holding the weapon in both hands as Pierce had taught her. Notch and peg bobbled on a hairy shoulder. She edged the barrel left, aiming for midchest. Her heart beat rabbit-fast, and she sought to slow her breathing. *"Squeeze the trigger,"* he'd said. *"Don't jerk it."*

"On three," he murmured. "One . . ."

Callie's SLuB wandered off target.

"Two . . ."

She brought it back, hands trembling.

"Three!"

*I can't do this!* She let the SLuB's barrel fall as Pierce's rifle spat its blue-green fire. His victim crumpled. He fired again, and the second Neanderthal fell, howling and writhing on the ground. It was the first time she'd seen Pierce fail to hit a target dead on.

Before he could fire again, the third Trog dodged behind a rock.

"Come on!" Pierce pulled her up the hill.

"I couldn't do it," she lamented.

His face was grim. "The hurt one'll need help. If we're lucky, he'll distract the other."

Behind them an earsplitting double wail rose from the ravine.

They were well up the mountainside when it dawned on Callie that Pierce's second shot hadn't been off at all. With both companions killed, the third mutant—the one she'd failed to take down—would have had no reason not to continue the chase.

She glanced at Pierce, respect for him rising another notch.

They rested in an open area surrounded by the tall pines. Callie stood gasping as her companion unzipped her pack—still on her back—and drew out a single bottle to share. His eyes never left the trees around them.

"Surely you don't think they're following," Callie said.

"They heal *fast* after the firewalk. And they cover ground like you wouldn't believe. We're way too close."

He took the bottle from her, gulped a mouthful of water, then screwed on the lid and slipped it back into her pack. The zipper whined shut.

"They're not howling anymore," she said.

"That's what worries me."

They continued upslope at a stiff pace. A thicket of underbrush gave them the option of following a game trail or circling into the open, and Pierce opted for the game trail. As they pressed through the sharp-tipped leaves, Callie became aware of the deep quiet around them. No birdsong, no insect noises, not even a breeze. Ahead Pierce eased into a clearing. She followed closely, hands trembling, every sense alert. A sudden animal odor provided an instant of warning before a hairy form reared out of the bush beside them.

Pierce fired as the beast howled and smacked the rifle from his grasp. He staggered back, and the thing leaped upon him. Off-balance, Callie stumbled sideways into the sudden hot awareness of another attacker on the off side. She glimpsed deep-set eyes, a flat nose, and a jaw full of dagger-sharp teeth. As she pivoted to avoid his grasp her heel caught on a root, and she pitched backward to the ground. Instantly the creature dropped upon her, straddling her hips. Seconds stretched into what seemed like long, nightmarish minutes as the clawed hand swung lazily up and back—

And she realized that by some miracle she still gripped her SLuB.

The hand floated down. With limbs turned to rubber, she brought up the SluB, closed her eyes, and squeezed the trigger. The gun bucked. Heat seared her belly and the backs of her hands as she sensed the beast recoil above her.

She opened her eyes. A bloody wound creased the Trog's side, but it seemed not to matter. The mutant reached angrily for her hands and the weapon in them. She fired again, into its chest this time. The creature's black eyes flashed, narrowed, fixed upon her own—

She shot it a third time, the SLuB's green fire drilling a hole between its eyes. As its head rolled backward, the beast collapsed forward, the full weight of its massive body pinning her to the ground. Gagging on the stench, hardly able to breathe for the weight on her chest, Callie struggled weakly to free herself. From somewhere close came the snarling of the second beast, and odd rasping whimpers that couldn't be Pierce—but must be.

In rising desperation, she gave a mighty heave and wriggled partly free of the dead Trog's body. Another heave and jerk and she was out, staggering upright—and still gripping the SLuB. Across the clearing, Pierce's rifle gleamed against gray humus. Between it and Callie, a black-haired monster had him pinned to the ground. She could see only his boots, part of one leg, and way too much blood.

"No!" Her own shriek brought the mutant upright and halfway around before she shot it, the shock of the beam knocking it off-balance and away from Pierce, who lay curled in a ball, head tucked, hands over his ears. The beast roared and flung wide its arms, pig eyes burning into her own, and she fired again. It reeled backward, stumbled over a root, and fell into the covering embrace of a thick growth of vine and brush. But still it wouldn't stay down. As the dark hulking shadow rose yet again, panic pushed Callie over the edge. She fired repeatedly, hardly even aiming, the foliage at the end of her beams leaping and quivering, little bits of leaves whirling up in a veil of smoke as, in the shadows, tiny flames burst into life and flickered out.

She didn't come to her senses until the weapon quit from overheating and agonizing pain seared her hands. The mutant lay still beneath a leafy shroud. At least for the moment.

Sobbing, she dropped the SLuB and stumbled forward to where Pierce still huddled in a fetal position, whimpering pitifully. She collapsed to her knees in front of him. "It's okay," she gasped. "I shot it. It's dead."

He gave no sign he'd heard her, but he didn't appear to be badly injured. Most of the blood must have been the mutant's. She touched his quivering shoulder. "Pierce?"

The quivers grew into great wracking shudders.

"It's all right," she said. "They're dead. They're both dead."

She was shaking almost as badly as he was and drew away, averting her eyes, dismayed by his loss of control. She picked up her still-warm SLuB, then sat down again, numb with shock.

Eventually the shudders waned. His breathing slowed. His face relaxed. Finally he opened his eyes. She watched focus sharpen in his expression, and then he started up.

"You're hurt!"

"No—" She held out her hands, warding off his panic. "The blood's not mine. It's the Trog's. I shot him." She held up the SLuB.

His gaze went from the blood on her jumpsuit to the weapon in her hand, then swept the clearing, lingering on the dark, still hump, half hidden in the bushes. Finally he lurched upright. His stride had stabilized by the time he reached for his rifle. She watched him switch it on and off, pop out the cube, and snap it back. Then he drew a long breath and glanced over his shoulder. "We'd better get going."

# CHAPTER

## 6

It took some time for the enormity of what Callie had done to settle in. She'd killed two people. Well, not quite *people*, but still. . . . Part of her was horrified and guilt ridden. Another part acknowledged she'd had no choice.

She had often wondered what she would do if someone were trying to kill her. As fearful as she was about so many lesser things, she figured she'd be paralyzed into passivity. That she had not buckled gave her a deep, if ambivalent, satisfaction.

Pierce's actions in the crisis, however, gave her anything but satisfaction. As she followed him, glancing up from time to time at his back, she realized that, though the rifle had been knocked from his grasp, he'd been wearing all his weapons when the Trog attacked. He had not been helpless—he had panicked. The same way he had panicked when they discovered the remains of his friends' camp.

The power of her disgust and the sense of betrayal she felt surprised her. She supposed she'd wanted him to be her hero, someone she could count on to protect her, and the disappointment of reality tasted bitterly familiar.

They refilled their bottles at a shallow stream, washed off the worst of the blood, and continued on. Come late afternoon, they were following a game trail through a thicket of prickle-leaved brush when a bald, red-bearded man stepped into their path. He wore leather britches and a vest and carried a rifle like Pierce's.

"Well, if it isn't the prodigal son come back," he exclaimed with a trace of an Australian accent. "Didn't expect to see you again, mate. Not after last night."

"We went to ground," Pierce said.

"You found our camp, then?"

"Yeah."

"Where'd you pick up the rookie?"

"Canyon by the harries' nest." Pierce introduced the man as Thor. This close, Callie saw the red stubble on his skull and the gray hairs threading his beard.

"The others are just over the ridge," Thor said. He paused. "We heard hunting cries earlier."

Pierce shrugged. "Not a problem anymore."

"You gonna go back and get them?"

"Nah. They were pretty big, and the main group's still out there."

Thor's eyes narrowed. "Well, Garth'll want to hear about it. And meet the girl, o' course." He winked at Callie.

Pierce moved by him without comment.

As they emerged from the brush and descended the slope, Callie asked, "Why would you want to go back and get them?"

"Towns pay out bounties for dead Trogs."

*Oh.*

At the foot of the slope, a stream curved through a grassy meadow, widening at one point to form a quiet pond. Beside it stood a black nylon dome tent amidst bedrolls, packs, pots, piles of tanned hides, and other paraphernalia. A man tended a spitted haunch roasting over a small blaze near the tent. Others sprawled or sat about the grass while, at the forest's edge, two men skinned the carcass from which the haunch must have come.

At Pierce and Callie's arrival all activity ceased. Then a blond woman threw aside the rifle she was cleaning and leaped up. "Hey, Garth! Pierce's back!"

Gazellelike, she bounded from stone to stone across the stream. Behind her a big dark-bearded man with a ponytail emerged from the tent.

Soon Callie was surrounded, feeling as if she'd fallen in with the Hell's Angels. From the stink she guessed they hadn't been to a Safehaven in some time. The men wore beards, mostly unkempt, though one man's was plaited into braids. Their long hair was worn loose or, like that of the one called Garth, tied into ponytails, and battle scars abounded. One man wore an eye patch. Another had lost part of an ear. All wore leather vests and boots like Pierce's, and all bristled with weapons—knives, crossbows, SLuBs, rifles—stuffed into belts and boots and pockets and strapped on in leather harnesses.

"So are they after us?" asked the blond woman. Long-limbed and full-busted, she had cover-girl-perfect features. Even with a dirty face and raggedly shorn hair, she was gorgeous.

"Not anymore." Pierce's guardedness returned.

"Did you take care of them?" asked Garth. A solid, muscular man with bristling brows and craggy features, his mien was one of long-accustomed command.

"I killed one." Pierce gestured at Callie. "She got the other two."

His friends exchanged glances.

The blonde pasted a smile on her face—to stunning effect—and said, "I'm Rowena."

"Callie."

"Well, Callie, two Trogs in one day is quite a feat for a rookie. How long you been down?"

"Ummm . . ."

"Three days," said Pierce.

Rowena's blue eyes widened. "And you did it with a SLuB? You must've been *close.*"

Callie thought of the creature's suffocating weight and shuddered. "Yeah."

Again there was that subtle exchange of glances and sidelong looks at Pierce. Then Garth smiled at her, the expression softening his features.

"Who'd ever believe such a pretty face could hide so much grit?" His gaze was so openly approving she flushed.

Rowena frowned at him and turned to Pierce. "Trogs hit us two nights ago."

"Who'd they get?"

"Killed Lem and Charlie right off. Took Josie, Jon-li, and the Parson."

"I've never seen so many of them," said the blond guy with the twin beard braids. "Like sand mites charging out of a burrow."

"We're lucky they were wanting a firewalk," said Rowena, "or they'd have gotten us all."

"Li and Jo and the Parson," Pierce pressed. "They're dead?"

"We didn't find any bodies," said Garth.

"Muties probably ate them," Rowena offered.

"So you're not sure."

"Pierce!" Annoyance sharpened Garth's voice. "They're *dead.*"

Another awkward silence ensued. Then Rowena slid her arm through Callie's. "Garth picked up a pair of boots for me in Harford that turned out to be too small. Maybe they'll fit you, and you can get out of those bedroom slippers. Your feet must be killing you."

As Callie let herself be led off, she noted Garth draw near to Pierce. "The three you killed," he said quietly. "They were the only ones?"

She didn't hear Pierce's answer, for Rowena was talking again. "I remember *my* first days here. If Garth hadn't found me, I would've died."

"You've been together awhile, then?"

"Four years." She pushed aside the tent flap and motioned Callie inside.

Beneath a scattering of paper and leather maps, a sandwich of wrinkled blankets took up most of the tent's floor space. Shoving the maps aside, Rowena sat and began rummaging through a large pack.

"Where'd you get all this stuff?" Callie asked.

"Oh, all over." Rowena pulled a bloodstained work shirt from the pack and continued to rummage.

"You mean they have tent and blue jean factories here?"

The woman looked up, puzzled, and then nodded as understanding dawned. "Our kidnappers supply them to those who serve them. *They* trade it to the rest of us. Boots, weapons, clothes—you name it, someone's offering it."

"And they trade it for. . . ?"

"E-cubes. Dragon hides. Redhorn. Blood crystal. We've done well on the hides this run. Got enough to make us all armor, with plenty to trade."

"Armor?"

Rowena pulled a pair of jeans partway from the bag, then stuffed them back in and followed them with the shirt. "Rock dragon hide is *tough*. Harries can't bite through it. Crossbow quarrels can't pierce it. Even SLuB fire can't get through. If we ever do find our way to the Inner Realm, believe me, we'll need it. Ah, here we are." She pulled a pair of hiking boots from behind the pack. "Hold on and I'll find some socks."

"The Inner Realm," Callie repeated. "That's the middle of the doughnut, right?" She recalled Pierce telling her about this. "Surrounded by the cliffs with all the gates."

"Right. Then there's the Outer Realm—where we are now—and then the mountains to guard the outer edge. But the exit's in the Inner Realm, so that's where we have to go."

She passed Callie a pair of thick cotton socks, then the boots. "Go ahead and try them on."

Callie sat and pulled off her dusty "bedroom slippers." "What about on the other side of the mountains?"

"Nothing. We thought for a while that there might be a way there, even launched an expedition." Rowena snorted. "Now there was a fiasco! The air's too thin, you don't go more than a day without a storm, and the winds are horrific. It took us four tries to reach the top. Only to find ourselves at the edge of a sheer vertical drop. Like when they thought the earth was flat, you know? It just falls into nothing."

Callie slipped her foot into the first boot.

"It's probably some kind of illusion," Rowena went on. "A cosmic moat or something. Still, not the sort of thing you want to go rappelling into." She gestured at Callie's foot. "How's it feel?"

"I think it fits." She snugged the laces.

"For years we heard talk of a canyon breaching the cliffs that guard the Inner Realm, but the terrain's so rough in the only likely spot, it's nearly impossible to find. We figured for a long time it was just a rumor, but last year we met a guy who'd actually found it. Almost reached the rim, in fact."

Callie put on the second boot. "Why didn't he go all the way?"

"Ran into muties coming off the top. Killed most of his party. He was about the only one who got away."

"And you're up for a repeat performance?"

Rowena shrugged. "Trogs don't come down the trail often; otherwise, everyone would know where it is. But that *is* why we want the dragon hide."

Callie tied the second set of laces. "I guess you haven't found the Benefactor the manual refers to?"

"Honey, I found four of them, and every one wanted years of my life in exchange for their 'help.' "

"The manual says there's only one who—"

"The manual says a lot of things. Most of 'em aren't true. So—they gonna be okay?" She gestured at the boots.

Callie flexed one foot and stood. "I think so. Are you sure you want to give them away?"

"They're no use to me."

Outside, the camp had settled back to normal, blanketed now in gloom. Pierce lay under a tree sound asleep. Garth perched on a log by the fire, poring over a map. Beside him, the cook shook a silver can over the spitted roast. A small black woman with a crown of dark braids sat across the fire. Two others stood at the pond's edge, skipping stones across the water.

As Rowena zipped the tent shut, Garth turned and, seeing them, smiled. "I guess the boots fit." He patted the log beside him. "Come talk to me, Callie."

As Rowena gathered the pieces of her rifle, Callie perched uneasily on the log's edge.

Garth leaned against her. "Now tell us what *really* happened with that mutant pack this morning."

He smelled of sweat and dirt and something vaguely sour. Uncomfortable with his closeness, she eased away from him, watching Rowena settle beside the black woman across the fire.

"The *whole* story, this time," Garth added.

Callie hesitated, wondering at her reluctance. Why should she try to cover for Pierce's shortcomings? Especially since these people appeared well acquainted with them.

She started with their discovery of the ruined campsite, but when she came to the part where the Trogs had jumped them, she faltered, glancing around at Pierce, still stretched out in the grass.

"Go on." Garth touched her knee. "The thing was on you."

"Well, I realized then I still had my SLuB, so I shot it. Then I shot the other one off Pierce."

"It had him pretty good, huh?"

"I thought it was eating him alive. . . ." She trailed off, puzzled. *It could easily have hurt him, but it didn't. Why not?*

"It probably happened so fast," Rowena ventured, "he didn't have time to draw another weapon."

"Yes, it happened very fast," Callie agreed. *Would I have remembered to draw my weapon if it hadn't been in my hand? Would I have been able to?*

*Why didn't that mutant hurt him?*

"Oh, come on, Row," Garth said. "You know Pierce's reflexes. He should have nailed him. But he lost it. Again."

Rowena studied her nails.

"Fact is," Garth went on, "he's getting flat-out unreliable. Somebody's gonna get killed 'cause of him."

"So what do you want to do? Leave—" Rowena swallowed the words, glancing guiltily at Pierce, slumbering on unawares.

Then the black woman murmured, "He may be unreliable, but if he'd been with us two nights ago, those muties wouldn't have surprised us."

Garth grunted. The two stone skippers joined them then, shifting the conversation to other things. Presently the rest of the group came in, too, and Rowena made the introductions.

The tall black man with the eye patch was Whit, once a star basketball player at the University of Illinois. John was the blond Viking with the twin beard braids and the gold earring. The black woman who'd come to Pierce's defense was LaTeisha. She was a nurse from Sacramento, and the group's official medic. The rest of the names Callie didn't remember longer than the time it took to get them all confused. It would be several days before she would sort them out.

As darkness settled, the cook sliced dripping slabs of pink meat and passed them from knife to knife. Callie used the opportunity to move across the fire, and Rowena took her place on the log.

"We could get mess kits in town," John explained as Callie awkwardly accepted a knifeful of the meat, "but the more stuff we have, the harder it is to move. And sometimes *moving* is the difference between life and death."

"I can appreciate that."

"It's cleaner, too," said LaTeisha. "No dishes to wash. Although"—she peered at her own slice, then picked off a four-inch-long hair—"sometimes you have to watch what the food is seasoned with." She glared at the cook. "Don't you bother to clean this stuff at all?"

The man kept his eyes on the meat he was slicing. "It's cooked, isn't it?" he grumbled in a Middle Eastern accent. "Fire killed all your little bugs."

"And if you dropped it in the dirt, would you trust the fire to take care of that, too?"

"You don't like it, you cook."

"Maybe I should."

"No way!" cried John the Viking. "We'd starve. You'd be sterilizing the knives and throwing out half the food."

"At least we wouldn't break our teeth on the rocks or die of food poisoning," LaTeisha retorted, pulling the blackened rind off her slice and tossing it into the fire.

"What is this, anyway?" Callie asked, biting gingerly into the seared flesh.

"Redhorn," Garth said.

"Another engineered bioform?"

"All I know is it's a big reindeer that roams the mountains. Horns are s'posed to be a more powerful aphrodisiac than dragon horn."

Pierce appeared out of the darkness, sliding around Garth's shoulder to accept a slice of meat from the cook. From every side Callie saw the others' eyes flick to him and away. He took the meat and a cup of coffee, then retired to the fringes behind Rowena and LaTeisha, avoiding eye contact.

"So, Callie," said Garth, when they'd finished eating, "tell us how they got you."

"Huh?"

"Your capture story. How you got here. Everyone has one. Was it a bogus experiment, or were you dead?"

"Dead?"

Rowena laughed and slapped Garth's back. "I told you it'd be an experiment."

"What do you mean, dead?" Callie asked.

"Well, some of us are here on a second-chance-at-life arrangement," Rowena said, cocking a brow at her seatmate. "Garth, for example, was mugged in south L.A. and left for dead before our alien friends found him."

"So what kind of experiment did they get you with?" John asked, rolling one of his beard braids between thumb and forefinger.

"It was supposed to improve decision making."

"Decision making?" Garth whooped with laughter. "*Decision* making? Oh, now, *that's* precious. And you just walked in and signed up for it?"

"I needed the money," Callie said, annoyed. "How was I supposed to know they were aliens?"

Garth held up his palms defensively. "Hey, I'm not tryin' to step on toes. We're all here, ain't we?"

"I was picked up at a workshop thing, too," John told her. "It was supposed to help me stop smoking." He made a face. "Well, I've stopped."

"Only because there's nothing to smoke out here," said Whit in a startling bass voice.

"Were you really dying?" Callie asked Garth.

"Babe, I was dead. Watched my blood run out in a big dark puddle around me. Things got all foggy, and I saw those bright lights people talk about. I thought, okay, you're finally cashing in, big guy. Gonna meet your Maker. Or maybe that other fella with the pitchfork!" He laughed, and so did the others. "Turns out it was these other guys.

Next thing I know, they're patching me up in their weird infirmary. Like Row said, I'm on my second life." He grinned. "Or maybe it's Purgatory."

LaTeisha, the nurse, had also died. Her small car had run off a country road, and she'd gone through the windshield. She woke up in the same alien infirmary.

"I was on a cruise," Rowena said, standing to pour herself more coffee. "Sun. Sea. Hours of nothing to do but work on my tan. It was heaven."

"I'll bet it was," Garth leered. The other men laughed.

Even here, in the worst of conditions, Rowena's sensuality throbbed. Her blue jeans molded a slender waist and curved hips like a second skin, and her scoop-necked T-shirt clung so tightly it left little to the imagination.

"Three days into the cruise," Rowena went on, "and well into the waters of the Bermuda Triangle, we sailed into fog."

Someone whistled the high-pitched four-note warble of the *Twilight Zone* theme song.

"All of a sudden the ship lurched, the deck tilted and everyone started screaming. Panic flew like swarming harries: *'We've hit a reef!' 'We've sprung a leak!'*

"We were all fighting to pile into the lifeboats when suddenly this handsome kid is standing beside me asking if I want to be part of his experiment. I thought it was sort of a strange pickup line, but what the hay! 'You bet,' says I. 'Anything to get me out of this mess.' So he dumps me here." She grimaced. "*Not* what I had in mind."

"It hasn't been all bad," Garth said, pulling her into his lap. "You found me."

She giggled as he growled and kissed her, one hand sliding over her skimpy tee.

Embarrassed, Callie averted her gaze.

LaTeisha rolled her eyes, and John the Viking said, "So did Pierce tell you where we're going?"

"To a canyon that cuts through to the Inner Realm?"

"Two months max, and we're home." John slapped his thighs.

"I understand the last party to try it ended up mostly dead."

"That won't happen to us," Garth said. "We got experience. And we're tough. What about you, pretty one? Wanna come along?"

"I, uh . . . was kind of set on checking the gates for myself."

"See?" Rowena elbowed him. "They always have to find out for themselves."

"Yeah, but so did we, babe." Garth grinned at Callie. "So happens, you're in luck. We'll be stopping at Manderia for supplies b'fore we hit the canyon. If you can wait a few weeks, you can check out your gate there."

"Manderia? Is that a town?"

"Yup. All the gates have towns. I guess people get that far and don't know what else to do."

"Did ya hear about those folks over in Devon who're building a dirt ramp?" John said. "Figure to walk right on up to the top."

"Morons," Garth scoffed. "They'll die of old age 'fore they finish. But we all gotta do what we gotta do. Me, I'll keep searching. There's a weakness somewhere in this bloodsucking prison, and I'm gonna find it."

He spoke with such sudden conviction Callie almost believed him. No one tittered or made snide remarks. They all just stared soberly into the fire.

Finally John and Whit went to rattle through the equipment out in the dark. Talk started up again, revolving around the day—observations, plans, private talk in which Callie had no part. Presently LaTeisha and three others left the circle, replaced by the four who had been on watch, including the bald, red-bearded Thor.

When it was time for bed, Rowena gave Callie a light brown sleeping bag that provided little padding against the hard ground, but amazed her with its ability to trap warmth. She'd hardly settled in before she had to peel the covers back. Eventually, though, she managed to get reasonably comfortable. Around her, soft rustlings faded to rhythmic breathing and, in some cases, snoring. The fire crackled, its smoke wafting intermittently over her, and somewhere an owl hooted.

She watched Garth pore over his map, tracing a thick finger across its surface. Firelight gleamed on his black ponytail and beard and flickered across his strong brow. He reminded her of the Marlboro man—

not as handsome, but powerful, capable, and utterly self-confident. He might be a little crude, but he was the kind of man you could respect— the kind of man other men followed.

Funny how much safer she felt tonight than last.

Yes, he *was* following a path opposite the one she'd been instructed to take, but if he and all his friends—who'd been trying to escape this arena for years—couldn't find the true Benefactor, was it reasonable to think she could?

———————

In subsequent days Callie's ambivalence mounted. Though she fully intended to read through the manual's unencrypted portion before week's end, she never found the time. Up at dawn and on the move till dusk, it was enough to eat and do her share of the camp chores before falling exhausted into her sleeping bag. And that was on the nights they actually made camp.

Nor did it help that the few times she did wrangle a spare moment to read, she received more ridicule than enlightenment for her efforts. While she paged through fine print detailing biomes, ASBs, and hand-warmer construction, her companions complained incessantly about people not pulling their weight, and idiot rookies who always had to "see for themselves," and the endlessly annoying mites that always emerged in force whenever the book was brought out.

"The thing's a nuisance," Garth grumbled. "You should give it to the mites and be done with it. It's not like you need it for anything."

He annoyed her with his pushing, but though she promised herself she would *not* let him discourage her, in the end the manual migrated inexorably to the bottom of her pack's lowest section, forgotten and neglected. As Garth said, she had no immediate need for it, and the less she read it, the less she thought about reading it. Days turned to weeks until, eventually, even when the opportunity arose and the thought occurred, she found herself unable to muster the effort to get it out.

What she did need to learn in order to survive in the wildlands off the white roads she received in full measure from her Outlander companions. Tough and canny, they knew all the tricks. Whether in trouble or at rest, they worked with an oiled efficiency that amazed her. They showed her how to recognize sand mite habitat and Trog spoor, how to spot redclaw runners under the sand, how to keep to the side of a ridge instead of walking along the top where she'd be sighted, how to run and drop when fired at, and how to handle SLuBs and rifles.

For her part, she was certain they were impressed with her ability to match their rugged pace. After a few days of proving herself not an imbecile, she was assigned her turn at guard duty, and Garth started sending her on scouting forays with Pierce. She suspected this was because no one else would work with him. He'd been sullen since the Trog attack, speaking only when spoken to, and then only in mono-syllables. Evenings he'd slip in to grab some food, then return to the fringes, keeping to himself.

Garth dismissed it as sulking, but it was clearly more than that. As the weeks passed, Callie realized Pierce was a deeply troubled man, plagued by horrific nightmares during which he jerked and grimaced and screamed, or curled whimpering into fetal position. Often, his cries woke the others, who'd watch him intently for a while and then go back to sleep as if they were long used to it.

----

One morning, after a particularly harrowing night, Callie asked Rowena and LaTeisha about it. The three of them were returning from the latrine, which at this site was positioned well up the hill from camp. She half expected them to shrug it off. Instead both women stopped and glanced at each other.

Then Rowena said, "I don't suppose he'd tell you himself, would he? Trogs had him for three weeks last winter."

Callie stared down the hill toward the jumble of camp, small figures moving back and forth as they packed. She felt suddenly cold.

"We'd given him up for dead," Rowena went on. "You know Trogs eat most everything they lay their hands on. But then we saw him two weeks later, shackled and walking among them. He's given them a lot of trouble over the years—maybe they recognized him and were paying him back. They get a charge out of torture, you know. And they didn't spare him a lick. You should see his back and chest."

"How did you get him away?"

"We didn't," LaTeisha said. "We found him a week or so later wandering the desert, dehydrated, covered with burns and welts, one arm broken. He was almost catatonic. It took weeks to bring him around. He still won't talk about it."

Rowena pulled a scalloped leaf off the oak at her side and ripped it into strips. "The worst part is, we never know how he's going to react anymore. Sometimes he's cool and collected, just like old times. He fights like a demon, and nothing can get to him. Sometimes he goes into a blind panic." She stopped and went on more softly, "Sometimes he just curls up like a baby. That's the worst."

She met Callie's gaze. "I expect you've seen that one."

The sick feeling returned, along with the memory. It was tempered now with a new, sharper pain of empathy. "I've seen all three of them," she whispered.

"Well, then, you know. The only good to come of it is that he can sense them now when they're near. It's saved our necks more than once."

Rowena tossed the remainder of the leaf to the ground. "Garth's right, though. Pierce *is* a liability. And it'll be worse in the Inner Realm. They say its crawling with Trogs twice the size and strength of those we've got here. If he doesn't get his act together, he won't survive."

She glanced at LaTeisha, then trudged down the hill. The black woman followed, leaving Callie behind, buffeted by memory—the sour stench, the massive body, the burning, inhuman eyes. . . .

Three weeks at their mercy. Three weeks to be their plaything.

*I've misjudged him. Badly.*

# CHAPTER

# 7

Crowded within the embrace of its thick outer guard wall, Manderia's jumble of stone buildings, wood-shingled roofs and narrow streets seemed straight out of the Middle Ages. Quaint shops beneath second-story living quarters offered bakery items prepared in wood-burning ovens. Others peddled hand-tanned leather, handmade shoes, pottery, tin pots, and armor—there was even an apothecary stocked with herbs. Donkey- and goat-pulled wagons abounded, and chickens, cats, and scrawny dogs roamed streets where raw sewage ran down a central gutter. Smoke veiled the rooftops, and soot coated everything.

The Outlanders planned to exchange their wares for supplies the afternoon of their arrival and depart by dawn the next day, so after settling into an inn near the east gate and staking out their sleeping quarters—the luck of the draw won Callie a berth in the stables—everyone set out on their various errands. Rowena's responsibility was to show Callie the Gate.

She'd gotten her first glimpse of it over a week ago, flashing on the cliff line like a beacon. Even from miles away, she'd felt an unexpected thrill—and then a rising, inexplicable attraction. More and more often she had found herself staring at it, transfixed by its shimmering beauty and longing to see it more closely. Ironically, now that she had arrived, she couldn't see it at all, as Manderia's grimy buildings obstructed the view. She'd see it again, Rowena assured her, when they reached the temple, perched on the hillside above.

As they walked through the surprisingly busy city the implications of its existence began to dawn on Callie with foreboding weight. Primitive as it was by modern standards, its construction had required considerable planning, time, and effort. No fly-by-night affair, it was a place of roots, a place people had clearly settled into for good.

"I guess they've resigned themselves to their fate," Rowena said when Callie voiced her observation. "They probably think they're making the best of it."

"You mean they've given up."

"That's one way to put it. But remember, some of these folks have been here almost twenty years." She glanced at Callie. "Blows your mind, doesn't it?"

It did indeed. So much so that Callie decided not to think about it further. They dodged a cartful of reeking cabbages as it trundled by, wooden wheels thundering over the cobbles. When they could hear again, she gestured at a storefront across the street, where machine-knit T-shirts and denim jeans were displayed in the window. "I thought our captors provided that stuff."

"They do. It just takes a lot of hands to get it out this far—traders selling to traders selling to traders. You know."

"But if the traders get it from the aliens, where do the aliens get it?"

"Some people say there are cities of civilized Trogs in the Inner Realm that make it all." Rowena stepped around a pile of fouled, chicken-pecked cabbages. "That's possible, I guess, but I think it's stolen from Earth. They steal people, after all, why not hiking boots?"

"Did you say *civilized* Trogs?"

Rowena grimaced over her shoulder. "Hard to believe, I know. Rumor says the trade route comes down through the canyon we're looking for. I don't know how 'civilized' they are, though, since I've heard they mainly trade in slaves."

"And this is where you guys want to go?"

"If it *is* where all the goods come from, and the goods *do* come from Earth, well . . ." Rowena grinned. "Where there's a way in, there's a way out."

Before long the street emptied into a square ringed by dull-colored awnings. On the far side, midway up a wide stone stairway, stood a young man in a pale jumpsuit. He was raving something about death and Mander, but most of his words were rendered unintelligible by the extreme passion with which he shouted them. The crowd ignored him.

"Watch this." Rowena crossed the square and mounted the stairway. The man appeared not to notice. Even when she was about to run into him, he ignored her, continuing to rant as she walked right through him.

Callie gasped, and Rowena stepped back into view, grinning broadly.

"Hologram," she said. "Isn't that something?"

Studying the image, Callie saw now that it wasn't as substantial as she'd thought. The stair and doorway showed through first an arm, then a leg, then a shoulder. "Where does it come from?"

"Haven't the foggiest." Rowena joined her again.

"Mander is not the way out!" the image screamed. "Don't let his lies ensnare you!"

"Not from the temple, I'd guess," she added as they left the square. "I've heard the aliens project them to confuse us."

They came finally to the gate road. Cutting straight through the city, its humped center and spongy white surface shed dirt, sewage, and debris like Teflon. Despite the surroundings and the heavy travel it received, it remained as white as the one Callie had first been deposited upon weeks ago. Two times wider than any Manderian street, it channeled a cool, fresh breeze and led them to the square where the walls of Manderia met the walls of the temple. Various flimsy booths stood outside the doubled gates, offering trinkets, modern clothing, and greasy-smelling food. Past that, the white road continued on, bisecting an empty greensward.

According to Rowena, every gate had a temple, every temple a benefactor, and every benefactor an angle. Some demanded service for their help; others required sacrifice or offerings—usually of items found only in the Outlands.

They passed through the double gates unhindered and crossed the yard. Stairs led to a colonnaded court crisscrossed with second-story, vine-clad walkways, but Rowena turned onto a secondary path before they got that far. The new path descended a forested hillside to a meadow, where it ribboned through silvery grasses to the cliff base.

Callie stood at the meadow's edge and tipped her head back, gazing up the soaring rock face. How high was it? A thousand feet? Two thousand? The cliff whirled, and she shut her eyes. When she opened them, the precipice still loomed over her, still very, very vertical. She could just barely see the Gate.

About eighty feet up something moved, and she made out a trio of men, hitched together with a bright green rope. "They're climbing it?" she gasped.

"Yeah." Rowena squinted up at them. "Won't work, though. Rock gets crumbly at about two hundred feet."

"You speaking from experience?"

Rowena nodded. "No one ever makes it past two hundred fifty. You ready to go back?"

"Let's check the end of the trail."

The pavement flared where it met the cliff, flanked by a jumble of fallen sandstone slabs. Etched into the rock at eye level was the familiar trio of interlocking circles now arranged around a central *t*. Callie fingered the carved grooves, then gazed upward again. The view was even more overwhelming from here. Carefully she studied the walls, the rock slabs, even the pavement. She had no idea what she hoped to find. A control panel? Cracks betraying a hidden passage? Some sort of instruction plaque?

"People say this is a map." Rowena traced the symbol with her index finger. "Some guy over at the Lunville gate made all these calculations—tangents, sun angles, the distances between the *t* and the center points of the circles. Supposedly if you added them together and went in the direction of the tangent to the cosine or something, you'd find a secret door. Far as I know he never has gotten it right."

Callie stepped back and scanned the cliff again. The climbers dislodged a brief shower of rock. A breeze whispered through the grass behind her and birdcalls echoed brightly in the quiet.

Slowly she turned, grit squeaking under the soles of her boots. *There's nothing here. There's really nothing here.* Her gaze swept the fallen slabs, the shimmering meadow, the dark forest cradling the temple's white walls, and then, once more, the rough, ragged cliff shooting straight up from her feet.

How could they do this? How could they put her down here, tell her to find this place, and have it be impossible to reach? It was outrageous, even downright cruel.

But everyone had been telling her that for weeks. It was the whole reason her new friends were looking for their canyon.

"Seen enough?"

Callie drew a shuddery breath and tucked her anger back into its box. As she glanced around one last time she was surprised to see a man seated amidst the boulders. His robe matched the rocks, but his skin was tanned mahogany. He sat ramrod straight, legs pretzeled yoga style, eyes closed. A sparrow landed on his head, pecked at his lank hair, and flew away. He never moved.

"A Sitter," Rowena said. "Every gate has a few of them. There's another to his right. And one behind the rock on his left."

"What're they doing?"

"Waiting."

"For what?"

"If I knew that, maybe I'd be sitting with them."

A shout rang out from above, followed by a sudden rush of pebbles. Callie looked up and saw one of the climbers dangling at the end of his rope, bobbing against the wall as his companions called down worriedly from above. Little by little he stopped swinging, and soon hammer blows rang against the rock as he began to climb back up.

"Idiots," Rowena huffed. "Can we go now?"

"I'd like to see the temple."

"What?"

"The manual says there's only one real Benefactor. Maybe Mander's the one."

"Maybe I'm the one."

Callie frowned at her. Rowena scowled back.

"You said yourself," Callie reminded her, "that you hadn't investigated this temple."

"I don't need to investigate it. It's obvious they require some sort of service or there wouldn't be a temple."

"Well, why do people go along with it?" Callie asked.

"Because they're idiots."

"You can't just dismiss it like that."

Rowena exhaled forcefully and rolled her eyes. "All right, let's go. I can see you'll be second-guessing forever if we don't."

As they returned to the green Callie glimpsed a brown-haired man in jeans and leather vest walking out the main gate. "Hey!" she cried. "Isn't that—" But he was already out of sight behind the wall.

Rowena stopped beside her. "What?"

"I thought I saw—" *Pierce? He'd been more disdainful of this temple than Rowena.* "Never mind."

They headed down the temple's gauntlet of colonnades toward a glass-walled sanctuary at the far end. Here and there, robed worshipers gathered in small groups, watching the newcomers with quick sidelong glances. Dim corridors led off into the recesses of flanking buildings, while overhead walkways supported large electronic screens bearing digital images of the gate on the cliff, now hidden by the temple itself. Callie was amazed. Considering the primitive state of the rest of Manderia, the temple was the ultimate in state-of-the-art technology. Where had all this equipment come from, and how was it powered?

The sanctuary was a large auditorium that stairstepped down to a window-backed stage overlooking a small grotto. Water trickled down the grotto's rock face to a pool nestled in mosses, vines, and sprays of grass. Inches above the pool's surface hovered a flat white stone surrounded by jets of water, while overhead, distorted by the building's glass walls and ceiling, they could just make out the shimmering gate atop the cliff.

"Must be siesta time," Rowena said, glancing around the empty hall.

"May I help you, ladies?"

A young man in an iridescent gray robe had come up behind them. Smelling faintly of sandalwood, he had thin blond hair, hazel eyes, and a round, cherubic face with a dimple in his chin.

Rowena waved him off, but Callie asked what people did at the temple.

The youth looked at them quizzically. "You are interested in serving Mander?"

"We're interested in getting through that gate up there."

He smiled. "Then you have come to the right place. The manual says no one can pass through the Gate without Mander's help."

"I don't remember it specifying a name," said Callie. Not that she'd read that much of it, but it seemed to her she'd surely have noticed a name if one had been there.

"Nevertheless," Wendell insisted, "Mander *is* the True Benefactor."

"How do you know that?" Rowena asked, propping a hand on one shapely hip. "I mean, no offense, but there are at least thirteen other benefactors who make the same claim."

The youth—man?—regarded her with surprise, a crease forming between his pale brows. "I don't know about them, but the manual says if you sincerely desire the truth, it will be made evident to you. Would you like to see the Grotto of Ascension?" He gestured with a pale hand to the stage and pond below.

Callie said they would—Rowena huffed exasperation.

As they descended he told them his name was Wendell, and that he had been serving in the temple over two years. In another six months his period of service would end, and then he could ascend to the Gate himself.

They reached the bottom as two robed supplicants entered the grotto and knelt beside the pool.

"Can we go down there?" Callie asked.

"I'm afraid only the Faithful are granted entrance. Those two are beginning their final purification for the Ascension ceremony tomorrow night. You're welcome to stay and watch." He smiled at her again.

"So what kind of service do you all perform here in order to earn this little ride?" Rowena demanded, scowling at the grotto.

"We serve in the meal dispensary or in the clinic, clean the temple, work the gardens, sing, meditate, pray." With his pale skin and soft grublike hands, Callie thought he must have done much of the latter and very little of the former. Was there a hierarchy, then, with new converts assigned to hard labor, while the experienced Faithful followed more cerebral pursuits?

"We also bring food to the Sitters," he went on, "and read *Mander's Meditations* to the climbers. We hope it will move them to cease their futile efforts, but it rarely works. When they finally fall, we bury them."

Callie recalled the spiderlike forms on the vast, rough rock, the dangling body struggling for a hold. What if that man had not found his hold? What if he'd pulled his friends down with him? She shuddered, glad that hadn't happened.

"So your term of service is what? Three years?" Rowena asked, fingering the short blond hair on the side of her neck. Her glance caught Callie's—*Told you*.

"It varies," Wendell said, "but three years is standard, yes." He paused. "How long have *you* been here?"

Rowena lifted her chin, her mouth hardening. "Long enough to know better."

"Longer than three years, I guess."

"At least we're free."

"No one in this world is free," Wendell said quietly, and Rowena had no response to that.

Callie watched the supplicants for a moment, then asked, "Did you say that in six months *you* will be ascending to the Gate?"

"If I decide so, yes."

"If?"

"I have a home here. And I find joy in helping others to ascend."

They stared at him. Finally, Callie said, "You've seen these ascensions, then?"

"Thousands of them. As I said, we'll be performing one tomorrow night."

"But how do you know they're going home?" Rowena persisted. "How do you know when they walk through the Gate, they're not just vaporized? Do you ever see them again?"

"Of course. They send us holograms assuring us of their arrival and encouraging us to persist."

"Holograms can be faked," Rowena pointed out.

He smiled. "I guess it boils down to faith."

"You mean check your brains at the door when you sign on."

The crease marred his brow again. "Do you ladies have a place to stay for the night? We have plenty of rooms."

"We've made arrangements, thank you," Rowena said. "And speaking of that, we'd better be getting back." She seized Callie's arm and steered her toward the stairway before he could say any more.

As they started up the stairs Callie pulled free. "Good grief, Row, you didn't have to be so rude."

"Aw, he would've kept us there all day—'Do you want to see the gardens? Do you want to see the dispensary? Can I show you the mop room?' "

"He was just being nice."

"He was just trying to get us to stay. They get points for new converts, you know."

"I thought you didn't know anything about this temple."

"They're all the same. I'm sure he gets points. He's probably trying to think of some way to call us back right now."

"He was only answering our questions."

Rowena wasn't listening. "It all boils down to faith, huh?" she muttered. "Faith in what, I'd like to know? Mander? The manual?" She snorted. " 'Serve me for three years and I'll release you.' You'd have to be an idiot to buy into this. I'll put my faith in myself, thank you."

"Well, you have to admit," said Callie, "it *is* a little nicer than sleeping on the hard ground and always worrying about Trogs."

Rowena cast her a disgusted look. "Maybe you oughta stay, then."

She took the stairs two at a time. Annoyed now, Callie followed more slowly. At the top, she glanced back. Sure enough, Wendell still stood where they'd left him, smiling up at her.

# CHAPTER

## 8

Back at the inn Callie took the bath she'd been anticipating for days and found it singularly disappointing. Since the inn had no bathrooms, she used a wooden tub set up in the room Rowena and Garth were sharing. The water, left over from Rowena's use, was tepid and scummy, the soap reeked of lye, and the small scrap of toweling was rough and already well dampened. Because there was no conditioner for her hair, she had to untangle the snarls with her fingers before she could use the wooden comb she'd borrowed from one of the tavern girls. By the time she finished, Callie was seriously considering Rowena's suggestion to cut it off. But she'd spent six years growing it, and Garth insisted they would be home in a month—she'd been here five weeks already; surely she could stand another four.

Back in the common room, smoke already hung in the rafters, and the evening's revelry was well under way. Men lined the wooden bar, jostling one another as they hoisted mugs of beer or tossed off shots of hard liquor. Some were eating, while others gambled at craps and poker and pool, underdressed women hanging over their shoulders. Callie spied the shaggy head and huge body of a fellow Outlander named Lokai among the men at the bar. Thor's bald dome gleamed beside him. For days the pair had talked of nothing but whiskey and girls— they were the last two she wanted to join right now. She didn't recognize anyone else, though, and for a moment she was back in Tucson, standing on the brick veranda of her sister's foothills home, surrounded by glittering, laughing yuppies who moved around her as if she didn't exist. No one glittered here, and these rough men and women were a far cry from her sister's high-class friends, but the same sense of being conspicuously alone writhed in her belly. Maybe she should go back upstairs. Or out to the stables.

"Callie!" Garth's voice pierced the low rumble of conversation. "Over here."

It was like being thrown a life preserver.

He was holding court at one of the plank tables at the back, with John, Whit, LaTeisha, and three strangers attending him.

"Where's Rowena?" Callie asked, squeezing into the space John made between himself and LaTeisha.

Garth shrugged and planted his right elbow on the table in front of the brawny man sitting across from him. "Ready?"

The black-haired stranger planted his own elbow and clasped Garth's hand. E-cubes piled the planking beside them.

"Did they have another fight?" Callie asked as the two began to push against each other.

LaTeisha glanced around at her. "Row and Garth? Yeah."

At the table's end the two men grunted, strained, and sweated while the others cheered them on. His arm muscles bulging and quivering, Garth seemed about to lose when suddenly he shoved his opponent's hand to the planking and ended the match. John banged the table and hooted as Garth pocketed the cubes with a grin. Scowling, the loser declined a rematch and went to console himself at the bar.

The aproned innkeeper arrived, a brooding man with a silver diamond tattooed into his forehead and a gold ring in his nose. Wordlessly, he laid out bowls of stew and dense black bread. He returned with mugs of ale and scowled when Callie asked for water instead.

The stew was lukewarm, greasy, and unpleasantly spiced, the meat gristly, the potatoes hard, and the bread so dense she could hardly chew it.

"Who do they get to cook this stuff?" LaTeisha complained. "The mules?"

"Keep your voice down, Teish," John warned. "Remember Logan-town?"

"Look at this." She gestured at the pile of gristle she'd accumulated beside her tankard. "Half of it's not even edible." She picked up the bread, broke off a piece, and frowned as she pulled the two portions apart with exaggerated slowness to reveal the hair connecting them. "It *is* the mules!" She threw the pieces into the stew bowl and stood. "I've got some jerky in my pack. Besides, all this smoke's giving me a head-ache."

Callie managed to force down half her portion before the stew's cool greasiness overwhelmed her. As she pushed the bowl aside, a shout of laughter erupted from the crowd at the bar where Lokai and Thor were apparently engaged in a drinking contest.

"They're doing it again," Whit rumbled in his deep voice. He had twisted around on the bench to see what was happening.

Garth shoved the last of his bread into his mouth. "They'll pay in the morning," he mumbled around it.

"And so will we. In lost time."

Garth glanced at him awry. "Do *you* want to try and stop 'em?"

With a sigh, Whit turned back, pulling at the strap of his eye patch.

"Let's just hope they don't tear the place up like last time," John muttered.

"They do and they're staying behind to work off the damages." Garth pulled a draught from his tankard. "I already told 'em that." He wiped his mouth, then set the vessel aside and laced his fingers on the planking. "So, Callie girl, you gonna sign on at the temple?"

"I don't know yet."

He waved a hand. "They're all cowards up there. Suckers who'll be here for life."

"The guy said they're transporting a couple people to the Gate tomorrow night," Callie said. "That they get messages back from those they transport."

"And you believed him?"

She fingered her tankard of water. "He has as much proof as you."

"I've got a map."

"Which may or may not be legitimate."

"Whoa-ho, Garth," John crowed, rocking back on the bench. "This lady don't care whose toes she steps on."

A half smile of approval lit Garth's face. "I like a woman who speaks her mind," he drawled.

Something in his manner sent the blood rushing to Callie's face.

He leaned toward her. "You gonna stay tomorrow and watch 'em?"

Callie dropped her gaze to her tankard, unnerved by his amused expression. Maybe it wasn't approval—maybe it was mockery.

He laughed. "No? Then I'd say you didn't believe the guy."

"I don't know what I believe," she said. "Maybe none of you is right. Maybe the answer's somewhere else entirely."

After a brief silence, Garth said, "Well, at least you know we weren't lyin' about the Gate and the cliff."

She continued to focus on her tankard, drawing lines up its battered side in the condensation. Across the table Whit drained his own vessel, then wiped the foam from his beard and mustache. He turned to Garth. "So what do you propose to do about this man in Hardluck? The one the innkeeper told us about."

"I don't like Hardluck," Garth said. "It's a vile little town, and they trade in slaves. Most of 'em are half Trog already."

"True, but they oughta know better than anyone about a route up the canyon. And Callie's right. You don't have much proof that map's legitimate."

Garth launched into a defense of his map and his judgment, and Callie's thoughts returned to the dilemma that had ripped at her all day—had ripped at her, in fact, since the day she'd met Pierce. Who *should* she believe? Nobody knew anything. The manual was no real help. And . . . and she was tired and frustrated, and maybe a night's sleep would clear it up. While the men continued their debate, she stood and slipped away.

Garth caught her at the door. "You aren't turning in already, are you?"

The crowd pushed him so close she had to tilt her head back to see his face. His breath stank of beer.

"I thought I'd take a walk," she said.

"Dangerous place for an evening walk. Want some company?"

She glanced over his shoulder, feeling trapped.

He cocked his head. "No, huh?"

"I need to sort things out."

"Maybe I could help."

"I doubt it."

His grin flashed in the dark nest of his beard. "You oughta come with us."

"Why?"

"Because it's the only way out. Because we need people who can keep their heads when things get hot." He tucked a tendril of hair behind her ear. "Because I like you."

His touch, his nearness, the dark intensity of his expression ignited an acute sexual awareness that again brought the blood to Callie's cheeks. Confused and a little afraid, she backed away. "I . . . that's nice, Garth. But I need time to think."

"Suit yourself." He sauntered back to his table.

The stables were blessedly quiet, redolent with the odor of alfalfa and manure and damp leather. Light poured through the big loft door above, washing over the tack and stalls across from it, and deepening by contrast the shadows beneath it. The stall she'd staked out for herself hid in that shadowy underloft, but someone was already in it. Two someones, in fact. Callie backed away, embarrassed, and stopped beside the loft ladder. Dare she try to climb it? Almost any height could trigger her phobia, but this was just a little ladder, with the wall beside it for support. True, it *was* almost vertical. . . .

She swallowed on a dry mouth.

The activity in the stall grew frenzied. Then, from outside, Callie heard a pair of slurred voices—men from the tavern. Had they followed her? Probably not, but she'd rather they not find her here.

She eyed the loft again. It *was* the best choice. *And it's high time you conquered this stupid phobia.*

With her gaze fixed upward, Callie climbed one careful rung at a time to the top, where sweet hay piled in silhouette against the brilliance of the open loft door. Here, though, the ladder stuck up past the floor. To get off, she'd have to step around and over it, with nothing to hold on to while she did.

Outside, the men's voices approached. Her stomach churned. Her wrists felt weak. Heat flashed across her back and shoulders. Gritting her teeth, she ascended another rung, bending double to keep hold of the ladder.

The fear burst out of nowhere, sweeping over her in dizzying waves, turning her legs to jelly.

*Just move through it. You'll be okay.* But she couldn't let go of the ladder. Already the ground was pulling at her, drawing her like a great magnet.

She was choking. Sweat slicked her palms, and her arms jittered to match her legs.

*If you don't go now, you won't go at all. Now, move.*

She lurched forward, planted a foot on the loft's edge, and let go. For a moment she teetered on the brink. Then the ground spun up at her, and she flailed backward—

Someone reached out of the darkness and jerked her to safety. She fell with him into the hay, smelled a familiar musky odor, felt the hard muscles of his chest and arms, and pushed away, her panic shifting focus. He backed off, a shadow crouching against the light.

"Are you all right?" It was Pierce, which part of her had known the moment he'd grabbed her.

"I'm fine." Even her voice shook.

"I thought maybe you were—"

"I'm not drunk!" All at once she was angry—at him, at herself, at the drunks outside, at Garth, at the aliens, at the whole situation. None of it was fair, none of it was right, none of it should *be*. She wanted out. And there was no out.

Loud voices pierced her frustration. The drunks were blundering into the stalls below, repelled each time by indignant occupants. They seemed to think this outrageously funny, and at last, roaring with laughter, they staggered back into the street.

As the silence returned Pierce stood and crossed to the back of the loft, where a rectangle of light flooded through the open doors. He sat down, his back to her, only a portion of his profile visible. She followed him to the middle of the loft and eased onto the straw, hugging her knees to her chest, but he ignored her, lost in one of his moods. She began to feel more than a little foolish.

Presently he stretched back in the hay, cradling his head in his hands, and her attention was arrested by the silvery light that bathed him. The Arena had no moon, and Manderia had no electricity. So where was the light coming from? The Gate?

Feeling a tingle of wonder, Callie stood and edged toward the opening, stopping with her feet just inside the light. Outside, Manderian rooftops tumbled toward the gleaming hulk of the city wall, the Inner Realm cliffs towering darkly beyond. The rim itself, however, remained blocked by the loft door's lintel, so she slowly squatted into the light.

The Gate was breathtaking. Its bright, clear radiance shimmered against the velvet night. Now blue, now gold, now silver, it flowed with intertwined rivers of light that waxed and waned and waxed again. Pierced anew by the inexplicable longing, she ached to be near it, to touch it, to feel its glory on her face.

*We intend this for your benefit*, Alex had said. For the first time she could almost believe it was true.

She didn't know how long she crouched there and wasn't aware of sitting down until she found herself beside Pierce in the straw. When she glanced at him, he was watching her.

The pale light softened his features and turned his eyes dark. His gaze flicked back to the Gate, and she saw in him a yearning that echoed her own. "That *was* you I saw at the temple today, wasn't it?"

He didn't move, hands still cradling his head, eyes still fixed on the Gate's arches. "Yeah."

She waited. He did not continue.

"So are you thinking of signing up with Mander?"

"Thinking of it."

Chills flooded her. "Don't tell me you believe the Manderians are right."

"Okay."

Confused into silence, Callie toyed with the straw at her feet.

"I hear it's not unpleasant," he added after a time.

"But the manual doesn't say anything about terms of indenture."

"No."

"So it's got to be fraudulent."

"Only if you believe the manual."

"If you take the manual out, nothing about this makes any sense."

"Nothing makes sense, anyway." His eyes met hers significantly. "And if you think the manual's so important, why did you let the mites have it?"

She frowned and examined her bootlaces. It had been almost two weeks since they'd taken it, and she still wasn't sure if she regretted that or not. A sudden rainstorm had caught the Outlanders by surprise, thoroughly drenching them. It was two days before they had time and opportunity to air everything out, and like the others, she'd emptied her pack, scattering its contents across grass, bush, and rock. For the first time in weeks, she'd actually held the manual, sodden and bedraggled after the rain.

She recalled thinking how much her attitude toward it had changed, how much she'd once risked—unknowingly, to be sure—to save it, yet somehow she still hadn't managed to give it even a good skimming. Guilt suggested she had time that very afternoon while they waited for everything to dry, but then John had suggested a target shooting contest and she couldn't say no—didn't want to say no, truth be told. She'd left the manual lying open on a rock to dry, and when she'd returned hours later, it was gone. She hadn't even seen them take it.

If anything, her reaction had been more relief than regret, though her sleep *had* been troubled that night. But surely if the manual held answers, her companions would've found them long ago. Why torment herself over the loss of something that really didn't matter?

And Pierce was right—manual or not, nothing in their situation made any sense.

"Has it occurred to you," he said, "that they might not intend for us to leave?"

"Then why put us here?"

"I don't know." Pierce sat up, stuck a straw in his mouth, and gazed at the Gate. Callie watched him covertly. Somewhere out in the city a tomcat yowled.

"Maybe they're testing us," he said at last. "Maybe they're planning to invade the Earth and want to learn about the opposition."

"Maybe they're hoping to contact us peacefully and want to find out if it's possible."

He huffed softly. "Or maybe it's all a show and we're the entertainment. An alien version of Roman bread and circuses." The straw twirled slowly between his lips. "You're too new to know how they play with us, offer us hope only to snatch it away."

"Those are pretty grim thoughts, Pierce."

"Yeah, but it makes the prospect of living in Mander under bondage considerably more appealing than mucking around in the Inner Realm."

She looked at him sharply, surprised again. "You think Garth's wrong?"

He snorted. "Aliens set up this arena. They traveled umpteen light years to snatch us off the Earth and bring us here. You think we're gonna escape on our own?"

He had a point.

"Are you going to back out, then?"

Silence answered her at first. Muffled voices drifted up from below. A mule stomped and snorted. At length he sighed and tossed the straw away. "Probably not."

He settled back and went to sleep. For a long time afterward she sat staring at the living Gate and the dark cliff and the sleeping city, wondering, come morning, what *she* was going to do.

# CHAPTER

# 9

Callie awakened the next morning to Garth's loud voice issuing cheerfully from the ground floor. Groans and protests greeted his efforts as she sat up, picking straw from her hair. Across from her, Pierce belted on his weapons, looking more rested than she'd ever seen him, and it occurred to her that last night was the first in weeks he'd slept without a nightmare.

"Pierce?" Garth called. "You up there?"

"Yo." Pierce slid on his new dragon-hide cuirass and headed for the ladder.

"You wouldn't know where Callie is, would you?" Garth continued. "Nobody's seen her since she left the tavern last night."

"She's up here, too."

Garth was a moment replying. His voice, when it came, sounded strangled. "Really?"

"It's not what you think." Pierce swung onto the ladder and started down.

Choking with mortification, Callie watched him disappear. She wanted to rush down and explain, but knew her babbled defense would only make things worse. Instead she lingered in the loft for a while and went to breakfast late. Only Whit and John remained by the time she arrived, and neither said a word, though John was definitely smirking at her.

An hour later Garth led them out of Manderia, following the Fire River south along the base of the cliffs. For three days they made good time; then the river tumbled into a steep-walled canyon choked with boulders, thick brush, and a particularly robust subspecies of redclaw. When John inadvertently stepped into a hidden capture pod, the thing retracted toward its digestive center with such force he was dragged six feet before they could cut him loose. After that, they kept to the canyon's rocky but barren sides.

No one mentioned Callie's night in the loft with Pierce, though she caught Garth watching her intently several times. His estrangement from Rowena was lasting longer than usual. Rowena repeatedly complained to Callie and LaTeisha that their relationship had soured, that he was too controlling and arrogant, that she wasn't going to let him use her anymore. Callie said nothing to encourage reconciliation, and felt vaguely guilty for it.

---

On the evening of the fourth day Garth approached her.

They'd camped on a wide ledge bounded by the soaring canyon wall on one side and a forty-foot drop-off to the river on the other. There was room to spread out and plenty of firewood in the juniper-oak forest that surrounded them. Some questioned the wisdom of building fires, but Garth assured them no Trogs would trouble them here.

Callie was heading out to gather wood when he stepped into her path from behind a juniper. "Hi," he said, smiling down at her. "Still sorting things out?"

She shrugged. "I guess not."

They started up the hill. "So what's the deal with Pierce?" he asked.

"Deal?"

"Your night in the loft—"

"I went up there to get away. I didn't even know he was there."

"But you stayed."

"Being with Pierce is like being alone." Not entirely true, but he'd avoided her these last days as assiduously as she'd avoided him.

"So . . . you didn't sleep with him?"

"No!" Indignation raised the pitch of her voice. "Not that it's any of *your* business."

Garth chuckled. "I gotta admit, I found it hard to believe. I mean, *Pierce?*"

Annoyed anew, Callie changed the subject. "How much farther do we have to go?"

"We should reach Hardluck tomorrow morning."

"Hardluck? I thought we weren't going there."

"We'll pass right by it, and Whit won't trust the map without confirmation." He stepped over a hummock of rock. "Not that Hardluck will give it to him."

"You have no doubts yourself?"

"I knew Tom—the guy we got it from."

"And the others didn't?"

"Pierce did. We met him after the trip to the Edge, while the group was split up."

Things had gone badly on that trip. She'd heard that many blamed Garth.

"Me and Row and Pierce decided to try the cleft on our own," he said. "All we did was get lost. We ran into Tom on his way down from the rim, hurt bad. We took him to Hardluck, and while he healed he drew the map."

"What happened to him?"

"Mutants got him. Same time they got Pierce, only they didn't let Tom go." Bitterness crept into his voice, and he fell silent.

They walked on. Callie picked up several dead branches before he spoke again. "But we're moving forward now, and that's what counts." He took the wood from her arms. "I'm glad you decided to come."

She smiled slightly, then stooped to pick up another branch.

He continued to watch her; she could see his half smile out of the corner of her eye. "You amaze me," he said.

She tucked a tendril of hair behind her ear, reluctant to meet his gaze. "I do?"

"You're so small and weak looking, but you never come unglued. The Ice Lady."

She had no idea how to respond.

He traced her cheek with the roughened finger of his free hand. Suddenly she could hardly breathe. Blood beat thickly in her throat. Again she felt that powerful sexual awareness.

"You feel it, too, don't you?" he murmured. "Fire burning beneath the ice."

She flinched away, unnerved at having her feelings read and noted so casually. His smile did not fade. He wasn't handsome, but he was strong and bold. A man who could protect you—or not, if he wished.

She backed another step. "I . . . uh . . . have to go."

Whirling, she strode blindly up the hill, desperate to escape him.

She didn't like the feelings he ignited in her, feelings she'd never had, didn't want to have—didn't think she *should* have. He was on the rebound from Rowena at best—more likely still involved and using Callie as a pawn. If she went on this ride he was suggesting, she would only be hurt. And he was suggesting—no way around that.

*"You feel it, too, don't you?"*

*Yes, yes!* Pulling at her like nothing ever had. How could this be? She barely knew the man, wasn't even sure she liked him. And she knew he didn't care about her. Yet she wanted to surrender, to let him carry her away and—

Callie stopped, drawn from her desperate musings by a sound— something that didn't belong.

Her companions' voices echoed as they searched for firewood. Their muffled voices were punctuated by the crackle of branches as they moved and the hollow thunks of their axes. In her immediate periphery, though, all was silent.

Her heart pounded. What had she heard?

*Trogs like to sneak up on a person, stalk them unawares.*

*Stop it!* But the sense of being watched persisted. It reminded her of her first day in the Arena, when she'd glimpsed the alien Watcher. Her new friends assured her that all the Watchers did was watch, thus presenting no real threat. Perhaps one was watching now. Except— she'd *heard* something.

There! A faint buzzing from the stand of juniper to her left. It sounded like electronic sputter. She started toward it, her mind cataloging possible explanations and coming up with few. The last thing she expected to find was Meg.

Her friend stood in the clearing, facing her, still wearing the cream-colored jumpsuit.

"Meg!" Callie cried. "What are you—"

"Callie," Meg interrupted. "It's me—Meg."

Strangely her eyes did not focus on Callie but instead on something beyond Callie's shoulder. And she was too bright, almost glowing in the lavender twilight.

"You must go back to Manderia," Meg told her. "The canyon is a trap. If you—" She wavered like water, her words drowning in static. "—all be killed—" More static. "—road and go back—"

Slowly the ivory jumpsuit turned gray. Meg's green eyes swelled and darkened. Her black hair became a bald dome. And suddenly, gleaming against the dark junipers, stood an alien, its black eyepits stalking her.

Gasping, Callie staggered back on leaden legs.

The Watcher lurched toward her, a swift, sharp feint, black pits probing. A dissonant tone rose and fell in her ears—laughter? Panic dissolved the paralysis, and she stumbled away, crashing through the brush, heedless of the branches whipping her face and tearing at her sleeves.

Pain in her throat and cramps in her chest finally returned her to her senses. She stopped and sagged against the rough bark of a silver-leaf oak, realizing suddenly that she had no idea where she was. Oak and juniper surrounded her, blocking the canyon rim from view. She couldn't even hear the river's roar. In fact, she couldn't hear anything— no birdsong, no insect chatter, nothing but her hammering heart and labored breathing.

But of course it was dusk, so the birds wouldn't be singing anyway, and she couldn't be that far from camp.

The sense of being watched still plagued her, and she searched the shadows intently, determined not to let panic have her again. What had happened? Obviously that wasn't Meg back there. But it wasn't all the Watcher, either, for why would it have interrupted itself? Unless it couldn't maintain the illusion of being Meg long enough. She didn't think that was the case, though. More likely Meg had tried to send a message—one the Watcher didn't want Callie to receive.

*"Go back. It's a trap."*

Was the answer in Manderia, then? Was Meg already through and sending Callie one of those holograms Wendell had mentioned? But she couldn't have served a term in Mander's temple—or any other temple—this soon. So there must be another way.

Unless it was a trick.

The sense of unseen eyes shivered between her shoulder blades. The shadows were thickening. Soon it would be too dark to find her way back to camp. Fresh fear revitalized her, and she pushed away from the tree, starting back across the ravine in which she'd stopped. As she stepped onto its sandy bottom, a rattle of rock downstream brought her up short. She stood rigidly, listening.

Another rattle. Panic swelled like a chemical reaction, bubbling up and out of its vessel. She was on the verge of bolting when a voice called to her.

"Callie? You okay?"

Fifty feet downstream, Pierce emerged from the oak trees, SLuB drawn. Relief made her weak-kneed. "I saw a Watcher," she said as she came up to him, embarrassment warming her face. "I guess I over-reacted."

His brow furrowed, but he only put away the SLuB and said, "It's getting dark. We should head back."

She went with him gratefully, her mind soon returning to the extraordinary visitation, or illusion, or whatever it was. "You know those holographic messages that are supposedly sent by those who've passed through the Gate?" she asked after a time. "Do you think they'd be able to send one out here?"

"Wouldn't they need a screen or projector?"

"I don't know. I saw one in Manderia, and there wasn't anything like that."

Branches snapped and leaves crackled under their feet, the sounds echoing around them.

"Why do you care?" Pierce asked.

She told him what had happened. "It seemed like an interrupted transmission," she concluded.

"Maybe it was."

"You think Meg *was* trying to reach me?"

"Or they wanted you to think that." He pushed aside a branch as they pressed through a stand of oak and held it until she took it from him. Moments later they came out of the woods into a wide, down-sloping clearing. At its far end, campfires sparkled through a screen of trees, and the warble of John's harmonica threaded the quiet air. The light was better here. It washed the cliffs a dusky blue gray, except at the rim itself, which was bright orange.

"She told me to go back to Manderia," Callie said.

"Maybe you should. Maybe we *all* should." He paused to study the rock walls looming around them and rubbed the back of his neck. "I have a bad feeling about this."

"Meg said it's a trap."

He looked at her sharply, his hand still on his neck.

She had a sudden suspicion. "It's not . . . you aren't feeling—"

"Trogs? Not yet."

Garth and Rowena had another shouting match that evening. It didn't last long, but it soured the mood, and most everyone turned in early, Callie included. Her sleep was fitful, though, plagued by unsettling dreams. She was motoring along the white road in a golf cart when Garth appeared beside her at the wheel. Suddenly the road turned steeply upward and she gripped his arm in fear, only to find he'd become her father, who told her not to be a baby and stomped on the accelerator. The cart engine squealed, and they lurched up the vertical road until gravity overwhelmed them, pulling the cart off backward, tumbling down and down and—

She screamed and woke up.

When the screams kept on she realized they weren't hers. The whole camp had roused, in fact, some resting on propped elbows, others sitting up, clutching their weapons and staring at Pierce. He thrashed and raved on his bedroll, and for the first time, Callie made out some of his words. "No! Leave her alone. Leave her—noooo!"

The last word keened out in an agonizing scream that abruptly cut off.

No one moved. Pierce lay on his back, panting, one arm flung up across his face. Callie felt sick and cold. What *had* he endured?

After that, sleep was impossible. The hard ground pressed against her hips and shoulders, and she couldn't get comfortable, could only lie there, mind racing from worry to worry. It was a relief when dawn finally came.

They crossed the Fire River using a hidden shelf tucked behind a waterfall. By noon they had settled at the juncture of two rugged canyons, waiting there while Garth, Whit, and Thor went downstream to Hardluck. They returned several hours later with the confirmation Whit had sought, Garth strutting and crowing his confidence. In three days, he declared—a week at most—they would reach the rim.

The trio brought back flasks of ale with which to celebrate, and before long things got wild and crazy. Callie sat in the shadows and watched. Afternoon cloud cover had turned the world gray, misting them with a light drizzle, and whether because of that or her dreams or the two Watchers she'd seen earlier that day, she found herself reluctantly sharing Pierce's sense of approaching disaster.

---

The next day they set out for the elusive Canyon of the Damned. As Garth consulted his map they crossed one deep ravine after another until they came to what the map labeled *Thornwall*. It was aptly named, for as far as they could see, thick, thorny growth scrawled across the slopes, curling around a graveyard of fallen trees. Sometimes they walked hundreds of yards without touching the ground, clambering over dead trunks and thickly matted branches. By midmorning Callie's dragon-hide vest was a net of scratches, the sleeves of her T-shirt torn in a dozen places. Her hands, arms, and face were bloody, and her right knee throbbed from when she had slipped and slammed it against a hidden log. She was battered, bruised, and exhausted, and her only consolation was that she was not alone.

Around noon they dropped into another canyon and came to a deep, swift-running river.

Pierce forded it first, riding the current downstream and across, and then returning to play anchor on the opposite bank as everyone else pulled themselves over. Afterward, as he and Garth stood together on the bank coiling up the rope and speaking quietly, Callie grasped something of the relationship they must have had before Pierce's encounter with the Trogs. Garth had been on a downslide after the failure of his mountain expedition, reviled and deserted by most of his friends. But not Pierce. It said a lot for Pierce's sense of loyalty and courage—maybe for the stock Garth put in him, as well. Or had at one time, anyway.

Leaving the river, they climbed again into the matted underbrush and fallen logs. After hours of toiling up and down and around Callie was ready to drop. More than that, she understood clearly how impossible it would be to find one's way through this nightmare web of drainages without a map. They spent a chilly, miserable night trying to get comfortable on beds of brambles. With no place to build a fire, they ate trail rations and drank cold water. Sleep, difficult before, became impossible.

—————

The morning dawned damp and colorless, and the group roused their stiff, protesting bodies to continue on. Mutiny rumbled in the ranks, as doubts about the map's validity were voiced with increasing frequency. The only thing stopping an eruption was the fact that going back was unthinkable.

And then, as the afternoon waned, they slogged over yet another ridge to find their troubles were just beginning. The thorn wall finally ended in an open meadow, beyond which rose the cleft they sought— an immense dark slash carved into the bowels of the earth. Massive curtains of stone overlapped in a gray giant's corridor hung with shifting mist. Distant harrylike shapes soared through its ragged fringes, and they could just make out the trail, snaking threadlike across the sheer walls until it disappeared into the clouds.

One by one they staggered to a stop, gaping in astonishment and dismay.

Callie swayed with dizziness. The thought of climbing that edifice, of perching on that narrow trail with all that space below made her stomach churn and her hands go cold and damp.

It was a long time before anyone spoke.

Then Rowena exploded. "A road? There's a road here and we've been busting our rear ends for two days over all this"—she motioned to the rear—"*garbage?*"

"That's not s'posed to be there." Garth pulled out his map.

Map or not, Callie could plainly see the wide earthen path beaten into the grass along the meadow's outer edge—headed back the direction they had come.

"It's *not* on the map," Garth proclaimed.

"I thought the stupid map was supposed to have been confirmed," Rowena snapped.

"It was. And anyway, why assume that road would've helped us? It probably peters out in a few miles."

"Ha! It probably heads right into Hardluck."

"Aw, you're just looking for something else to gripe about. If you don't like it, go back. You can always kiss up to one of those wimps at the temple."

"Better than kissing up to you!"

Rowena stalked down the hill toward the road. The rest of the group shifted uncomfortably, exchanging uneasy glances. Then Pierce struck off toward a group of trees on the far side of the meadow, triggering a general exodus. Before long they'd made camp, their fires snapping cheerily beneath bubbling stew pots.

The group was uncharacteristically quiet that evening. Sight of the canyon had sobered them, Callie most of all. She had expected a boulder-clogged cleft in whose bottom they would walk, not this ghastly, sheer-walled gash with its spider's thread of a trail. The appeal of returning to Manderia beset her with a vengeance, countered immediately by the knowledge that she'd never be able to find her way back. Not over the terrain they'd just come through. And she couldn't imagine Garth agreeing to copy his map just so she could go back.

*There's the road, though,* she thought. Rowena had not yet returned from her investigation. Maybe it did lead to Hardluck.

She stood up.

And sat down again. *How can you be such a coward? The only reason you're considering this is because you're scared of the heights. Which is pretty sorry, don't you think?*

Rowena had still not returned by the time Callie finished eating, so she went out into the dusk to look for her. Following the road along the base of the ridge they'd labored over earlier that afternoon, she came eventually to the edge of the thorn wall, and sure enough, the road tunneled straight into it, dead and living branches woven into dense walls around a passage whose end she could not see.

"Having second thoughts?" Garth's voice startled her, and she turned to find him coming up behind her.

"Yes."

"Reckon you're not the only one," he said. "But this doesn't look much better."

"No." Rubbing her arms against the chill, Callie started back toward camp, uneasily aware of the fact that they were alone out here.

"The hardest part's behind us, though," he said, moving in step beside her.

*Not for me.* She considered telling him about her acrophobia. It helped to have one person who understood—a "safe person," one therapist had called it. Someone to talk sense to her when the fear overwhelmed her, someone to cling to until the panic passed—or get her to safety should she need it.

"We'll be at the top in a day," Garth said. "Two at the most."

"And then what?"

He smiled at her. "Why, I'll walk you through the exit gate myself."

"But you don't know where it is."

"I'll know when I need to. I can feel it." He gazed up the road toward the ominous cleft, obscured by the gathering gloom above the trees and the slope of the meadow. "Of all the things I've done, all the ways I've tried to escape, this one feels most right. Come on." He caught her hand and led her faster along the road. "I wanna show you something."

They passed the camp and the trees, then crossed a grassy slope downside of the road and entered another grove of spindly pines. "I figure they put us here to test us, see," he said as they entered the wood, "to find out which of us will figure it out."

She regarded him doubtfully.

"It makes perfect sense. The stories about the Inner Realm, the fact that every single false benefactor has forbidden his followers to try the cleft, all the mumbo jumbo about not being able to get out on your own. It's a ploy."

*And Meg? Was she a ploy?*

"And even if it turns out we do have to go through one of those Benefactor's gates, at least we'll be up there. Ah, here we are."

She came around him to find a quiet glade and a gleaming pool of water. In the gathering darkness it glowed with a green phosphorescence. "It's beautiful!" she cried.

"Warm, too. Feel it."

She dropped to her knees. "Incredible! How did you know about this?"

"It's on the map." He sat on the grass beside her.

"And you didn't tell the others?"

"I'll tell 'em in the morning." He leaned back on his elbows, grinning at her.

A thrill went through her, excitement and fear—and a small voice telling her she was a fool.

"Do you ever wear your hair loose?"

His regard was so frank and suggestive, Callie blushed and averted her eyes. "Sometimes. It's not very practical out here, though. I'd probably get it caught in a bush and have to cut it off to get free."

"And what a shame *that* would be." He fingered the end of her braid, rubbing the plaited texture. She sat very still, galvanized by his touch, its indirectness all the more stimulating.

"Rowena had long hair when I met her. She cut it off a few years ago." He lay there, tugging at her braid, then said, "There are no bushes around here. Least not that you'd get caught in."

She shifted uneasily and glanced around. "Maybe we'd better go back."

He released her braid and sat up. "Maybe we should."

Somehow he had gotten very close to her. Blood pounded through her again. A wild, sweet song surged to override her voice of reason. *You're getting in over your head. You really don't want to do this.*

Garth watched her intently and, when she didn't move away, leaned forward and kissed her.

# CHAPTER

## 10

He pushed her to the ground, kissing her hungrily. Her body responded with treacherous enthusiasm, her flesh burning, blood pounding. But when his hand slid under her shirt she came to her senses.

*What am I doing?*

She pulled her lips from his. "Garth, wait."

He kissed her neck.

"I don't want—this isn't what—"

His mouth closed over hers—she pulled away again. "Garth, stop. I don't want to do this."

He pushed himself up to gape at her with glazed eyes. "What?"

"I don't want to do this."

He stared at her stupidly, then bent to kiss the hollow of her throat. "Are you kidding? You can't lead a man to the water hole and not let him drink."

"I didn't lead you here."

"Oh, yes you did, babe." He nibbled her ear. "You want this just as much as I do."

"Come on, Garth." She pressed her hands against his chest, trying to wriggle out from under him. Her efforts only seemed to impassion him. He told her how beautiful she was, how much he loved her, how he couldn't live without her. His caresses grew rougher, his breathing ragged, and she began to struggle in earnest, but it was like being pinned by the Trog. Apprehension uncoiled in her belly.

Then, out in the dark wood, a branch cracked, followed by a soft voice. "She said *no*, Garth."

Garth froze, and Callie pushed away from him, gaining her feet as she frantically attempted to straighten her clothing. Her face burned and her hands shook.

Garth stood up, frowning into the darkness. "Pierce?"

A figure detached itself from the shadows and approached.

"We need to talk," Pierce said. His eyes flicked to Callie, his face like stone.

Mortified, she whirled and plunged into the trees. She stopped at the forest's edge, panting, willing the frenetic pace of her heart to slow. Atop the rising meadow, campfires flickered against a backdrop of spruce, casting giant macabre shadows over the Outlanders. She felt cold and dirty and horribly guilty, for even though she knew she had not led Garth on, she *had* responded.

She shut her eyes and rubbed her face with both hands. Never in all her life had she responded to a man as she had just responded to Garth Copeland. The way she had leaned into his early caresses, pressed herself against him . . . She groaned in misery, hating herself.

Worst of all was Pierce's expression as his gaze flicked to her and away in that dreadful mask of stone.

She'd never be able to look him in the eye again.

The low staccato of argument that had been chattering in the forest behind her grew suddenly loud. Before she could pick out any words, it broke off, and someone came thrashing through the woods toward her. Pierce burst from the shadows to her left and stalked up the hill toward camp. She expected Garth to follow. When he didn't, she climbed the hill herself.

Pierce was stuffing his things into his pack, his face tight with anger. She stopped at the line where light met darkness, hoping he wouldn't notice her, and he didn't. His things stowed, he slung the pack over his shoulders, picked up his rifle, and disappeared into the night, every eye in camp upon him.

*He's leaving,* she thought, alarmed. *I should go after him. Go with him.*

Then Garth appeared at her side, grinning. "Sorry if I got carried away."

"Carried away? You'd have raped me if it wasn't for Pierce."

She turned her back, but he jerked her close and whispered, "It wouldn't have been rape, babe, and you know it."

Trembling, she tore free and stalked away.

"I love a woman who plays hard to get," he called after her.

Her stomach was a hard knot by the time she reached her bedroll. At first she could only sit there, caught in a matrix of conflicting emotions, too scared to leave, too outraged to stay.

"I wonder what that's about," LaTeisha drawled, breaking into her distress.

Callie looked up to see LaTeisha sitting nearby on her own bedroll. Her SLuB lay in pieces before her, but her attention was on something across the camp. Callie looked around to see Garth stand up from where he'd been talking to Lokai and Thor and walk to his tent. Behind him, the two men frowned, then Lokai arose and lurched into the forest.

"Garth's driving folks away left and right," LaTeisha muttered. "You gonna be next?"

"What?" Callie returned her attention to her friend.

"Rowena, Pierce, Lokai. They're bailing like rats off a sinking ship."

"I don't think Lokai's leaving. He didn't take his things."

"Maybe he's just going to take a leak. Sure looked like Garth was chewing him and Thor out, though. Or were they just getting the fallout?" She cocked her head at Callie. "Did he make his move on you, and Pierce interrupted him?"

Callie's face flamed.

LaTeisha laughed. "Guessed that one right, did I? Don't be shocked, honey. We were all waiting for it." She wagged a piece of the SLuB at Callie. "And don't think Pierce didn't know exactly what was going on."

"You mean he was spying on us?"

"I wouldn't call it spying, but if he broke it up, it wasn't any accident. I imagine *he'd* call it a rescue."

*No question it was that.*

"I see you would, too," LaTeisha said.

*What am I, an open book to everyone?* She turned away and wrapped her arms around her legs.

"And I thought you were falling for him," LaTeisha added.

Callie shuddered. "Why didn't you warn me?"

"Would you have listened?"

"Yes!"

LaTeisha snapped the SLuB barrel into the handgrip housing and rubbed it with a cloth. "Okay, then, here's more—rejection eggs him on. It won't seem like it at first, but you're a challenge now. Specially with Rowena gone."

"Great." Callie lay back on her bedroll, resting her head on her hands.

"He can be very charming," LaTeisha added.

"You speaking from experience?"

Her friend snorted. The pieces of the SLuB snicked and clicked as she reassembled them.

"How long before he gives up?" Callie asked.

"Honey, he doesn't give up."

Callie exhaled a long, slow sigh and pulled her hands from under her head, folding her arms across her chest. More than ever she wanted to leave. Pierce had. Rowena had. Why couldn't she?

Because, as much as she dreaded the climb and loathed Garth, she knew going back would get her nowhere. Pierce would probably sign up with the Manderian temple, and she wanted that no more than she wanted Garth's attentions.

She was still awake when Thor and Lokai returned, surprising her because she hadn't realized Thor had left. They had their weapons with them, which, inexplicably, they passed to Garth in his tent before seeking their beds. She wondered about it for a while, but her thoughts kept returning to her own concerns, and finally sleep claimed her.

She awakened to a groggy head, burning eyes, and a grim sense of foreboding. The clouds had lowered during the night, and the scent of moisture hung heavy in the air. Neither Pierce nor Rowena had returned, but no one commented. Within an hour they had all shouldered their packs and started up the cleft.

At first the trail climbed gently through a boulder-clogged channel grown thick with willows, not much different from what Callie had first imagined. Garth was often out of sight, walking at the head of the line with Thor and Lokai, which suited Callie—bringing up the rear with LaTeisha—just fine. All too soon, though, the path left the comforting presence of the willows to climb the left wall of the canyon, angling across increasingly vertical faces. Callie hugged the inner wall and stared at the place where wall met trail, sometimes glancing up at LaTeisha's back ahead of her, but careful never to look toward the trail's edge. Even so, she sensed the well of space gaping at her side and clenched the shoulder pads of her pack straps as if somehow they could hold back the rising panic.

Then they came to the bridge.

The trail curved around the wall and through a U-shaped cut in a shoulder of granite. Four large iron rings, two on a side, had been secured to the rock as anchors. The bridge, a narrow, frayed-rope affair, swooped sickeningly from edge to edge. Only its upper handrails were visible from Callie's vantage, and those dropped swiftly out of sight. As the first man started across, he seemed to step off into nothing. She watched him disappear section by section—legs, waist, chest, head— then reappear far out on the span, struggling to keep his balance on the swaying, undulating structure. Against the sheer rock face beyond him, he looked unbearably tiny, an insignificant mote suspended over a gulf of swirling lavender.

Callie's legs started to shake. Nausea clawed the back of her throat. The world spun, and the gargantuan space pulled at her, sucking her toward it like a black hole. Desperately she clutched the wall beside her, struggling to breathe. Her vision began to flash, and she knew if she did not get away from here *right now*, she would die. Gasping, she fled back to the boulders and the willows, where Garth found her a few moments later, sitting beside her pack at the road's edge, hugging her knees and weeping miserably.

"Callie? What are you doing?"

He stood over her, rifle in hand. Whit, Lokai, and Thor loomed behind him. When she didn't answer, he slung the rifle over his shoulder and squatted before her. "What's wrong, babe? What's happened?"

She closed her eyes and turned her face from his, sick with shame. "I'm . . . not going with you," she whispered.

"What?"

"I can't."

When he said nothing, Callie forced herself to look up, brushing the tears from her cheeks. "I'm going back to Hardluck."

He frowned suspiciously. "Because of last night?"

"No." She looked at the trees, the boulders, the sky. She wiped her face again. "Because I can't"—her voice was high and shaky—"cross the bridge."

"What do you mean you can't cross the bridge?" His frown deepened. "You gutshot a Trog at point-blank range, girl. Why can't you cross a little bridge?"

"Because I'm acrophobic."

He had no response to that. Behind him Thor hawked and spat. Whit shifted his grip on his rifle, leather armor creaking.

Finally Garth exhaled in annoyance. "That's it? You won't even try?" Censure rankled in his voice.

She averted her gaze. For a few minutes he squatted there, then opened his mouth to speak, closed it, lifted his hands from his thighs, let them drop back again. Finally he stood.

"Okay. If that's what you want, it's your life." He held out his hand. "But first give me your SLuB."

She looked up in surprise. "Why?"

"Just give it to me."

Puzzled, she drew the weapon from her waistband, then hesitated. He seized her wrist and jerked the weapon from her grasp. "We'll need this more than you will, babe." Tucking the gun into his waistband, he picked up her pack and handed it to Thor, who slung it over his shoulder.

She leapt to her feet. "What are you doing?"

He walked away, Thor and Lokai following. Whit frowned at her, then at Garth, as if he might protest, but in the end he followed the others.

"Wait," she cried. "You can't do this. What if the Trogs come? I don't have any water. Garth!"

"Come and get it," he called back at her.

She followed a few steps, then stopped, pounding her fists against her hips and screaming epithets at him. He ignored her and walked around the bend. She stared after him, sobbing with frustration and fury and desperate fear. He'd left her alone in the middle of nowhere with no defenses and no provisions.

*I have to go with him*, she thought, walking a few feet up the trail.

A vision of the rope bridge stopped her. Pressure built in her chest, a sharp, expanding pain that crawled up into her throat. Around her the willows and rocks pulsed in the damp morning air, shimmering as if reality was twisting out of its boundaries. *He left me . . . with nothing. . . .* The pressure exploded all at once in a scream of rage and desperation, echoing off the rocks and coming back to taunt her. She screamed again and again, until her throat was raw and she realized she couldn't just stand there and scream. She had to think.

*Why? What good will it do? I'm going to die out here. Never see my family again. Never marry. Never have children.* "Stop it!" she cried aloud. "Think."

She'd go back to Hardluck. The road appeared well used. It undoubtedly led there. The clouds would keep her cool, and she could drink at the river they'd forded yesterday. But, oh, Lord, how would she ever cross that torrent alone? She thrust the thought from her mind. If she started now, she might reach the town by afternoon, since she wouldn't have to work through the brambles. It was going to be okay. It was.

As she turned Callie spied the Watcher crouched on a rock twenty feet off the trail. The dark eye pits sucked her gaze into them, holding her cold and motionless. Then the mocking laughter bubbled up in her head. Her stomach boiled with nausea, and she had to wrench her eyes away, had to force herself to breathe again and walk down the trail.

*It will be okay*, she told herself. *It will.*

The thorn-wall tunnel was less intimidating by day than it had been at dusk the night before. Light filtered through the woven branches, and a chorus of twitters, rustles, and cracking twigs provided a welcome sense of company. Callie took comfort in the rabbits and squirrels darting across her path and tried not to dwell on the fact that, should she encounter Trogs, she'd have no place to hide.

She'd walked some ways when a distant crashing brought her to a standstill. Shortly the new noise stopped, too, and when it did not resume, she continued on. Probably just an animal—and not even a predator, since no predator would make so much noise. Besides, it was far away.

But then it started again, closer than before, a staccato of snapping twigs somewhere ahead. She slowed and considered waiting while whatever it was went its way. Again the crashing stopped, making her wonder if she'd somehow been sensed.

The silence lengthened. Impatience gnawed at her. The longer she waited, the greater her chance of meeting up with *something* unpleasant. Whatever was ahead was on top of the brambles anyway—perhaps it had gone to sleep or changed course and left.

She eased forward and was well past where she judged the unseen intruder to have stopped when the ruckus erupted once more, now directly overhead. It so startled her she cried out, and immediately the sounds ceased. Aghast, she stood motionless, willing whatever it was to go away. Instead, a rush of breaking twigs and falling debris preceded the emergence of a nightmarish face through the branches—red and misshapen, one round eye staring right at her.

Swallowing a scream, she whirled and ran.

"Callie?"

The voice sounded hoarse, but familiar.

"Callie, wait!"

An avalanche of snapping sounded behind her as astonished recognition brought her to a halt. When she turned back, he was limping after her. Trepidation warred with hope. His face was unrecognizable, the left eye a closed, puffy lump, colored black and purple and bright red. His swollen lips were crusted with white, the lower one split and blood-caked. Shiny bruises lashed cheekbones and jaw, and one ear swelled shapeless and purple. Nevertheless, the voice was right.

"Good heavens, Pierce! What *happened?*"

He stopped before her. "Thor and Lokai jumped me last night. Brought me out here and dumped me. Maybe they were afraid I'd retaliate, though what they thought I could do unarmed is anyone's guess."

It had been Pierce's weapons they'd passed to Garth last night, not their own.

He touched light fingers to his injured eye. "Looks pretty bad, huh?"

"I had no idea skin could turn such colors."

"So what're *you* doing here?"

Shame swept her. "I'm going back, too."

He frowned. "Without your stuff?"

"Garth has it."

His gaze probed her, seeing the truth she wasn't telling. "He left you out here defenseless."

"He said they'd need the stuff more than I would." Bitter anger twisted in her chest. How could he have said he loved her last night and do this today? She'd been such a *fool!*

Pierce swore softly. "He's lost his mind."

"He wants to get home," Callie said.

"Is that supposed to be an excuse?"

"An explanation. Can we go now?"

He regarded her evenly, and she was seized with a compulsion to explain about last night, how it had been Garth's idea, not hers—that she'd had no idea what he'd intended when she'd gone with him to that pond. Except that wasn't entirely true, so she said nothing.

At length he exhaled. "Yeah."

They reached the river before noon. By then it was hot, the clouds having shredded away as the day progressed. A cable rigged with a small raft served to ferry travelers across the river's sparkling green surface, and soon they were in the opposing bramble tunnel, confident the road did indeed lead to Hardluck, though they wouldn't be going that far.

By early afternoon they'd left the road and bushwhacked their way to what they assumed was another branch of the Fire River. Meandering in multiple streams through a broad, graveled bed, it ran relatively shallow here. The near bank descended in wide tiers, the far rising in a line of red cliffs.

"There should be a gate road on that bluff across the river," Pierce said, gesturing.

"What about supplies?"

"I think there's a Safehaven, too."

"You think?"

He shrugged. "I've never been in it."

They crossed the river where it was forty feet wide, calf-deep, and moving at a good clip. Its rocky bed made for slippery footing, and Callie held tightly to Pierce's hand as they lurched and slid their way across. Then, midchannel, he froze, that blank, faraway look on his face. She peered downstream in alarm but saw nothing. When he finally moved on, Pierce tugged at her to hurry. Slogging out of the water, they clambered over the boulders along the river's edge, careful to avoid the massive redclaw pods hidden throughout the tumble. Overhead a few puffy clouds played with the sun as Pierce stopped at the base of the far bank, studying the twenty-foot-tall face of ridged rock.

"It looks lower downstream," Callie said.

"We can't go downstream." Tension clipped his voice. "Come on."

He led her upstream along the bank to a rock slab lying aslant the cliff, which he climbed to take a look around. "There's a cut in the bank up the way," he said, descending to her side. "We might get out there." He flinched and his eyes went blank again—Callie's pulse accelerated—then his fingers closed around her hand. "We'd better hurry."

She swallowed. *We have no rifle, no SLuB, no protection at all.*

They slid and jumped and bounded from boulder to boulder, then ran down a sandy side wash, willow branches slapping their arms and legs.

Callie saw the cut up ahead, the one Pierce must have seen from the rock. No sounds had erupted from behind, so the Trogs must not have spotted them. They might just make it.

Something snagged her left foot, and she flew forward, face and hands driving into the sand. The wind knocked out of her, she lay gasping and spitting sand as the world seemed to slip by. Abruptly she realized it *was* slipping by—she'd blundered into a redclaw pod.

"Pierce!" His name came out a croak—she dared not risk a full yell. Grabbing at spindly weeds, which broke off in her hands, she twisted onto her back and tried to brace her free foot against a boulder or stump to stop herself—couldn't. Ahead she saw the gray leaves of the plant's central body, smelled its sweet-vomit stench. Her fingers clutched a willow branch that bent but held, and immediately she felt a pull in ankle, hip, and shoulder. Pain flared up her leg and back. The branch tore her palms, slid through her fingers. . . .

Then Pierce was there, chopping at the runner with a long knife— where had he gotten *that?*—in swift, powerful blows. Purple juice welled from the woody stem. The pressure on her leg released, and Callie sagged against the sand, dizzy with the pain. She shook her head to clear it, then sat up to attend the pod, still clamped to her foot. Pierce already crouched beside it, knife in hand.

A thin, distant shriek brought both their heads up.

Callie kicked frantically at the pod.

"Wait," Pierce said. In seeming slow motion, he inserted his knife tip between the pod's serrated lip and her instep, then twisted outward, away from the boot, sawing laboriously through the fibrous material.

Another howl split the air, closer now.

The knife broke free of the pod. He returned it to its initial place and sawed toward her toe, paralleling the boot. Meanwhile, Callie stuffed her fingers into the first slit he had made and peeled off a chunk of juicy green flesh. He finished the second cut and pulled the top part free. She ripped off the section on her heel, and the final piece fell away. Stuffing the knife into his boot, Pierce pulled her up, and together they raced across the sand, jumping hidden pods and keeping to rock when they could.

In moments they stood at the base of the cut, finding it not nearly as deep as they'd hoped. The bank sloped away from them, about fifteen feet high now, not exactly vertical, but close. Deep slashes, clefts, and gleaming knobs scattered its horizontal striations.

"Can you get up this?" he asked.

She swallowed heavily. It wasn't that high. And there were good hand- and foot-holds.

Behind them the howls sounded again, much closer.

*If I keep pressing at the problem, I'm bound to master it*, she told herself. *This'll be just like the ladder in the stable.* She licked her lips. "Sure."

"You go first, then. I'll hold them off if need be." He had the knife out.

Resolutely Callie mounted the rock. *Just find one handhold and then the next. . . . It's not that bad. No reason you can't do this. No reason.*

She reached overhead, feeling for a crack, and started to climb. The stone bulged in her face, brushing her nose, forcing her head back at an awkward angle. She heard Pierce start up after her. An image of what lay below drifted through her mind, and the fear began—a curdling deep in the pit of her stomach, a tremor tickling her limbs. Sweat slicked her brow and upper lip, stung the cuts on her cheeks.

Another howl ululated up the riverbed.

She reached with her right foot for a hold, found a knob about knee height, and was easing her weight onto the swell when it gave way, pebbles cascading down the rock face. Clutching the cliff with both hands, eyes tightly closed, she scrabbled with her dangling foot, found a hold, and clung, panting.

*You're okay*, she told herself. *You're almost to the top.*

Taking a trembling breath, Callie forced herself to open her eyes— the worst thing she could have done. She was looking down, and the ground seemed a hundred feet away. Adrenaline fired in hot prickling waves. She closed her eyes and clenched her teeth. *Not again. Please, not again. I have to do this.*

Her palms were slick with sweat, her fingertips slippery on the stone. The soles of her boots teetered on their purchase as memories of the Disneyland Skyway resurfaced—vivid and awful as the day they were born—the small car swinging in the breeze as her panic rose along with her father's rage.

"You're doing fine, Callie," Pierce murmured from somewhere below and to the right. "Don't stop."

She couldn't open her eyes. Couldn't move her arms or legs. Couldn't do anything but cling to the wall in desperation. *I can't do it! I can't do it!* The words shrieked like a whirlwind through her mind. A violent trembling overtook her.

*Oh no . . .*

Her foot slipped from its knob. She clutched harder to her handholds, but her efforts only made her situation worse. Both hands began to slide off the ridges they clung to. Then the other foot gave way—and she was falling.

Images whirled through her mind—the Skyway's chrome railing, the puffy clouds, the dark things pulling at her as she cried and clung to her daddy's arms. They could not make her lose hold of him, would *not*. She would hang on with all her might. . . .

The arm to which she clung was suddenly warm and slick with sweat and Callie opened her eyes. Pierce was bent over her, gently slapping her face. She blinked and released her grip on him.

They were in a shadowed cleft. Rock walls soared on either side, framing a narrow rectangle of sky. Pierce's brow ran with sweat and he was panting. He must have carried her.

She started to speak, but his fingers pressed her lips, and shaking his head, he mouthed, "Are you hurt?"

Her knee throbbed and her back ached, but neither injury seemed incapacitating. She shook her head.

"They're just below," he whispered, "searching for our trail. I ran through the stream to confuse them, but it won't last. We have to get to the road."

She eyed the sheer rock faces, the slit of sky above, then shook her head again. "I can't. You saw what happens to me."

"It's only about six feet of vertical, then it slopes back. Just wedge yourself into the chute and work your way up. I can help you." He regarded her soberly. "If you won't try, we might as well slit our throats now."

Callie rubbed her palms on her thighs, staring down the narrow cleft to the green slash of willows and weeds below. Faint sounds drifted up—splashing, snuffling, the rattle of pebbles. She closed her eyes and breathed deeply, squeezing down the fear as she squeezed her fists. Finally she swallowed hard and nodded.

He helped her up. Bracing her back against one side of the chute, her booted feet against the other, she inched her way upward. It wasn't long before her legs shook from the effort, and pain shot from both knee and spine, but she gritted her teeth and kept on. She was past the halfway point when Pierce started up. Soon she heard him breathing right below her.

The facing wall became harder to press against as the chute widened. Her legs straightened, and she had to use her toes and the upper part of her back. Panic fluttered in her belly.

"You've done it," Pierce said. "Now shove with your legs and roll over the edge. I'll help you. On three."

At the end of his count Callie pressed hard with both legs, twisting and arching her back as she did. The movement wrenched a smothered cry from her lips, and she teetered on the lip of rock, not quite strong enough to roll all the way. Then she felt his hands on her bottom, thrusting her up and over. And all at once she lay facedown on the rock, a prickly weed in her face.

"Here I come."

Wincing, she scrambled aside as Pierce shoved out of the chute and rolled to his feet in one fluid movement. From there, as he had promised, a narrow, easily managed path ascended to the rim, not twenty feet ahead of them.

As a snarling ruckus erupted below they hurried up the trail, Callie in the lead. When she reached the stand of oily-smelling willows on the rim and pressed through it to a grassy flat—there it was. Fifty yards ahead, the broad white surface of the gate road gleamed like a beacon.

Exultant, she was about to emerge from cover when she spotted four Trogs approaching from the right. She dodged back into Pierce, and he saw them at once. Using the foliage as a screen, they circled the clearing, the sounds of their passage lost in the commotion being made by the mutants still searching the riverbed. But when they came to the end of the willows, thirty yards of open grass still separated them from safety.

"We'll have to run for it," Pierce whispered.

Callie looked at the four creatures gathered across the clearing at the edge of the cliff, hooting and bellowing at their companions below, then met his gaze and nodded.

CHAPTER

11

Terror overrode the pain in her knee, and Callie ran all out, dodging and leaping clumps of sage and yellow grass. Pierce ran behind and to the side, shielding her from the mutants, whose cries of discovery they heard all too soon, the road still an eternity away. Her breath tore at her throat, and her chest burned. The round weights of a Trog's bola whirled past her head. Another clattered behind her, followed by a heavy thump. She glanced back. Pierce rolled in a cloud of dust, legs entangled as his knife flashed.

"Run!" he yelled, the bonds already falling free.

As she obeyed, a third bola clattered around a sage plant, its heavy black head slamming her ankle. She staggered, vision flashing with the pain as she regained her balance and dashed on. Two dark giants burst from the trees to her left, so close she could see their eyes and hear their grunts as they ran. Then Pierce caught her arm and hurled her forward as he dove for the road. They sprawled in a tangle on its far side.

Shoulder and cheek stinging fiercely, Callie rolled back against Pierce, and his arm tightened around her. Along the river side of the road, a mere four feet away, nine huge Trogs leered down at them, their chests broad and solid, their hands big as dinner plates. Lank, greasy hair hung over their shoulders, framing mostly bearded faces with pig-gish eyes and heavy brows. Ragged, too-short britches wrapped their bodies, exposing furry shins above worn boots. Surprisingly, one of them was female, an oddity among Trog populations since most women did not survive their initial months of capture. This one had grown almost as big as the males, so coarse and heavy of feature her gender was only distinguishable by the most basic of female accoutrements, and even that took a second glance.

Gagging on the stench of urine and old sweat, Callie cringed against Pierce, feeling unspeakably small and helpless. And yet, though the mutants grimaced and growled, they did not advance or lift their weapons, though bolas dangled from several hands, and all had knives and crossbows.

After all its inconsistencies, the manual appeared to be right in one thing: The road *was* a safe zone.

As her terror waned, Callie took note of the mutants' deformities, side effects of their exposure to the fire curtain. The one in the tight red trousers had a flared, piglike nose with a large, oozing, dark-crusted mole. Another sported two hornlike knobs sprouting from his forehead. A third had a clubbed hand so large it resembled a flipper. And a fourth continually changed form before her eyes, alternating between a handsome, almost stark-naked blonde and a lizardlike creature squatting at the roadside.

They hooted and snarled and roared, made threatening motions with bolas and knives, but not one of them set foot on the white pavement.

*We can probably get up and walk away.*

She was preparing to test that theory when the creatures ceased their fussing and murmured, "Andrews . . . come with us. . . ."

Andrews? Wasn't that Pierce's last name?

"Taste the fire. . . ."

The wind kicked up a veil of dirt around them as overhead one of a growing number of cotton-ball clouds blotted out the sun.

"You know you want it. . . ."

Pain in her bicep drew Callie's attention to Pierce's hand, tightening viselike around her arm. His bruised face had paled, his good eye darted wildly, and he panted like a trapped animal. She sensed he was near to breaking, that any moment he might bolt, panic-stricken, or curl up inside himself and seal it all out.

"Andrews . . ."

Fear for him tightened her throat. She pried his fingers off her arm and turned to face him. "Pierce, they can't hurt us. Don't listen to them."

He gave no sign he'd heard her.

"Come on." She took his hand and stood and, when he did not respond, bent to shake his arm. "Pierce! Come *on!*"

Behind her the mutants jeered. "Won't do no good, babe."

"He's not listening, girlie."

"Give it up, sweet cakes. He knows what he wants, and it ain't you."

"Forget them!" She grabbed his bearded chin and forced him to look at her. He was trembling, and sweat sheened his brow as the wind fanned locks of hair at his temple.

"Don't," he said in a small, tight voice. "Don't let them . . ." His eyes flicked to the Trogs, came back to her, full of terror, then glazed.

"No!" she cried, shaking him hard. "You're not giving up now." She stood again and tried to pull him to his feet, but he was dead weight. "We're on the road!" she cried. "They can't hurt us. Come on, Pierce! Don't do this."

Her vehemence must have gotten through—for a moment his eyes focused on her, and then he helped her pull him up, let her tug him into motion. But after that he marched mechanically, his hand limp in hers, face blank.

The Trogs followed alongside, taunting and hooting, and after a while they even included Callie in their abuse, offering obscene comments and lurid suggestions of what they wanted to do with her. Occasionally the shapeshifter leaped ahead and, assuming his lizard form, screamed wildly. It scared her at first, then became mildly amusing. With time, even the taunts ceased to unnerve her—being nothing but noise and bluster. As long as she stayed on the road, they couldn't touch her.

She wondered why they persisted. Did they really expect them to panic and bolt? Maybe. It seemed the mutants weren't strong on brains—the enlargement of their bodies appeared to work a reciprocal shrinkage of gray matter.

Up on the rim, the clouds knocked together and rumbled with thunder, but they offered little relief out here on the plain. The sun beat at her like a mallet on a gong, burning her exposed skin and raising a sweat that stung the raw spots on her face and shoulder while pain stabbed her knee with every step. The river's cool shimmer grew increasingly tempting, especially since the Trogs frequently went down to douse themselves, returning wet and pungent smelling to offer her bags of water, which they then laughingly drank in front of her.

Callie's mouth grew dry, and the sun's heat intolerable. She floated through spells of dissociation, caught up in visions of a cool, sweet plunge into one of the river's deep eddies, and finally found herself stopped at a break in the bank where a path led down to it. It wasn't far, and she ached for a drink and a rest.

Surprised by the silence, she glanced around. When had the mutants left?

Oh well, what did it matter? They were gone. And she needed water. She'd come right back, just be a minute.

The voice at the back of her mind—the one she always seemed to ignore—told her not to be foolish, that she wasn't *that* thirsty. But look—Pierce was already running down the path, so she might as well follow him, right? As she started after him, she wondered at his sudden recovery. And several steps off the road, she realized he hadn't recovered at all. Whirling back, she saw him standing where she'd left him, staring blankly back in the direction from which they'd come. As she raced to his side, a bola sailed after her, flying over the road and pinwheeling around a sage bush.

Reverting to his lizard form, the shapeshifter came back up the bank to watch them. Callie seized Pierce's hand and glanced over her shoulder. Sure enough, the Trogs were hiding in the willows along the bank's edge. And not just Trogs. Beyond them, also in the willows, stood three gray, spidery-limbed Watchers.

Waiting for her to walk into the trap?

Shuddering, she limped on with Pierce in tow. One thing was certain—they weren't leaving this road until they reached the Safehaven.

As the shadows lengthened, the anvil of clouds building above the cliffs finally spilled out over the plain, lightning raking its black underbelly as thunder rumbled across the land. The wind kicked up and rain scent rode the air. Callie reflected sourly that, where earlier she would've welcomed the storm, now it only promised a wet and miserable night—to say nothing of the possibility of their being electrocuted. But when she topped a rise, the sight of a low white building awash in warm light revived her flagging spirits. Although she tried to pick up the pace, Pierce continued to walk like a zombie, so by the time they plodded through the gate in the Safehaven's outer wall, fat silvery droplets were splatting the pavement around them. Even then he wouldn't hurry, mechanically crossing the white flagstone patio to the pair of entry doors, which slid open before them in a rush of foliage-scented air.

"We made it!" Callie cried as they stepped into the plant-choked atrium and the doors slid shut. Smiling, she turned and almost crowed with joy to see Pierce emerging from his shell.

His gaze roved the hanging ferns, the fishpond and fountain, the blue-and-white tile—and came to rest upon her. He looked long into her eyes, then drew his hand from hers to touch her cheek. "Thank you."

His words came out ragged, more breathed than spoken, and she stared at him, vibrating with unexpected emotion. Suddenly her eyes teared and she turned away, swallowing a lump in her throat. Perplexed and embarrassed, she hurried through the atrium into the common room beyond and stopped in amazement.

State-of-the-art appliances lined the left wall beyond a curved freestanding counter, and to the right, an oak dining table stood before a wide rain-pecked window that looked out on a walled garden. Gleaming blue-and-white tile paved both areas, ending at the edge of a sunken sitting room carpeted in beige and furnished with sleek white sectional couches. A semicircle of floor-to-ceiling plate glass afforded a view of the rumpled landscape, and an entertainment center stood left of the window, stocked with books and compact discs. Soft, jazzy music tinkled from hidden speakers, but the place, though well serviced and obviously awaiting guests, appeared deserted.

Following directions on a screen among the appliances, they obtained two large glasses of water, followed by two of root beer, then toured the premises in search of beds and showers. Two opposing hall-ways led off from the common room, one accessing several bedrooms, the other a breezeway leading to a windowless side structure. The wide horizontally sectioned door at the front and the smaller people-sized door in the breezeway suggested a garage, but since both doors were locked, they couldn't be sure.

"What would they need a garage for?" Callie asked. "Delivery trucks?"

"Maybe it houses a swimming pool."

"All locked up? And without windows? No, I think it probably holds the workings for this place—supplies, generators, that kind of thing."

"And the little robots that come out in the night and clean up?"

Callie glanced at him, surprised. He was not acting in the brooding manner that usually followed a mutant encounter. And was that the ghost of a *smile* on his face?

"Why not?" she said. "Somebody's gotta do it."

"Yeah, right."

"Well, I'm heading in. It doesn't look like this building's gonna yield its secrets today, and *I* want to try out one of those fancy show-ers."

She chose suite seven, right off the main room, and immediately discovered the door had no lock. At least not on the knob. Etched into the wall beside it, though, was the familiar triangle of golden circles surrounding a central dot. Maybe that secured the door.

Pressing her hand to it, she felt a thrum of electric current but noth-ing more. She tried pressing the dot, then the centers of each of the circles, first one at a time and then simultaneously. She even tried out-lining each of the circles while positioning her thumb on the dot in the middle. Nothing. Finally deciding it was probably a recognition logo and feeling foolish for her antics, she gave up and left the door unlocked. Pierce wasn't likely to barge in on her anyway.

The suites were each furnished with a king-sized bed, desk and chair, CD player, and a private bath. The latter was a marvel, awash in soft illumination without visible light fixtures. The basin faucet was motion activated, and the toilet, while familiarly shaped, held no water and no controls for flushing, yet disposed of the waste instantly, silently, odorlessly. Across from it a chute labeled Laundry instructed her to empty her pockets before depositing her clothes, assuring her the apparel would be returned when she emerged from the shower.

"You guys thought of everything," she muttered, shaking her head.

She had one foot in the shower when a tone sounded and the chute door reopened, her jeans and shirt still lying on the tray at the bottom. A soft voice insisted, "Please empty all pockets before depositing garments."

Frowning, Callie felt through her clothing until she found the crystal stylus she'd made weeks ago, long forgotten in her back pocket. Her garments now acceptable to the laundry chute, she stepped into the white-tiled shower and swore she'd gone to heaven. She stood under the beating spray long after she'd finished washing, letting it massage her aching back and shoulders. The hot water never diminished, and in the end she had to force herself to get out. Fans kicked on as she toweled herself dry, sucking out the steamy air in minutes. A white terry-cloth robe hung on the back of the door, sweet smelling and soft. She belted it on, reentered the bedroom, and collapsed onto the bed with a sigh.

*This is so much better than the last place we stayed! Wonder what dinner will be. Wonder if there's room service.*

A ping drew her attention to the wall beside the closet where a shelf extruded to present her clothing, clean, mended, and neatly folded. Once redressed, she set about finger combing the rat's nest that was her hair—as usual, an exercise in frustration.

"I take it back," she muttered as she worked. "There is something they didn't think of—a comb."

She was working out the twentieth snarl when the design by the door began to flash. She frowned at it. The last time one of those things flashed at her, the road had disappeared from under her feet. Was the whole Safehaven going to vanish this time? She seemed to recall the manual saying they were allowed twenty-four hours here, but maybe she was mistaken.

She waited. After a few minutes the symbol went dark, and the whole thing faded into the wall.

"I wonder what that was about." She scanned the room, floors, ceiling, mirror. Was it some kind of test? Or warning? Or . . . *Well, who cares so long as we're not being evicted!*

When she returned to the main room, Pierce was already there. With his face clean and his wet hair combed back from his forehead, his black eye looked worse than ever. At least the swelling had gone down, though his lips were still red and chapped. He was fiddling with the kitchen appliances—various panel lights glowed red and green—and the aroma of melted cheese and chili filled the room. As Callie slid onto a stool, he glanced over his shoulder.

"If I've got this figured right," he said, "it should be about ready. I hope you like enchiladas."

"Love 'em."

"And what to drink?" He turned back to a panel and read off a list that could've come from any restaurant menu.

"I'll have iced tea," she interrupted.

He punched a button. Moments later a small door opened in the wall to reveal a tall glass. "Here you go, ma'am." He handed her the tea.

Callie marveled again at the change in him. It was as if the brooding, cynical man she'd known had washed away with the dirt while he showered. In fact, she felt a little changed herself. Surrounded by this clean, friendly, almost normal environment, the horror of the last five weeks took on the unreality of a fast-fading nightmare.

The buzzer rang, and a panel opened to reveal two plates of sizzling, sauce-drenched cheese enchiladas.

"These are huge! And they smell grea—ow!" Pierce jerked his hand away and searched for a hot pad. She found forks while he put the food on the table.

They ate hungrily, intently, exclaiming at the food's excellence. Callie couldn't remember when she'd been so ravenous, or when enchiladas had tasted so good. Afterward they stayed at the table, watching the lightning show above the cliff. Callie wondered how the others were faring. Was it raining on them? Had they met up with Trogs? How far up the canyon had they gotten?

Despite the humiliation of being rejected and abandoned, part of her was glad it had happened. It was nice not to feel scared or hungry or desperate, and she wouldn't trade places with them for anything—unless they found deliverance from this strange world.

She sipped her tea, ice cubes tinkling.

Beside her, Pierce shifted in his seat. "This reminds me of home."

Callie lowered her glass and waited for him to continue, watching him carefully. His brown hair had dried into soft waves that curled over the top of his collar. His beard looked fuller than she remembered, curly with strands of red and gold in it. From this side, all she could see of his eyes was the injured one, a riot of yellow, green, and blue now joining the black and purple.

He kept his gaze on the cliffs. "Our ranch is in the southeastern Rockies. There's an escarpment like that just beyond our backyard. I used to climb it all the time. Loved the view."

She shuddered.

He noticed. "How long have you been acrophobic?"

"Since I was seven." She rattled the ice in her glass. "It started after my father left. I thought I was cured, but lately it's come back."

"You mean like today?"

"Back on Earth, actually. Little things at first—trouble with elevators and overpasses. And then, a few weeks before I was brought here, I had an attack while hiking one of the peaks near Tucson. My friends had to carry me down." She played with the drips of condensation on her glass. "I was an idiot to think I could ever climb that awful canyon."

Pierce said nothing.

"In any case, I'm glad it's over. I needed to turn back. I want to talk to those people at the temple. I have a feeling the answer's there."

He shot her a dubious look.

"Remember that transmission I got from my friend?"

"Your friend was brought in when you were." He stroked the soft, clean whiskers on his chin. "And the service period for the Temple of Mander is three years."

"Not always. Wendell said it's different for different people."

"But your friend didn't tell you to join the temple, did she? She just said to go back to Manderia."

"And that the canyon was a trick."

"Maybe *she* was a trick."

Callie scowled at him. "So what are you saying? You don't want to go back after all?"

He snorted. "It's not as if there's anything better."

"Well, if you don't believe the answer's there, why did you give up on Garth's plan?"

"You know as well as everyone else. I was scared witless." He snatched up the glass and drained it, then stood and took his dishes to the receptacle in the kitchen. A few minutes later she heard the breezeway door open and close as he went outside.

The music from the CD player drifted around her. She sat toying with her glass and ice cubes, beset with bitter memories of her own. If she were honest, she'd have to admit fear had turned her back as well— not some growing conviction the answer lay in Manderia. She'd been there. She *knew* it offered nothing. But once again, she'd let fear close the door on opportunity. Shame and bitter frustration welled up in her, spilling out in tears that streaked her cheeks and made her glad she was alone.

Over the cliffs, multiple forks zigzagged against the blackness, lighting up the clouds and silhouetting the cliff line. Raindrops spattered the glass, and a distant howl ululated on the wind, quickly drowned out by a growl of thunder. Another splat of rain preceded a second howl and Callie sat up straight, pulse accelerating. Pierce was outside. Alone.

The howl sounded a third time, definitely closer now.

She stood up so fast the chair fell against the bar. Ignoring it, she made for the breezeway.

Pierce stood by the outer wall nearest the cliff, hands resting on the waist-high barrier, staring toward the cliffs. Wind tossed his hair and parted his beard, flattening his clothes against his chest. She stopped beside him as the howls chorused again, sending chills up her back. *They're down in the riverbed. Coming this way.*

She laid a hand on his arm. "Pierce?"

He did not move. His eyes saw nothing. She repeated his name twice before he took note of her.

"Let's go inside."

He complied without a word.

Back in the main room he went immediately to the big window and stared at the night while she rummaged through the cabinets for a game or movie, something to distract them. Finally she pulled out a box of Chinese checkers and, when she'd set all the marbles into place, invited him to play. He came and sat on the couch.

After only two rounds she knew her plan wasn't going to work and slouched back on the L-shaped sofa, regarding him thoughtfully. He held a red marble, turning it round and round between his fingers.

"Those mutants out there," she said. "They knew your name."

"Yeah."

"Were they the ones who caught you?"

"Maybe." He spoke softly, turning the marble faster. "I don't remember much of it. We were looking for blood crystal, found a good solid vein and set up camp. We had no idea they were around. They attacked at sundown. Tom and I were the best shots, and we had the weapons, so we covered the rear while the others ran. They got us. Got Shara, too."

His voice caught when he said the name. Callie leaned toward him, her attention riveted, but she kept silent for fear of shying him off.

Presently he resumed. "They staked us out that night—Tom and me. Used hot irons, whips, knives—I remember that. I remember trying not to scream. . . ." He trailed off again, his gaze fixed on the wall above her head, his fingers frantically turning the marble. When he spoke next, his voice was faint and distant. "They must've killed Shara and Tom, and eaten them. That's what they usually do. I don't remember. The last thing I can recall was this Trog who came up and cut off my thumb."

Callie stared at him, horrified.

He stopped turning the marble and placed it on the tray in front of him. "Maybe I fainted and dreamed that, though, because I still have my thumb." He fell silent again, massaging the digit in question.

When he did not go on, she risked asking, "Why did they let you go?"

"I don't think they did. I think I escaped. I remember running through the desert in the darkness and hiding in a cave. And begging"—his voice choked—"begging the aliens to save me. When I think back, they must have. Mutants were all around me. I was injured. I must've stunk to high heaven. But I got away. I guess Garth and Whit found me wandering in a daze. They said the Trogs had me for three weeks, but I don't remember."

The CD player had gone off, and they sat without speaking, listening to the thunder and the rain and the wind. A loud chorus of howls temporarily overlaid the other sounds, then faded. With a low cry, Pierce exploded off the couch and returned to the window, standing with his back to her, arms folded across his chest. His reflection stared back at him, pale and haunted, a skull-like mask.

Blue-white light lit the room, followed by a swift loud crack that made her jump and left her ears ringing. Pierce seemed unaware of it.

At length Callie said, "So after that—after they got you back and you recovered from your wounds—that's when you started sensing the Trogs?"

He didn't move.

And just when she'd decided he hadn't heard her, or wasn't going to answer, he said, "Yeah. And that's the worst of it. Because it's not them that scares me so much as me. Something inside me wakes up every time I'm near them. Something that wants to be with them."

She frowned. "How could you want to be with them, knowing they'd torture you again?"

His gaze moved upward, toward the boiling, flickering clouds. A gust of wind shook the window in the dining nook, spattering it with rain.

"I think," he said, "they made me pass through one of their fire curtains."

She felt the blood leave her face and trickle down to an icy pool in her middle.

"It would explain what happened to my thumb," he went on. "Maybe even why I can't remember anything."

He looked over his shoulder at her. "If that's what happened, they weren't calling me this afternoon because they want to kill me. They want to finish the transformation. It'd be the ultimate revenge for all the trouble I've caused them—to make me one of them." He grimaced at the clouds. "The kicker is, part of me wants to do it."

Horror gripped her hard, churning acid in her stomach. "Oh, Pierce . . ."

"You forget how long I've been here." He faced her, eyes blazing. "Five years. Five. I've been to every gate there is, walked all over the Outlands searching for a way out. I've watched my friends die one after the other, yet I'm still here, and I haven't the vaguest idea why.

"Yes, I'm cynical. Hope is a temptress. And it hurts so much when it dies, after a while you learn not to let it in. At least as a mutant I'd be strong—one of the feared, instead of one of the always fearing."

He held her gaze defiantly for a heartbeat, then stalked past her to his room, the first one in the hall opposite her own. The door closed behind him with a snick, and she was alone.

After a moment Callie let out her breath and sagged back on the couch.

# CHAPTER

## 12

Callie awoke to her own screams, and she lurched up, gasping in the darkness. It was just a nightmare. There were no mutants. And Pierce . . .

Was not one of them. Yet.

She closed her eyes and clenched her hands in the sheets. "Alex," she whispered, "if you really meant what you said . . . don't let that happen to him. If there's anything, *anything* . . ."

She sighed and the passion waned. "What am I doing? You don't care."

Maybe that was their intent—to see what it took to get humans to turn themselves into monsters. The thought made her so uncomfortable she didn't pursue it. Besides, she was thirsty. Mexican food always did that to her. It had probably brought on the dream as well.

A thin band of blue light ran horizontally along the kitchen walls, providing faint illumination, and when she stepped onto the tiled floor, the main lights kicked on. She keyed in her request and was removing her glass from the dispenser when the screams started in Pierce's room—no surprise, considering what the day had brought. Sliding onto a stool, she rested her bare feet on the rung and stared at the tiled counter.

How could he want to be a Trog? No matter how frustrated, how dejected, how defeated one might feel, there was no reason to stoop to that. It horrified, perplexed, and frightened her. How many times could they have put him through the curtain in three weeks? How far would he be from transformation? Did it happen slowly, or all at once? If they came tomorrow, could she stop him from going with them?

Mercifully, the tortured cries cut off. Were they worse tonight, or was it her imagination?

The storm had exhausted itself while she slept, and in the silence she heard a thump. Then Pierce's door opened, and he entered the kitchen. He stopped when he saw her, blinking in the bright light as if trying to remember who she was. He wore only pajama bottoms, his lean, well-muscled torso crisscrossed with shiny white scars.

Callie set down her glass. "Are you all right?"

Her voice jarred him fully awake. Recognition lit his eyes, and the tension bled out of him. Exhaling deeply, he shoved a hand through his tousled hair. "Bad dream."

He shuffled to the dispenser for his own glass of water, and Callie couldn't keep her eyes off him. His back was covered with scars, too.

Pierce drank the water in one long gulp, got a refill, and drank some more. Halfway through he stopped, wiped his mouth with the back of his hand, and met her gaze. "What's the matter?"

She studied her glass, that inexplicable lump once again pressing against her throat. "Nothing."

He came around the counter and slid onto the stool beside her. She felt his eyes on her face.

"It's nothing," she said again.

Somewhere in the building, something whirred and clicked.

"It's just—I don't know." She forced a laugh. "Just the strain of it all, I guess." But she couldn't meet his eyes. She kept seeing the Trog version of him from her dream.

He sighed. "I shouldn't have told you that stuff. It wasn't your prob—"

"I'm glad you did. Now I know what you're going through." She drew a steadying breath and made herself smile. "Maybe I can help."

"*No!* Whatever happens, you stay on that road. If I walk off, just let me go."

"I know I couldn't stop you. I just mean—" Her voice betrayed her, choking into silence.

He stared at her, his good eye wide, his face pale around the bruises.

Sudden tears blurred her vision. Angrily she wiped them away, seized her glass, and moved around the bar. "I don't know what's wrong with me. Everything, I guess. You, Garth, nearly getting killed. I'm probably in dire need of sleep, and here I am wasting the night away."

Desperate to stem the flow of her babbling, she gulped down the rest of her water, then set the glass on the counter. He watched her soberly. "See you tomorrow," she said, and fled to her room.

Later, when the edge of her mortification had worn off, she lay in bed staring at the ceiling, contemplating what they faced tomorrow. The Trogs would surely come. How could she just let him go to them?

"If we can get to Manderia," she said to the room. "If we can just make it that far . . ."

When she awoke in the morning, the design by the door had returned. With a yawn, she ignored it and limped into the bathroom, wincing with every step. Her body ached, and her face—scratched, bruised, one cheek dark with scabbing—looked almost as bad as Pierce's.

As she went about her business, she noticed the crystal stylus on the counter where she'd set it when she put her clothes in the laundry bin. She'd thought once it might be a key. Now as she picked it up, a wave of goose bumps washed over her.

Seconds later she was back in the bedroom, facing the mysterious design. Breath held, she aligned the rod with the dot amidst the circles. The circumferences were a perfect match, and a current leapt through thumb and finger where they held the pad. Gently she pushed. The rod's end sank into the wall.

She opened the bedroom door and yelled for Pierce, who was in the kitchen conjuring wonderful breakfast smells. He came warily into her room. When half the rod's length had vanished into the wall, the three circles blazed white.

"Do you have the vaguest idea what you're doing?" he murmured.

"One of the five rules at the beginning of the manual said that ASBs would supply all our additional needs. Later, I remember reading about Auxiliary Supply Boxes. But since we never came across any boxes in our travels cross-country, I forgot about them. The manual said they were marked with an identifying sign, and you had to have a key to open them." She pushed the rod all the way home. As the key's grip pads touched the wall, a glowing rectangle appeared around it.

"Try turning it," Pierce suggested.

She did, drawing the circles inward. Guessing at the final configuration, she adjusted them until each joined with the other two, the key port at dead center. Nothing happened. Then, just as she'd concluded she was wrong after all, the insignia flared, the front of the box vanished, and the key fell to the floor.

Eagerly they peered into the exposed niche.

"A comb?" Pierce squeaked as Callie pulled it out.

"Well, I did need one." It was carved of ivory, a tracery of green vines running along the top and handle, the large tines perfect for her fine, thick hair.

"Talk about anticlimactic," he said, heading back to the kitchen.

She turned the comb in her fingers, not nearly as disappointed as he. This was a little thing, perhaps, yet its very insignificance impressed her, like the small touches of a gracious host—the rose on the nightstand, the chocolate on the pillow.

Alex's parting words sprang to memory. *We intend this for your benefit. Don't let fear and stubbornness keep you from finding something better.* If she had accepted his orientation and stayed on the road, she might have reached a Safehaven that first night. Might have had this comb weeks ago. Might be home now.

As she worked the tines through her hair, she realized the box was still open. Was there more? Yes: a second key. When she removed it, the box disappeared.

The smell of bacon drew her to the kitchen, where Pierce sat at the counter eating eggs, pancakes, and sausage. She laid the extra key beside him. "This was in there, too."

He picked it up. "It's just like yours."

"Yes."

"Why would you need a second one?" He set it down and resumed eating.

"Maybe it's for you." Callie keyed in her breakfast order.

"There wasn't a box in my room. Nor anywhere else I've seen."

"The boxes seem to come and go. It might be there now."

"If it is, I'm not playing. I don't like their little games."

"Maybe it's not a game. Maybe they're just trying to be helpful."

He snorted and returned to his eggs.

A buzzer announced the arrival of Callie's Belgian waffles and syrup. She settled at the counter opposite him, and they ate in silence, the tension deepening between them. Every bite brought them closer to leaving, closer to their rendezvous with the Trogs.

Finally Pierce's stool stuttered across the tile as he got up and took his dishes to the receptacle. "You gonna be ready soon?" he asked.

"I'd like to comb out my hair."

He hesitated, watching her. She continued to eat in slow, deliberate bites.

"It's a long walk," he said. "The earlier we get started, the better." He went outside.

Too soon her plate was empty, and she retired to her room to work on her hair. Once during that time she heard him come in and go out again, but he didn't call for her, didn't say anything at all.

At length she finished, and there was nothing left but to get ready to leave. The wonder kitchen had provided a sack lunch—sandwiches, fruit, Snak-Paks, and pouched juice drinks all packed in a carrying bag and delivered to the service window at the touch of a finger. When Callie set the bag on the counter, she noticed the key she'd left for Pierce was gone. As she keyed in her request for a second lunch, he appeared in the hall leading from the breezeway, his face flushed.

"You won't *believe* what I just discovered." His voice was soft, almost reverent.

He led her to the people-sized door in the side of the building they had puzzled over yesterday. Though the door remained closed, the significance of the design gleaming in the wall beside it struck her like a blow. When Pierce inserted his key and aligned the circles, the door slid open, revealing a rectangle of shadow. Uneasily she stepped into the oily scent of machinery and was all but blinded as lights flared on overhead. Then, blinking in the brightness, she gasped. It *was* a garage. And it held ten small bubble-windshielded cars, each accommodating maybe four riders. On the side of the vehicle nearest them, the three-circle design invited her key, which opened the door. A pleasant voice bade her get in.

"We'll make Manderia by nightfall," she murmured.

"Yup."

When she returned with the lunches, Pierce was already in the car. As she climbed in beside him, he slid his key into the dash slot, igniting an array of red lights. Following the voice's instructions, they fastened their seat belts and closed the doors. Then the car vented itself with a hiss, the red lights vanished, and they jolted forward. As the garage's rollback door lifted before them, they glided into the courtyard.

"There's no steering wheel," Pierce noted as they circled the buildings. "No brake pedal, either."

"Maybe we don't need them."

"I suppose we could always pull out the key." He peered under the dashboard, then straightened. "You know, I've seen cars like this before. I just assumed some benefactor had provided them."

"Some Benefactor did provide them."

"I mean a phony one. You'd think there'd be more of them—cars, that is."

As they turned onto the main road Pierce suddenly twisted around to stare out the back window. And when Callie saw the four figures walking up the road, she almost panicked. Then reason asserted itself. Trogs could not walk on the roads. Besides, this bedraggled foursome had a familiar look about them.

She squinted into the sunlight, wishing for the thousandth time that she had not lost her glasses. "Is that Whit?"

"Yeah." Pierce pulled the key from its slot. The car slowed and sank to a stop.

They popped open the doors and got out as the foursome—Rowena, LaTeisha, John and Whit—approached, heads down. Muddy, bruised and blood streaked, they appeared exhausted. Makeshift bandages wrapped Whit's thigh and LaTeisha's arm.

Ten yards away John glanced up and stopped, his jaw dropping open. One by one the others followed suit.

John recovered first. "How'd you get out of Hardluck?" he cried, hurrying toward them. "We thought you were dead."

Pierce and Callie exchanged a glance. "Hardluck?" Callie said.

"Garth told us you were afraid to cross the bridge," LaTeisha said, staring at Callie. "Said that you'd had a breakdown and were blubbering at the side of the road."

"He was just covering for his stupidity," John countered. He cocked his head at Callie. "It was obvious you'd decided his plan was nuts. Or maybe you'd decided *he* was." He grinned and she flushed. "Whit told me how Garth took your stuff and left you. At first I didn't believe him. But then we noticed Thor had an extra rifle with notches on the stock." He glanced at Pierce. "Just like yours. We figured he'd done the same to you, and that we'd be next if we crossed him, so we sneaked away while he was out scouting. Figured you'd be in Hardluck—that's where we found Rowena."

Rowena wasn't telling her story. She hung back from the others, face turned down, luscious figure concealed by a baggy gray shirt. A blue bruise colored one cheekbone and her lower lip was swollen and cut.

"The place was crawling with Trogs, so we got out fast," John went on, tossing windblown hair from his face. "We thought they'd gotten you, since you had no weapons."

"We didn't go through Hardluck," said Pierce. "Just headed straight for the road."

LaTeisha motioned toward the Safehaven. "And you stayed here last night?"

"First time for everything, huh?" Pierce said. "It's pretty nice."

"It's done wonders for you, man," said John.

LaTeisha gestured at Pierce's black eye. "Did Garth do that, too?"

"Actually, Thor."

"Where'd you get the car?" Whit asked, speaking for the first time. His deep voice was hoarse and weary. "Does it come with the Safehaven?"

"Yup."

LaTeisha laid a hand on Rowena's shoulder. "Let's go inside, okay? Looks like they have showers and beds and food."

They walked through the gate toward the front door.

As LaTeisha's voice faded John said, "Muties had her."

The group stood in silence, absorbing the ramifications of his statement. Then John slapped Pierce's arm and said, "Hey, why don't you guys come back in? We can exchange war stories."

"We can't," Callie said before Pierce could agree. "Our twenty-four hours are almost up, and we're on our way to Manderia."

John's gray eyes narrowed. "You're not gonna sign up at the temple, are you?"

"Maybe," Pierce said.

The other man regarded him thoughtfully, beard braids swinging in the wind. Callie couldn't tell if he was considering it as a viable option, or if he was simply disgusted. In the end he nodded brusquely. "Well, take it easy, man. And good luck."

Callie watched him follow the women. And then Whit towered over her, his one eye fixed upon her, his dark face grim. "I'm sorry I let them get away with that," he told her. "There's no excuse for my cowardice, and I'm not very happy with myself. I came back to make things right—but I see you weathered it just fine."

She shrugged, watching John enter the Safehaven, trying not to feel bitter.

Pierce said, "There were mutants outside Hardluck?"

Whit nodded. "Hundreds of 'em. With more coming in all the time. All I can say is I'm glad we got out of that canyon."

Both men surveyed the windblown grasslands, neither willing to speak the thought they shared. Finally Whit said good-bye and turned away. Pierce stopped him, holding out his newly acquired stylus. "It'll let you get one of these cars when you're ready. There's no steering wheel, so they must be programmed to take you only to Manderia, but it's better than walking."

As Whit took the key Pierce explained how to use it.

Callie watched the interchange with surprise and mounting disapproval. "I can't believe you did that," she said when they were on their way again. "Here you've barely gotten it, and already you're giving it away?"

He shrugged. "We still have yours."

"But that key was meant for you." She scowled out the window at the river and the soaring cliffs. "You shouldn't have done it."

"Callie . . . he came back to help you."

"I know." She fingered the end of her braid. "It's just hard to forget how he walked off without a word."

"It's hard to argue with Garth. You of all people oughta know that." Though his tone was neutral, Callie's face flamed with unpleasant memories. Again she wanted to explain, and again she couldn't get the words to form. In the end, she turned her face to the window and watched the cliff wall whiz by.

Eventually the road curved away from the river and the scenery grew dull—endless grassy hummocks on one side and the gray escarpment on the other. Pierce settled back for a nap and Callie yawned, her mind wandering aimlessly over old ground: Meg's mysterious message, the temple's offer, the possibility she'd missed something at the cliff where the white road ended.

Her eyes snapped open—when had they closed?—and she sat up, staring at the key in the dashboard. "Pierce?"

No answer. "Pierce? Are you awake?"

His voice came muzzily. "What?"

"You know how these designs appear and disappear? The ones the keys open?"

"Yeah."

"There's one at the end of this road. I'll bet the key unlocks it."

She watched comprehension drive away his sleepiness, saw the light of hope zing across his face, then vanish as he squelched it. He shifted onto his side and closed his eyes. "I guess we'll find out."

Yesterday his apathy would've annoyed her. Today she understood. And she had seen that light come into his eyes, if only briefly. Suddenly the car was not going fast enough.

She awoke from a nap to find Manderia's gray walls looming ahead and the Gate glimmering on the rim against a backdrop of white clouds. Its beauty—silver, gold, and ruby crystal plaited into rivers of light—

struck her more forcefully than ever. The old yearning resurged, and she promised herself that this time she'd find a way up to it.

When the road dropped into a tree-filled gully, she glanced at Pierce. He was reading a manual. "Where'd you get that?" she asked in astonishment.

"From the box in my room."

"The box in your room." He'd said nothing about any box. "Have you been reading it the whole time I slept?"

"Yup."

She hesitated. "Anything about the key?"

"Well, it does talk about the supply boxes, like you said. I hadn't remembered those."

"Is that all?"

"No." He brushed the hair back from his eyes.

"Well?"

"You're right about the key."

"I am? Let me see!" She grabbed the book.

"It also says we need the Benefactor's help."

She insisted he show her the passages, and after she'd read them several times, she sat back bubbling with excitement. "Well, obviously we've already gotten his help."

Pierce lifted a skeptical brow.

"At the Safehaven. He gave us the key."

"Callie, you had a key to begin with."

"But I didn't know what to do with it. Now he's shown us."

Pierce remained unconvinced.

She grinned. "Go on, be skeptical. You've earned the right. But this *is* the answer."

He went back to his reading.

Half an hour later the car rolled to a stop at the temple gate in Manderia. As the vehicle sank to the ground, the key popped from its slot and clunked on the floor. Pierce picked it up and laid it in her hand. "Guess we have to walk from here," he said.

The scene at the base of the cliff had not changed. The Sitters still sat, and the climbers still climbed, though this new group had red ropes, instead of green, and was nearer the bottom. Callie wondered what had become of their predecessors. Had they given up? Or were they laid out under new white headstones in the temple graveyard on the hillside?

Wendell sat on a rock near the road's end. He glanced up from his reading of a large book as Callie and Pierce approached. Callie ignored him, focused now on the design, which was as she remembered: three circles and a *t* etched into the stone. As they stopped in front of it, Pierce clearly struggling to remain indifferent, it occurred to her that this device was different from the one in her room. Here the circles were already pulled together, and it was not lit up.

She thought the key's touch might activate it, but it didn't. Nor could she push the rod into the central *t*, though she tried for several minutes.

"Well, that's that, I guess," Pierce said, stepping back from the wall.

She turned, gesturing with the key. "It's not lit up. That's the problem. We just have to wait until it is."

He cocked a brow and glanced meaningfully at the sitters.

"This is different," she said. "I think if we wait, if we're patient . . ."

He sat on the white pavement and leaned his head back against the rock. After a while she sat as well, but facing the cliff so she could see the device. The shadows lengthened. The light faded. Eventually Wendell stopped reading and went back up the hill.

After a few minutes Pierce got up, too. "I'm going to the temple."

She didn't try to stop him.

Darkness gathered around her. One by one the Sitters arose, left their places, and disappeared in the rocks, returning shortly to take up their posts again. The stench of fresh urine drifted on the evening air. Insects chittered in the woods as, directly above her, the climbers bivouacked for the night. Their voices muttered softly for a while, then faded away. She dozed off, awakening with a start, terrified the light had come and she had missed it. Doubt and guilt plagued her. Had she missed her chance by not going with Garth? Was this not the answer after all? She had little trouble staying awake after that.

In the morning Pierce returned, clothed in one of the Faithfuls' ubiquitous gray robes. A silver strand encircled his neck, similar to but plainer than the one Wendell wore. He looked haggard and clearly dismayed to see her. The sight of him made her want to cry.

"So," she said. "You've signed up, then."

He sat on the rock beside her, smelling of sandalwood. Though the flesh around his eye was still colored green and yellow and purple-black, the swelling had gone down, and he could open it a little now. He regarded her soberly. "I told you they were like this."

She gazed at the sky, layered with sodden clouds, and stroked the key in her hands. "It might come. Any minute now, it might come."

"You don't believe that."

She swallowed, tears burning her eyes. Her voice trembled. "Oh, Pierce! Is there *really* no way out of here?"

He sighed. "I don't know. I haven't given Mander a chance yet."

"You think he *is* the true Benefactor?"

"I don't know that, either. Why don't you come and have some breakfast, at least." He stood and held out his hand.

At first she just looked at him. Then she put her hand in his and let him pull her to her feet. They'd gone a little way up the path when she turned back, staring at the sheer, implacable cliff with the glittering gate at its top. As much as she yearned for it, it seemed she'd never have it.

Pierce was right. They *were* cruel. And she hated them. *Hated* them.

Fury burst up in her, and she flung the key at the wall with a scream, the outburst echoing in the silence that followed. Then she turned to Pierce and burst into tears. This time she made no effort to stop them, and he drew her into his arms, holding her until the storm had passed.

# CHAPTER

## 13

Callie ate little of the corn pudding they gave her in the temple dining hall and finally left Pierce in conversation with Wendell to wander the grounds alone. A graveled path wound through a formal garden—past rosebushes, topiaries, and reflecting pools—then outside the wall to a series of tiered fields where crops were grown for food and clothing. Here workers in sleeveless linen tunics hoed, weeded, and raked along rows of tall green cornstalks or harvested bean pods from short freestanding plants.

Callie stood under a willow and watched them work, mesmerized by their movement, until one woman finally approached her and asked if she was seeking service to Mander.

Callie did not answer at first, struggling to process the words and find her tongue. "I don't know. . . . What's that on your neck?"

The young woman touched the silver chain in which were set six blood crystals of varying sizes. "It's my Strand of Service."

"And the stones?"

"The tally of my reward. When I have enough, I'll get to Ascend."

"How many do you need?"

"It depends." The woman lifted her dark hair off her neck and fanned herself. "The harder you work and the purer your motives, the larger your stones. The larger the stones, the fewer you need." She drew a leather thong from the front pocket of her tunic and tied her hair into a ponytail.

"So it isn't just the time you serve, then," Callie said. "I mean you don't sign on for three years and automatically get out."

"No."

"And you're almost done?"

"Yes." The woman fingered the stones and smiled again, wistfully now. "Though I'm not so sure I want to go back anymore."

Callie said nothing.

Her companion drew a deep breath and wiped her palms on the front of her linen shift. "Well, back to work."

She returned to the harvest, pausing to confer briefly with a couple of her fellow workers, their glances darting Callie's way. A little later, she saw them trudging back to the temple, their sacks full. A tolling bell drew the remaining workers after them, most likely a summons to the noon meal, if the baking bread and hot grease she'd been smelling were any indication. She wasn't hungry, so she kept wandering, returning at last to the meadow at the foot of the cliff.

The climbers were a little farther up now, showering the ground with an almost continuous stream of pebbles. None of the Sitters had moved, and though they gave no sign of it, Callie felt as if they were staring at her. She settled among the rocks above the trail where she could watch both wall and gate, and waited. A couple came down the path to investigate the road's end, but soon wandered back up to the temple. The birds chirruped. Insects buzzed near the trail. The sun beat upon her. Listlessly she lay back against the rock, staring at the Gate. As before, it danced in constant flux, now red, now clear, now silver and gold. From blood to living fire, it changed and changed again, filling her with that inexplicable yearning.

The afternoon passed. A group of people came down to the wall, but she ignored them, engrossed in the Gate, as if by staring she might make it draw her up to it. After a while they went away. Later, Wendell came to feed the Sitters. He called to her from the path below her perch, but she pretended not to hear him.

It was late when Pierce found her. He climbed to the flat rock on which she sat, then stood beside her, but she ignored him as she had ignored everyone else. "Callie," he said softly, "you can't just give up."

"You have."

He squatted, bringing his bearded face even with hers, sandalwood scent wafting from his robe. "I'm just trying another option."

"I don't want to serve Mander," she said.

"You'd rather sit here for the rest of your life?"

She watched the Gate flicker and shift. The temple bell tolled. "Did you know," she said after it faded to silence, "that you have to wear a collar if you serve him?"

Pierce shifted his weight back and sat down, wrapping his arms about his knees. "Yeah."

That's right. He already wore one. She'd seen it last night. She finally looked at him. His left eye socket was bright green around the brow and temple, purple on the lid, and there were dark shadows under both eyes. His lip was still scabbed, his skin gray, his eyes flat.

Her gaze dropped to the silver strand at his throat.

From the cliff came a shout and a rush of pebbles. Another climber dangled at the end of his rope. She felt just like him, banging helplessly against the rock, too tired to haul herself up again.

After a long silence Pierce stood. "They're holding an Ascension tonight," he said. "Why don't you come watch?"

"I can't. The device might come on."

She felt his reproachful gaze. It *was* a lame excuse. Without the key, she couldn't access the device even if it did appear. "I'm too tired," she added, as if that would be a better excuse.

He sighed, then started down, stopping after a few steps. "Whit and the others are here."

"They gonna sign on, too?"

"Already have."

The climber righted himself and once more inched up the rock. Pierce said no more and left as the tiny figure rejoined his companions. All that work, and for what? In another fifty feet they'd hit the band of sandstone and have to quit. Or die.

"I should've stayed with Garth," she said, then laughed at the absurdity of the sentiment. "Like I had a choice." Bitterness ignited into frustration. She lifted her face to the darkening sky.

"Why have you told us to do what cannot be done?! You're not being fair." Her echoing voice sounded embarrassingly whiny, but if the Sitters heard her, they gave no sign, and the climbers were too far away. Only the crickets took notice, having cut off their high-pitched chirps when she spoke, and now starting up again.

Pierce was right. She couldn't just give up. The Sitters' long hair and beards showed the uselessness of staying here. And while Garth's Canyon of the Damned might well be the way, *she'd* never climb it. Which left only Mander.

It was dark when she arrived at the temple for the Ascension, and though the ceremony would not begin for another hour, the main court already hummed with activity as Manderians settled everywhere with their blankets and picnic dinners. Determined to watch this miracle in the flesh, Callie traversed the long court and climbed a staircase to one of two balconies flanking the Grotto of the Ascension. There a single monitor offered a canned view of the Gate and would presumably provide close-ups of the Ascension. She peered over the balcony wall into the grotto, but found little to see for the moment.

Gradually, though, both the grotto and the glass-walled sanctuary overlooking it filled with gray-robed Faithful. She was watching the crowd idly, when a tall black man with an eye patch stepped through the balcony door. His companion, sporting beard braids and an earring, followed. The two of them joined her by the wall. Like Pierce, both wore gray robes and empty Strands of Service.

"Gave up on the cliff watch, did you?" John said.

"For a while," she admitted as LaTeisha and Pierce came through the door next.

Pierce drew up beside her, his gaze sober. "I'm glad you came."

She managed a small smile. "Where's Rowena?"

"We haven't seen her since before dinner," LaTeisha said, self-consciously touching the silver chain that gleamed against her dark skin.

"She was talking to some girl," said John.

"Trying to figure a way to wiggle in with Mander, no doubt," LaTeisha added.

The balcony filled to overflowing, the air growing heavy with heat and stale sweat. Callie stood pressed between Whit and Pierce as they peered over the wall. Looking back and stretching on tiptoe, she could just see the monitor between the score of heads now obscuring her view. As the ceremony got under way the screen's shimmering image of the Gate changed to a close-up of the grotto pool and its hovering shelf. The lights dimmed, the crowd stilled, and a stirring melody presaged the emergence of a tall, bearded, gold-cloaked man with flowing blond curls. He glided across the flagstone, climbed the low stair to the platform, and turned, spreading his arms.

"Mander!" the Faithful called, reaching out to him. "Mander!"

The man's charisma was undeniable. His face, his manner, his expressions—his whole presence—commanded attention and approval. Yet the mindless way his subjects called his name drove a chill up Callie's back. She murmured in Pierce's ear, "He's bearded, so he must not be an alien."

"The beard could be false," he murmured back.

She glanced up at him, pleased he was not swept away like everyone else.

"Faithful servants!" Mander cried. "What a joyous day this is!"

"Oh, joyous day!" they repeated.

Behind her a woman whimpered, reaching past Callie's shoulder and over the stone wall toward her . . . Savior? Lord? Manipulator?

Callie's aversion mounted.

"We are gathered here," Mander intoned, "to witness the glorification of two of our body."

"Bless you, Mander . . . Thank you . . . Savior . . ."

Two robed figures entered by the same doorway Mander had used and joined him on the platform.

"Jacki Lohman and Brian Fitz, faithful servants, what shall I give you in reward?"

"Please, our Master," they said together, voices amplified by unseen microphones, "send us home."

"Whoever asks me for the way," Mander cried, arms raised, "I will deliver. Let it be as I have said. Tonight you will see the Gate of Freedom."

He helped them onto the hovering stone, then faced the crowd. "Let this be a sign of my love."

*A sign.*

Callie glanced about. There were no triple circles here. Not in the rooms, not on the doors, not anywhere in the grotto. If Mander was the real Benefactor, surely the circles would be in evidence. A wild relief swept through her. This wasn't the answer, after all. The only place marked by the true Benefactor's sign was the cliff at the end of the road.

Her rising triumph collapsed. That was no answer, either. The design was on the cliff, yes, but it still offered no way to access the Gate.

The stone upon which Jacki and Brian stood glowed with a blue-white light as Mander pointed at it, and slowly it began to rise. If cables were pulling it, Callie couldn't see them. Breathless, the crowd watched the two glide upward, Jacki sobbing tearful *thank-you*s while lines of moisture streaked Brian's cheeks.

Callie wanted to scream, *Stop! It's wrong! Don't go!*

But she didn't.

The stone bore the couple to the rim, where they stepped off and walked out of sight.

"As they have asked," Mander said, "so I have done."

"As they have asked, so you have done," the crowd repeated.

Slowly the stone descended.

Callie frowned. They hadn't vaporized. They'd been carried to the rim and stepped onto it. Maybe this wasn't so bad after all. Maybe—

But why were there no circles? The manual was marked, the supply boxes were marked, every bit of equipment was marked, the car was marked, and the Safehaven had it—why not this place?

And anyway, she didn't know they hadn't vaporized. Maybe they weren't even real. Maybe they were holograms, like Meg. Or aliens, impersonating Jacki and Brian. Or maybe . . .

She didn't know. And worse, she still had no other way of ascending the cliff.

Mander intoned some parting words and left. The stone was half-way back as the lights came up and the balcony cleared. Callie stayed put, partly to let the crowd thin, partly because she didn't know what to do.

Pierce leaned his forearms on the wall and looked at her. "Well?"

"There are no triple circles, Pierce."

He laced his fingers and scanned the grotto. "I noticed that."

"And we never saw them actually walk through the Gate."

"No." The stone stopped just above the water and the fountains kicked on. "Still, they *are* up there."

"Maybe."

"Come on, Callie," John burst out behind her. "You saw it with your own eyes."

"Yeah, but with their lasers and holograms and computer-generated realities—how can we know what we saw was real?"

"You have a better idea?" Whit folded his arms across his chest, frowning down at her.

"I think the answer's at the end of the road," Callie said. "Where the symbol is."

"So what do we do?" LaTeisha demanded. "Walk up and ask to be levitated?"

The others laughed, but Callie went rigid, awash with tingles. She seized Pierce's arm. "Those things Mander said tonight—something like, whoever asks me for the way . . . and as you have asked—is that in the manual?"

His brow furrowed. "I remember something about asking him to help, but—"

"That's it!" she interrupted. "It's gotta be. I asked for the comb and the box appeared. I asked for you to be protected, and we found the cars."

She turned to Whit. "Do you still have the key Pierce gave you? The one that runs the car?"

"Key?" He shook his head, brows knit as if he were still two steps behind her. "No," he said finally. "Rowena took it."

"Rowena?"

"It fell on the floor when the car stopped, and she picked it up."

"Callie—" Pierce touched her arm.

"What were you saying about not giving up?" She pushed away from the wall. "I'm going to find Rowena." She half expected them to let her go alone, but they didn't.

Rowena was in the chapel, talking to a dark-haired woman Callie didn't know. "Where did you put the key?" Callie demanded, stopping in front of them. "The one from the car."

Rowena regarded her blankly. "I gave it to Mander." She arched her slim brows at LaTeisha and Whit. "He called it the Key of Life. Said it was the most valuable offering anyone can bring to him. It's bought my passage home." She smiled, fingering her Strand of Service where an egg-sized blood crystal rested in its setting. "I go up day after tomorrow."

They gaped at her.

"Sorry I couldn't take any of you along—it's only good for one."

"It's a trap," Callie said. "He tricked you."

"You're just saying that because you can't go."

Callie ignored her, already turning away. Maybe she could find the key she'd thrown at the cliff.

The meadow gleamed like ice in the Gate's light, the road a golden ribbon. Ninety feet up, the climbers hung bivouacked in their slings. One of them must have been reading, for a tiny light glowed against the dark wall.

Callie raced to the tumble of boulders where she had thrown the key. It could not have landed in a worse place, for the rocks were small enough to be numerous, but large enough to form inaccessible crevices into which the key could easily have fallen. She knew the chances of finding it were slim—even assuming it hadn't shattered on impact or disappeared with time like the boxes it was supposed to open or been seized by a mite.

Pierce and the others scrabbled about the rocks, calling to one another, getting in the way more than helping. If the key hadn't already fallen into a crack, someone would probably knock it there in all the bustle. She was about to call them off when she found it, caught in a weed where three boulders met. Another half inch and it would have slid into a crevice too slender to get an arm into. Trembling, she seized it and stood, her cry of triumph silencing the others.

They gathered quickly around her, faces alight with hope. Beyond them, at the meadow's edge, a handful of the Faithful had followed them down from the temple—Wendell and Rowena among them. Just behind them stood a trio of Watchers, and to the right, another trio. And another up on the rocks. In fact, Watchers surrounded her, some even clinging to the cliff above, their pale skins gleaming in the ghostly light. Among them, here and there, other forms—transparent, luminescent men dressed in white—faded in and out like holographic transmissions. All of them watched her intently.

Did that mean she was right?

Callie licked her lips, swallowed on a suddenly dry throat, and approached the cliff. "Okay, Mr. Benefactor. You say we must find you and ask for your help. Well, I think you're here now, so I'm asking: Help us get up to that gate."

Silence swallowed her voice. Her pulse throbbed in her ears. *Please, please, please, be right.*

Moments passed. Someone stirred behind her, sighed deeply. Out in the meadow, Rowena's voice muttered, and the crickets started up again.

*It takes a while,* she thought. *It took a while for the box—*

The triple circle flared crimson, molten light in the thin engravings. The others gasped behind her and one of the Sitters cried out, a rush of pebbles betraying his movement.

She set the key's rod against the central *t*, and immediately the rock grabbed it, sucking it inward. Slowly the circles moved away from each other, two separating horizontally, the third heading straight up. When the cross-facing circles were five feet apart and the top one seven feet off the ground, they flared orange-red. A line of fire shot crosswise, connecting the side circles. Another blazed downward, forming a *t*. The slits opened to reveal a shoulder-wide stairway angling up into the rock. The cross-facing circles had carved opposing shelves into each side of the passage wall, paralleling the stair and imbedded with lines of red light.

Awestruck, Callie stared for a full minute without moving, afraid even to blink. Then a warm, copper-scented breeze blew out of the opening and coursed around her, pushing her from behind. Warily she mounted the red-lit stair.

At first the staircase didn't appear long enough to reach the rim. But by the time she'd ascended fifty paces she saw no end to it at all, just a blurry red line disappearing into dark distance. Looking at it made her dizzy, so she fixed her gaze on the step in front of her and realized that the stairs were moving, carrying her upward like an escalator. A wave of disorientation wobbled her knees, and she groped for the wall, trailing her fingers along it for balance and reassurance.

Up and up and up she went, until it seemed she'd gone much farther than the height of the cliff. She dared not look back, dared not even imagine how high she had to be. As it was, the end of the ride sneaked up on her. One minute she saw only the interminable red line, the next, a white doorway loomed before her.

It opened into a granite basin where a pool of snowmelt reflected a star-spangled sky. The Gate swept upward out of the pool, radiant streams of crystal, silver, and gold woven together and sparked with spears of crimson. A film of silver-and-gold flecks shimmered across the opening, and the air and ground thrummed with an immense power, tingling across her skin and deep into her vitals.

Trepidation seized her. This gate was something alien, something mighty beyond imagination—as different from any power she had known as light was from dark. To even approach it seemed sacrilegious—to pass through it, suicidal. Surely no earthly flesh could touch this presence and live.

And yet, though the pulsing brightness was almost palpable, though the organs in her chest vibrated in resonance with its power, Callie felt no heat and heard no sound beyond the soft rush of the wind—still swirling around her, still urging her onward. She swallowed and clenched her fists. He *had* opened the rock for her, and his stairway *had* carried her up here. If he intended to kill her, he could've done so long ago. Besides, what else could she do? Go back and serve Mander?

She lifted her chin, straightened her shoulders and stepped off the granite shore into the water. It was unexpectedly warm and effervescent, fizzing playfully around her shins. The arch loomed closer, and the humming vibration intensified. At its threshold she stopped again, her heart pounding, her hands icy, palms slick with sweat. She tilted her head back, lifting her gaze to the shimmering, blinding, living gateway above her, and caught her lip in her teeth. It was going to change her. She did not know how she knew that, but she did.

A whisper of air caressed her cheek and memory bloomed—Alex offering her the day pack. *We intend this for your benefit.* . . . For the first time, the expression in his eyes registered—compassion, sadness, resignation. There was no anger in him, no malice. He had been telling the truth. He really wanted to help her.

Setting her will, Callie dropped her gaze, clenched her fists, and plunged across the threshold.

A man stepped into her path so suddenly she couldn't avoid him. Blinding light flared at the impact, and an intense heat sizzled across her, something that should have birthed agony, but didn't. For a moment she was blinded, lost in a well of shimmering whiteness, her other senses as numbed as her eyesight. Then shapes began to emerge from the light, a corridor of crystalline arches stretching before her into an infinity of brightness. The wind rushed around her, carrying the sweet ring of chimes and words that danced just beyond comprehension—though she felt if she listened closely enough, all the secrets of life would be hers.

The corridor vanished as swiftly as it had appeared, and solid ground once more pressed against the soles of her feet. Then she was gasping and staggering in the shin-deep water, her vision throbbing with the red afterimage of lost brightness. When her eyesight cleared, she saw she had come thirty yards past the Gate in a single step.

# CHAPTER

## 14

*I've made it*, Callie marveled, blinking at her surroundings. Humps of granite sporting smiles of old ice reflected the Gate's light, and the basin's placid pool held its perfect mirror image, radiant against a starry sky. Who was that man she'd run into? An alien? Alex? What had happened? What did it all mean?

A breeze stirred around her, and she realized she was soaking wet and should have been cold with evaporation in the night air but was not. It took her a moment longer to notice her hands. Where seconds ago there had been cuts and scrapes and torn nails, now lay smooth, unblemished skin shimmering with a golden iridescence. Even her cheek was soft and whole, the scab sloughed off in the passage.

The breeze stirred again, ruffling the water and drawing her attention to a white path leading from the pond to the ridge above. Stars sprinkled the black sky beyond, bright and piercingly brilliant. In fact, everything seemed brighter, clearer, more . . . significant. As if her eyes were seeing it all in a new way.

Pushed encouragingly by the breeze, Callie waded ashore and followed the path to the ridgetop, where she stopped again. A starlit valley lay before her—spiring evergreens, pale meadows, and a silver lake, all ringed with snowcapped peaks. On the slope directly below stood a multileveled complex of buildings that reminded her of college dormitories—except for the fortresslike tower-studded wall encircling them.

Most amazing of all was how clearly she saw it. Where distant objects had previously looked like a wet-in-wet watercolor, now every window, every line, every tree stood out in sharp detail. She saw as well as if she had her glasses back, her eyes apparently fixed along with her scabs.

The path switchbacked down the hillside to the complex in clear indication of where she was to go. And yet she felt reluctant to leave the Gate. So much had happened here that she didn't understand, so much wonder and joy. More than ever, its power pulled at her—

But when she turned around to gaze at it again, she found with a stab of profound dismay that it had vanished, the pool along with it. All that remained was a dry, unremarkable mountain basin. For a moment she almost cried. Then the breeze curled around her comfortingly, nudging her toward the walled complex below. "I'm supposed to go down there, huh?"

The breeze nudged her again, almost playfully.

"Okay," she relented. "I'm going."

It was only as she descended the hill that she began to wonder why the pool had disappeared—and why her friends still hadn't joined her. Were the two events related? Had the others been afraid to enter the cleft? Had it closed before they could? Had Mander come and stopped them?

A clatter of rock brought her around, eyes scanning the hillside. Then a familiar voice called, "Callie! Wait up!" and she saw John bounding down the starlit switchbacks toward her, beard braids flapping around his shoulders. She climbed back toward him, giddy with relief. "What happened?" she cried as they met. "Did the doorway close? Did you need another key?"

"I just followed you." He looked around. "Can you believe this? After all this time? And it was so easy!"

An echoing whoop heralded LaTeisha's arrival. She was soon followed by Whit, Rowena, and someone who was obviously one of the climbers. Short and wiry with close-cropped brown hair, he still wore his climbing harness and bubbled with excitement.

"When I saw the light and y'all going through, I knew I'd found the answer. My friends couldn't see it. I had to rappel down alone and cut m'self free, but here I am! What a rush!" He turned full circle, taking in the landscape. "This is *out*standing! And who was that guy in the Gate?"

"You saw him, too?" Callie exclaimed.

"Walked right into him," the climber said. "Couldn't help it!"

"I think he was the Benefactor—the *real* one," Whit said. The healing powers of the passage had not, Callie noted, replaced his lost eye.

"I remember a corridor of endless arches," LaTeisha said.

"Yes!" Callie exclaimed. "But it was so bright I could hardly see."

"I ended up thirty yards away," Whit said, "and I only took one step."

"Me too," John said. "But I feel fantastic. All my aches and pains— they're gone."

"I feel like I could climb Everest in a day," the climber agreed. "By the way," he added, sticking out a hand. "Gerry Felder from San Antone. Pleased to meet y'all."

The next person to come through was Wendell. He stood among them in his gray robe, smiling sheepishly, as if he couldn't quite believe it all.

"What happened to Pierce?" Callie asked.

"He was just standing there when I went in," LaTeisha said.

"Maybe he couldn't see it," Gerry suggested.

"It might have scared him," Wendell added. "My friends thought it was a trick and ran away."

"With Pierce, who knows?" Rowena said. "He may stand there brooding for the next ten years. Me, I'm heading home!" She started down the path.

The rest of them followed, marveling at their good fortune. Only Callie remained, filled with a mounting sense of loss. Surely of everyone, *he* would see it. The way he'd looked that night in the loft, that undeniable yearning on his face—how could he not come through?

But as the minutes crept by and he did not appear, she began to fear the pull of the Trogs had been too strong. Or that passing through the fire curtain might somehow preclude passing through the cleft. Or the Gate.

She was turning away when movement caught her eye, and there he was, standing on the ridge. "Yes!" She shook her fist and called to the others. They waved and shouted to him, but she alone went back.

He seemed not to see her, standing like a captain at the prow of his ship, straight and tall as if some awful burden had lifted from his shoulders. He was staring over the valley, the breeze ruffling his hair and beard, his black eye having vanished in the passage like her own injuries.

"What kept you?" she asked, coming up beside him. "I was starting to worry."

He did not answer at first, the breeze hissing through the grass around them, laden with the sweet, moist scent of night. Then he turned to her. "After everything we've tried. . . . For it to be so simple."

So simple. *As you have asked, so shall it be. . . .* It was right there in the manual all along. But they'd been so busy looking for someone they could see, or something they could do—so busy blaming and hating their kidnapper—that they'd missed the simple truth.

"I don't think it was so simple for him, though," he added softly. His gaze caught her own. "Did you hear the screaming?"

"Screaming? There wasn't . . ." Wait. In that instant when the light had overtaken her, there had been something. She had been too overwhelmed by what her eyes and balance were reporting to pay much attention to her ears. There'd been singing, yes, but before that . . .

"Why would he have screamed?" she asked. It must've been the man she'd run into.

"Couldn't stand to touch us, maybe? It's obvious our bodies are different from theirs."

"Then why step in our way?"

"I don't know." Pierce's gaze swept the valley, and he sighed. "I feel as if I've been stumbling around with my eyes closed, and finally I can see."

She knew what he meant. It was as if something dead in her had come alive, a part never recognized, never named, just waiting for the right kiss of power to awaken it. It wasn't just an increased ability to sense and appreciate the world, but an awareness of . . . something more, something wonderful just beyond what she had always known. It sparked in her a renewed yearning, not for the Gate anymore, but for the one who'd made it.

"You two gonna stand up there all day?" John's voice echoed up to them. "We're not home yet, you know."

Pierce smiled down at him. It was the first time Callie had ever seen him smile, and the expression changed his entire face, taking her breath away.

His eyes came back to hers, and he sobered. "I wish I'd listened to you sooner. And now I almost wish . . ." He trailed off, then sighed and turned away. "Well, John's right. We've got another gate to find."

He left her staring after him, reeling from his smile. *I'm going to miss that guy,* she thought. And laughed aloud. *Here I'm on the brink of victory, and I'm wishing I didn't have to leave!*

Inside the compound they joined the others on a cypress-lined patio fronting a building marked with the familiar triple-circle symbol. They were trying the building's locked doors when two men and a white-haired young woman, all in white jumpsuits, approached.

"We've just come through the Gate," said Rowena, gesturing up the hill.

"Yes," said the taller, auburn-haired man. "Welcome to Rimlight."

"Is this some kind of Safehaven?"

"Sort of." He had a boyish face, a slight paunch, and a receding hairline. "I'm Tucker," he said. "This is Alicia. And Ian."

Rowena shook their hands, introducing herself and the rest of them. "I gather the exit portal isn't here?"

"I'm afraid not."

She cocked her head. "You're kidding, right?"

The auburn-haired man, Tucker, shook his head. "There's a guide that's supposed to lead us to it. We're waiting for him now."

LaTeisha stepped forward. "A guide?"

"You mean," asked Callie, "like an alien?"

"We don't know. We were told to gather and wait—that someone would come to show us the way."

"So coming through the Gate was for nothing?" Rowena cried.

"Oh, not for nothing. The exit will kill you unless you've gone through one of the Benefactor's gates. We do know that much. Apparently our molecular resonance has to be realigned or something.

Anyway, you've made it to the halfway point. That's more than most do."

John tugged nervously on one of his braids. "How long have you been waiting for this guide?"

"I've been here about two weeks. But the others—" Again Tucker glanced at his companions. The girl, Alicia, clung to Ian like a wraith, so pale of skin and hair she hardly seemed solid. She stared at something in the middle distance, ignoring them all.

"Some longer than that," Ian volunteered.

"How much longer?" John asked.

Tucker's eyes consulted Ian again. "Morgan's been here, what? Four months? And Evvi longer than that. Then, of course there are those who've already tried to cross the Inner Realm and failed. Some of them have been here a long time. Working up their nerve to try it again, I think." Tucker nodded at the woman. "Alicia here is one of those. She went out with the Leyton party a couple years ago. They were ambushed and she was about the only survivor, the way I hear it. She won't talk about it, though."

Alicia continued staring into space. Everyone shifted uncomfortably. No one seemed to know what to say. Finally Tucker exhaled. "Well, let's get you settled in the dorms—"

"Wait a minute," Callie said as he turned away. "Why can't we just follow the white roads?"

"Because there aren't any."

He left her staring after him, perplexed but not as upset as she thought she ought to be. True, they were facing yet another perilous journey without even the roads to lead them, but after unlocking the secret of the first gate and finding it so embarrassingly simple, she was confident the rest of the trip would continue in kind. So long as they followed the instructions, anyway.

Rowena was not so confident. "No roads?" she murmured as the others moved on. Her blue eyes glittered with rising tears as she turned to Pierce. "How could they do this? After all we've been through!"

"A lot of what we've been through was our fault," he pointed out mildly.

"But surely we've paid our dues by now."

"This isn't about paying dues, Row."

"Then what *is* it about?"

He eyed the building beside them. "Following instructions, maybe?"

"Pierce, we've been here almost five years!" Her voice broke. Tears spilled down her cheeks. "We finally make it through the Gate, just to find out we have to start *over?*"

"We've been here five years because we didn't do what we were told, Row. We didn't have to struggle. We only had to ask."

She pushed away from him. "How can you defend them?"

"The manual told us what to do from the very beginning."

"If they wanted us to ask, they should've put up a sign." She dashed her tears away and gathered her composure. "They're sadistic, is what they are. Garth's right. The only way we'll get out of here is by our own efforts."

She strode after the others, disappearing around the cypress.

"Did we all go through the same gate?" Callie asked after a moment.

"We must've."

"Then how can she—"

He shook his head and shrugged. "Everyone's different, I guess."

They caught up with the others on a narrow stairway at the back of the building, crossed a small green, and entered the lobby of one of the complex's three two-story dormitories. Beside the elevators Tucker showed them a layout of hand-sized panels duplicating the building's floor plan. He explained that pressing one's palm against an unlit panel would program the corresponding room door to open at a touch.

"After you're settled, come on over to the rec hall and meet the others. The dispensaries are always open for snacks."

"I want to know more about this guide, first," John said. "You say you don't know if he's human or alien?"

"He'll be human," Alicia said softly.

Tucker frowned at her. Ian's dark brows arched. Again that uneasy pall settled over them. Then Pierce asked, "Do you have any manuals?"

The others stared at him.

Tucker waved a hand. "There's one in every room, and a whole shelf of them in the library. But most of what we can read applies to life in the Outer Realm. The rest is still gibberish."

"You mean the encrypted stuff in the second part?"

Tucker nodded. "We've tried to decode it. Some of us have made some headway, but it is a slow, difficult process."

"And we will never fully understand it," Ian said. "Not until the Guide shows up."

Tucker flashed him a dubious look.

"I don't care what Morg says," Ian protested. "If we could do it on our own, they wouldn't have told us to wait for the Guide."

"Who's Morg?" Rowena asked.

"Our unofficial leader," Tucker told her. "He's the one who got the Holographic Transmission Station running." He paused. "Maybe you all should come to the rec hall now and meet some of the others. They serve a great hot fudge brownie sundae, too."

That sold John, and in the end, everyone followed Tucker downhill from the dormitories to the glass-walled Recreation Hall. An indoor swimming pool and weight room occupied the ground floor, a high-ceilinged game room the one above it. Amidst the fragrance of popcorn and old grease, the complex's inhabitants had gathered around Ping-Pong tables, pool tables, and blinking arcade games.

Now they flocked to the newcomers as Tucker made the introductions. Soon afterward, he found a manual and challenged Whit to read a section that had been indecipherable in the Outer Realm. He still couldn't understand it. Neither could John, nor Gerry, nor Wendell.

Finally Rowena snatched the book away. "Why don't you give us girls a chance?" She flipped a few pages. "Shoot, I can read this."

"It's the portion at the back." When Tucker showed her, she did no better than the others, and as she peered over Rowena's shoulder, neither did Callie.

As the crowd dissipated, Tucker led them through the cafeteria, which opened for breakfast at 6:00 A.M., and downstairs to The Fountain, where he and John got their sundaes. Then they crossed the yard to the library, where six blue-screened computers welcomed them in white text and informed them that they'd know the Guide when he unlocked the "hidden places of this installation."

"What does that mean?" Rowena demanded, pointing at the words. "Hidden places? Could the exit portal be in one of those locked buildings?"

"I doubt it." Tucker scraped the last of his sundae sauce from his plastic bowl. "The whole thing seems more like a training installation to me. There's a park in the lower left quadrant with rappelling cliffs, dry stream beds, and steel cables strung between the trees. Looks for all the world like an obstacle course. You'll see it tomorrow."

They headed next for the Holographic Transmission Station, or HTS, where residents donned virtual-reality helmets to contact participants in the Outer Realm.

"Most commonly we speak to those who have gotten off the road," Tucker explained as they exited the library, "trying to get them back on it."

*This is what Meg must've done!* "Can you send messages anywhere, then?" Callie asked. "You don't need a receiver?"

"No. But you have to find the person you're sending to. Which isn't easy."

"I have a friend—Meg. She might—"

But Tucker was shaking his head. "I'm terrible with names, and there's over fifty people here."

Before she could launch into Meg's description, Wendell said, "The holographs we received at the temple told us Mander was the true Benefactor."

Tucker grimaced. "There's a whole army of aliens who don't want anyone to get through these gates. And we don't have a corner on this equipment."

"But Mander brought people up here."

"Just 'cause you've gotten up the cliff doesn't mean you've gone through one of the gates." Tucker led them up a short bank of stairs. "In fact, you can't even *find* one apart from going up that miraculous stairway in the cliff. And even then, once you've gone through, the Gate vanishes."

"Yes!" Callie said. "I saw that! But I thought it was just to keep me from standing there staring at it for the rest of my life."

Tuck smiled at her. "You might be right—who knows? Anyway,

we just had a couple like that come through a few hours ago, Unchanged and still looking." He stopped in a small courtyard at the top of the stair and turned back as the others drew around him. "I told them they'd have to go back down and come up through the cliff like the manual says, but they didn't believe me."

"So it was all a fraud," Wendell murmured, his round face pale, his gaze turned inward.

Tucker nodded soberly.

"Hey," LaTeisha cried. "I'll bet that couple was Brian and Jacki! Are they still here?"

Tucker shook his head. "We offered 'em a place, but they were determined to find the Gate and moved on. At least they were honest about it. Some try to pretend they've already gone through, when it's obvious they haven't."

"You can tell they're Unchanged just by looking?" Callie asked.

Tucker nodded. "Changed folk like you all have a glow about them. It fades after a few days, of course, but at first it's obvious."

He was right. Now that Callie looked for it, she saw it—her companions shone with the same iridescence she'd seen on her hands. Even Rowena had it, for all her bitter complaining.

"*Is* there a way to get back down from here?" Wendell asked as they started walking again.

"Sure. There's a portal up at the HTS they can use. They never do, though. Least not that I've seen. Maybe some of them go down at one of the other complexes—there's thirteen more, just like this one," he added with a grin, heading off the inevitable question. "One for each gate. Maybe after they've gone to all of them and found nothing, maybe then they believe. More likely, though, they just head inward for the Exit. After all, they're up here, aren't they?"

"But didn't you say," Callie asked, "that you can't pass through the Exit unless you've been Changed?"

"That's right. And if you try it, you're toast, so I'm told. But they never believe it, so you just have to let them go."

The HTS was shut down for the night, so they got no active demonstration of its capabilities. They did get to see the portal that would return one to the Outer Realm in order to pass through the Gate properly. It looked like a simple elevator car, though Tuck said it apparently only worked for the Unchanged.

After touring the HTS they returned to the dorm and there met Morgan Dunway. Tall and broad shouldered, he had small, close-set brown eyes and a large nose. He smelled of aftershave, and his shoulder-length blond hair had been styled and sprayed into position. He was in excellent physical condition—a big man who exuded the same kind of charisma Garth had. Callie disliked him the moment she met him, and his way of sizing them all up and declaring their group to be another "strikeout" did nothing to change her impression.

"Are you the Morgan who's putting together the trip to the Inner Realm?" Rowena asked.

He grinned. "Tuck's told you about that, huh?"

"Just that you're thinking—"

"Callie?"

Callie's head jerked up, her gaze darting across the gathering. *Meg?* Meg pushed around Morgan and fell upon Callie with a shriek.

# CHAPTER

## 15

"No wonder I couldn't find you today," Meg cried as she let Callie go. "I was searching that horrid canyon, and you were already back at the Gate. I am *so* glad to see you!" Before Callie could speak, Meg turned to the white-haired man shadowing her. "Look, Mr. C! She's come through."

The man smiled warmly. "Welcome to Rimlight, Miss Hayes."

Callie took to Mr. C—for Chapman—as quickly as she had reacted to Morgan. He had a friendly face—not nearly as age lined as his white hair and beard would indicate—and laughing brown eyes. He was one of those people you instantly like because they seem to instantly like you.

"Mr. C's been helping me track you," Meg offered, hooking a black curl behind her ear.

"And Mr. Andrews, as well," Mr. C added. He glanced around. "I don't see him, though."

"Mr. Andrews?" Callie asked. "You mean Pierce?" She glanced around, too.

"He's gone up to his room," John said.

"He's not much of a socializer," Callie explained.

"He's a head case is what he is," said Rowena.

Callie frowned at her. "I wouldn't call him a head case."

"What would you call him?"

Awkward silence ensued. Then Meg plunged on. "So what happened, Cal? You were so far from the Gate when I saw you—"

"Didn't you know?" Rowena persisted, her tone acidic. "She's an acrophobe. Couldn't hack the heights and turned back."

Callie gaped at her. Meg frowned.

"That was Garth's story," John said.

"She hasn't denied it," Rowena countered. "Nor Whit, for that matter, and he was there." She looked to the black man for confirmation, but he ignored her. Her gaze returned to Callie and she laughed. "It's a good thing, though. If not for her, we'd all be dead. Right, honey?"

Callie regarded her in bewilderment. Rowena was smiling now, as if her scorn had never been, and when Callie did not reply, she turned to Morgan. "So. About your plan—?"

He grinned. "I've been studying the maps in the manual, and I've got some ideas."

"When do you intend to launch this expedition?" She was coming on to him strongly, and he couldn't seem to keep his eyes off her. Perhaps with good reason—with the glow of change upon her, Rowena was more attractive than ever.

"Haven't decided yet," he said.

"Are newcomers invited?"

"Certainly."

Rowena took his arm, and as they sat down on one of the side couches, Mr. Chapman started conversing with John and Whit, and Meg drew Callie away.

"Is she always that catty?" Meg asked, settling on a blue sectional behind a screen of potted palms.

"No. I have no idea what her problem is." It seemed unlikely she was jealous over Garth, since he'd clearly rejected Callie. But what other reason could there be?

"I s'pose you're pretty mad at me, huh?" Meg asked, worrying a hangnail. Her hair was longer, and she wore the standard jumpsuit, but she was still Meg, and it was vaguely disorienting to find her here.

"I was furious at first," Callie admitted. "But now . . . well, you couldn't have suspected the truth. And it's not like you aren't in this mess, too." She shook her head wryly. "Though I must say you've done better than me."

"At least I've had an easier time. So far." Meg's hands twisted around her interlaced fingers, then fell apart as she heaved another sigh and let the subject go. "So why *did* you turn back? Was it my message?"

"Partly. The transmission wasn't very good—"

"I was afraid of that. I'd forgotten to program the ground shielding. The Watcher was on it before I'd even stopped transmitting. Then it was too dark to start again, and the next morning I couldn't find you. I found the others halfway up that canyon, but you weren't with them anymore. I had a feeling you wouldn't be. . . . I mean, *I'd* have a hard time climbing that trail. But I was afraid they'd murdered you, or you'd fallen off a cliff or something. How in the world did you hook up with those people, anyway?"

"It's a long story."

Meg hooked the recalcitrant lock of black hair behind her ear again and grinned. "We've certainly got the time, girl."

So Callie told her. She said nothing of her ill-considered attraction to Garth, but Meg was aghast all the same to learn how he had abandoned her. Thankfully she dismissed him with an unladylike word, then honed in on Pierce. "So. Is he cute?"

"Good grief, Meg!" Callie collapsed back on the sectional with a laugh. "Is that all you think about?"

"Is he?"

"He's a friend."

"You aren't answering my question."

"This is silly! No, he's not 'cute.' He's just an ordinary guy with a brown scraggly beard." *And a gorgeous smile. And eyes the color of the sky.*

"But you've got feelings for him."

Callie grimaced. "He's a *friend*, Meg. A plain, regular guy." *With a lot of problems. Change the subject.* "So what about you? How long have you been here?"

"About six weeks."

To Callie's chagrin, Meg had done everything by the book. Deposited in a small side canyon similar to Callie's grotto, she'd accessed a car by means of the Auxiliary Supply Box glowing in the glass wall beside the Drop-Off sign and ridden all the way to the Gate. From the safety and comfort of her vehicle, she'd observed a pride of rock drag- ons sunning themselves on the cliffs, eaten a tasty box lunch, watched the eerie flight of a group of harries silhouetted on the skyline in late afternoon, and reached Manderia by evening.

"The whole temple thing was so *obviously* a trick. The TV screens, the robes—I just couldn't buy it. So I backed up, and sure enough, the road forked."

"But how did you know what to do when you got to the cliff?"

"Same way I knew about the car—Alex told me in the briefing. Though it *is* right there in the manual." Meg's tone was gently chiding.

Callie made a face. "Well, it's sure not something that screams out at you. And I was pretty upset about it all, especially at the beginning— to think they'd kidnapped us like that!" She frowned at the end of her braid. "But that never bothered you, I guess."

Meg drew her legs up, encircling them with her arms. "I didn't think of it as kidnapping. We did walk in and sign up."

"I signed up for a few hours of negotiating an obstacle course and solving some problems." She gestured around. "This is . . . something else entirely."

"True." Meg rested her chin on one knee. The lock of hair had fallen free of her ear again, dangling now against her cheek as she gazed into the darkness beyond the window. "But I suppose I was looking for something more from the beginning. Romance. Adventure. Fulfill- ment." She sighed. "I thought I wanted Alex, but I think I really wanted a new self." She tilted her head to glance at Callie. "A new life."

Callie kept silent, thinking her own reasons hadn't been much dif- ferent. And while she had expected a smaller course than the one she'd encountered, it wasn't because they'd lied about it. She supposed it was the part about not being able to back out that had disturbed her the most. And yet they had warned her of that, too. . . . Odd how clear that had become.

*"We intend this for your benefit, Callie."*

She believed that now. Completely. As if somehow she had entered

Alex's mind and had seen his true thoughts. Or maybe not Alex's but . . . whoever she'd run into there at the Gate. The Benefactor?

"Anyway," Meg said, releasing her legs and slouching back on the sectional, "I'm not sorry. I love it here. The scenery's gorgeous. The food's terrific. There's all kind of things to do." She paused. "Helping someone find the Gate is pretty exciting."

"And sometimes pretty frustrating, too, huh?" Callie grinned.

Meg shook her head soberly. "That's been my one curse—worrying about you. When I discovered you'd left the road, I was frantic. If not for Mr. Chapman, I'd have gone crazy." She faced Callie directly. "I was so afraid you were dead, or that the Guide would get here before you did. Then what would I do? I felt guilty enough as it was. When we finally spotted you in the temple at Mander I was ecstatic, but before I could figure out how to send a message you'd actually notice—the Tohvani run interference like you wouldn't believe—you'd vanished again."

"And the Tohvani are—?"

"The Watchers. The other side. The ones that don't want us to get out."

"And the side that does?"

"They're the Aggillon. Actually, I think they were all Aggillon once, and there was a war."

*The men in white standing with the Watchers at the base of the cliff,* Callie thought. *Were they Aggillon?*

"That's what Alicia says anyway," Meg went on. "Have you met her? White hair, kind of an addled look?"

Callie nodded.

"She knows a lot, but she won't talk." Meg flicked her fingers through her hair. "They say the Trogs put her through a fire curtain."

The couch seemed to shift under Callie's weight. "We're not going to have to face Trogs and fire curtains again, are we?"

Meg shrugged. "It's just a rumor. No one here knows much of anything. The real answers are all in the manual."

"Which only the Guide can interpret."

"Right. Anyway, Mr. C suggested I search along the river." She smiled. "He was almost as caught up in it as I was! And he didn't even know you. But that's Mr. C. He is one impressive guy. Been every-where you can imagine. And the jobs he's held! Writer, fisherman, nat-uralist—he's got degrees in astronomy, psychology, and physics, even dabbled in art. He knows just about everything, but he's still really nice."

"He reminds me of someone—"

"Dr. Haller from Algebra I, right?" Meg grinned.

"Well, yeah, now that you mention it. But I was thinking of some-one else."

She glanced through the palm fronds at Meg's new friend. He and the others had settled together on the central U-shaped sectional, with Morgan and Rowena conspicuously off to themselves. Someone had apparently cracked a joke, because the group burst into laughter, even Whit, who was usually sober as a monk.

With his white hair and neatly trimmed beard, Mr. Chapman was easily the oldest of them. In fact, he was close to being one of the oldest people Callie had seen in the Arena. She wondered how he came to be here. Had he been seeking life's answers, or was he one of those people who'd died and was getting a second chance? On the surface he looked as solid and satisfied as they came.

The laughter faded and Rowena began to talk, drawing everyone's attention. She leaned forward in her chair to project across the gap sep-arating her and Morgan from the others. Morgan nodded approvingly, but Wendell and Tuck frowned.

"Well," Meg murmured, "looks like Morg's won another convert."

Callie stood. "I want to hear what they're saying. Do you mind?"

They took up positions behind Whit and John. Rowena frowned at Callie but finished her speech without a break: ". . . see no reason to wait. Haven't we wasted enough time? At this rate, when we get home no one'll remember us."

"You must've led an awfully shallow life, Row, if you're worried about that," John said, fingering the gold hoop in his ear.

She made a dismissive face. "You think you'll just step back into things the way they were?"

" 'Course not, but it's been years for some of us! What's another few weeks?"

"And you're assuming time works the same way here as it does on Earth," Mr. C pointed out. "Maybe it doesn't."

"You mean like a month here is equal to a day back home?" Rowena asked. "I wouldn't count on it. And the fact it's been five years is exactly the point."

"How can you talk like this?" Callie burst out, exasperated. "I mean, what was the main lesson of the Outer Realm? Follow the manual's instructions! We haven't even been here a day and already you wanna go traipsing off without the Guide. Has it occurred to you the Exit may be right here?"

"This is a training facility. You heard him." Rowena gestured at Tucker. "No doubt meant to prepare all the people who got into their little cars and motored straight to the Gate. Well, we've had our training, babe. Years of it. I don't think we need any more."

"Actually we haven't even begun," Pierce said.

Startled, Callie turned to find him standing behind the sectional to her left. He held a dark book in one hand, and his face wore a pinched expression that made her stomach tighten with sudden concern.

No one said anything, not even Rowena, until John broke the tension in his oblivious way. "Pierce buddy! You missed the grand tour. Not that we saw much of interest, since most everything was locked, but—"

"Those are armories and shooting ranges," Pierce said.

His statement took John aback. "How would you know that, bud?" He glanced at the others, smiling indulgently. "I mean, you haven't seen—"

"We're going to have to be in prime shape, mentally and physically," Pierce went on, ignoring him. "Because the Exit is at the middle of the Inner Realm in a Trog city called Splagnos. The route will have to be worked out from information in the manual along with direct guidance from our Benefactor." He drew a deep breath and let it out. "It's not going to be easy."

By now Morgan was standing, Rowena beside him, all of them staring at Pierce.

Morgan said, "How do you know this?"

Pierce's face was expressionless as his eyes flicked over the gathering. Callie looked again at the book in his hand, and understanding dawned. "He can read the manual," she said softly, her voice clear in the silence. "He's the Guide we're supposed to wait for."

There was a long moment as her words were digested, as everyone took hold of them and wrestled with them.

Then Rowena spat an expletive and sat down hard on her sectional.

# TRANSFORMED

"HE GAVE SOME ... FOR THE EQUIPPING OF THE
SAINTS ... [TO] BE TRANSFORMED BY THE
RENEWING OF [THEIR MINDS ... TAKING] UP THE
FULL ARMOR OF GOD, THAT [THEY] MAY BE
ABLE TO RESIST IN THE EVIL DAY."

EPHESIANS 4:11–12;
ROMANS 12:2; EPHESIANS 6:13

# CHAPTER

# 16

As Callie stepped from the chilly spring twilight into the main auditorium, the sudden warmth made her cheeks burn. Though the snow was melting and the days were getting longer, the evening air still had a bite. She flung back her hood and sidled down the crowded aisle toward her seat, people congratulating her as she passed.

"Hear you're in the running for a medal on the short range," Mr. C said. "Good work."

Wendell said, "Did you *really* score a perfect 50 today?"

Callie smiled and nodded and moved on. It had been a good day. On the range and elsewhere. She had a chance for a bronze in the short-range shooting competition—if Morgan didn't beat her out.

Gerry grabbed her arm and spoke in her ear, "Outstanding run on the O-course, today, Cal. I saw you go down the rappelling cliff." He gave her a grin and a callused thumbs-up. "You looked like a pro."

She grinned back at him. He'd been working with her on that cliff. Though her scores on the obstacle course would never win her any medals, today she had completed the hand-over-hand and cable slide in personal record time. Even more incredibly, she'd plunged off the cliff without the slightest hesitation.

"Callie!" Meg wriggled between two opposing backs and scampered down to her. She wore tight jeans and a yellow silk blouse, and her dark curls, held back by a yellow ribbon, bounced to her shoulders. She seized Callie by both arms. "Great job on the range, girl. I'm jealous. The most I've ever made is 26."

"If you'd practice—"

"I don't have your eye." She leaned closer, the light fragrance of her perfume wafting on the warm air. "Don't have your teacher, either. I assume he *is* going to announce the departure date tonight?"

"I have no idea. And he's not just *my* teacher. He'd help you if you asked."

Meg only smiled. "You going to the party?"

"No."

"Have you been to the fair at all this spring?"

"Haven't had time with this push we've been on to finish the map. And I have some HTS projects that—"

"You can't transmit at night, Cal, and the map's done. Come."

Callie grimaced. "You know I hate that kind of stuff."

"This isn't one of your sister's stuffy parties." As Alicia and Ian pressed through, murmuring *excuse-me*s, they stepped apart, Meg talking all the while. "You'll know everyone there. And it's fun. There's food, craftsmen, musicians—they've even put down a dance floor."

"Like *that's* supposed to make me want to go?"

Meg grinned. "You can wear the dress I gave you for Christmas."

The Christmas dress, bought with Meg's weekly discretionary spending credits, had triggered a huge fight. Meg had given it to her so Callie would "have something for the New Year's party." Callie had interpreted the gesture as another matchmaking attempt. It took them weeks to forgive each other.

Now Callie frowned suspiciously. "You'll be going with Brody. I'd just be a third wheel."

"Whit's going. And Teish. And John and Evvi. And Wendell."

They were forced together as three people squeezed by.

"You're setting me up with Wendell now?"

Meg rolled her eyes. "I'm not setting you up. Why do you always accuse me of that? Even if I was, it wouldn't be with Wendell."

"Well, anyway, I hate crowds. And I don't know how to dance."

Meg frowned at her.

"Really, I'd rather paint."

"Okay, okay." Meg's gaze slid to something behind Callie. "Um, would you excuse me a minute?" And she was gone, slithering through the crowd toward the dark-haired hunk coming through the door. Brody Jaramillo had arrived last month, and Meg had fallen hard for him. Callie had disliked him from day one and was unhappily aware they were already sleeping together. She wasn't certain what bothered her most. Perhaps it was Meg's abandonment of common sense in the face of unbridled emotion, or that Callie had believed her when she promised to save her virginity for marriage. Perhaps it was because their relationship reminded her of how close she'd come to doing the same thing with Garth. Or perhaps—

Perhaps somewhere deep inside she was jealous.

She spied Whit down the aisle, head and shoulders above the crowd. He was talking with Morgan, John, and Rowena. Clean and clad in regulation white, they appeared considerably more respectable than when Callie had first met them. Whit had shaved his beard, leaving a drooping mustache. John had clipped his own beard close to his face and cut his hair to collar length. In the uniformlike jumpsuit, he looked quite militarily proper, except for his gold earring.

Rowena was gorgeous as always. She wore her jumpsuit skintight, the front zipper pulled so low her cleavage looked as if it might burst free at any moment. Cosmetics highlighted her perfect features, and silver starbursts dangled from her ears, sparkling with every movement. She made Callie feel like a potato. It did not help matters that she was also the best athlete and markswoman in the compound.

The only thing that made the situation tolerable was that Rowena's antagonism toward her continued unabated. If the woman had been friendly and pleasant, the guilt would've been unbearable.

" . . . showed him the whole migration pattern," Morgan was saying, waving a vellum flimsy in one hand as Callie joined the group. "It's right there in red, blue, and green. If we don't leave within two days, we'll run into a horde of Trogs—or have to wait till fall. And then we'll have problems with the harries swarming. And the weather. And who knows what wars will have erupted among the Nine Cities by then."

"Was he convinced?" Whit asked.

Morgan shrugged. "You know Pierce. But I told him flat-out—if we don't leave now, we'll have to wait another year."

"Maybe that's what he wants," Rowena suggested.

"Why would he want that?" Morgan asked.

She studied one of her long pink nails. "Maybe he doesn't want to leave. Maybe he likes it here."

A chill tickled Callie's spine.

"That's ridiculous," Morgan said, frowning. "He's talked of nothing else for months."

Rowena tilted her head, earrings shimmering. "Then why is he stalling? It's been two weeks since the snow cleared out of the passes." She glanced toward the still-empty dais and lowered her voice. "What if he has no intention of leaving? How long are you willing to wait for him?"

John and Whit stared at the floor. Morgan's frown deepened. He didn't seem to know what to make of Rowena's talk, but then, he was the only one in the circle who didn't know about Pierce's humiliating terror of the Trogs. Callie wondered how long it would be before Rowena enlightened him—and everyone else as well.

Thankfully, Tucker stepped onto the dais just then. "Looks like we're about to get started," Callie said, stepping through the circle toward her seat. The others glanced toward the front, and the moment was lost. As she pressed past Rowena, Callie felt the other woman staring at her, but she only looked back when she had settled beside LaTeisha, ten seats down the row of folding blue theater chairs. By then, Rowena had left.

"Well?" LaTeisha asked as Callie struggled out of her jacket. "Did Morgan present his big plan?" Her notebook lay open on her lap, today's date already recorded in her precise handwriting.

"Yeah."

"And?"

Callie shrugged and twisted around to hang her jacket over the back of her chair.

LaTeisha flicked her pen back and forth. "Okay, what's wrong?"

"Rowena."

"She on Pierce's case again?"

"Yeah." Callie sank back into the chair and picked up her braid, studying its end. "I know she's disappointed that he's the Guide. But it's so obvious the Aggillon chose him, why does she fight it?"

"He's gonna have to prove himself."

Before Callie could reply they were interrupted.

"Great job on the range today, Cal." Evelyn Albion collapsed into the seat beside her, dropping pens and scraps of paper as she did. "Now if you can just hold on against that windbag Morgan. It's eating him alive that a woman's beating him, you know."

She struggled out of her coat, almost hitting Callie in the face and dropping her notebook in an explosion of fluttering papers. Pens rolled everywhere, sending Callie and LaTeisha scrambling to retrieve them. The coat off, Evvi hung it carelessly over the back of her chair, where it fell into the aisle behind as soon as she faced front.

She scrunched her papers together and spoke around the pen in her mouth. "Have you heard about his window for departure theory?"

"Who hasn't?" Callie asked dryly. Sometimes she wondered if Evvi took little trips into outer space, she seemd so out of touch.

"Something about Trog migrations. I haven't paid much attention, 'cause what difference does it make? Pierce is the Guide, after all. When he says go, we'll go."

It was not easy to reconcile Evvi's spaciness with her unflagging support for Pierce's leadership. She hung on his every word, believing everything he said without question. Callie *wanted* to like her but had never quite overcome her almost reflexive aversion. Lately, with Meg focused on Brody, Evvi was following Callie around like an adoring puppy, and there seemed no way of discouraging her short of playing dead.

"You know what?" Evvi said. "I bet he *doesn't* announce a departure date tonight, precisely because everyone is demanding he do so."

"He's waiting for Elhanu's go-ahead," Callie reminded her. Elhanu, they had learned early on, was the Aggillon leader—the mysterious man they had walked into when they passed through the Gate.

"That's what I mean," Evvi said. "If I were Elhanu, I wouldn't do it."

*Thank heaven you're not*, Callie thought, eyeing the woman's long disheveled hair and smudged jumpsuit. Evvi bent to grope for another pen, and her notes and vid-discs crashed to the floor. Callie glanced at LaTeisha, who rolled her eyes.

During the commotion of Evvi's arrival, Pierce and Mr. Chapman had joined Tuck on the dais. The trio was deep in conversation beside the podium.

Like John, Pierce had changed greatly. He'd shaved off his beard months ago, revealing a strong jawline and a face of wonderfully angular planes that set the artist in Callie afire. The jumpsuit showed off his lean form, accentuating narrow hips and broad shoulders, and she didn't need Evelyn Albion to tell her he was an attractive man. Even Meg thought so. And they weren't the only ones.

But it hadn't always been so, especially at the beginning. If not for the fact that Pierce had "unlocked the hidden places of the installation," as their instructions said the Guide would do—and that his jumpsuits alone bore the triple-circle, three-barred device of his authority—few would have given him the time of day. The first night he'd addressed them as a group had been a disaster. Pale and nervous, he'd rubbed his fingers distractingly along the podium's rim, stared fixedly at his notes and stumbled over his words, punctuating them with long uncomfortable pauses. Too often his voice had trembled or dribbled away to a barely audible murmur, and by the time he had finished, some in the audience were openly mocking him. The second session went no better, and Callie had ached for him, knowing how much he loathed his position of responsibility. Why the Aggillon had chosen him, no one could guess. *"Someone's idea of a joke,"* Pierce had suggested in one of his darker moments.

It didn't help that what he was teaching sounded like science fiction. As Meg had suggested, the Tohvani had indeed been Aggillon, part of a peaceful, galaxy-spanning empire ruled by Elhanu. Based on a universal reverence for truth, Aggillon culture knew no war, no crime, no poverty, no suffering of any kind. Without need of working to live, they lived to work, their work centering around trade and discourse, science and math, art and sport—all of it translating into great reverence and appreciation for their emperor, Elhanu, who had brought it all to pass. It was a time of stimulation, challenge, and wonder.

Nevertheless, dissatisfaction sprouted. Prince Cephelus was the brilliant, talented, and respected head of the noblest of Aggillon families. Though he had everything, including the ear and heart of Elhanu himself, it was not enough. Nourished by self-absorption and watered by jealousy, the seedling of his arrogance grew. Why should he have to submit to Elhanu? He was just as intelligent, as learned, as capable. Why should one Aggillon lord over the rest, with all the approbation going to him, when others were just as worthy?

Blossoms of pride gave forth seeds of contention and deceit, which, sown into the hearts of his fellows, yielded a harvest of rebellion. War swept the universe. Brother battled brother in a conflict of light-based weaponry that loosed lethal curtains of energy—blasting star systems to rubble and hurling their remnants light-years in all directions to destroy, deface, or destabilize whatever they encountered.

The manual didn't say how long it lasted, just that in the end, the usurpers lost—Cephelus and his followers were found guilty of treason and sentenced to be eternally imprisoned in a magnetically sealed plasma well, their bodies caught in an unending—and agonizing—cycle of forming, unforming, and forming again.

They protested immediately. The sentence was cruel and unfair, one Elhanu could not possibly impose and still keep his vaunted integrity. Had he not claimed for time unmeasured to be a ruler who knew and loved deeply every one of his subjects? Who wanted only the very best for them? Who was incapable of committing a wrong against even the least of them? Had not his subjects trusted him in this, reveled in it, and worshiped him for it? How then, could he now consign some of those same subjects to an eternity of torment?

In an expression of the very love to which his enemies appealed, Elhanu offered to pay for their disobedience with his own suffering, thereby absolving them of their crimes. But to accept that offer, Cephelus and his followers would have to admit their inferiority, their failure, and their need—a humbling they refused to consider. They appealed the sentence, certain Elhanu could not mean it.

And so a new phase of the trial began. The Arena was constructed as a representative universe, with Homo sapiens—lesser beings in all regards—brought in to serve as witnesses. Allowed the freedom to obey or disobey the instructions they were given, the humans would, by their own decisions and actions, provide opportunity for Elhanu to demonstrate to his watching Aggillon the fact that, while he was loving, he was also good and just, and not one of those characteristics could ever be exercised at the expense of the other two.

He himself oversaw the selection, preparation, and insertion of individual participants to ensure it was done in accordance with the rules and that those who took part should suffer no loss, save that which their own volition incurred. All they needed to do was walk through the Arena to its exit. So long as they stayed on the white road Elhanu provided, they would be returned—with great reward for their trouble—to their lives on Earth.

Cephelus and his cronies, now styling themselves as Tohvani, or "Enlightened Ones," mocked such an easily thwarted plan. Did Elhanu think them fools? Indeed, Tohvani cleverness lured the first witnesses off the road in no time, enticing them with the seductive, mutative fire curtain. Once exposed to the energies of that device, the participants' bodies were corrupted. When, later, they tried to pass through the exit, they were flung back, burned to ash and bone. Worse, the portal itself was corrupted by their contact and rendered impassable. Not only was the remainder of the original party trapped, but all who came after, as well.

Where was Elhanu's love in that? Cephelus had mocked. Bringing in people who had nothing to do with the conflict and causing them, by his own ineptitude, to lose their lives? That was no fairer than the sentence he had pronounced upon the Tohvani!

Elhanu answered with his Gates of Change, liberally placing them around the Arena to provide maximum availability and ease of access. When willing participants passed through any one of the fourteen gates, he took them into himself and rearranged the molecular structure of their bodies so they could pass through the damaged exit. At the same time he made them immune to the Tohvani-manufactured poisons that would soon saturate the air and ground around the exit. Most important of all, he forged a link between their minds and his—a channel through which flowed not only his insights and understanding, but also his power. It was an act that astonished his followers and antagonists alike, done at great pain and cost to him. Merely touching men's dark minds and bloody flesh was bad enough—merging with them was unthinkable.

For a time Cephelus feared all was lost. Since their new link with Elhanu would provide his human adversaries with a power and understanding even greater than his own, how could he ever get them to do anything but trust and obey the one they were bonded to? About to cry foul again, he realized Elhanu, ever the gentleman, would allow his human witnesses the same liberty he allows his Aggillon. They could use the link only if they wanted, only if they learned by their own choice how to use it. And it was Elhanu's way, always to give his subjects the freedom to say no. Cephelus would exploit that freedom to the fullest.

Cursed with an inflated sense of their abilities, humans had a predilection toward self-reliance and disliked depending on anyone else. Curious, emotional, and immensely distractible, they were easily duped, even with the link inside them. And the Tohvani took full advantage. Free to sculpt the Arena for their purposes, they set to work, eradicating much of the white road, re-engineering the original bioforms into dangerous predators, and developing a new, more potent line of fire curtains for Arena-wide distribution. All the dangers and deceptions participants encountered in the Outer Realm—sucker paths, rock dragons, mites, temples, false benefactors, fire curtains—came courtesy of the Tohvani. More of the same awaited in the Inner Realm.

Even Changed, many would fail to reach the Exit. But every now and then a group of participants came through who did not fail, who learned to use everything Elhanu had provided for them, who understood exactly why they were in the Arena, who even came to ally themselves with his cause and make it their own. These were the victors in this contest, the truest, brightest witnesses of who and what Elhanu was, not merely Changed but devoted servants and friends. Men and women who, though inferior to the Tohvani in almost every way, could understand and love what the Tohvani would not. For this their reward would be very great.

But to become victors, Pierce said participants must understand that the true struggle, the true advance lay in the mind. They must set aside their self-reliance and learn to access the link, then make the consistent and conscious decisions to use the power it provided no matter what the circumstances. Such learning would take time, effort—and lots of practice.

Of course, no one wanted to hear that, and for two agonizing weeks Pierce and his message were ridiculed unmercifully. People were interested in routes and defensive fortifications and how much opposition they might expect. They did not want to hear about learning to control their emotions and their thoughts, and they most especially did not want to hear about how weak and helpless they were without their alien sponsor.

Pierce's audience dribbled away to a third of Rimlight's residents. He began to brood and snap. One day Callie was working with him on an early draft of the map, and when she offered in idle conversation a suggestion to improve his public presence, he'd gone ballistic—yelled hateful things, thrown the manual across the room, and stalked out of the office, vanishing into the steep, forested slopes outside the compound.

He had returned three days later, at peace.

That was when he shaved his beard, as if to mark the change. After that, he threw himself into studying, and let the rejections roll off his back. Gradually a quiet conviction took hold of him. His speaking confidence increased. He looked at his listeners and stopped fidgeting with the podium. He grew more committed to Elhanu every day, and the more confidently he explained, the more his explanations made sense.

In addition, he was constantly unlocking computer files that gave credence to his teachings. The coup had come when he discovered a cache of logs from previous expeditions—not only of groups that left from Rimlight, but of those who had embarked from the other training compounds scattered around the rim, as well. A shocking number of the records detailed gruesome debacles wherein many of their participants were taken captive and tortured. Though death itself was no longer a threat—whether they "died" in the Arena or walked out the Exit, all who had been Changed would return to their lives on Earth—the prospect of capture was. Many of the Trogs in the Inner Realm were Changed participants, taken prisoner en route to the Exit and tortured or enticed until they agreed to submit to the fire curtain. It did not take many exposures to develop addiction. And though the possibility of recovery did exist—if the effort was begun soon enough—it was a long and painful process, fraught with danger and uncertainty, and few negotiated it successfully.

The records effectively squelched any ideas of leaving without the appointed Guide. Within a week most were giving Pierce another chance. Somehow they'd stuck with him all winter.

Now, as Mr. C took his seat in the front row, Pierce sat in one of the platform chairs and Tuck approached the podium to make the announcements. The armory, he informed them, had shut down that morning—surely a good sign. The current standings for the obstacle-course competition had Morgan and Gerry in contention for the lead. Callie was one of the medal contenders in the shooting tournament. The Aggillon entertainers who had encamped outside the compound's lower gates two weeks ago were hosting a celebration after tonight's meeting. There would be entertainment, food, and drink for all. After a few more odds and ends relating to cafeteria and maintenance sched-ules, Tuck yielded the stage to Pierce.

The silence electrified with anticipation.

For a long moment Pierce regarded them with that stone-faced expression that was so exasperatingly unreadable.

"I know what you want to hear from me," he said finally, his ampli-fied voice echoing through the auditorium. "I'm afraid I can't oblige. I've told you from the beginning, we leave when we're told to. Until then, it's business as usual."

"But Pierce—" Morgan stood up several rows behind Callie. "Aren't *you* supposed to decide that? As our 'leader'?"

Pierce regarded him evenly. "I'm to decide when Elhanu tells us to go, and so far I've received no such clear directive."

"What about the armory closing?"

"It's only one of many criteria to be considered."

"And the stats I gave you? Are you just going to ignore those?"

"I appreciate the work you've done, Morg, but the fact remains—"

"The fact remains—if we don't leave now we're going to run into a swarm of mutants!" Morgan's voice, grown loud and emphatic, echoed in the shocked silence that followed it.

Then Pierce said calmly, "We can't know that for sure. And if we do run into them, I'd assume we were supposed to."

Morgan laughed incredulously. "Oh, now *there's* a plan."

"Forget it, hon," Rowena said, standing beside him. "His mind is made up. And I don't think this has a thing to do with stats. I'd say the problem is a lack of courage."

Callie's heart constricted, but before Rowena could elaborate, Tuck burst out laughing. "Courage? I'd like to see you get up here and teach this group anything."

"At least *I'd* listen to people," Morgan snapped.

"You're just jealous," Tuck cried, "because he was chosen and you weren't."

"That's enough!" said Pierce, his voice low and firm over the speakers. "Morgan, if you aren't interested in what I have to say, perhaps you should leave."

Rowena tugged his arm. "Come on."

"Yeah. It's not like we'll learn anything new."

They picked their way past the row of knees to the aisle.

"Anyone else?" Pierce asked. A few more followed, but the majority remained.

Pierce braced both arms on the podium and regarded his audience. "I didn't ask for this job," he said. "But the fact is, I have it. And I answer to Elhanu, not you." He shook his head. "This is the kind of thing the Tohvani delight in—divide and conquer. If we can't maintain our unity here, what are we going to do out there?"

No one answered him. After a bit, he readjusted his notes and said, "Well, you came for a lesson, so let's get on with it. Tonight has turned out to be an excellent time to review what we know about our enemies."

"Psst! Callie!" Evvi jabbed her arm. "Do you have a pen? Mine are out of ink."

Stifling her annoyance, Callie pulled an extra pen from her pocket and handed it over, keeping her attention on Pierce.

An hour later he concluded. As people filed out, Evvi stood beside Callie, clutching her notepads and struggling to pull her coat out of the crack behind her chair. "He makes them sound so scary," she said as she tugged at the jacket. "I almost don't want to leave. Morgan should've heard this." With a grunt she pulled the garment free, and it slapped Callie in the face. "He's such an arrogant jerk."

"He *has* spent a lot of time with the video logs," Callie said. "He knows the Inner Realm."

"We need to know Elhanu." Evvi's gaze fixed upon the knot of people surrounding Pierce, and she got the same distracted expression Meg had evidenced earlier. "See you at the fair," she said absently. And she was off, trailing papers.

As Callie picked one up, LaTeisha leaned close. "Better watch your flank, girl," she said, eyeing Evvi as she pressed into the crowd around Pierce. "I think someone's moving into your territory."

"Territory?" Callie stuffed the paper into her own notebook. "What's *that* supposed to mean?"

LaTeisha only laughed and moved off down the row, leaving Callie to frown after her, annoyed all over again. Everyone seemed to think she and Pierce had some kind of romantic relationship going, when that couldn't be further from the truth—they were friends, nothing more. Maybe if she encouraged Evvi in her "move," people would finally believe her and quit with the oblique comments and sly winks.

Tuck intercepted her as she headed for the door. "Pierce wants to see you. Something about the map." He drew back to let people pass. "You coming to the party?"

"I doubt it."

He grinned. "You'll miss the best meat pies on Earth."

"We're not on Earth, Tuck."

He laughed and left her.

Pierce was in his study, fielding the last few questions as she came in. Seeing her, he thanked the questioners for their interest and herded them into the hall.

"I think some of them would wash your feet if you asked them," she said as he closed the door behind them.

He frowned. "I know. I've tried to dissuade them, but . . . well, at least they're eager to learn. You can't fault that."

"I guess not. . . . What'd you want to see me about?"

"More changes to the map." He went to the desk and picked up a rolled parchment.

"I'll put them in tonight," she said, taking it from him.

"Tomorrow will be fine."

"I don't mind." Unrolling it, she checked the revisions. "Is this all?"

"Actually, no." He straightened the papers beside his keyboard. "The Aggillon are leaving for Rimtruth tomorrow, you know, and I thought . . . well, that is . . ." He drew a deep breath, then looked her in the eye. "Would you like to go to the fair with me tonight?"

Callie was caught completely off guard. Her automatic response was negative, but she realized a flat refusal would hurt him, and she swallowed it unspoken. Annoyance flared. First Meg, and now Pierce. What was this? Some kind of conspiracy?

"I know you don't like parties," Pierce said. He leaned against the desk and puttered with the papers again. "Neither do I. We can always leave early."

"Why go at all?"

He looked up at her. "I'm curious, for one, and . . . it might be fun." He smiled, and as always she melted before it. "Will you go?"

*It won't hurt you*, she told herself. *And you have to admit you're curious, too.*

"Oh, all right. For a little while. Let me drop this stuff off in my room first."

"Fine. You'll need to change clothes, anyway. Aggillon rules," he added when she frowned at him. "No uniforms in their camp."

"Oh yeah." Well, that had happened neatly. Now not only was she going to the party, but she also had to wear the dress. And wouldn't the rumors fly after this! She'd better encourage Evvi's pursuit of Pierce as soon as possible or she'd never hear the end of it.

# CHAPTER

## 17

When Callie returned to the lobby half an hour later, only three people remained in the main salon—a couple watching a video on the large freestanding screen and a man in western garb facing the window. He turned as she stepped off the elevator, but only as he approached did she recognize him.

"Wow!" Pierce said as he joined her. "You look terrific."

She laughed, feeling her cheeks flush. "You don't look so bad yourself, cowboy."

"All I need is my hoss." He doffed his hat and grinned, and she wondered how she had ever thought him ordinary looking.

The Aggillon had parked their gold-gilt wagons and colorful tents in the flat outside Rimlight's front gates. Electric heating columns warded off the chill, and strings of tiny lights festooned the wagons, their soft light glinting off the booths and tables of wares—clothing, jewelry, trinkets, audio discs, vid-discs, knickknacks, gadgets, and food, food, food. Meat pies, fruit pies, fry bread on sticks, French fries, tacos, hot dogs and hamburgers, soft drinks, beer, mulled wine, and cider— the air was redolent with the mingling aromas, alive with laughter and the music of roving minstrels.

Pierce had long been easy company, and Callie quickly relaxed. Friends and acquaintances jostled around them, calling out congratulations or greetings or witticisms. They ate meat pies and honey-glazed

fry bread on sticks, drank mulled cider, and watched jugglers and tum-
blers, then listened to a minstrel with a voice so exquisite it raised goose
bumps on Callie's arms. A tooler worked intricate designs into a silver
bowl, while beside him an Aggillon illusionist performed the deftest
sleight of hand she had ever seen.

At the end of the performance Pierce confessed he'd drunk too
much cider and went searching for a bathroom. Callie waited for him
by a glassblower's stall, first watching the man finish a delicate blue
vase, then turning her attention to the crowd as it milled between the
booths and streamed in and out of the red-striped tent set up for dancing. Music drifted from the tent in a lively, foot-tapping tune.

The faces were familiar, even those of the Aggillon merchants and
entertainers. Traveling a circuit that also included visits to each of Rimlight's thirteen sister training compounds, most had come through
before as circus performers, and before that as a theater troupe.

Their arrival had surprised her the first time. Knowing the Aggillon's power and intellect, she found it incredible that they stooped to
the task of entertaining participants. Gradually, though, she'd perceived
that their entertainment was anything but frivolous. Forbidden to speak
to participants except in superficial business interaction, their stories
communicated what their conversations could not. Their songs
recounted their history. Even the magician's show was instructive—a
warning in disguise of what lay ahead. For the Tohvani were once
Aggillon, sharing the same abilities and intellect. And while the Aggillon would never deceive participants beyond the benign illusions of a
magician's act, the Tohvani would.

Roving idly across the bright colors and moving figures, Callie's
gaze snagged on something out of place—a gray, spindly-limbed form,
barely visible, like a wisp of shifting fog. It stood between a blue-
cloaked Gerry Felder and LaTeisha, elegant in a red velvet dress. As
Gerry watched the crowd, he had his back to the apparition, but La-
Teisha should have seen it. Apparently she didn't, even though the
minute Callie focused on it, it sharpened into solidity. The black eyes
bored into her own, and she felt a gust of fear. Then Gerry stepped in
front of it, and when he moved again, it was gone.

She scanned the crowd, seeking another glimpse, wondering in the end if she'd imagined it. Tohvani Watchers supposedly couldn't manifest in Rimlight, and in the nine months since their arrival, she'd seen not one—even outside the walls. And between her hiking and cross-country skiing, she'd seen a lot of the outside.

"Ah, Miss Hayes! So you did come down."

She turned at the familiar voice, grinning as Mr. Chapman joined her. "Meg said you weren't planning to attend."

"I changed my mind."

"Good. You and Mr. Andrews work far too hard." He glanced around. "Where is he, anyway?"

"Why do you think I'd know?"

Mr. C grinned. "Where there's one of you, the other's usually not far."

"Really."

His brown eyes twinkled. "Am I wrong?"

"He's in the bathroom." She gestured toward the portable tucked between the armorer's wagon and a cart serving fry bread.

"Ah." He leaned closer. "How was it for you going over that cliff today? You looked strong."

"Thanks. It was good."

"Did you have to count?"

"No. I used the link, like you suggested. Or tried to." Counting backward by threes from one hundred was the method Gerry had suggested to help her control her panic. At first it was the only thing that worked. Lately, though, she'd been focusing on her link with Elhanu instead. "Once I went over the edge, I forgot all that and just concentrated on my technique. The next thing I knew I was down. Do you suppose I've got this licked?"

He squeezed her shoulder affectionately. "If not, you're very close. I'm proud of you, lass. It's not easy to overcome deep fears. Speaking of which"—he turned as Pierce rejoined them—"I see you managed to ask her."

Pierce grinned sheepishly under the broad brim of his hat. "She said yes, too, just like you said she would."

Callie cocked a brow at Mr. C, bemused. "I almost didn't."

" 'Almost' doesn't count, lass." He clapped a hand on Pierce's shoulder. "It's good to see you down here, son."

Pierce regarded him quizzically. "Afraid I'll start brooding again?"

"Or studying—searching for that tidbit you think will convince everyone you're right."

"Which, of course, is nonexistent," Pierce added, laughing.

Mr. C tilted his head in acknowledgment.

Pierce hooked a thumb on the front pocket of his jeans. "You were sure right about Morgan. It's a miracle half the group didn't troop out after him tonight."

"You're still the Guide, though," Callie said. "And contrary to what you may think, most of these people do respect you."

"Yeah, but for how long?" Pierce gazed over the crowd. "Everyone's getting restless. And let's face it—I don't have Morgan's charisma."

Callie frowned, wondering where he'd gotten this charisma business, and how he could think there was any comparison. Before she could reprove him, however, Mr. C was already doing so.

"Don't sell yourself short, young man," he said sternly. "These people don't need charisma. They need hard work and the truth—exactly what you've given them. You've done very well here, and I believe you'll do even better out there. Popularity isn't everything. In fact, it isn't anything when you get right down to it. The majority is rarely right."

Pierce snorted.

Mr. C squeezed his shoulder and released him. "But, hey, you two are supposed to be having fun." He turned his head as a new burst of music erupted from the tent, glanced at Callie with a sly grin, and said, "Why don't you take her dancing?"

Pierce caught the grin. "Good idea, sir." He grabbed Callie's hand and pulled her toward the tent.

"But, Pierce, I don't know how to dance!"

"So I'll teach you."

She looked back helplessly at Mr. C, who grinned and waved and told her *this* would be a good time to count.

The tent held a varnished wooden dance floor made of interlocking plates. At its far end, a band of drum, pipe, and fiddle played, while couples twirled in complex patterns around the floor. Callie suggested they sit at the edge and watch, but Pierce would have none of it. "Best way to learn is jump in."

"But—"

"You told me yourself you always wanted to do this," he said, dragging her amongst the others. "You just lacked the nerve. Here, stand like this."

"What makes you think I have the nerve now?"

"If you can throw yourself off the edge of a cliff, my dear, you can handle this." He took her hands, smiled his wonderful smile, and she surrendered.

"Watch my feet," he said. "Here we go. One, two, three—one, two—that's it."

Before long Callie had the hang of it. It didn't matter that she'd never done it before. Pierce was good enough for both of them. He twirled her this way and that, her skirt and hair whirling around her. When she made a mistake, they just laughed and went on. It was exhilarating, intoxicating—she loved it!

But after the fourth song, she collapsed against him, breathless. "Enough! I'm so dizzy I can't stand up, and I *have* to get a drink." She staggered to one of the tables surrounding the dance floor, where an Aggillon waiter brought them water, then colas.

As they watched the others move in time to a slow song, she admitted it was fun. "Even if I did make an idiot of myself."

"You did fine."

"I had a masterful teacher." She leaned her chin on her palm and regarded him bemusedly. Could this be the surly, filthy stranger she'd met that first day on the sucker path? "Where'd you learn to do that, anyway?"

He grinned. "I wasn't born in the Outlands."

"I suppose you play the violin, too."

"Actually, the piano. I don't do gymnastics, though."

"Seriously?"

"I was too clumsy."

She blinked. "I mean the piano."

"Do I play the piano seriously? Sometimes."

She was laughing now. "No—are you any good at it?" And when had he turned into a tease?

He fingered the brim of his hat, now lying on the table. "My mother wishes I was better, I'm sure, but I never liked competition. I play for myself mostly."

He became pensive, lost in his past. She studied him, fascinated. Competition was an option? With those long fingers, it was easy to see why. *A pianist*, she thought. *Here I think I know him, and then another door opens and I see a whole new side.*

"I was supposed to go to the state finals my junior year of high school," he said after a few moments, "but I broke my hand a week before the competition."

"Broke your hand?"

"Mountain lion jumped me, knocked me off my horse."

She stared at him wide-eyed.

He shrugged. "He was half starved. I felt bad for shooting him. Anyway, that ended my musical career."

"What about the next year?"

"By then the ranch was in a bad way. Dad had already let most of the hands go. I didn't have time to practice, much less spend a week in Denver. I never wanted to be a professional musician, anyway. They're inside too much."

The slow dance ended and the band took a break.

Callie sighed. "I always wanted to play the piano, but we couldn't afford it. And Mom said I lacked the discipline to practice."

"Your mother said *that*? About *you*?"

She ran a finger around the rim of her glass. "I taught myself to play the guitar, but it wasn't the same. Someday I'm going to get a piano and take lessons." The intensity of Pierce's gaze made her self-conscious. "Anyway, I'd love to hear *you* play."

"Maybe that could be arranged sometime."

He looked up as a couple squeezed by their table. Once again she was struck by the elegance of his profile, the lines burning into her memory with an insistence that made her itch to start drawing. She had long ago admitted to herself that his face and form fascinated her— almost embarrassingly so. She hated to think what Meg would say if she ever found the sketchbook hidden under Callie's bed.

"Hullo." As if conjured by the thought, her friend's voice interrupted their silence. They looked up to find Meg and Brody Jaramillo standing beside their table.

"I'm Meg Riley," Meg announced. "I don't believe we've met." Immediately her mock seriousness dissolved. "Was that you I saw out there *dancing?*" She turned to Pierce. "And your date here—surely not our serious and stoic Guide to the Inner Realm?"

Pierce cocked a brow.

"It's an amazing feat you've accomplished, Mr. Andrews," she added. "To my knowledge no one has gotten this girl onto a dance floor in her entire life."

"Harvey Bellum," Callie said dryly. "Sixth grade."

"That was square dancing, and Mrs. Wareheiser assigned him to you. Hardly the same thing."

"Harvey Bellum?" Pierce asked.

"A cute little blonde with big brown eyes," Meg said. "Callie had a crush on him."

"*Meg,*" Callie said between clenched teeth.

Meg grinned. "Am I embarrassing you? Sorry. Pierce, have you met Brody?" She tugged her date forward and made the introductions.

"I understand we're about to start for the final portal," Brody said without preamble.

Pierce's expression became guarded. "Could be."

"Good, 'cause I've got a lot of things cooking back home, and I wanna finish this as soon as possible."

Callie snorted. "Like the rest of us don't?"

He regarded her with half-lidded eyes. "Some of you've been in this place for years. I'd never have hung around that long."

"I'm sure you wouldn't," Pierce said. He leaned back and folded his arms.

"Hey, I'm committed to those prime directives you explained the other night." Brody waved a hand. "Forward momentum, never look back and all."

"Forward momentum isn't always physical," Pierce said.

Brody looked blank.

"You've seen the Leyton record?"

The young man shook his head, shooting a questioning glance at Meg.

She blushed. "That one's awfully gross."

"Calvin Leyton's group moved out too soon," Callie explained. "Most were captured. They tortured Calvin for six hours, and in the end, he pleaded for the curtain. They're probably all Trogs now."

Brody swelled before them. "I'm not afraid."

"Good thing," said Pierce, "because your armor won't work if you are."

The other man's eyes widened, and again he looked to Meg.

"The belt's sensitive to fear," she explained. "The minute you're afraid, off it goes, and without the field it generates, the breastplate and helmet are useless."

He looked surprised, and Callie wondered how he could have been here even the three weeks he had—having been issued his own set of armor besides—and missed that information.

"You know, you might consider waiting for the next Guide to come through," Pierce said after a moment. "'Cause if you're not ready, you could spend a good deal longer than a year here."

Brody stared at him, nonplussed.

Pierce shrugged. "It's your call." He glanced toward the dance floor. "Ah, here's the band coming back." He put on his hat, stood, and held out a hand to Callie. "You ready to try again?"

She let him lead her onto the floor and, as he faced her, said, "Goodness, Pierce. You were kinda rude, don't you think?"

"Is that the guy Meg's all in a tizzy over?"

"Yes."

He glanced over her shoulder at them. "Can't say I'm impressed."

"Well, no . . ."

"Poor guy's gonna have a tough row to hoe."

Callie couldn't argue with that, and she quickly forgot about Brody as the band warbled a sultry, languorous selection. "Oh no, this is a slow one."

"I think we can handle it."

He slid his hand around her waist and suddenly she was in his arms.

Her mouth went dry, and the blood hammered in her ears and throat. She fixed her eyes downward. "What do I do with my feet?"

It took her a few minutes to get the pattern down, and then she had nothing to think about except how close Pierce was, and how awkward and jittery she felt. She stared over his shoulder and tried to relax, searching for something to say.

Then Morgan and Rowena stepped through the tent's entrance. They sat at a floor-side table to watch the dancers, and Rowena quickly spotted Pierce. She touched Morgan's arm, and when he turned, Callie knew she'd told him everything.

"What's going on back there?" Pierce asked.

"Rowena and Morgan just came in." She risked a glance at him. "I think Rowena—"

"Spilled her guts?" He grimaced. "You knew she would eventually."

"What're you going to do?"

"Swallow whatever they dish out, I guess."

When the song ended, she immediately stepped away from him. "Let's go."

"I'm not running, Cal." From his expression, she knew he wouldn't be persuaded otherwise. And as it turned out, running would only have made things worse.

Morgan confronted Pierce as they stepped off the dance floor. "You lied to us!" he said, his voice low with outrage. "All that garbage about Elhanu was just a cover for your own cowardice."

"It wasn't a lie, Morg."

Morgan jerked a thumb at Rowena, standing just behind him. "She told me how you froze up and couldn't fire your weapon. How your friends never knew if you were going to cut and run, or curl up and mew like a baby. No wonder you hid all the records."

"Hid the records? What're you talking about?"

"Don't play dumb with me. Anyone can find them if he knows how to get around the blocks."

"There are records of the Outlands?"

"There are records of everything. All in living color."

Pierce had gone pale, but he met Morgan's gaze unflinchingly.

Callie scowled at Rowena. "Why did you open this up again?"

Rowena lifted her chin. "People have a right to know what kind of coward they're trusting their lives to."

"He's not a coward."

"Callie." Pierce laid a hand on her arm, then said to Morgan, "I'm not proud of what I did. I can't even promise I won't do it again. But that's not why we're not leaving."

"What kind of a fool do you take me for?"

Around them, the others had stopped dancing, and now the band fell silent. Familiar faces stared wide-eyed—Wendell, Gerry, Tuck, Ian, Brody, Meg. Callie wanted to scream at them to mind their own business and keep on with what they were doing.

"You're not the only one who can read the manual around here, you know," Morgan said. "Or the only one who knows how to access the link to Elhanu."

"But I am the only one who wears the circles and bars."

"That doesn't guarantee you're infallible. Calvin Leyton wore them, too."

"And left too early."

"And Jason Puala, fearful of sharing his fate, left too late—and shared it anyway." Morgan leaned toward him, rigid with intensity. "We need to go *now*, Pierce. The signs are everywhere, if you'd just open your eyes and look."

"Then go."

Morgan's eyes narrowed. "Without you?"

"If you believe I'm deliberately refusing the directive to leave," Pierce said, "why would you trust me to find the exit portal?"

"Those are two different matters."

"No, they're not." Pierce moved for the door.

Morgan stopped him. "It's true, isn't it? You like it here, lording it over the rest of us, and you have no intention of leaving."

Pierce was white as death now, but his voice remained calm. "I'll leave when Elhanu tells me to. That is my only intention."

Callie caught up with him outside the tent. He wore his stone face like a shield and said nothing as they walked back to the compound. It was a relief to leave the light and noise and stifling warmth for the chilly, quiet darkness of the front square, a relief to escape the crowd's curious glances. How many of them would be reviling Pierce by morning?

They followed the path that wound around the obstacle course, deserted now in the starlight, and stopped when they reached the pool at the base of the climbing cliff. Here the camp's music was a distant wheedle, overlaid by the water trickling down the rock face and the breeze hissing in the trees. Pierce leaned against the railing and gazed at the silver pond shimmering against the dark masses of foliage and the cliff's pale bulk. The air carried the scents of moisture and verdant growth.

After a time he sighed. "I'm not going to be very good company anymore. Do you mind if we call it a night?"

"Of course not."

He made no move to leave, however, and neither did she.

At length he said, "I guess it's better this happened now rather than on the road. At least no one will be surprised. If there's anyone around for it to matter."

"There'll be plenty of people around," Callie said softly.

He stepped back and braced both hands on the rail. "This is probably what Elhanu's been waiting for. It sure gives everyone a choice. And choosing *is* what the Arena's about, isn't it?"

He studied his boots a minute, then looked up at the trees again. "Gives me one, too: Will I go with what I believe and lose the group, or will I rationalize my way around to doing what Morgan wants?" He snorted and straightened. "Maybe I've been rationalizing all along. Maybe I *am* just using the manual to justify my own cowardice."

"I don't believe that."

Pierce laughed bitterly. "You of all people? You've seen me in action. I'd be dead if not for you."

"And I'd be dead if not for you. So would a lot of other people."

"Things are different now. I'm supposed to be the leader. What if I lose it again out there, with everyone depending on me?"

She watched the treetops' scalloped edges sway in the breeze and said softly, "Isn't it Elhanu we're supposed to depend on? Besides, you're not the same man. And you have the link now."

For a long moment Pierce stared at the pond. Then sighing, he said, "You're right. I'm being an idiot." He turned and stiffened with surprise. "You're shivering! Why didn't you say something?"

Callie insisted she was fine, but he took her back to the dorm anyway, walking her to her door on the third floor.

"Thanks for going with me tonight," he said.

"Hey, it was fun. Even if you did make me dance."

He grinned. "*Especially* because I made you dance."

They stood looking at each other, and his grin faded. His eyes were very blue and solemn beneath the thick lashes. Her heart began to gallop as once more she became aware of how close he was, his face inches from her own, his familiar, pleasantly musky scent making her light-headed.

*He's going to kiss me.*

A wild fear rose up in her. Abruptly, she stepped back and immediately saw the hurt flash across his face. It felt as if a knife had twisted in her chest. She wanted to apologize, to explain—except she had no explanation, and he was scaring her. No, she was scaring herself. This was too much like what happened with Garth.

"Well, thanks for everything," she mumbled, unable to meet his gaze. She touched the lock pad and her door slid open. "See you tomorrow."

"Yeah."

The door slid shut between them.

# CHAPTER

## 18

They were showing videos of Pierce's failings next morning in the rec hall, and the cafeteria buzzed with reaction. Morgan announced he would set out tomorrow, and that all were welcome to come. "But you'd better be ready to *travel!*" he concluded with a laugh.

Everyone cheered.

Sickened by the enthusiasm with which Pierce was being ridiculed, Callie lost her appetite halfway through the breakfast line. No one showed his being tortured, or any of his moments of heroism, just his failures. Worst of all was seeing Meg at Brody's side, spouting abuse with the rest of them.

Callie approached her privately afterward, and they went round and round until Meg suggested Callie's feelings were blinding her. Callie erupted like a land mine, hotly denying the charge and saying something about the pot calling the kettle black. The conversation degenerated from there.

Later when her anger had cooled to stomach-twisting regret, she acknowledged Meg's accusation had hit a sore spot. Last night she'd tossed for hours, tormented by memories of that almost kiss in the hallway, and the look on Pierce's face when she'd stepped away. Sleep, when it came, was filled with dreams of being trapped in various vehicles racing toward destruction. She'd awakened depressed and irritable. Things had only gotten worse as the day progressed.

Callie knew that with her ill-considered words she had destroyed all hope of changing Meg's mind. She stewed about it for a time, then went to lunch early, hoping to avoid the crowd. Pierce had evidently had the same plan, for he sat alone at a window table in the deserted cafeteria. Her first inclination was to pretend she didn't see him—she had no idea what to say to him and wasn't even sure she wanted to try. But when she reached the end of the food line, she knew she couldn't abandon him, not with everything else that was going on.

*Maybe if I treat him as if nothing happened*, she thought as she sidled between the tables, *it'll blow over and we can go back to normal.*

He wore a red flannel shirt, jeans, and hiking boots, and his face was flushed from a morning hike. When she stopped beside his table, he glanced up and wariness leaped into his expression.

"Want some company?" she asked.

He shrugged, his stony mask dropping into place.

"I'm sorry about last night," she said, setting her tray on the table. "I didn't mean to—"

"You needn't apologize." He scraped up the last of his eggs. "I'm the one who overstepped."

She slid into the chair across from him. "I've hurt your feelings."

"Sometimes the truth hurts."

*I shouldn't have come. This is only making things worse.* But stalking away didn't seem like much of an answer either. She broke off a piece of tortilla, scooped up scrambled eggs and salsa, and focused on eating, stealing glimpses of him as she did. He finished his blueberry muffin and leaned back in the chair, gazing out the window as he sipped his coffee. Sunlight streamed onto him, casting long, dramatic shadows off to his side.

A handful of newcomers entered, ostensibly ignoring them, though Callie noticed their furtive glances and quiet comments.

"So," she said finally, scooping up more egg. "Where'd you go this morning?"

"Window Rock." A stiff climb that offered breathtaking views, she knew Window Rock to be one of his favorites.

He did not elaborate, however, so she tried again. "Morgan's leaving tomorrow."

"You going with him?"

"Of course not!"

Finally he met her gaze, his eyes joltingly blue. She thought he would say something, but he only set the cup on his tray and stood. "I better get to work."

"It's your day off. You're supposed to rest."

"I like studying."

She watched him weave between the tables and exit through the glass door, then sat sipping her coffee, feeling grumpier than ever. She needed very much to talk—about Meg, the Morgan crisis, her own confused feelings. Yesterday she would've confided in Pierce. Maybe not about her confused feelings for him, but all the rest. Now that was impossible, and the loss of their comfortable relationship made her want to cry.

More people filtered in, and the noise of conversation rose. Callie had sat there half an hour when Evvi Albion dropped into the seat across from her, licking a strawberry ice cream cone. "Mind if I join you?" she asked.

*Would it matter if I did?*

"Can you believe those videos? What a pack of lies." Ice cream dripped down the back of her hand onto the table. "It's obvious the Tohvani made them up. Pierce would never act like that. He's not that kind of man." She licked the cone, then picked up a napkin to smear the spots around. "I'll bet word comes to leave the day after Morgan goes. And it'll be good riddance, too."

She crumpled the soiled napkin into a ball and left it beside the smear as she pulled another from the dispenser and licked her cone again. More drips splattered the brown Formica, but she didn't notice. "Um, Callie, there's something I've got to ask you—" She licked her cone. "Do you and Pierce, well, like, are you really lovers?" Unheedingly she laid her arm in the ice cream drips.

"We're friends."

Evvi fixed her with round owl eyes. "You're sure."

"Of course." Callie fingered her coffee cup. "Why?"

"Oh, no reason." Finally noticing the ice cream on her sleeve, Evvi daubed at it with the clean napkin while the cone dripped elsewhere.

"You're interested in him yourself!" Callie cried, feigning surprise.

The other girl flushed. "Well, if you're really just friends . . . yeah. I mean . . ." She daubed at her sleeve again. "You're sure, now. Because I wouldn't want to . . . you know."

"We're strictly business," Callie assured her. "If you want to pursue him, be my guest."

Evvi's eyes went wider than ever. "Really?"

"Really."

Crumpling the second napkin, she grinned broadly. "Oh, wow. Thanks, Callie!"

Callie watched Evvi maneuver between the tables, feeling smug. *That should take care of the rumors of romance. Maybe make Pierce feel better, too.*

A burst of laughter drew her attention to a group shoving two tables together nearby, and she decided to leave. Fifteen minutes later she was climbing the trail behind the compound, laden with sketchbooks, watercolor blocks, and paints. One of the many wonderful things about Rimlight was how it provided for its residents. Once she'd discovered the art supplies in her office, she'd begun sketching everything in sight. Whether it was the exceptional clarity of light or the novelty of snow and mountains or the simple freedom of making art for the sake of making it, something had broken loose. This work would be left behind when they departed. It didn't have to win an award, impress a gallery manager, or even bring a sale. It only had to please her, and that not too much. She hadn't had such fun since she was a child, and that had brought a corresponding looseness to her work—and lately, an unexpected authority.

Even more unexpected was how it had been received. Pierce had hung one of her sketches in his office—matting and framing supplies had appeared along with the paper and paints. He'd suggested she hang some pieces in the auditorium's lobby. Others saw them and wanted works for their own rooms, and before she knew it, she was feeling like a real artist.

Today she set up on a familiar windswept knoll and began a large painting of the massive rock thrusting out of the slope above her. She'd often painted this rock, drawn by its creamy contrast against the blue sky, its angularity against the surrounding plumes of grass. As always of late, she let herself go, using a big brush and lots of paint and water.

When she was done, she set it aside to dry and picked up her sketchbook, flipping through the used pages to the back, where she began a new drawing. The image had nagged her since lunch—a figure lounging in a chair under strong light, the cast shadows streaming on a dramatic diagonal. She paid particular attention to the features—features she had studied and drawn so often, they took form effortlessly.

She was so absorbed in memory and distinctions of light and shadow that she didn't hear Mr. Chapman's approach, didn't know he was standing behind her until he spoke.

"That's very good."

She flinched and had to exert conscious effort not to flip the book shut. "Thank you."

He crouched to study it more closely. "I like the way you've put him between the light and dark. Kind of symbolic, don't you think?" She frowned at the sketch, symbolism having been the farthest thing from her mind. "And you've captured his expression perfectly. Pensive, thoughtful—I've seen that look on his face."

Settling on a nearby rock, he unclipped a water bottle from the belt of his gray shorts. "Beautiful day, isn't it?" He took a long drink, using his free hand to hold in place his Tyrolean hat with its long russet-colored feather.

"That it is." She closed the sketchbook and set it on the ground, then dug into her pack for her own bottle. A sudden breeze tousled tendrils of hair about her face.

He waved his bottle at the painting of the rock, propped against an outcropping a few feet away. "That's nice, too. You must have done quite well back on Earth."

"Actually, I was drowning in rejection and paralyzed by a perfectionism that didn't even make good paintings. This year's been good for me."

A gust of wind caught the block, flipping it into the grass. She leaped to rescue it and, when she turned back, was mortified to see the same gust had thrown open the cover of the other book, displaying the images one after the other right before her companion's eyes. Already he was bending to pick it up. She swallowed her protest as he lifted it onto his lap. "These are wonderful. May I look?"

What could she say? He was already looking. "Go ahead. They're pretty rough, and the subject is a bit repetitive. . . ." She trailed off, blushing.

As he paged through the book, she washed her brushes and gathered her things. He took his time, studying each image intently. Finally he handed it back. "You capture the man well."

"Thank you."

"I'm surprised you got him to pose for you. He doesn't seem the type."

"These are mostly from memory."

His white brows arched. "From *memory*?"

*Oh, please, let's change the subject!* Callie stuffed the book under her day pack and tried. "So where are you headed today, Mr. C?"

He leaned back on his rock, rubbing bony knees and gazing about. "I thought I'd catch the sunset at the Window. Get away from all the ruckus." He gestured toward the compound below them. "What they are doing to Mr. Andrews is most distasteful."

"You don't believe the videos?"

He shrugged. "The past is past. Why drag it into the present?" He took off his hat and perched it on his knee. "People just want an excuse to leave."

"And who cares if they humiliate a good man in the process?"

He nodded sadly.

"Meg's leaving, too," Callie blurted, the words taking her by surprise.

Mr. C's brown eyes turned serious.

"We had a fight this morning," Callie went on.

"And that's why she's leaving?"

"No." Callie sighed. "It's just—I don't understand. Pierce wears the circles and bars, he's unlocked most of Rimlight, and he can read the manual better than any of us, but he still studies his head off to make sure he won't lead us astray. How can she—how can any of them—think Morgan's right?"

He fingered the white whiskers under his lip. "People believe what they want to believe, lass. And it isn't always the truth. Sometimes it has nothing to do with the truth."

"That's Meg. She's so dazzled with Brody, I feel like I don't know her." Callie recapped her water bottle. "And she had the gall to say *I* was blinded by feelings."

"For Pierce, you mean?"

Her face warmed. "It's not what she thinks."

"Ahh."

"It's not."

"You don't fill a sketchbook with pictures of someone you don't care about, my dear."

"I find his features artistically interesting, that's all." She slid the bottle into her pack, avoiding his gaze, her heart hammering against her breastbone. What was it about this man that made her see herself so clearly? He'd done it first with her fear of heights, making her acknowledge it didn't really burst out of nowhere but arose from her own thinking. She could control it, he said, by controlling what she chose to think about. And choice was always the issue with him, but choice based on fact—not hopes, not self-delusion, and most of all, not fear.

*And I am afraid of this, aren't I?*

Meg had accused her of scuttling past relationships as soon as they hinted of getting serious because she was afraid of love. Meg had made her mad. Mr. C hadn't even mentioned the matter and somehow led her back to it. But after Garth's betrayal—and her own father's—didn't she have good reason? Besides, it wasn't just fear. . . .

"It's true, Pierce and I work well together," she said at length. "And sometimes it's scary the way we read each other's mind. I admit I enjoy his company. I respect him to death, and I've trusted him with my life more than once. But that's not love."

A corner of his mouth crinkled. "If that's not love, what is?"

She waved a hand. "I'm talking about romantic love. Sparks. Chemistry. Knight-in-shining-armor stuff. I don't feel that with him."

"Doesn't mean you couldn't."

She looked up at him, surprised.

"That stuff is fun," he went on, the breeze ruffling his hair, "but it has no staying power. Respect is what matters. Respect and rapport and integrity. If you have those, the sparks will follow."

He stroked the russet feather in his hat, then met her gaze, brown eyes piercing straight to her soul. "Don't let fear rob you of joy, lass. If you can trust him with your life, why not with your heart?"

She had no answer, but he didn't seem to want one. Instead, he put on his hat, reclipped his bottle to his belt, and stood. "Well, the afternoon's a-waning. Good luck with your painting."

She did no more painting, however. Instead she sat in the sun, smelled the grass, drank in the quiet, and thought. After a while she pulled out the sketchbook and paged through it, conscious of a strange new feeling welling up in her. The breeze whispered about her, caressing her face and making the flowers dance. She sat there until the sun hovered over the distant peaks and a chill crept into the air.

Finally, reluctantly, she shrugged on her pack, gathered up her pads and blocks, and started for the trail—only to freeze, adrenaline washing through her in a hot, prickling wave.

A Watcher stood four feet in front of her, blocking her way and radiating menace. Small crystalline scales covered its body, reflecting the fading light in places, absorbing it in others, so that parts of the creature's form disappeared from time to time. Its eyepits were not holes, but rather black orbs with blacker pupils that reminded her of a shark's eye—soulless and uncaring. She sensed it could devour her in a heartbeat if it chose to, that she was nothing more than prey.

Originally assured the Watchers were harmless voyeurs, she now knew better. They were the Tohvani—brilliant, clever, seductive. And while they couldn't physically touch participants, that did not lessen the threat they posed.

How long had it been standing there? What did it want?

Slowly the creature bent, picked up the sketchbook she hadn't known she'd dropped, and held it out to her. She took it hesitantly, then stooped and retrieved the block as well. Except for returning its arm to its side, the alien never moved. Callie backed away, skirted a rocky outcropping, and stepped onto the trail. The Watcher pivoted, keeping her in sight. Nape hairs prickling, she turned her back to it and descended toward the compound, part of her wanting to bolt, part refusing to give the creature the satisfaction of seeing her panic.

*They're right, you know. He is afraid.* The words formed so clearly in her mind, she thought at first she'd heard them with her ears.

*He's tasted the curtain. Even here he longs for it.*

Her treacherous feet brought her to a stop. The compulsion to turn back pressed her.

*We hold his leash, you see. When we call, he'll come running, all his sheep behind him, right into our hands.*

Her knees wobbled violently, compulsion urging her to turn, to gaze into those bottomless eyes. She hugged her drawing pads to her chest and plugged her ears, finally seeking the link. The creature's laughter echoed in her mind.

*It's a little late for that, Callie. Even if you could find it, you'd still be listening to me. Because part of you isn't so enamored with your sponsor as you'd like to pretend. He put you into this, after all, without your consent. And deep down, you're still angry—still scared to death you won't survive.*

Images tumbled through her mind—cliff-side trails, ripping winds, lavender depths pulling her down, down, down—

"No!" She hurled herself down the trail, not stopping until she reached the compound. Finally, breathless and quivering, she glanced back. It was still there. Shuddering, she stepped within the protective walls, and only then was she released, only then did she realize the full impact of the Watcher's strength. Pierce had sobered them last night with his warnings about the powerful mental pressure Tohvani could wield. She guessed she hadn't believed him—until now.

The worst of it was, the thing was right. Something in her *had* leaped in response, something that still squirmed against what they had done to her—and still feared desperately that she would be like countless others who had tried to cross the Inner Realm and failed, who'd betrayed themselves and the Benefactor and had gone over to the other side, allowing themselves to become the very monsters they'd started out fighting.

Instinctively she went looking for Pierce and found his office door open. The light was on, but no one was there. He wasn't in the library, either. She checked the weight rooms, the dormitory, the big-screen video room, the HTS station, and finally returned to his study. It was as she'd left it—the computer on and the manual open on the desk, blued by the light of the screensaver.

She stepped forward to see what he'd been working on. His notes were cryptic, half of them recorded in the same code as the manual, which she found difficult enough to decipher in print, let alone handwritten. Since nothing indicated where he had gone, she decided to leave him a message.

In the search for something to write on, she found more notes tucked under the manual:

> f.c.= portable rejuvenating energy field; causes profound physio chngs; passage through first gate reverses changes, but desire and vulnerability to seduction remain.
>
> degree of change determined by frequency of exposure
>
> possibility of reversion to original state if expo cut off before too far—what's too far?
>
> p181 "defiled" = physical chg?
>
> p267 anyone who tastes defilement will always crave it
>
> p145 defiled cannot pass through the final portal—what is "defiled"?

Callie stared at the words, feeling as if someone had slugged her in the stomach.

"We hold his leash, you see . . ."

No! Elhanu wouldn't choose him as Guide if he was doomed to surrender to the fire curtain!

Unless Elhanu wasn't as benevolent as she wanted to believe, or there was nothing he could do about it. Doubts leapt up from the floor of her mind like debris in a whirlwind. What if it were all a monstrous deception and—

No. I won't believe that—I mustn't. Callie closed her eyes and pressed her clenched fists against the table. I have no proof for any of this—

And no proof the other way, either—

It's just the Tohvani getting to me. Besides, I have the link—

Which you still can't find with any reliability—

I will in time. And I have the way we were brought here, and this last year, and all the ways he's provided for us—

*But how do you know—*

And here Callie cut off the doubt, refusing to consider it further.

Voices and approaching footsteps penetrated her absorption. She straightened, replaced the papers under the manual, then stepped into the hall, nearly colliding with Pierce and Evvi. As they dodged and apologized she saw from Pierce's expression that something was wrong.

He frowned at her. "What's the matter?"

"I ran into a Watcher. I thought you ought to know." She glanced at Evvi. "What's going on?"

"A Watcher?" Pierce looked down at Evvi. "I had one following me this morning, too."

Evvi smiled at him. "They always come around when something big is about to happen, and I'd say this is pretty big."

Callie frowned, annoyed as much by the smile as by the fact that she was out of the loop.

"We've just come from the armory," Evvi explained. "It's closed."

"Yeah. It closed yesterday. Tuck announced that last night."

"No," Evvi said. "I mean it's all closed. The dispensary, the ranges, everything. Even the obstacle course." She cocked her head. "Don't you get it? It's the signal we've been waiting for."

Callie turned to Pierce for confirmation. He wasn't nearly as delighted as Evvi, and she understood immediately—in spite of the obvious signs, the timing would make it look like he'd caved in to Morgan's demands.

"Better start packing," he said.

# CHAPTER

## 19

One hundred fourteen of the inhabitants of Rimlight left the next morning, following a graveled trade road across the valley and into the mountains. They stayed on that route for a week before Pierce struck off cross-country toward a forbidding barrier of cloud-swathed peaks. Though Morgan protested vigorously, Pierce insisted the manual clearly said to leave the road and head for a canyon called the Devil's Cauldron. There a slit in the rock would access a safe zone where they could rest and restock. When Morgan continued to object, Pierce merely walked away, ending the argument.

Maybe it was the fifty Watchers clinging to the roadside cliffs, or maybe people weren't ready to reject Pierce's leadership outright just yet, or maybe the participants who were reading the manual confirmed the fact that it was pretty clear about the instructions. Whatever the reason, everyone continued to follow Pierce—but not cheerfully. As Callie had predicted, many believed he'd left Rimlight to save face and saw his abandonment of the road as just another attempt to prove his courage.

The increasing signs of mutant presence did not help matters. Along with tracks and warm campfire ashes, they found shriveled, feather-trimmed human hands dangling from tree limbs, a freshly decapitated stag's head set dead center in a pass, and eerie lines of skulls standing guard over lakes and waterholes. Whether these were territorial markings, offerings to the gods, or totems of cursing, no one knew. But they made everyone uneasy.

Pierce said the Trogs wouldn't attack so great a force as themselves, and so far he'd been right. Nevertheless, he routinely chose strategically defensible campsites, always set up the perimeter alarms and electronic fencing, and insisted on backup shifts of flesh-and-blood sentries. Thus far, however, the only things that tried to crash their perimeter had been the ubiquitous mites.

Three weeks out of Rimlight, they stopped for the night beside an ice-fed lake in a glacial moraine overlooking a long, spruce-filled valley. The valley was to have led them to a passage through the spine of lofty, snowcapped peaks blocking access to the south—until they saw the columns of smoke arising throughout it.

Morgan threw a fit, insisting they return to the road at once. Pierce refused. If worst came to worst, they would try a mountain route, but they were not going back. Alarmed and angry, and in defiance of Pierce's command otherwise, Morgan took a party to scout out the mutant camps, apparently thinking additional evidence would change things. Meanwhile the others set up their three-man tents, rigged and readied the alarm system and perimeter shields for later, gathered firewood, and scraped out latrines. In less than an hour, a blanket of domed tents arced across the basin's lower, flatter portion, and cook pots roiled with steam.

When Callie went down to the lake for water, she thought the campsite looked like a geothermal area. Hardly discreet, but Pierce figured the mutants would count them as more of their own, en route to the intertribal religious rites held each summer in this wilderness.

It was nearly dusk, and the lake mirrored the surrounding peaks and sky in a breathtaking fire of pink and peach. In the stillness she could hear the hissing of the cookstoves, the murmur of voices, and occasional laughter from up the hill behind her—a peaceful, quiet moment. But as she squatted on the granite bank and dipped her first bottle into the icy water, a sense of being watched drew her gaze to four Tohvani, pale against a backdrop of dark spruce, on the opposite bank.

Watchers had dogged them in increasing numbers since they'd left Rimlight, and several people had had encounters with them similar to what Callie had experienced. Was their presence tonight just more of the same? Or was it an omen of approaching disaster?

Uneasily she finished filling her bottles, then turned to find Meg on the slope above her. Like everyone else Meg wore the camo-patterned breastplate and belt over a drab olive undershirt and baggy camouflage trousers. The matching helmet hid her black curls. She held a couple of her own bottles, already full, and as Callie met her gaze, her green eyes slid away. They'd not spoken to each other at all during the three-week trek.

"Hullo, Meg."

"Hi." Meg's gaze darted back to Callie's. "How ya doing?"

"Fine."

Again Meg's eyes danced away. Then she drew a breath, as if to nerve herself. "Listen, uh, I, uh . . . well, some of us are going back."

"To Rimlight?"

"To the road." Meg gestured with a sloshing bottle toward the smoke-threaded valley beyond the lake. "If we go marching into that, we'll surely be caught."

"Not if that's the way Elhanu wants us to go."

"Big if."

Callie hugged her water bottles to her chest and said nothing.

"We've passed a lot of natural fire curtains the last few days," Meg went on. "And, well, Brody saw Pierce at one last night." She met Callie's gaze evenly. "Said he just stood and stared at it."

"So?"

"Come on, Cal. With his history he's got no business going near one of those things. If the Watchers get to him"—she held up a hand, stopping Callie's protest—"if they get to him, he'd lead the rest of us into their hands."

Her words were so close to what the Tohvani had said on the hill above Rimlight that Callie shuddered. Unfortunately, she had to admit she'd harbored the same suspicions. Worse, she wasn't close enough to Pierce anymore to know for sure—if one ever knew for sure. "Did Brody see him walk through it?"

"Callie—"

"Being tempted is not giving in. And the manual says we're to go to this Devil's Cauldron."

Meg scowled. "I don't think it says that at all. And I've seen too many vids of Trog prisoners screaming and begging. There's no way I'm committed enough to resist that."

"Well, I guess it's your choice to make."

"Come on, Cal. Be reasonable."

"I am. And if—"

Meg stiffened. Her eyes fixed on something across the lake. Alarmed, Callie turned to find four more Watchers had joined the group on the bank.

"In the trees," Meg whispered. "It wasn't a Watcher."

Callie searched the shadows. All this time, all these miles, and they had yet to be attacked. It couldn't last. Had Morgan stirred up trouble? Carefully, she shifted the bottles to her left arm, felt for her belt's control, pressed it on. She felt the vibration sweep up through her breastplate and into her helmet.

Something was out there. Something dark and evil. Something that wanted to hurt her.

*It's the Watchers*, she assured herself. *Trying to unnerve you. That's all.*

She stood rigidly, watching the trees. Beside her, Meg switched on her own belt.

A stag crashed out of the copse to the right, and Callie jumped so violently she dropped her bottles. The beast bounded across the rose-lit basin, zigzagged up the steep slope, and disappeared over the pass, leaving an eerie silence filled only with the camp stoves' hissing in its wake.

Gradually voices and actions took up again, and Callie finally released her breath, chagrined to find she'd drawn and powered on her SLuB. So had Meg. No doubt the Watchers were having a good laugh. Grimacing, she knelt and fished her bottles from the icy lake.

"We'll leave when Morgan comes back," Meg said as Callie stood. "Please think about coming, okay?"

Callie stared at her. Grim faced, Meg turned and climbed the bank. On the way back to her own tent, Callie detoured by Pierce's, wondering if he was sensing anything unusual. Something had spooked that stag, and it wasn't the Watchers. Animals always ignored them.

Pierce sat with Evvi on a rock near his tent. They were bent over the manual spread across their laps. As Callie approached, Evvi leaned against his shoulder, laying her hand on his back. Annoyed, Callie changed course. Clearly Pierce was relaxed, so either he could no longer sense the Trogs or the stag had spooked at something insignificant.

She found LaTeisha sitting Indian style by their tent eating macaroni casserole out of an aluminum trail cup. "You seen Ev?" she asked as Callie walked up.

"Yeah. Why?"

"She threw this macaroni together and barely stirred it before she lit out. I wondered what was up."

"Pierce is what's up." Callie unhooked her own cup from the front of her pack. "Every waking moment." She straightened, sniffing the air. "What is that *wonderful* smell?"

LaTeisha groaned. "Tuck's beef stroganoff."

"Does he have to spread the smell around like that?" Callie squatted beside the cook pot, where a pan of cheese macaroni and beef sat scorching over the flame. "We oughta make him camp on the other side of the lake."

"Or else cook for all of us."

"Now *there's* an idea." With a grimace Callie slapped gooey yellow pasta into her cup. "Eyugh! Why does she always burn it?"

"She doesn't always. Last night it was hard in the middle, remember?" LaTeisha frowned into her cup, then pulled out a long hair. "I'm getting awfully tired of this." She draped it over a tiny plant. "If I thought she could set up the tent, *I'd* take on the cooking."

"I don't even want to think about her and the tent."

In the last weeks Callie's aversion to Evelyn Albion had blossomed into full-fledged dislike. Not only was Evvi all thumbs and heedless of everything in her periphery, she had launched an all-out pursuit for Pierce's attentions. Every night she sat at his side, draping herself over him, patting his legs and arms and shoulders until Callie had to remove herself to some other part of camp. It wasn't just embarrassing, it was deeply annoying, and she had no idea what to do about it. For days she'd tried to ignore it, but lately she'd had to acknowledge, at least to herself, that she was not merely annoyed. She was hurt. And, Lord help her, she was jealous.

Abruptly the macaroni's scorched, spoiled-cheese taste gagged her.

"I can't eat this." She dumped the stuff on the ground. "Is there any more soup in the bag?"

LaTeisha rummaged through the food sack and drew out two brown packets. While they waited for the water to boil, Callie took out her sketchbook. Today had been another twenty-miler, but after twenty-one days she was getting used to it. Her blisters had healed, and the agony of overused muscles and joints had eased into the simple ache of fatigue. She no longer wondered with every step whether she'd make it to camp without collapsing.

Now she roughed in a sketch of the camp, Whit and Mr. Chapman perched on rocks in front of their tent, with Wendell and Gerry crouched before them eating from the ubiquitous trail cups. Behind them, others gathered in similar circles—eating, washing dishes, cleaning weapons—the perimeter alarm system poles gleaming over all in the fading light waiting for dark—and the return of Morgan's party—to be activated. Her eye caught on a familiar pair not far away. Evvi had her hand on Pierce's shoulder as she whispered into his ear. Frowning, Callie flipped to a clean page and turned to face the shadow-cloaked mountain looming over them.

"Here's your soup." LaTeisha handed Callie her cup. She set it on a rock to cool and returned to sketching.

They didn't have mountains like this around Tucson—bursting out of the tree line and jabbing into the sky. This was all barren slopes and steep, angular planes, thousand-foot drops and bulging overhangs. Callie imagined clinging to that high, almost vertical face, slipping on iced rock, surrounded by mind-boggling space—

She swallowed and made herself start drawing, concentrating on shape and line, on light and shadow and form.

"Found a route up yet?" Mr. C asked, looking over her shoulder.

She chuckled. "Ask Gerry, not me."

"Oh, Gerry's already lined out his choice." He traced along the rock faces she had sketched. "He thinks we could angle across these slopes to get above the cliffs, then head up this chute. After that I'm not sure."

Gerry was now standing over her, too. "We'll decide when we git there." He pointed at the drawing. "But you've skipped some things, Cal. There's a jag here and a drainage here."

"I'm summarizing, Gerry."

"Oh. Anyway, looks like the hardest part's up top."

She twisted round to peer up at them. "You really think we're going up that?"

Mr. Chapman shrugged. "We need to get to the Cauldron. The mutants can't take the heights. Sounds like a solution to me."

"Why do ya think they had a rappellin' cliff back at the base?" Gerry drawled, eyes twinkling. "Looks like an outstanding climb, if you ask me. Can you imagine the view?"

Callie shuddered.

Mr. C patted her shoulder. "You'll do fine, lass."

John strode up, looking peeved. "Well, it's finally happening, just like Pierce said. A group's going back to the road soon as Morg returns."

"Idiots!" Whit rumbled. He sat beside the cookstove he shared with John and Mr. C, cleaning the pan they'd just used. "We'll be lucky if he doesn't bring back a pack of Trogs."

"I can't believe he was stupid enough to go down there," John said.

"Stupid isn't the word," Whit said, dumping the dirty water from his pan. "He can't sense 'em, and he's had no real experience with 'em. What does he think he's gonna do?"

They went on grousing, and Callie returned to her drawing, assuring herself that the mountain route would be okay, that she'd do fine, just like Mr. C said. But she kept remembering that horrible moment on the trail up the Canyon of the Damned when she'd turned and run. This was that canyon turned inside out. Maybe worse.

She was adding the final touches when a sense of malevolent presence hit her so powerfully she dropped her pencil. Her mouth went dry and her heart knocked against her ribs as the sensation swept over her in smothering waves. Everyone around her went silent and still, all of them scanning the gloom-shrouded trees across the lake, and nearer, to the left of camp. The compulsion to run seized her—it didn't matter where, just out, away. Fast. It took all her willpower to calmly stand, step to her pack, and slide the journal inside.

When she straightened, she glanced at Pierce and Evvi. The girl babbled on, focused on the book in her lap, but Pierce sat ramrod straight beside her, staring into the nearer grove of trees.

Suddenly certain that an attack was imminent, Callie snugged up her helmet and reached for her long-barreled SI–42 as LaTeisha did the same. She had just pulled a handful of extra E-cubes from her pack when Morgan and his company raced out of the trees.

"They're right behind us!" he gasped as he reached them.

"What happened?" Pierce strode up with his SI.

"They surprised us. We took a few of 'em down, but another group came to help. We gave 'em the slip for a bit, but I'm sure they're following."

"Get the perimeter shield turned on now," Pierce shouted, starting toward the control box.

"No!" Morgan seized his arm. "There's too many of them. They'll surround us and wait for our energy supplies to give out."

"We'll go over the mountain," Pierce said. "Take it easy. Panicking isn't going to help."

"I'm not panicking," Morgan snarled. "And to blazes with the mountain. There'll just be more of them on the other side. Our only chance is the road." He whirled to address the others, now congregating around them. "Move out, people! Fast—or we're Troggie toys!"

He strode toward the rear of the encampment, where his supporters waited, the crowd parting before him. Silence fell in his wake. He yelled at them again. "You heard me! Get your stupid carcasses moving!"

The people jolted free of their shock. Three-quarters of them ran to their things, tearing down tents and stuffing gear willy-nilly into their packs. The rest milled uneasily, arguing among themselves. Pierce, Whit, and John went to move the perimeter lines inward, and before they were done, Morgan's followers were climbing out of the basin.

Callie and LaTeisha were just setting the final perimeter pole into its relocated socket when a rain of quarrels flew down from the mountainside, zinging by like bullets and bouncing off the granite. One plunged through Ian's breastplate into his heart. As he toppled backward, Callie dove for her SI and rolled behind a knoll.

But the Trogs were well hidden in the rocks, difficult to see, impossible to aim at, and the perimeter lines needed to be on *now*. Crouching, she zigzagged through the tents toward the control box, the twilight flickering bright blue as her companions returned fire. She reached the box a step ahead of Pierce and found it swarming with red mites. As he covered her, she jerked them off with her bare hands, her efficiency compromised by the need to dodge their snapping pincers. Frustrated, she looked around for a stick and spied movement up the hill under the trees just as a line of Trogs burst from the copse. They carried clubs, scythelike blades, and heavy, studded maces.

Pierce stepped in front of her, his steady fire dropping mutants one after the other. It made little difference. He yelled something at her, but she'd already abandoned the box, scrambling sideways, crablike, searching for cover and firing her SI continuously. With her friends screaming on every hand, and with crossbow quarrels plunging into one armored body after another, Callie could hardly control her rising panic. At length she found herself crouched behind a granite hummock, shaking violently and sucking in deep draughts of air as she sought the calm that would enable her to reactivate her belt.

The sense of something bearing down upon her made her glance up just in time. Both her shots hit the attacking mutant, but as she rolled away, she knew she'd missed the kill spot and braced for the inevitable blow to come. Instead, a third beam drilled out of the darkness into its head, and the thing collapsed backward into the gloom.

Another deep breath, and Callie shoved up, firing at the attackers coming in from the flank. Behind her Whit was shouting. Pierce answered from somewhere above. LaTeisha yelled for her to come back down, where a group of them were retreating around the lake.

Callie squinted up the slope where Pierce had gone to ground behind a swell of rock, the flashes of his SI betraying his position. She waved Teish on and raced up the hill but was only halfway to Pierce's position when two figures bore down upon her. Dropping to one knee, she took one out. The other crashed into her, slamming her backward onto the granite and exploding her world into a kaleidoscope of colored starbursts. She glimpsed something dark and smelly bending over her and kicked at what seemed to be its legs. It staggered back when she connected, and then a blue lance shot out of nowhere, blinding her yet again. When she regained her sight, the Trog was gone.

She staggered upright, her helmet falling away in two pieces, as another score of mutants burst from the trees. Blue fire peppered them, originating from Pierce's granite hummock. Hunching her shoulders, she sprinted toward him, quarrels zipping by her, and was still ten feet away when the outcropping exploded, slamming her to the ground and raining rock upon her.

She lay gasping, pain stabbing her chest, a red haze filling her head. It took longer to recover this time, and when she finally pushed herself up, a fog of dust hung in the air and three lifeless figures sprawled on the slope above her. What had happened? Had the Trogs acquired grenades?

Someone fired from a position upslope, aiming at the mutant flank as it engaged with Morgan's group, now spread out along the rim to capitalize on higher ground. In daylight, they might have prevailed, but Trogs saw better at night than humans—even Changed humans—a fact Morgan evidently realized, for the flashes marking SI positions were retreating rapidly over the brow of the pass.

Callie's immediate periphery, meanwhile, had quieted. She ran to where Pierce hunkered on the slope behind a grassy hillock. As she dropped belly down beside him, his SI flashed, illuminating the dark form of a mutant as it crumpled to the ground. A few of its fellows ransacked the camp below and searched for the wounded, who would become their prisoners.

Pierce tugged her backward. Quietly they retreated up the hill to a grove of wind-sculpted spruce. In the pass above the basin, Morgan's combat line had disappeared, but occasional distant flashes told Callie the fight continued.

Abruptly four Trogs clambered over the ruined rock in front of them. Silhouetted against the pale backdrop of the basin and lake, they milled around, grunting and laughing. Hidden beneath the prickly evergreen, Callie felt Pierce's fingers bite into her arm, warning her not to move. As the mutants poked and prodded at her dead—or stunned—companions, she barely breathed. Two of them picked up bodies and went back down, but the other pair turned to the mountain, facing Pierce and Callie. They seemed to look right through the twisted branches into Callie's eyes. Any minute she expected them to lift their crossbows and shoot, or else charge up the hill and rip them from their hiding place. One stepped toward them, muttering.

Then rough voices from down in the camp claimed their attention. They turned, one yelled a reply, and both went back down.

The sounds of their passage soon silenced, but Callie knew better than to be impatient. Moments dragged by. Her forearm ached where Pierce still gripped it. A branch poked into her hip. Her hand beneath the SI had gone to sleep, and her head throbbed where it had struck the granite. No more flickerings showed in the pass now. Trogs moved around them occasionally, the ground thumping with their passage, their guttural voices echoing in the night, but more and more, the sounds grew distant and finally dwindled to silence.

At length Pierce released her arm, told her to stay put, and eased out of their sanctuary. He returned with a pack, two parkas, and a new helmet. Wordlessly she slipped on the helmet, then the parka. Pierce donned the pack and they set off. Darting from one group of spruce to the next, they ascended the mountain. Eventually they ran out of trees, and with the starlight reflecting brightly off the pale granite surrounding them, Callie felt horribly exposed. But if the Trogs were aware of them, they didn't appear to be following.

According to the manual, mutants avoided heights. Not only was the mountain daylight too strong for their sensitive eyes, but their rapid metabolisms and increased brain tissue also made them susceptible to severe bouts of altitude sickness in the thin air. Perhaps the risk was not worth the capture of just two people. Especially when they had so many on lower ground to chase.

Callie's headache worsened, but they couldn't stop to dig out the med kit, so she endured, counting her steps as she trudged after Pierce. They crossed a small moraine, passed a row of stunted spruce clinging to the banks of a lakelet, then climbed across more granite domes. Through it all, the wind never died, varying from a stiff breeze to a gale that nearly plucked them off the mountain.

At length Pierce suggested they go to ground. Though Callie's heart pounded from exertion and her breath burned in her throat, her fingers and toes were numb from the cold. Even with the parka, the thought of huddling under some rock did not appeal to her. If they kept walking, at least they'd stay warm.

"But the slope's getting steeper," Pierce said. "We need to see where we're going or we'll fall."

She acquiesced without further protest.

They found a hollow under a fallen slab that was roomy enough for them and the pack. Animals had nested here in the past. One corner was lined with a mattress of dried plants—thick stems with fuzzy leaves, wide-bladed grasses, and an occasional dried flower. The insulation extended along the back of the space, some of it stuffed into the chinks where the slab rested on support rocks.

Pierce left, and Callie stripped off the stiff, rubbery breastplate of her armor, then redonned the parka, shivering from just that brief exposure. She stood the neoprenelike plate in the opening to block the wind, braced it with her helmet, then dug out the med kit, muttering heartfelt blessings on her companion when she found it. She gulped down two red pain pills as he returned with a pan of snow. While he set up the stove, she went to relieve herself.

When she returned he had the field lamp lit, the water boiling, and was dumping chocolate pudding mix into their aluminum cups. As she maneuvered into the back of the chamber, he set up the pack frame and his own breastplate in the doorway alongside hers. Already the hollow was much warmer than the outside air.

He'd unrolled the single sleeping bag he'd been able to salvage from the campsite and one of the light plastic sheets that were the Arena's version of space blankets, reserving the latter for himself and leaving the bag for Callie. She considered arguing with him about it, but only briefly. She'd probably be colder than he, anyway, and the plastic sheet was plenty warm.

As she settled in her corner, Pierce poured hot water into the cup and handed it to her with a spoon, then served himself. She would have prepared tea, but the chocolate was better—hot, thick, and fragrant. They ate without speaking and when they finished he made the tea, too, pouring it into the used cups. As she sipped the calming brew he removed the pot from the stove, turned the dial to its lowest setting, and laid the device on its side. Its red coil pointed toward them, radiating heat directly into their faces. It felt wonderful, but Callie disliked the glowing head's proximity to the dried grass. As she drew breath to mention it, he pushed the grass aside.

Now, with nothing left to do, he sat staring at the coil. The pain pills had done their job. Callie's headache had eased to an ignorable background throb. She'd been eyeing a gash on Pierce's forehead ever since they'd stopped, and now she said, "That cut on your face is still bleeding. You want me to look at it?"

He touched the trickling blood, frowning as if he hadn't noticed it. "I'll do it."

"It might need stitches. At least a butterfly bandage."

"I'll take care of it."

He dug through the pack and pulled out a coil of turquoise rope, then the med kit and a sock. As he set up a pan lid for a mirror and dipped the sock in some of the warm water, Callie said, "That's a climbing rope."

"Yeah." He surveyed his face in the lid, tilted his head to see the cut, and daubed at the blood.

"So we're not going back down to the valley?"

"You have a problem with that?"

"What if I did?"

He stopped what he was doing and studied his reflection. "Then I guess we'd have to go down." Annoyance colored his voice. "Is that what you want to do?"

"You think there's a way over this mountain?"

"Yeah."

She hugged her knees, frowning. "What does the map say?"

"You tell me. You drew it."

"I don't remember. We were planning to go down the valley."

"Well, unfortunately, memory's all we've got." He set the sock aside and grabbed a tube of antibiotic.

She gaped at him. "You don't have the map?"

"They ransacked the camp, remember? And it wasn't like I had a lot of time."

"You don't have a map and you're planning to. . . ?"

He put the tube down and finally looked at her. "You want to go back?" Anger, frustration, and a vein of despair warred in his expression. "You think I don't know what I'm doing now, too?"

"No! I mean, yes. I mean—I thought you did. But now—everything's changed."

"You're darned right everything's changed." Savagely he tore open one of the butterfly bandages and turned back to his reflection in the pan lid. "I don't think it could be much more changed. Or much worse."

He taped the cut with two butterflies, then sat looking into the pan lid. After a time he sighed. "So what do you want to do?"

"Go back. Find some of the others. They didn't all go with Morgan."

"Is that objectivity or fear speaking?"

"We don't have the map, Pierce. We don't know if we can get over this mountain."

"I think we can. In fact, I think this might be the way we were supposed to come all along. The map wouldn't have helped anyway. There wasn't much about the mountains. Besides the Trogs won't be bothering us up—"

"You don't know that for sure."

"Well, there's a lot less of them up here than down there." He packed up the med kit.

"But what if there are others who got away? Whit or Teish."

He did not answer at first, but when he did, the angry edge had left his voice. "How would we know which way they went? I'd never be able to track them over all this rock. Besides we're supposed to go to the Cauldron, and they know where it is as well as we do."

"What if they've been captured?"

He stared at the kit in his hands for a long time before he spoke. "Then they'll be brought to the Cauldron, and we can rescue them there."

"The Cauldron? You think the Trogs are—"

"The Tohvani don't want us to reach that slit. Of course it will be guarded." He slid the med kit into the pack. "In the morning I'll go up with the binoculars and see if I can see anyone, any sign. Then we can—"

A deep thumping reverberated through the ground, cutting him off. They both went rigid, listening to the wind's thin whine.

Slowly Pierce reached for his SLuB while Callie turned off the field lamp, leaving only the red glow of the stove's coil. The thumping came again, rapid, rhythmic, as of running steps. With their daylight-sensitive eyes, if the mutants were going to do any tracking, now would be the time for it.

A chill skipped up Callie's spine, as if she had brushed up against something cold and evil. Again she felt that sense of malevolence, stalking her. She glanced at Pierce. "Can you. . . ?" she whispered. "Are they. . . ?"

He nodded and turned off the stove. The red light faded to darkness. The coil ticked erratically. Outside, the wind keened, and down the mountain the thumping sounded again, definitely coming closer.

# CHAPTER

## 20

They sat very still, listening. A fine sweat broke out on Callie's brow. The SLuB thrummed against her palm. She reached down to check her belt, then recalled she had taken it off. An eruption of snorts and thundering footfalls made them both flinch, and the sounds halted right outside their hideaway.

"Mountain goats," Pierce whispered.

As the musky smell enveloped them she knew he was right. Goats were the only mountain creatures big enough to make those kinds of noises. But they sounded spooked, and she gripped her weapon tightly, knowing her first shot would have to be a good one if the Trogs found their hiding spot.

Gradually, though, the sense of malevolent presence faded. Outside, the goats grunted and rustled as if bedding down. Finally, Pierce put his SLuB aside and pulled the plastic blanket around him. "They're gone," he said. "The goats must have obliterated our scent trail."

"So we should be thankful for this stench?"

A smile twitched his lips as he settled. "I'd bathe in it if I thought it would keep the Trogs away."

———

Morning dawned cold and foggy. Though Callie's headache had

abated, the back of her skull was tender, and she was stiff and sore and bruised in a hundred places. They breakfasted on hot tea and cold biscuits, peering out of their hollow at the seven white goats that had saved them last night. There were five adults and two kids, their coats long and silken, the adults sporting short pearlescent horns. Against the foggy background, they seemed as insubstantial as wraiths and flew up the slopes in alarm when Callie and Pierce stepped out among them.

With visibility cut to thirty feet, Pierce scrapped his plan to use the binoculars, but he went down the slope a bit to look around and returned with confirmation that Trogs had indeed been in the area last night. After his news, Callie was not so eager to go back to the valley, especially when they couldn't see anything.

They followed a game trail over the ridge and along the trickling runoff of yet another alpine lake. An oblong of reflective pewter, the lake was bounded by steep granite walls on one side and a forty-five-degree slope of crusted snow on the other. Pierce tackled the snowy slope without hesitation, following a path cut by the goats, which were now traveling ahead of them just at the edge of sight. The path wound some fifty feet above the lake, and Callie could not help observing that a fall would take her right into the icy water, where the shock of cold would drive the breath from her lungs and paralyze her limbs. Her legs trembled, and she blanked the image before fear unhinged her. *One step at a time*, she told herself. *One solid step at a time.*

Carefully she kicked into the snow, testing each purchase before she committed to it. Pierce was sitting at the field's edge when she caught up, and though she was ready to rest, he sprang up as soon as she joined him and started off again. Sighing, she followed.

A basin curved behind the lake, ringed by ragged peaks on all but one side. At the gap, a crescent of snow arced beneath a low cliff, which the goats were already climbing. Some had stopped to watch, as if waiting for the humans to catch up. By the time Callie and Pierce reached the cliff base, the mists had closed to a ten-foot pocket of visibility that Callie welcomed heartily. If she had to climb, she'd rather not see what lay below her.

A sharp crack from behind brought them both around.

"Was that rocks hitting together?" Pierce murmured.

"I heard a thumping," she said, glancing at him. "More goats, maybe?"

"Could be."

But as they continued, she realized if the Trogs were going to track anyone into the heights by day, these foggy conditions were ideal.

The cliff was rougher than it appeared. They climbed swiftly, angling left across its face, then right, forced at the end to use hands and feet to scramble over the top. Callie made it, but by then she was shaking, dismayed to find herself dogged by the old crippling fear.

They stood in yet another grassy basin. The goats were still ahead of them, lingering, as always, at the edge of sight. Leaning his SI against a rock, Pierce stripped off the pack, pulled out the water bottles, and sat down. Callie settled gratefully beside him. Her headache was back, and she was short of breath, so she figured they must be pretty high. Maybe ten thousand feet. Maybe more.

Pierce sat rigidly, scanning the mists. Presently he got up, SI in hand. "I'm gonna look around," he said. "Stay put."

She glanced at the weapon and nodded, content to rest her still-trembling muscles. As he disappeared into the fog she realized things were going from bad to worse. On a clear day, they could've studied the peaks from a distance and picked out the most promising route. Today they didn't have that option. Leaning back against the rock, she sipped from the bottle. Fear, her most faithful companion, clawed at the pit of her stomach. She tried to push it away with imaginings of an easy route opening before them, sunshine and flowers on every side, all going well—

But how could she, when the landscape was anything but? This was not the world of *The Sound of Music*. It was a barren, inhospitable moonscape, just rock upon rock and the impenetrable mist. They were going to get into trouble. She knew it. And though she'd supposedly conquered her fear at Rimlight, she saw now she hadn't—not totally. Perhaps she never would. *I'm going to freak. And then where will we be?*

*Stop it.* She closed her eyes and clenched her fists. *Stop thinking like this. How can you be such a wimp?*

*Easy. I've had lots of practice. All my life. If it was too scary, I just didn't do it.*

*Well, now you don't have that choice.*

A thudding, clacking sound came up from the cliff they'd just ascended, and she stiffened, her hand closing on the SI. As she slowly stood and turned she imagined Trogs climbing the same rocks she'd just scaled.

The soft thumps of approaching footsteps jerked her around, weapon leveled. But it was only Pierce. "You ready to go?" he asked, picking up the pack.

"Did you hear that noise from down the cliff?"

"Yeah." He buckled the hip belt and turned away.

"Do you have any idea where we're going?" Callie asked.

"Not really. But I figure the goats do."

"The goats? They could be leading us anywhere. Even around in circles."

"Or to better pasture on the other side of the mountain." He glanced back at her. "I don't believe it's a coincidence we've found them. And they do seem to be leading us."

The thought had crossed her mind. "You think Elhanu sent them?"

"Yes. I do."

They crossed the basin and ascended a talus-covered slope. As they climbed, the shattered rock gave way in localized slides so that each step took them back almost as far as they went forward. The mist thickened. Numbness crept into Callie's extremities. She gave thanks there was no wind but wondered if it would snow. The small ice fields and the crescents and commas of crusted snow testified that flurries would not be impossible, even in summer. How ironic if, after all her concern about falling, she succumbed to exposure.

The talus was eventually replaced by five-foot chunks of rock even more difficult to traverse, and her limbs soon shook with exhaustion. She gasped almost fruitlessly in the thin air, blood all the while pounding in her temples, a painful timpani of altitude sickness. At length they rounded a slope and found a ragged cliff looming out of the clouds. On a ledge a goat perched bright against the dark rock. As they watched, it jumped from perch to perch, scaling the wall as if gravity did not exist, until it disappeared into the mist above.

Pierce started after it at once, but Callie hesitated, staring up at the wall, swallowing the thickening in her throat. *You can do this*, she told herself. *You can*. But already the black things flickered at the edges of her vision, and she had an unnerving recollection of preparing to climb the vertical bank of the Fire River and saying much the same thing.

Composed of ragged ranks of layered rock whose slant pitched inward toward the mountain, the cliff was more of a steep hike than a climb. Following the goats in a diagonal route across its face, they were able to ascend at first with shoulders to the wall, not even needing to use their hands. With the mist holding them close, Callie kept her focus on the rocks and climbed carefully, steadily, confidence rising within her.

Then the breeze kicked up, and light followed shadow as the clouds shredded, reformed, and shredded again. They came to a ledge sprinkled with goat droppings. It curved around a ragged granite face, then dipped under an overhang that forced Callie onto her hands and knees. Her confidence waned. The clouds continued to pull back. From the corner of her eye she glimpsed yawning spaces out beyond the rock's edge and angled her face more toward the wall. Her heart pounded with exertion and altitude and rising anxiety. She felt shaky and light-headed. Again and again she was swept with the sensation that something clung just beneath the ledge, preparing to leap up and grab her.

Pierce waited for her on a good-sized bulge. Reluctantly, one hand holding to the rock, she climbed beside him, keeping her gaze turned down on—

Nothing. Just beyond Pierce's booted feet the ledge sheered off into dizzying space and vertical rock faces, plunging so violently she couldn't see bottom, though she stood almost at the edge. She gasped as with a roar, the demons hurtled out of that space, flapping darkly around her and filling her with the familiar compulsion to hurl herself over the edge. Whimpering, she dropped onto hands and knees and inched back to the overhang where the ledge was wider, and where, shaking and weeping, she huddled and clung to the rock.

"Callie?"

She flinched as Pierce touched her shoulder.

"Callie, we can't stay here."

"I can't do it," she moaned into the rock.

"You must."

"No."

He gripped her shoulders to pull her up, but she fought him, squealing and struggling to break free until he wrapped his arms around her and held her tightly. After a few minutes she stopped struggling and clung to him instead, sobbing hysterically. He held her and said nothing, and after a time the hysteria gave way to exhaustion. She fell silent, sniffing, still shaking, pressing her face against him so she wouldn't have to see that they were still on this awful cliff.

Presently he said, "I can't carry you up this."

"Then leave me."

His arms tightened about her. "Can't do that, either."

After a moment he pushed her gently away, cradled her face in his palms. "There are Trogs behind us, Callie. We either have to keep on or go back and fight. Is that what you want to do? Go back?"

If they went back, he would very likely die—or be caught—trying to protect her.

She swallowed. "You really think there *is* a way up?"

"I do." His hands dropped back to her shoulders. "Elhanu has promised to lead us through this, Cal. We've got to trust him."

Her fingers tightened on his breastplate, and she shook her head. "It's hard."

"You can do it if you want to."

"I do want to! It's just that when I look at that drop—"

"Don't look at it, then. Look at him instead."

"Look at—"

"Use the link."

The link. Of course.

She pressed her forehead to his chest and shut her eyes, seeking the elusive connection, trying to remember all she knew of the one who made the link possible. It was like groping down a dark hallway in a strange house. And then, as if a door had opened to the outside, light and strength and blessed calm poured into her. Suddenly she knew with startling clarity that they had been led here, to this time, this place, this situation, so that she could face this choice. Would she trust him? Would she use what she had been given?

Over and over Pierce had reminded them the battle was waged against thoughts and feelings more than material things. And so it was. She could let herself be carried away by visions of the terrible things that might happen, or she could willfully concentrate on the fact that she carried Elhanu's power in her body, that he had promised to deliver her from this place and was capable of keeping that promise, and that she had climbed a cliff wall like this at least fifty times at Rimlight and knew very well what to do.

Decision hardened within her. She lifted her head and managed a half smile. "Okay. I'm ready."

The expression that flashed across his face was one of relief and something more. Something deeper and more profound than simple satisfaction. It vanished before she could identify it, and then he was squeezing her shoulders and stepping back. "I'll get the rope."

He shrugged off the pack, slinging it around to brace it on his knee. After he helped her drink some water, he tied them together at the waist, putting about twenty feet of slack between them, and they started off again. Callie concentrated fiercely on the link with Elhanu, on the granite wall beside her, on the rocks beneath her feet, and on Pierce, who never got so far ahead that he couldn't help her if she needed it. More than once she was impressed by the strength with which he hauled her over the rough spots. Rock by rock, bulge by bulge, they inched up the cliff's face.

The light shifted constantly, brightening, dimming, brightening again as the mists drew in and out. A breeze gusted around her, tickling her face with tendrils of her hair, wafting the tangy musk of the goats. Occasionally she spied dark grapelike clusters of droppings caught in the cracks and took comfort in knowing the animals had preceded her. Then the path petered out completely and the slope went vertical. Pierce pounded a piton into the rock, hooked on a carabiner, and looped the rope through it. They were anchored now. Nothing to fear.

She started up with inward trembling—and a rising sense of hope. The vertical portion was only about ten feet, and still hardly more than Gerry's steep hike. Not bad at all. Something she'd done many times before. Light brightened and blue sky peeked through the clouds in promise.

Then a quarrel smacked the cliff wall to her right. She gasped as she watched it skitter down the gray rock beside her. Its descent dragged her eyes downward to the great bowl yawning below her. She gulped and pulled her gaze back up, but her arms and legs were already shaking.

*It's just a feeling. I will not give in to it. The arrows can't hurt me as long as my belt's on.* But was it? She let go with her right hand and pressed the switch to be sure. Breathing deeply, she dove inward, seeking again the precious window of strength and calm.

The rope tugged on her waist, breaking her concentration. Pierce had reached the top and now peered back at her. "Come on, Callie," he said, his voice low and urgent. "You've got to hurry."

She reached for the next handhold, pulled herself up, and groped for a foothold. Her legs shook deep in the calves. Her shoulders burned. The rope slackened, then tightened again. She heard a distant howl and refused to look down, but the skin between her shoulder blades crept in anticipation of being shot.

She reached for another handhold, clinging to Elhanu's inner presence as the rope went slack again. Her knee banged into a rocky knob, and she lurched for balance, rough stone tearing at her fingertips. Clenching her teeth to still their chattering, she lifted her leg again, out and over this time, gaining purchase on the knob. Abruptly the rope tightened, jerking her upward. She lost the knob, the ledge, everything. Gasping and flailing, she was jerked up again as another quarrel bounced off the rock beside her. She grabbed an out-thrust shelf and hauled herself up. Two more quarrels hit somewhere close below her as she scrambled over the edge and into Pierce.

They landed in a heap, gained their feet in unison, and, still bound by the rope, sprinted across the mist-bound flat. Only after they had rounded the base of another slope did they stop for breath.

"I can't believe they came this far," Pierce gasped, gulping water and wiping his mouth with his sleeve. Rope burns lashed his wrists and the backs of his hands.

"Do you think they'll follow us up that cliff?" Callie asked.

"I don't know. They looked like they were hurting, so maybe not. On the other hand—"

"Maybe we could sit up here and pick them off as they come over."

He shook his head. "If the clouds close in we might miss them. I doubt they'll go much farther. Like I said—they're hurting." He stood, pulled her to her feet, untied the rope from her waist, and they started off.

They had not gone far when the rocky corridor they were following widened into yet another basin. The goats ranged up ahead and then disappeared into the mist on their left. Pierce stopped abruptly. Callie dodged around him, adrenaline firing for fear the mutants had cut them off.

But there was nothing there.

*Wait.* She stepped closer and saw a thin film of light stretching between neighboring rock faces ahead, smears of green and blue undulating across it like a misplaced jellyfish. Dark ink churned between the colors, spilling in and out of the spaces, and a high-pitched hum rode the air, alternately masked and revealed by the errant breeze.

It was a natural fire curtain, hypnotic and vaguely repellent, yet generating an undeniable allure. It pulled at her, promising respite from the headache, the aching muscles, and the rising nausea of altitude sickness. She turned away, shivering.

Beside her Pierce stepped tentatively toward it. He had balled his fists and clenched his teeth, and the expression on his face made her heart quail.

"Pierce?"

He shuddered and turned off the trail. "We'll go around it. That's why the goats were over there, I guess."

The goat tracks led across a wide, snow-crusted shelf to another valley where Pierce called a rest. Callie fished two pain pills from the med kit and washed them down with a gulp of water, wishing she could wash away the memory of the fire curtain as easily. Even now a perverse longing stirred in her.

Pierce sat with his SI across his lap, staring back the way they'd come. After a few minutes, he got up. "I'm going back."

She frowned at him. "But you said—"

"They may be sick, but if they get through that curtain we're in big trouble."

"I'll come, too, then."

"They'll be less likely to spot me alone," he said. "You stay here and rest."

"But—"

He was already gone.

She scowled after him. "I'm not going to stay here," she muttered and stood—

A little too quickly. The world tilted, her head felt about to split, and she nearly retched. By the time she'd recovered, Pierce was long gone, and all she could do was wait, trying not to dwell on the way he'd stared at the fire curtain.

She sat there a long time. The pain pills finally kicked in, and she was again thinking about going back, when a low boom rolled between the peaks, shaking the ground and spreading the goats like buckshot up the hillside. Peering nervously at the opening across the valley, she picked up her SI and switched it on. Shortly Pierce emerged from the clouds, carrying two bags of E-cubes.

"I got them both," he said when he joined her. He smelled oddly sweet, almost like actone.

"Don't they usually travel in threes?"

"The third one probably couldn't make it up the last cliff." He set aside the bags and his SI and slung on the pack.

"What if it's just slow? Once it gets to the curtain—"

"The curtain's gone."

"What?"

"I walked through it with the belt on." He gestured at his waist. "The field acts like a reflector. Sends the waves back to their source and burns it out."

"You walked through the fire curtain?"

"I blew it up, Callie. Didn't you hear the boom?"

She regarded him doubtfully, battling unpleasant suspicions. "Why didn't you do that before, when we were both there?"

"I didn't think of it. But I wouldn't have tried it with you around, anyway. I wasn't sure what would happen. If it worked, I didn't know how big the explosion might be. Come on. I think we're almost to the end."

They descended a narrow chute past a chain of lakelets, silver hued in the misty light. All around them rock lay against rock, dark and ragged, accented with dirty ice fields. Callie wondered how Pierce could say they were almost to the end. Even if they were over the top, who knew what horrors of descent lay before them?

But the slope was not as steep as it had been on the other side, and when they found their first bunch of yellow columbines, she felt a glimmer of hope. Skirting a granite dome, they descended a slope covered with short, thick grass and more yellow flowers and, at long last, stepped out of the mist. Callie staggered to a stop, unable to believe her eyes.

The mountainside tumbled away from her feet, grassy flanks dotted with white humps of granite rolling down to a wide, spruce-blanketed valley. A great crack of a canyon ran up its middle, sections of the green river at its heart gleaming here and there. From this vantage she could even see the tawny cliffs that marked the Gap—just as she had drawn them on the map. Beyond those lay the Devil's Cauldron itself.

Pierce stopped just behind her. "Wow."

She glanced over both their shoulders at the wall of mist swirling around the peaks, then again at the spectacular vista before them. Relief flooded her, and on its heels, pure joy. With a whoop she turned and threw her arms around his neck, hugging him so hard he staggered. Laughing, she released him and ran down the slope to the sun and the grass and the bobbing wild flowers. There she stripped off her helmet to let the breeze run through her hair, spinning with a delight so intense it brought tears to her eyes. She tripped and went down laughing, then lay flat on her back reveling in the sun's warmth and the blue sky and the life that bounced and shone and smelled so pungent around her.

Pierce came more slowly, eventually dropping the pack and stripping off his own helmet as well. He pulled out the water bottles, handing her one as he settled beside her. It was a perfect spot for lunch, so they got out the ration bars and Snak-Paks.

Pink and lavender flowers danced around them and the scudding clouds played the land with roving shafts of sunlight. Her headache all but gone, her stomach no longer churning, Callie again stretched out on the slope and closed her eyes. She'd made it! She'd come over the mountain and survived. The link was still open, and now she channeled gratitude and newfound appreciation through it. What a remarkable gift she'd been given!

She opened her eyes and grinned at the sky, then tucked a hand beneath her head and regarded her companion. Pierce lay beside her, propped on one elbow as he surveyed the landscape and drank from his bottle. The wind lifted the hair off his brow, reminding her of the day they had come through the Gate, how he'd looked like a captain at the prow of his ship—strong, wise, capable.

"We've come a long way, haven't we?" she said.

He glanced at her, smiling. "Yeah."

Sweat had kinked his hair and plastered it to the back of his head, and his jaw wore a few days' growth of beard, but to her he had never looked better. A wave of deep affection swept her. Impulsively she drew her hand from beneath her head and laid it on his shoulder. "Whatever would I do without you?"

He went rigid, a strange light flickering in his eyes. Then the mask fell into place. "You'd manage." He squinted out over the valley.

"No," she said softly. "I wouldn't." Beneath her palm, his shoulder trembled.

"You're tougher than you think." Water sloshed in the bottle as he lifted it to his lips.

"You saw how it was for me back there."

"I saw you overcome it, too." He capped the bottle and laid it down between them. "And it's not me you can't do without, it's Elhanu."

"Maybe. But if you hadn't been there to make me think of that, I'd be dead. I'm such a wimp. I always have been. Afraid of everything—heights, people . . . my own feelings." She stroked his shoulder with her thumb, felt hard muscle beneath the knitted undershirt. Then she sighed. "Oh, Pierce, I'm sorry I hurt you that night. I was scared. I didn't know what to do or even what I was feeling."

He turned to snare her gaze, his eyes that deep turquoise that made her breath catch. "And do you now?"

She felt poised at the edge of another precipice. Her heart raced. Blood pounded in her ears. "I think so."

The wind whipped up around them, setting the wild flowers to frenzied bobbing. He smoothed the dancing tendrils of hair back from her face, fingers trailing moth light along her cheek and jaw. His thumb paused under her chin, and then he leaned down and kissed her.

She felt as if she'd exploded into a thousand pieces of light that whirled up and up into the vast cloud-scudded sky. When he drew away, she was spellbound with wonder. His eyes traveled over her face, his fingers caressing the contours of her lips and again pressing back the dancing tendrils of hair. She touched the grizzle on his jaw, the brown curl by his ear, then drew him to her, drinking him in, shivering with feelings she'd never dreamed she had.

She heard the rattle of stones a second before he broke away. Pushing up onto his knees, Pierce reached for his SI and stared up the hill, while she lay frozen, watching him closely.

"Someone's coming," he murmured.

"The third mutant?"

"Maybe. Come on." He rolled back onto his feet, gave her a hand up, and they were off as if nothing had changed.

# CHAPTER

## 21

They hurried downhill, taking cover behind a granite hump. *It's going to smell us,* Callie thought. *The goats are gone, and we've been here almost an hour. But there's only one, and it's sick. Pierce destroyed the fire curtain—*

A horrible suspicion knifed her. What if he hadn't?

He laid a hand on her arm. She looked up to find him listening intently, and instantly she heard distant whoops and shouts that didn't sound like Trogs. Warily, she peered around the rock. On the slope above, a group of helmeted figures in camouflage danced and cavorted at the mist's edge.

"Well, how about that?" Pierce murmured, stepping into view.

"They must have been right behind us."

One of the figures pointed at them, and more whoops rode the wind. Evvi reached them first, long hair flying. She flung herself onto Pierce and spun him around. Then the others were there—Tuck, Gerry, Wendell, and Mr. Chapman—slapping their backs and exclaiming with delight.

They'd seen the rocks explode, Tuck explained, and thought Pierce and Callie were dead. "We split and ran. They got Whit and LaTeisha and John—"

"Killed or captured?" Pierce asked.

"Captured."

A moment of silence ensued as they pondered the awful signifi-cance, then Tuck continued. "Anyway, few as we were, we could only go up and hope they wouldn't follow."

"We wandered around for quite a while," Evvi added, "trying to figure out the best way to go. When we saw three Trogs ahead of us, Gerry figured there must be a route, so we followed them."

"Then we heard the explosion," Tuck continued, pulling off his helmet and combing freckled fingers through his auburn hair. "When we got to the top and found them dead—two with clean head shots— and that blasted-out crater, I'll tell you the backs of our necks crawled. I guess you picked 'em off. Did you make the crater, too?"

Pierce nodded. "You say all three were dead?"

Tuck replaced his helmet. "Yeah. I think the altitude got to the one. What I can't understand is what they were doing up here. They had to know the air would kill them."

"There was a fire curtain there." Pierce braced the butt of the SI on his hip. "I blew it up."

Tuck cocked a brow at him. "What'd you use? A howitzer?"

So Pierce explained to them about the belt.

"You were right in the middle of it, and you didn't get hurt?" Evvi asked, her brown eyes wide.

"My ears rang for a while."

Gerry edged in front of her. "What I'd like to know is, how you found your way over that pass."

"The goats led us over." Pierce squinted up the mountainside. "You must've scared them off."

"*Goats?*" Tuck pulled a peanut butter ration bar from his pocket and unwrapped it.

"They could've been over the mountain in an hour," Pierce explained. "Instead, they took their time, making sure we followed. I think Elhanu sent them."

The others considered this in silence. Tuck started eating his bar, and Gerry said, "Well, it was a great route. I was sure there was no way over that thing without some serious rope and piton work." He grinned at Callie. "Outstandin' job, Cal. I am impressed."

Evvi was bent over, struggling with the zipper on her pack. "Me too. I nearly came unglued myself on that one cliff."

Callie smiled at Pierce. "I had help." Abruptly all those newly discovered feelings welled up in her, and for a moment she was back in his arms again, tasting his kisses—

"Well," Gerry drawled, jarring her back to the present, "I'd say you're cured of acrophobia."

"Indeed," Mr. C chimed in, squeezing her shoulder. His dark eyes understood as no one else's. And then he flicked a knowing smile at Pierce, as if he understood what had happened there as well. Was she that transparent?

Evvi's zipper finally gave way and she fell to the ground with an *oof*, then pulled out her water bottle. A rations wrapper skittered away. Callie stomped it and put it in her pocket. Evvi never noticed, pulling out lunch things and chattering about their trip as the others settled around her.

Their break didn't last long. By dusk they were well below the tree line, and though they had seen no Trogs, the smoke rising from innumerable points throughout the valley confirmed the mutants' presence. They built a lean-to, warming it with a tiny fire over which Tuck made a meal of two grouse they'd shot earlier in the day.

After dinner Pierce and Callie went out to a rocky bluff to glass the valley below. The air lay still and quiet. Long shadows striped the tumbled forest at their feet, and here and there the river gleamed between tree-cloaked promontories. They stood in the shelter of several pines and passed the binoculars back and forth, discussing the best route for tomorrow. Two bags of E-cubes wouldn't go far given the number of Trogs in the valley, so they wanted as little enemy contact as possible.

Finally the decisions were made and the binoculars put away, yet still they lingered, ostensibly admiring the sunset. It *was* breathtaking, but Callie barely noticed. Although Pierce had spoken privately to Evvi, and the news had clearly hurt her, he'd been so coolly professional toward Callie since the others had joined them, she feared he'd come to regret his actions. Hoping for reassurance from him once they were alone, she'd gotten nothing and ached now to ask him about it. Except she didn't know how, and was, in the end, afraid to. Her anxiety had risen to a fever pitch when his fingers brushed her temple and smoothed the hair behind her ear. When she turned, he was looking down at her, his eyes green in the golden light.

"Was what happened on that hillside today real?" he murmured. "Or did I imagine it?"

The anxiety drowned in a flood of relief. "If you did, I must've imagined it, too."

He took her into his arms and kissed her. It was a long, gentle embrace, and when he pulled away, she was so full of emotion she thought she would burst.

"I have wanted this ..." he breathed, "dreamed of this for so long. ...." He kissed along the edge of her jaw and down her neck. Electric thrills radiated from his touch, weakening her knees so that she clung to him giddily. "And just when I decide there's no chance of ever having it, here it is." His lips found hers again.

He was hard and lean and smelled of sweat and pine and smoke, and all of a sudden she fiercely resented the spongy double layer of breastplates that stood between them. This was so different from the way it had been with Garth. It was so right. So real. With Garth there had been a crazy sensuality that had swept her away, a trumpeting of her body's need that almost blotted out the protests of her mind. This was the opposite. Her mind knew and appreciated all that Pierce was, all that he meant to her, and her body responded to that appreciation with a firestorm of desire that made what happened with Garth seem like nothing. In that moment she believed if he had asked she'd have given him anything he wanted. But he didn't ask.

Instead he pulled away with a shudder and relaxed his embrace, holding her gently now, chin against her forehead. "I hope I'm not dreaming," he whispered.

She drew back to regard him. His face was flushed, his eyes shining, his feelings for once transparent. She smiled. "You were so distant after the others joined us, I was afraid you'd changed your mind."

"I didn't trust myself. I am supposed to be leading these people. And I wasn't sure you hadn't changed *your* mind."

"Not likely." She touched his whiskered cheek, his brow, brushed back the wing of hair that fell over it—saw the pair of butterfly closures on his forehead.

She fingered them, frowning. "This cut has already healed."

He went very still. The stone mask dropped into place. Suddenly she was as frightened as she had been at any time during the last two days.

He touched the small bandages, then dropped his hand and stepped out of her embrace.

The world heaved under her feet. She couldn't breathe—had to force the words from her throat. "Did you go through that curtain before you destroyed it?"

He turned to the gloom-filled valley, spangled with firelights, and said nothing.

She went around to face him, grabbing both his arms. "Pierce? Please. Tell me you didn't."

He wouldn't answer her.

"Oh no! Why?"

"I . . . wanted it," he said softly.

She stared at him, feeling as if some great wave had slapped through her, washing away all emotion, all thought, leaving her an empty shell. Light flickered at the edge of her vision, and everything got far away. Her knees wobbled, and she would have fallen if he hadn't caught her.

Easing her to the ground, he knelt beside her. "I know it was wrong," he said tightly. "I knew it the minute I did it. But it was a small one. A natural one. The effects aren't as great—"

"Don't try to make it less than it was. If it was smaller, its allure was less, too."

He let go of her, dropped his hands into his lap.

"How could you do this?" she cried. "You of all people—you know better than any of us!" Her voice shook. "Elhanu changed you, healed you. But now—how could you do this to yourself? To me?"

"To you?"

"Make me fall in love with you, just so I can watch you turn into one of those things!"

"I am not going to turn into one of those things."

"No? What are you going to do when we come to a big one?" She wiped the tears from her face, then hugged herself miserably.

"Callie, I won't do it again."

"How can you expect me to believe that?"

He pressed his lips together. A crease formed between his brows, but he said nothing. After a moment he got up and walked away.

Callie sat for a long time, inwardly railing at him, at herself for letting him go back alone when she knew his temptation. She should have insisted he take her. And now . . .

When she returned to camp, she sought him out. "Does this mean you can't go through the portal?" she asked.

He shook his head. "One time isn't enough."

"One time."

"I told you, Callie. I won't do it again."

Never had she wanted so much to believe him. Never had she been more afraid she couldn't.

*"We hold his leash, you see."*

————————

Late in the afternoon, four days later, a well-torn riverside trail led them into the Devil's Cauldron. Switchbacking alongside the river as it plunged down a narrow chute, they proceeded with great caution, Tuck and Pierce leapfrogging on point, with Wendell and Gerry covering the rear, and the others watching the group's flanks. Having already encountered five bands of Trogs, they were excruciatingly aware of the potential for disaster, and with woodsmoke hanging blue in the trees, they knew they were close.

Nevertheless, it was a surprise when they rounded a rocky curtain and found the Cauldron gaping before them. Its sheer walls embraced a broad meadow shaped like an uneven hourglass, the larger bowl closest. At its waist, on the left, a graceful arch leapt from the cliff, just as the manual had described. Directly beneath that arch, cut into the wall where the stream curved around a rocky spit, lay the passage to their Safehaven, still out of sight from this vantage.

As Pierce had predicted, the Trogs had set up camp in front of it, denying all hope of easy access. Their leather teepees, lean-tos, and stolen dome tents filled the meadow beneath a haze of smoke. A few mutants lay sprawled on the ground, apparently sleeping, and more squatted in groups, talking or playing games. Here and there others stoked the fires and tended cook pots in preparation for the approaching night. At the midst of it all stood a massive, antlerlike fire curtain, its heavy main shafts looming some thirty feet high, curved toward each other at the top, with secondary tines branching off at intervals. Gleaming pale blue, each shaft was a good five feet in diameter at the base. Waist-high power boxes stood to one side, cloaked, like everything else, in blue dust. Farther away, a large wooden pen held prisoners.

Though the device was clearly turned off, Callie could still feel its aura, as if residual energies lingered. It appalled her how powerfully it conjured the memory of her encounter with its smaller cousin. She could almost see the undulating swirls of color, feel that warmth and sense of promise. . . .

She shook her head, breaking free. Pierce stood beside her, white faced and rigid, transfixed, until his gaze shifted to hers. His jaw tightened, and he glanced at the others. They were all going through the same thing.

On his signal they returned to the top of the chute, where they left the trail and ascended the side of the ravine to hold quiet conference. Pierce wanted to wait till morning, but Gerry protested they could be discovered at any moment. Or the weather could change, or a thousand other things could go wrong.

"And they've got Whit and the others," Callie added, her eyes on Pierce. "If we don't go tonight—"

"If we go now," he said firmly, "we'll end up prisoners ourselves. There are too many of them, too fresh out of the curtain. We'd use up all our E-cubes, and they'd still get us." He braced the butt of his SI against his hip. "In the morning they'll be nearly unconscious. We can slip through and free the others, then."

"But if they put them through the curtain—" Callie began.

"It'll have worn off by the time we reach the portal."

She frowned at him.

"We might as well throw our weapons aside and surrender if we go down there now."

Finally agreeing that he was right, the band found a wooded hollow in which to settle. With the possibility of a new group of Trogs coming down the trail at any time, dinner was limited to cold ration bars and water, and conversation stuck to necessities. They huddled against trees and rocks in their parkas and helmets, and everyone kept his armor on, his SI at hand, his SLuB holster unbuttoned.

Callie drew first watch and stationed herself on a rock below the hollow, the dark wooded slope sheering down before her. Overhead the sky faded from lavender to dusky blue as the crickets started up. Behind her, someone was already snoring. Probably Pierce. He was still the only person she knew who could fall asleep in a matter of minutes, no matter what the danger.

On the trail below, thudding footfalls approached, accompanied by various creaks and cracks, and once, a curse and a cry of pain. She listened tensely, but the sounds passed by without incident and faded, lost in the crickets' symphony. Continuously she scanned the darkness, pulling out the rough verticals that were trees, the pale humps of rocks. Her belt's energy field, amplified and integrated by helmet and breastplate, not only protected her from being shot, it extended her range of visible light—at both ends of the spectrum. With it on she could tolerate light that would normally blind her, could see Aggillon and Tohvani manifestations that unenhanced eyes would miss, and enjoyed a significantly improved level of night vision.

A sound drew her eye to the left—it was Pierce shifting onto his side. She could see his face with its week's growth of beard and placid brow. He'd made peace days ago with his failure at the fire curtain, but she still struggled with it. Of course, it was none of her business. It was Elhanu he'd offended, Elhanu he answered to. And since he was still alive, still wore the circles and bars, and had even used the belt immediately after his failure to destroy the curtain that had beguiled him, she had to conclude Elhanu had forgiven him. And if he had, how could she not?

She had tried—really tried. Except . . . somehow she hadn't been able to return to that place of giddy warmth she'd known on the mountainside. Instead she'd been cool toward him, unfailingly professional, and without conspicuously avoiding him, managed never to end up alone with him. He'd borne her reaction stoically, patiently, saying nothing. But though she knew she was hurting him—again—she couldn't seem to do anything about it.

Stars blanketed the night sky when the voices in the Cauldron rose to a dull roar. That, plus a high-pitched tone that stabbed deep in her ears and buzzed over her skin, told her the Trogs had turned on the fire curtain. The screams started soon after. Some were from the Trogs— savage vocalizations of strength and power and pleasure. But then came the wails of their victims, betrayed by the high-pitched edge of hysteria and the fade-out into ragged breathlessness.

Callie tried not to think about her friends, but it grew increasingly difficult. Doubt assailed her like a cold wind snatching at the shutters of her soul, rattling the door, gusting down the chimney. What if Pierce was mistaken after all and they *were* in the wrong place? What if they should have left earlier? What if there was no passage or it was blocked? What if he was unwittingly being drawn here by his craving for the fire curtain? What if it wasn't unwitting at all but a deliberate conspiracy?

The night air carried a stench of burning flesh, the screams raking her nerves as the pestering doubts interwove with nightmare visions of her friends' torture. She pushed the images away, but they returned again and again. This was what awaited them if they were caught tomorrow. Perhaps she could use her weapon on herself before it came to that. A head shot would kill her just as certainly as it killed a mutant, wouldn't it?

But Elhanu had forbidden suicide as a means of exit from the Arena. And in the heat of battle her shot might go wild. . . .

Pierce rolled over, moaning, and a new concern seized her. What if he had a nightmare? What if he started one of those screaming fits?

She swallowed, grimly put the notion aside, and flipped on her belt again. As it purred back to life she set herself to find and focus on the link within, wishing she dared close her eyes.

Her breath caught and she stiffened, hands tightening on her SI. Something had moved. There. A stealthy form glided from one tree to another, melting into the darkness. Her heart drummed against her chest. Her hands ached from the intensity of her grip. Around her the crickets droned on, and the distant snap of a branch echoed through the night.

Moments dragged by.

She was about to exhale when she saw it again, lurking behind a tree ten yards downhill—a lean, pale-skinned form, naked despite the chill. Tohvani. Its eyepits were blacker than shadow, and they pierced right into her, snatching up her mind.

They were doomed. All of them. No one had ever penetrated the full congregation of Trogs. Only those who found the meadow empty could pass. Pierce had made a mistake, and they would pay. Mocking laughter sounded in her soul, then silenced with a cold wrenching as the creature vanished, leaving her gasping. Then something dropped onto her shoulder, and she lurched violently before she realized it was Mr. C come to take the next watch.

"Sorry," he whispered as he settled beside her. "Didn't mean to startle you. What's up?"

"Just another Watcher."

"Ah." He peered into the darkness. The number of Watchers had tripled over the last few days. "Did it speak to you?"

"Not directly." But all those crazy fears had not been of her own making. It had used seeds from her thinking, yes, but they were magnified, embellished, saturated with emotion. Callie switched on her belt again, the vibration spreading warm comfort up her torso. Somehow she had to learn to keep it on longer. Preferably before tomorrow.

"It'll be easier," Mr. C said, "once you actually start." His white beard glowed in the gloom.

"If I could just turn off my mind as easily as I turn off the belt. I don't know how I'm going to sleep tonight."

"There's always the link. And exhaustion is a powerful soporific."

"I don't feel tired at all."

"But you are." He patted her shoulder. "You'll make it tomorrow, lass. Your heart's in the right place, and I have every confidence in you."

She flushed with pleased surprise and gratitude. Even through the parka, his hand warmed her shoulder. Then, snorting, she drew her feet under her. "You'd think differently if you could see the wartorn battlefields of my mind. Good night, Mr. C."

She joined the others and had just gotten comfortable when an ear-piercing wail arose from the valley. Guilt whipped at her, though she knew she could do nothing tonight. Whoever it was, she prayed they would hold on, that Elhanu would protect them. Her friends had the link within them, too, after all.

Folding her arms across her chest, she exhaled, searching for that blessed contact herself, and found it almost at once. As its quiet assurance spilled into her soul her doubts subsided. She relaxed, snuggling into the comfort, aware of a curious warmth in her shoulder where Mr. C had rested his hand. It radiated down her arm, across her chest, and up her neck, bringing with it an oily lethargy. Her eyelids drooped, her muscles sagged, her breathing slowed, and despite her earlier protestations, despite the awful noise, which was oddly distant now, she slept.

# CHAPTER

## 22

They split up the next morning. Gerry set off along the Cauldron's rim with Pierce's turquoise climbing rope looped across his chest and six ceramic carabiners clinking on his belt. He would circle around and rappel down the cliff, hopefully undetected, to find the slit and direct the others when they got there. He would also lay down covering fire if needed.

The rest of them descended the trail, stopping at their first closeup view of the Trogs' camp. As Pierce had predicted, the mutants sprawled everywhere, sleeping off the night's reveling. Around them, untended fires had smoldered to ash. Threads of smoke rose to join the blue pall overhead. Except for a couple of half-dozing sentries, nothing moved.

"Look at all the Watchers," Dell whispered over Callie's shoulder.

They clung to the Cauldron walls, gathered on the spit, stood in the trees and the water, and slunk throughout the fallen mutants. There were hundreds of them, and their presence was at once heartening and disturbing. This was most certainly a test, but one the Tohvani didn't want them to pass. Would they alert their mutant servants? Could they?

Pierce's gaze slid over them one by one—Tuck, Dell, Evvi, Mr. Chapman, and finally, Callie. He hesitated, as if he wanted to say something, then broke eye contact, drew a long breath and expelled it. "All right. Let's do it."

They eluded the inattentive sentries easily and spread out as they pressed toward the camp's heart. Trogs lay everywhere, snoring vigorously, and the air reeked of liquor and urine and smoke, the stench worsening as the morning warmed. It was the most unnerving experience Callie had ever endured, not only because she was so visible—and so *small*—but because with every step she thumped and clinked and squeaked, and some of those steps took her directly over a mutant's leg or hand. The fact that none were armed offered little comfort. This close they wouldn't need weapons. Even the SI on automatic wouldn't stop all of them. But she couldn't worry about that or her belt wouldn't work.

She turned it on. Again.

By now they were deep into the camp, well past the point of no return. She dodged a fallen mutant, slipped under a line of drying hides and around a skin teepee, and stopped in horror. Directly ahead, a stout wooden rack stood in the shade of a huge birch. On it hung a row of human bodies, clearly—

Grimly she tore her gaze away, fighting sudden dizziness. She was breathing a mile a minute and vomit clawed the back of her throat. She swallowed hard, drew in a deep shuddering breath, and hurried on, trying not to focus on the horror she passed. A Watcher's laughter invaded her mind, drawing her attention back to where it stood among the bodies on the rack, enjoying her discomfort.

Distracted, she blundered into a pile of bloodied pans and rags and fell headlong in a clatter of metal. For a moment she lay gasping, stars pinwheeling across her vision, choking on the fear of discovery. Nearby, a mutant gagged, then went on snoring. She leaped up and hurried on, sweat hot and slick under her armpits. Her stomach hurt from the tension, and every time she checked her belt, she had to switch it back on. She kept trying to find the link, but there were too many distractions and no way could she stop and close her eyes.

The fire-curtain poles towered over her like the antlers of some monstrous beast, its ghostly emanations promising succor from the filth, relief from the tension and fear. The tents stood closer together here, the walkways occluded by bodies.

Then the pen loomed ahead, a lattice of roughly hewn poles twelve feet high lashed together with a top grating. Pierce melted the gate chain with his SLuB, and they stepped inside. The prisoners—bloodied, battered, and almost naked—clung to one another, regarding the intruders warily.

Whit, Teish, John, and, incredibly, Ian sat together on the right side. Behind them sat another familiar group—Karl, Jesse, Anna, and Brody Jaramillo, all Morgan supporters. They all still had their clothes, now filthy and tattered, and though they appeared unharmed, there was no doubt Ian—since Callie had seen an arrow pierce his chest—had been put through the curtain.

Whit gained his feet. Beside him, John blinked furiously, his earring glinting in the shadow. "Pierce?" he said. "Is that you?" He was up now, too, hurrying toward them, disbelief warring with hope. "Man, we thought you were dead! How did you get here?"

"Came over the mountain. Can you walk?"

"Yeah. But some of these others can't."

"We haven't been able to see the slit," Whit said. The Trogs had taken his patch, exposing the shriveled socket of his lost eye.

"It's there." Pierce turned to the others in the pen, explaining, "There's an escape passage in the cliff across the river. We'll take you there."

Gaunt, pain-wracked faces gaped at him. Some people whimpered and drew away, but a few got up.

"Come on, folks," Whit said. "Hop to."

"NO!" A huge bare-chested man burst out of the group. "You're lying," he yelled, eyes rolling wildly. "You only want to—"

Pierce shot him through the heart. As he crumpled to the ground, Callie was not the only one to turn in horror.

"He'll be fine," Pierce said. "He's healing already."

And so he was. As they watched, his skin glowed yellow-green, and the hole stopped bleeding, then drew closed.

"He's more mutant than human," Pierce said. "He'd only try to hinder us." He looked at the others wearily. "You're free to come or stay, as you wish."

As he strode from the pen, some of the prisoners shook free of their paralysis. They rose and stumbled toward the gate, voices lifting in soft exclamations of wonder until Whit's rough command silenced them. Of the thirty captives, sixteen chose to go. Five were so far gone they were unable to choose and thus were brought along by their fellows, and the remaining nine were too terrified to move. Once they saw they were being left, however, they began to scream and bolted from the pen, blundering among the tents, stumbling over the sleeping mutants.

Without the prisoners, the rescuers might have made it to the cleft anyway, but their rescuees were injured, weak, and disoriented. They were only halfway to the river when a roar from behind signaled trouble. The first flight of quarrels came shortly thereafter, pelting the ground around them. Callie saw one bounce off Dell's shoulder just ahead, repelled by the force of his armor. Beside him another slid through a skin tent. From somewhere to her right she heard Pierce yell for them to scatter.

She needed no second urging. Fortunately the only mutants yet awake were behind them. Those through which she careened were only beginning to stir. Another flight of quarrels rained upon her. She jumped a prostrate Trog, wove between two tents, and saw the cliff face looming ahead. The front-runners were already disappearing over the high bank along the river. One of the captives ran ahead of her, twisting and dodging. A quarrel appeared, as if by magic, in the middle of his back, hurling him forward to flop facedown beside a mutant.

Horror and fear rose up in Callie's chest. She quenched them both, sought the link, and slapped on the belt just in time. Something slammed into her back, knocking her headlong into a tent. Dazed and gasping, pain radiating from her left shoulder, all she could think was that she was down, and panic nearly claimed her.

Desperately, painfully, she sucked air and groped for her belt. It was off again, but she might have just done that. And there was no blood. She decided it must have been a deflection. Sometimes the force of the blow could knock one down even if the quarrel was prevented from penetrating.

Something stirred beneath her, galvanizing her to action. She pushed up, seized her SI, and stumbled out of the tent, shaking away the dizziness. Then on the riverbank ahead, a mound of rock exploded, the boom reverberating across the valley. Clearly, Inner Realm Trogs had more than crossbows at their disposal.

Mutants were rousing around her now, still groggy enough for her to elude them before they reacted, but gaining their senses all too rapidly. A pair of giants lurched into her path, and she ducked around a tent. But they cut her off, closing in. She shot them both as three newcomers closed from the right. She jerked the SI around, but they fell before she fired. Somebody on the bank ahead was helping.

Racing into the opening, she was hit by another quarrel at the bank's edge. The blow hurled her down the slope in a rolling, bouncing tumble that ended in the river. Its icy chill shocked away the pain and brought her senses back. She staggered up coughing and dripping, her SI lost. People scrambled onto the opposite bank, aswirl in dust. Figures crouched behind rocks, and the blue-purple spurts of the SIs flashed there and there and there. Others splashed across the river past her. Someone called for her to hurry. As she slogged across the water, a high-pitched whine sliced the tumult and a chair-sized rock at the base of the talus slope began to jump around. She stopped in amazement and watched as it exploded, a wave of hurtling shards flinging her backward into the river. She came up sputtering as gravel banged hard upon her helmet and splashed the water like rain. Staggering onto the bank, she scrambled up the slipping talus under a withering rain of arrows, taking two more hits before she managed to fling herself behind a boulder. Whit crouched there, too, surrounded by expended pink E-cubes. Someone must have fallen for him to have a weapon. He wore no armor, and his dark skin was gray with dust and streaked with sweat and blood.

Drawing her SLuB, Callie peered around the boulder. A three-man rear guard stood on the opposite bank, their body armor and camos blending with the mottled earth. Beyond them Trogs fell on every hand, but for every one that fell, two more staggered upright in the rear. Worse, the rest of the camp had finally organized, two groups now closing rapidly on the defenders' flanks. A few more minutes and the trio on the bank would be cut off.

Apparently they saw that, for one by one they raced across the river to take up new positions among the boulders. The last was starting across when another rock exploded somewhere behind Callie, pelting them all with fragments.

"Where's that coming from?" she asked Whit as he fired.

"I don't know," he growled. "Why don't you get to the slit? You can't do a thing with that SLuB."

He was right, but she didn't want to leave. Not yet. "Come on, you guys!" she heard Ian yell from behind. "They're trying to close the opening!"

"Get out, Cal," Whit said, firing over the rock.

She ignored him, watching as the last rear guardsman joined his comrades on her side of the river and they scrambled up the slope. She moved aside to make room as Pierce and Gerry dove in beside them, ejecting E-cubes and slapping in new ones as Whit told them what was happening.

"I can't pinpoint the weapon," he said.

"They're doing it telepathically," Pierce said. And then Callie remembered: The fire curtain produced more than physical mutations—there were mental ones as well. Some mutants could levitate objects, create fire—or cause stones to blow up.

As if in confirmation, another rock exploded, and a whole slab slid free of the cliff wall, crashing down mere yards away from them.

Gerry yelled, "We can't stay here!"

Two more rocks burst simultaneously to either side of them.

"He'll get tired," Pierce said. "This won't last much longer."

"Neither will we."

"I think I know which one it is." Pierce laid the barrel of his SI across the rock. "I'll see if I can take him out. Callie, get out of here. I can't concentrate, and you're not accomplishing a thing."

He bent over his weapon, taking aim. Beside him, Gerry and Whit started firing. Already the mutant frontline was spilling down the face of the bank, climbing over the fallen bodies of their comrades without hesitation.

Suddenly Pierce pushed away from the rock, grabbed Callie's arm, and shoved her toward the cliff wall. "Get *out* of here!"

Another boulder exploded, and they hunkered down, shielding faces and fronts. As the thunder faded, Callie ran.

She hadn't gone ten steps before a quarrel slammed her to the ground. She came to, struggling to drag air into her lungs and spitting dirt. Pain knifed her chest as she staggered upright, uncertain in the dust where the slit was. And then another explosion ripped out of the rock behind her, the concussion hurling her into the dirt again, battering her with a deluge of rocks and gravel.

# CHAPTER

## 23

Someone yanked Callie up by the arm. As she tried to get her sluggish legs under her, she was shoved through a narrow opening, her helmet clunking the wall, rough rock rasping her shoulder. As the impetus from behind stopped, she staggered toward the dim light ahead and came out in a chamber with twenty-foot ceilings and fire-blackened walls. It smelled of sweat and blood and something foul. Field lamps stood at various spots, casting ghostly illumination throughout the room, as well as the one adjoining it. Across from her, a milk white river of rock, streaked with red crystal, flowed from ceiling to floor. A passage led off beyond it.

People had congregated in the second chamber, four of them laid out on blankets and parkas, six more clustered nearby, moaning. One man's foot had been smashed to a bloody pulp. Wendell had a quarrel in his rear, and Brody had one in his thigh, which John was in the process of removing. Evvi lolled against the wall behind them, dead eyed, blood trickling ominously from her ears. LaTeisha and one of the women they'd rescued were working on a man who was the source of an awful sucking sound, his chest working grotesquely as he labored to breathe.

John called Callie to help him with Brody, instructing her to hold the gauze padding in place while he wound a bandage around the man's leg.

Brody's handsome face was scratched, his dark hair was coated with dust, and he smelled of sweat and faded aftershave. Beneath the shadow of his beard, his jaw muscles rippled over clenched teeth. Still he managed a sneer for her. "I thought this was supposed to be a Safehaven."

Callie glanced around. He was right—it wasn't what she'd expected. "There's probably a door somewhere." She eyed him again hesitantly. "Do you know what happened to Meg?"

He hissed as John tied off the bandage, shaking his head. "I think she got away with Morg." John handed him a pair of pain pills and a cup of water. "She was one of the first to go. I was keeping up the rear." He tossed the pills into his mouth and washed them down with the water.

A series of thunderous explosions rocked the cave, the ground, the air. Dust and rocks cascaded from the ceiling as a new chorus of screams began. But the ceiling held. The dust settled. The rumblings faded.

Tuck emerged through the slit, Whit following closely with a body draped over one shoulder. Gerry barreled in behind them, and he and Tuck turned back to cover the opening. Whit carried his burden to where LaTeisha was finishing with the chest injury and laid it down.

Suddenly everything but that form faded from Callie's awareness. "No," she moaned. "Oh, please, no!"

Pierce was laid out on his side, his back to Callie, a crossbow quarrel sticking out of it. The way LaTeisha dropped what she was doing and knelt beside him slew any hope that his injuries weren't serious. By the time Callie reached him, Teish was slicing through the shoulder straps of his armor to remove the breastplate, and Whit was unfastening its Velcro sides.

"What happened?" LaTeisha asked as Whit lifted the front away. Though there was little blood, Pierce's skin gleamed an unhealthy gray.

"Rocks blew right beside him," Whit said. "Threw him into the cliff like a rag doll."

"There's probably internal injuries, then." She lifted away his undershirt, revealing the quarrel's head protruding from his chest. Blood streaked the skin around it. "And he's going into shock. Okay, we'll cut off the back and pull it through."

Swaying with nausea, Callie averted her eyes. Her hands hurt from clenching each other.

After Teish removed the back of the shaft, Whit pulled the quarrel through Pierce's chest, blood puddling the ground beneath it. Muttering about the filth in which they worked, LaTeisha applied gauze pads and strips of torn undershirt to the wound.

"Here, roll him onto his back—"

"Where's the Safehaven?" Whit asked.

"Ian's searching for a passage now," LaTeisha said. "Oh, look at this—busted ribs. And maybe a ruptured spleen. He needs a hospital."

Pierce coughed, and bright blood foamed over his lip. Callie turned and fled, bouncing off Ian as he came around the flowstone curtain.

"The passage!" she said, grabbing his arms. "Did you find it?"

"No. There doesn't—"

"Then we have to keep searching!"

"Callie, there isn't any passage."

She gaped at him.

"There are only three rooms here," he said, waving a big rawboned hand. "They're all dead ends."

"That can't be."

But it was. Callie examined all three passages herself. Two were obvious dead ends. The third led into a crawlway that accessed a room behind the main chamber. Gerry was already there, in the process of conducting his own search.

Their field lamps cast bright circles around them, sluing off a ceiling hung with ranks of short flowstone draperies and glistening nets of red-orange crystals. To the left, tiny blue-green box crystals encrusted an entire wall, but at the top of a talus slope ahead, the light bounced off flat ochre rock. A dank mineral smell tainted the air.

"The manual said something about the Devil's Window and the Blood of Sacrifice," she said.

"Well, if the arch is the Devil's Window," Gerry drawled, hands on his hips, "we're under it." He looked around. "There's a breeze in here. Feel it? Must be another opening."

"Could that be the Blood?" She spotlighted the red crystals on the ceiling.

"Where's the door?"

She swept the room again with her lamp.

"Maybe we have to ask," Gerry suggested.

But their request only faded into silence. No device glowed in the wall, no door opened, not even the air stirred. She clenched her teeth against the scream trying to rip out of her throat and said, "Maybe we missed something in the other passages. Or maybe we should try asking there."

But though she went back again, and again after that, nothing had changed. There was still no device, no door, no way to get through. When she returned to the main chamber, Pierce had regained consciousness. As she knelt beside him he tried a smile—the effect was ghastly.

"You're not dead," he whispered.

"No."

"I thought you were." His voice rasped like dry leaves. He seemed distant and distracted. "My belt went off. . . ." He lay listless and horribly gray, a vacant gleam in his eyes. "I guess you didn't find the passage?"

She brushed hair back from his bloodstained face, desperate to touch him. His skin was cold, clammy. "No."

Disappointment flitted across his face and vanished as if forgotten.

She told him about the red crystals in the central room. "I'm thinking that could be the Blood of Sacrifice. Remember that passage in the manual?"

He swallowed. "I'm thirsty."

Catching her lip between her teeth, she went to get him some water. LaTeisha stopped her on the way back. "He can't have that, Cal. He's bleeding internally. If you give him—" She glanced at Pierce, then at the men by the slit, and sighed deeply. "Never mind. You might as well make him as comfortable as you can."

She went back to stitching up a gashed arm. Callie stared after her, cold to the core. By the time she got back to Pierce, she was shaking. It was all she could do to lift the vessel to his lips and let him sip.

The water revived him. He wanted more, but she refused. After that he grew restless, his gaze shifting around the room. He reached for her arm, his grip weak and so very cold. "Did you find the passage?"

"Not yet." She felt brittle, unreal, as if this were a very bad dream from which she would soon awaken.

"The Door of Hope," he quoted, "lies beneath the Devil's Window, where the water of life mingles with the Blood of Sacrifice. . . ." He coughed and that bright foamy blood flecked his lips. She wiped it away with her fingers, rubbed them on her pants leg.

"I shouldn't have walked through the curtain," he said. "That's why this happened. My belt was off. If your belt's off, you can't see."

She squeezed his hand.

He smiled. "You know, for not being able to die in this world, this sure is uncomfortable."

"Don't talk like that. You're not going to die."

"Don't worry. They'll send someone else."

"I don't *want* anyone else!"

His eyes fixed upon her gravely. His bloodied hand touched her cheek, fell to her shoulder, and slid down her arm. "Do you have your key?"

"Of course."

"Well, then—" He swallowed and his eyes wandered away. "You should open the door."

"We don't know where it is."

"He who has eyes to see . . ." His voice dropped to a whisper. ". . . let him see . . ."

"There's nothing here."

"It's here." His hand fell to his side, and he faded before her, his eyes half closing, his breathing so shallow that for a moment she feared he was dead.

Gerry returned with her to the central chamber, and they searched every inch of it. Nothing. She ended up back at the wall atop the talus slope, where she pulled out her key and touched the smooth surface— here, and here, and here. Still nothing. She asked again and was reduced in the end to tearful pleading.

Gerry stood by silently, his lamp aimed at the floor.

"If Pierce was here," she said, "I'm sure *he'd* see something—"

"There's no way we can bring him through that crawlway, Cal. Not in the shape he's in."

"No." It occurred to her that even if they found the passage, they wouldn't get him through it in time to save his life.

Her stomach churned. *Don't think about that.*

She swept the beam slowly across the chamber again, searched the yellow wall beside her for indication of an opening. Finally she turned her focus inward, seeking the link, but her thoughts kept straying to images of Pierce lying gray-faced on the floor, and to the horrible notion that they'd been mistaken, or tricked, that there was no Safehaven.

No, there had to be something, something important that she was missing.

As she turned toward the exit, the sense of being watched prickled up her spine. Realizing with a start that Gerry had left unnoticed, she hesitantly flashed the lamp left and right—and spied a Tohvani, standing at the base of the talus slope about twenty feet away. It did not flinch or blink in the light but just stood there, staring at her. Was this proof the door was here? Was the creature waiting to see if she could find it? Mocking her because she hadn't?

Anger erupted. Though she had been watched by these creatures since her first day in the Arena, she never got used to it, and she hated it now more than ever. Those cold, empty eyes, so devoid of expression, so . . . so superior. It was their disdainful attitude, more than their appearance, which made them seem so alien.

She turned her back on it, feeling for cracks in the wall again.

*We can't help what we look like. He won't let us appear any other way.*

She froze.

*We're as much victims as you are. He's the one who runs things, after all.*

She should leave now.

*Makes you wonder why he's gone to all this trouble, doesn't it? I mean, bringing you here, demanding you jump through all his hoops?*

*Get out now*, she told herself.

*Ah. You're telling yourself you shouldn't be listening to me. I might make you think, and we can't have that. When puppets start thinking, it's no time until they're trying to cut their strings.*

Her legs trembled. Her heart pounded.

*Why are you still here, Callie? You know I'm evil.* The word was drenched with mockery, even in her mind. *Why aren't you running away like a good little witness?*

She clenched her fists and took a step down the slope. When had she turned around?

*Is it because for the first time you're beginning to grasp the fact that "truth" depends on who you're talking to?*

Confusion rattled her. It was as if everything she believed had come loose from its moorings and now swirled around in her head, nothing more certain than anything else. From the beginning she'd seen the Tohvani's side of things only through Aggillon eyes. They had been dismissed as evil, and she had been warned not to speak to them. Was that for her own good, as she'd been led to believe, or because the Aggillon feared she'd learn the truth of the other side's plight?

If he made them look like this, if he forbade them to speak, was that not unfair?

The black eyes bored into hers. *We're all in this together, Callie. We want to help you.*

She blinked. "You made the fire curtains."

*He made the Arena, fire curtains and all.*

"You're lying."

*Am I? Or is he?*

She swallowed hard.

*He brought you here, Callie, not us. He's letting your man die, not us.* The creature paused to let her absorb the truth of that, then added, *He could easily save him. But no. First you have to find the secret door. Does that sound like someone who really cares about you?*

The words fell like drops of acid, eating into Callie's soul, exposing a long-buried vein of resentment. He *had* brought them here—snatched them away from Earth for his own purposes, not for theirs. How could she have forgotten that? How could she have stopped being bothered by that?

She licked dry lips. *"Is* there a door here?"

*There are doors all over the Arena. How do you think they collect the bodies?*

"I mean, is there one here, in this cave?"

*He could save your man. But he won't. Can't you see he's just playing with you?*

"If there is a door here, can you show it to me?"

Laughter burst through her brain and the creature vanished. Callie stood there, reeling, feeling strangely empty, as if something vital had been ripped out of her. Her knees wobbled and gave way. She held her suddenly splitting head in her hands and took deep breaths. Gradually the pain passed, and when she looked up again, a faint nausea was all that remained.

The maelstrom of confusion had settled, but it had reduced her convictions to ashes. Suddenly she didn't know what she thought. Elhanu *did* seem to be toying with them. To bring them all this way, lead them through that awful camp, promising safety and succor if they just reached this slit. . . . The taste of betrayal lay bitter on her tongue.

She flashed the light around the room and sighed. There was nothing left but to go back to the others. Yet she hesitated, afraid of what she might find in the next room. *Oh, please,* she thought fervently. *Don't let him die. I couldn't go on without him. . . .*

Back in the main chamber, Pierce was still with them, but even Callie's untrained eye saw he was failing. Every so often he would rouse, grope for her arm, and mutter, "Can't see . . . belt . . . belt's off . . ." Then he'd lapse into unconsciousness. She sat with him, stroking his face and hair, holding his hand as if their connection might keep him from slipping away.

Besides Pierce, four others had sustained life-threatening injuries. Karl was in shock, bleeding internally. He lay on the ground beside Jesse, whose chest wound would certainly kill him without treatment. Anna had wandered around for half an hour before collapsing. La-Teisha suspected a brain injury, and the woman now reclined beside the others. Along the near wall, Evvi lay eerily still on a sleeping bag, her glazed eyes fixed on the ceiling. Her skull had been fractured when she fell down the same bank Callie had, and LaTeisha was surprised she lived at all.

Teish herself lay stretched out beside Evvi, sound asleep, her dark face hollow with exhaustion. The others, about fifteen of them, were spread out between the slit opening and the flowstone. Fatigue pulled their faces and flattened their eyes. Surveying them, Callie suddenly realized who was missing.

"Where's Mr. C?" she demanded, her voice sharp and loud in the silence. The others roused and blinked at each other.

Dell said, "He didn't make it." His cherubic face was pale around the bruises and grubby whiskers. "He was behind me when we set off, but I don't know what happened."

The others mulled this over in silence. *How could we have lost Mr. C?* Callie thought. His humor, his steady patience, his understanding—they'd been the glue that held the group together. And more than that—in so many ways he'd been the father she'd never had. . . . A wave of grief swept through her, and suddenly she was fighting tears, struggling to think of something else.

At the slit Tuck unwrapped a chocolate chip rations bar and bit into it.

Whit stood. "I'm gonna have another look around," he said.

"You've already looked three times," Brody protested, scowling up at him. "And Callie's scoured the place bare. Why bother?"

"Maybe we missed something."

Brody snorted as Whit walked past him and disappeared around the flowstone. In the lamplight, its crystalline veins glowed like fresh blood. As the sounds of his footfalls faded, John leaned his head back against the wall and closed his eyes, his earring gleaming in the lamplight. Tuck crumpled the rations bar wrapper and stuffed it in his pocket. Ian continued to stare blindly out the slit. For the first time, Callie realized Alicia wasn't with him. She hadn't been with the prisoners either, though, so maybe she had died and had finally gone home.

Before the night was over, would the rest of them be home as well? Or would they be in mutant hands? Strengthened and rejuvenated by the fire curtain, their enemies could sustain an assault until the defenders had no more E-cubes. Or, even easier, they could just wait for their water to run out.

Callie swallowed and closed her eyes, fighting hysteria. Pierce stirred, muttered. She smoothed the hair from his face. The new scar on his temple gleamed pink against his skin.

She kept coming back to the same thing. Why had they been brought here? Were they supposed to wait for a door to open? Or had something gone wrong? Perhaps the Tohvani had gained the upper hand offstage, and now Elhanu couldn't carry through on what he'd promised.

The light from the slit was fading when Gerry slapped his knee and cried, "We can't just sit here!"

"What do you suggest?" John asked, lifting his head. "A frontal assault?"

"We could surrender," Ian said.

Everyone stared at him.

He studied his big hands. "I went through it. It wasn't that bad."

"They didn't torture you first," Brody sneered. "Or rape you or cut off your—"

"Shut up, Brody," John said.

"What, afraid to face the inevitable? Maybe a frontal assault isn't such a bad idea. We take out as many of 'em as we can, then blow our own brains out."

Whit came around the curtain of flowstone then. His face was haggard, his ruined eye socket still shocking. He hunkered down beside Callie and Pierce. "Has he said anything?

"Nothing new."

Whit's dark brow furrowed. "I don't get it. Why bring us here and hide the passage?"

"Obviously your great leader miscalculated," Brody sneered.

Whit shook his head. "I'm certain we're where we're supposed to be." He looked at Callie. "John said you all were led over the mountain pretty deliberately."

"Yeah, by a bunch of goats," Brody said. "Real deliberate." He shifted against the wall, grimacing. "Man, you guys are stubborn. Isn't it obvious this is a mistake? We should've followed Morgan."

"Following Morgan didn't do *you* much good," Callie said dryly.

"If we'd listened to him in the first place, we'd still be on the road." He snorted. "I would've been better off staying back in that pen."

"Yeah," John said, "but then you wouldn't be able to blow your brains out."

Brody scowled at him.

The air pulsed with a familiar nauseating disorientation, and then came the high-pitched, brain-spearing tone and the antlike crawling of the skin. But there were no ants, and no amount of thrashing would diminish the sensation. The Trogs had turned on their fire curtain.

"What did the manual say?" Whit asked. "Beneath the Devil's Window where the water of life mingles with the Blood of Sacrifice? I thought it was that flowstone, but there's nothing there."

Callie shook her head grimly. "Nothing we can see, anyway."

The irritating buzz backed off to a soft vibration of almost pleasure, promising relief, empowerment, ecstasy. Pierce stirred, opened his eyes, and moaned about his belt. Outside, the Trogs began to shriek and howl. Soon after, the first of their victims screamed. The sound crawled up the scale, ululating with agony. It cut off briefly, and then began again as the Trogs roared approval.

Brody's wide eyes were fixed upon the slit. His swarthy face was gray beneath streaks of dirt and blood. Gerry lifted his head, and Ian stepped into the opening, resting a quivering hand upon the rock beside it. After that, no one moved. They just listened in silence as the screams went on and on and on.

Callie's fingers dropped to her belt, flipped the switch from long habit. She felt the vibration as it started up and quickly died. She did not turn it on again. It had been off for hours. What good would it do her now? It couldn't ward off sound.

The keening degenerated into dreadful animal gruntings, then momentary silence, swiftly followed by the roar of the mutant spectators.

Callie's eyes strayed back to the glittering flowstone. Blood of Sacrifice—water of life. Was that the door? Had the Trogs or Tohvani somehow obscured it? They could have entered this cavern earlier and somehow covered over the telltale marks.

"There's something I keep wondering about," Dell said, drawing everyone's attention. His hazel eyes flicked around the circle, his baby face drawn. "Those bodies we saw hanging in the camp—the human ones. If they're destroying our bodies, how can we be sent home?"

The question unnerved them all, and no one had an answer. Callie looked down at Pierce, his face lined with pain even in unconsciousness. A vision of that awful rack assailed her, and her stomach knotted.

John leapt to his feet. "Gerry's right. We can't just sit here. Maybe there's another slit outside. With all the explosions, who knows how much it was changed? That must be what the mutants intended all along."

Whit glanced at him. "You're suggesting we blunder outside in the dark?"

John gestured at Pierce. "He's dying, Whit. If we don't do something soon, we're gonna lose him. And the others, too. And ourselves. All given up to that thing out there."

Whit had no answer to that.

"I could use Pierce's armor. You could use Dell's, and Gerry and Tuck still have their own. With the belts, we'd be protected—"

"Not from their bare hands," Whit said, frowning. "Not from exploding rocks—"

"They're distracted right now. And it shouldn't take long with the belts enhancing our vision."

Callie gasped. "The belts!" Letting go of Pierce's limp hand, she leapt up. "Of course! How could we have been so *stupid?*"

Whit looked at her in dawning comprehension, his hands going to his own waist, which had been stripped of its belt when he'd been taken prisoner by the Trogs.

Callie was already fumbling with the switch on her own belt, turning to face the flowstone.

*"Water of life . . . eyes to see . . . belt off . . ."*

Pierce hadn't been out of his head. He'd been trying to tell her all along. And she'd been too dense—maybe too upset—to figure it out.

*If he dies because of my*— She felt the initial vibration as the belt's power cells burst to life—and died.

*Calm down!*

"I can see it!" Tuck cried. He was standing in front of the flowstone, one hand on his belt. "I don't believe this! It's been here all along. I can *see* it!"

"So can I!" Gerry exclaimed, standing beside him.

Callie drew a deep breath, forced all the fear and recriminations from her mind, and switched on the belt again, trying this time to maintain it. Something flickered in the flowstone behind the two men, then vanished. Tuck had his key out. He plunged it into the stone and turned it slowly—

Hope rose in Callie, and this time her belt stayed on. She saw three red circles in triangular array drawing together as Tuck turned the key. The entire stone glowed neon bright, red crystals streaking down its face like streams of blood. *Where the water of life mingles with the Blood of Sacrifice.* The circles contracted into perfect intersection and a blinding light flared as a group of gray-uniformed figures burst out of the exposed corridor, gurneys floating in their wake. As Callie blinked away tears, one of them knelt beside Pierce and checked his pulse while the other waved the gurney to the ground beside him.

"He's still alive," the Aggillon murmured. "But barely. I don't know if we've made it in time or not."

He inserted an intravenous drip pack, and they moved him onto the gurney. Callie started to walk with them, but they waved her back, herding patient and platform ahead of them into the blue-lit corridor. Four other pairs hurried after them with their own patients and float tables, and they all disappeared around a bend in the corridor.

The passage remained open in their wake, and now the rest of them stirred.

"Well, I'll be," Brody said, gaping at the opening.

"Outstanding!" Gerry agreed with a broad grin. Then he and Tuck helped Brody up, while John assisted Dell. Whit led the way, and there was nothing left for Callie but to follow.

# CHAPTER

## 24

The corridor led to a platform where a train of open-topped cars awaited. Seeing no sign of the Aggillon, who had evidently taken their patients another way, the rest of the group could only board the train in hopes it would bring them back together. Gliding silently on a single rail, it bore them through a serpentine tunnel past stunning rock formations illuminated by hidden lights. Beds of tiny red teeth gave way to walls of short green knobs, then to vast stretches of slender white fibers that crumbled at the touch and shimmered in the glow of the train's lamps.

Though the sights were beautiful, Callie couldn't enjoy them for worrying about Pierce. The Aggillon's words kept recycling through her mind. *"Alive . . . barely. I don't know if we've made it in time."* She could hardly stand not knowing where he was, or how he was, or what they were doing to him, and the train's leisurely crawl only stoked the fires of her impatience. More than once she considered getting out and running up the track ahead.

After what seemed like an eternity, the train stopped at a second platform, where an elevator whisked them upward for so long that Callie's ears popped. Finally, though, the car stopped, its doors opening on a white-stone courtyard illuminated by tall globe lamps beneath the dark sky. A graceful two-storied building surrounded the courtyard, and twinkle lights sparkled across the vine-hung balconies, while a jasmine-scented breeze tinkled through the wind chimes hanging along the eaves. Several white-and-gray-uniformed Aggillon stood near tables laden with punch bowls, cups, cheeses, crackers, fruit, and cookies.

As the travelers entered the courtyard, the closest man smiled in greeting. "I am Nahmel," he said. "Welcome to Hope."

Like all the Aggillon Callie had encountered thus far, Nahmel was incredibly handsome—dark skin and hair, dark eyes, perfect features.

"And congratulations on your progress," he continued. "We salute you."

The Aggillon behind him smiled and nodded, and Callie felt a peculiar rush of satisfaction, as if they had somehow conferred upon her the warmth of their feelings. Tall or short, well muscled or slender, dark or fair, they were all gorgeous. She wondered what they *really* looked like.

Then wondered if it mattered.

Three of them came at once to help Brody and Dell, leading them and the other injured down a side passage. "Help yourselves," Nahmel said to the rest of the group, gesturing at the table of goodies. "We have prepared rooms for each of you, when you are ready."

"What of our friends?" Whit asked. "Are they all right?"

"They are in surgery now, sir."

Callie pushed around Whit to confront Nahmel. "Will they be back?"

"I'm afraid I can't answer that, Miss Hayes." Nahmel paused. "If they don't, you may rest easy knowing they have resumed their lives on Earth well-compensated."

He seemed no more cheered by this prospect than his listerners.

"How long can we stay here?" John asked.

"You have three weeks." Nahmel lifted his voice to address them all. "Our dining room serves breakfast, lunch, and dinner, and there are always snacks in the lounge." He spread his hands. "*Hope* is yours. Enjoy it as you will."

As the others made for the tables, Callie cornered Nahmel. "I want to see Pierce."

He spread his hands. "You can do nothing for him, Miss Hayes. No more there than here."

"I would feel better there."

The Aggillon studied her expressionlessly. "Very well."

He led her through a lighted garden to a circular building and left her in a small salon looking out on an artfully lit and landscaped patio. She stood before the window, staring at her blood-and-grime-smeared reflection, feeling cold and jittery. Her stomach was a hard, painful knot, and every time she thought of Pierce, tremors swept along her arms and legs so powerfully she finally had to sit down. As much as she tried not to consider it, the possibility of losing him loomed very large. If that happened, she didn't see how she could go on. It would be like having her heart and soul wrenched from her body. The worst of it would be knowing she might have saved him had she kept her wits about her.

She sat there a long time before she realized someone had joined her. Turning, she found a white-haired, bearded man regarding her soberly from the bench beside the door. He wore one of the Aggillon uniforms, though his had gold piping along the yoke and was all white. She recognized him immediately and leapt to her feet.

"Mr. C! We thought you were lost. How did you get through?"

He stood to meet her enthusiasm, his dark eyes crinkling in amusement. "Get through?"

"All those Trogs."

"Ah." His smile faded. "Callie, I couldn't go through the Cauldron with you. At least not in this form. It wouldn't have been a proper test."

She stared at him, grappling with his words until understanding dawned and her mouth fell open. He was an Aggillon. An *Aggillon!* She'd trusted him, confided in him, loved him—grieved him, for heaven's sake!—and he wasn't even human. Never had she felt so betrayed. His care, his concern, his friendly manner—all an act to worm his way into her confidence so he could . . .

Her outrage sputtered away. No. That sober, dark-eyed gaze proved his care was genuine. And his counsel, his actions, had never been less than supportive. Without him . . . without him, she wouldn't even be here.

She studied her clasped hands, feeling suddenly awkward.

"You wanted to see Pierce?"

Pierce! Old concerns wrenched at her, and she looked up. He smiled. "He's going to make it. Come." He led her down a long white-walled, beige-carpeted corridor. "You understand you won't be able to talk to him."

"I don't care. As long as he's going to be okay."

Awkwardness closed about them again. Mr. C's presence reminded her of her failures, how she hadn't even remembered the most basic policy of keeping her belt on.

"You needn't flail yourself about it, lass. Everyone fails."

He never ceased to surprise her with his uncanny ability to read her mind. "Perhaps," she said, "but that's no excuse."

"No. But any penalty associated with failure has already been paid." He stopped in front of a door. "He's in there."

She hesitated, torn between the curiosity his cryptic words had roused and the sudden intense need to see what lay behind the door. The door won. Beyond it, she walked into a dimly lit room lined with monitors and smelling of oranges and spice. At its midst stood a transparent capsule holding a man submerged in amber fluid.

A blond Aggillon turned from the capsule as she entered. "Miss Hayes, I'm afraid—"

"It's all right, Jaalel," Mr. C said, coming in behind her.

The Aggillon bowed. "Of course, my lord. Shall I leave you?"

Callie didn't hear the answer, her attention riveted on the man in the capsule. He lay naked in the fluid, eyes closed, arms drifting at his sides, hair floating around his head in a dark nimbus. As she drew near, she saw his ribs rising and falling ever so slightly—somehow he was breathing that stuff. He was shockingly thin, and his beard was far thicker than a few hours would account for. Dark amber coagulations floated at the puncture in his chest, hovered along his broken ribs, and completely obscured his pelvis.

It was hard to see him like this. If he hadn't been breathing, she would have suspected a hoax. As it was, she kept wanting to take a deep breath, and never had she longed to touch him more. She laid a blood-stained hand on the capsule. It was cool beneath her palm, thrumming softly. She felt shaky again, close to losing it.

"This is why we discourage visitors," Mr. C murmured. "He's actually responding quite well."

"I thought he was going to die in my arms," she whispered.

"His injuries *were* severe: broken ribs, broken pelvis, ruptured spleen, punctured lung, concussion, plus that crossbow quarrel nicked an artery. The vessel burst just as they got him into the operating chamber."

She took a moment to absorb the information. "What is this stuff he's in?"

"Post-op growth stimulation gel. It's nutrient rich and charged with a slight current to enhance absorption and stimulate tissue regeneration. He'll be here for another ten hours, at least."

Callie shuddered, and her gaze returned to the beloved face obscured by the beard and the red-gold fluid. How had she ever believed she did not care about this man? She splayed her hand on the box, and suddenly tears spilled down her cheeks. She hardly knew why she was crying. Grief, gratitude, relief, shame—it all roiled together and took her by storm. Mr. C wrapped an arm around her, and she leaned against him gratefully.

Her composure was slow in returning. At length she wiped the moisture from her face and chuckled. "All that outrage I nursed over his walking through that curtain, and here I've blown it ten times worse."

His arm tightened around her. "It does no good to compare, lass. You're not the same person. You don't have the same weaknesses."

She leaned away to see his face and he released her.

"Besides," he added, "it's behind you. Best learn what you can from it and leave the rest in the past."

"You mean like remember to keep my wits about me and my belt activated?"

He regarded her soberly, his hair and beard glowing amber in the light. "I think it goes a little further than that."

Yes. She should've trusted Elhanu. Except . . .

Callie shook her head, frowning. "Why didn't you open the door? We'd made it across the meadow."

"The doors only open from your side."

"You come in to collect the bodies."

"Those passways are configured for Aggillon frequencies, not human."

"Well, then, why didn't you remind us? That Tohvani was there. Why couldn't one of your people come? We were upset and frightened. We needed your help."

"You had the link, Callie. Right there inside you."

"But I—"

"It was a test, lass. You knew that going in."

"I . . ." She frowned. It was true. All of it. She'd had everything, known everything she needed. The fault was hers. Why was it so hard to admit that?

The rhythmic hiss of the fluid rushing through the tubes filled the ensuing silence.

He squeezed her shoulder. "You're exhausted. How about I take you to your room?"

She glanced at Pierce's unconscious form, and again Mr. C knew her thought. "My people want him well as much as you do. They'll take good care of him. And your spending the night beside this capsule isn't going to do either of you any good."

With a sigh, she acquiesced.

A bath—steaming at just the right temperature—was drawn and waiting in the room to which he brought her. After a long, delicious soak, she stumbled to her bed and was asleep before she knew it.

She awoke to daylight filtering past the floor-length, rose-colored bedroom curtains. For a while she lay there, savoring the smoothness of the bed sheets, the soft comfort of the mattress, and the sweet sense of being safe and loved. She'd expected nightmares after what she'd been through. Instead, her dreams were filled with light—glorious, wonderful radiance so intense it had physical substance. Even now she could feel the pressure of it wrapping about her like a pair of strong, gentle hands. Never had she felt more content. Or more at peace.

Time and reality reasserted themselves when she glanced at the bedside clock. She'd slept nearly sixteen hours. Pierce would be out of the goop by now.

Arising, she pulled open the curtains—and gasped. Her room

perched at the edge of a sheer cliff overlooking ranks of pale blue ridges that marched down to a vast plain webbed with silver ribbons. The sun stood high overhead, two hours past its zenith, its strong white light flattening and expanding the landscape.

She stared in wonder, her heart swelling with a sense of space and freedom that was almost like flying. And she wasn't afraid. For the first time in memory she stood at the edge of a precipice and felt no fear. Even when she went onto the balcony.

The demons were gone. In their place the link glowed like a door of light in her soul, a haven of joy and comfort and clarity of thought.

She turned from the balcony, eager to find Pierce.

Her tattered camos and boots were nowhere to be found, so she chose a loose white sleeveless gown and white slippers from the selection her closet provided. Leaving her hair unbraided, she set off for the infirmary, bubbling with anticipation.

The coffinlike capsule lay open, drained of its fluid and missing its occupant. The Aggillon attendant told her Pierce had been moved two hours earlier and warned her he wasn't likely to be awake much for the next day, at least.

She still wanted to see him, so the alien escorted her to Pierce's new room and left her standing just inside the door.

Dressed in a light blue hospital gown, Pierce sat reading in a railed bed, its head raised to support him. At first she hardly recognized him, for his brown hair curled past his shoulders, and his beard had grown thick and long. Then he looked up and smiled. It was a shadow of his usual expression, lopsided and weary, but it was Pierce.

"Hi," he said in a papery voice.

"Hi." She came to the side of the bed, staring at his long hair and beard. "My goodness. You look like a homeless person."

"Thanks a lot."

"If it keeps growing like that, pretty soon it'll be as long as mine."

"It's a side effect of the gel." He set his manual aside. "Don't get too attached to it."

Callie rested her hands on the railing between them, hardly knowing what to say. "So how are you feeling?"

"Tired." He wiggled his toes. "Weak. A little light-headed."

As he scratched his ribs, she noticed his nails were as incongruously long as his hair and beard. An IV pouch clung to his inner arm.

"They say I should be able to walk tomorrow," he went on, "but when I tried to stand up coming in here, everything gave way. Hurt like the dickens, too. So I don't know." He glanced at her and smiled. "It does seem kind of fast, considering I had a broken pelvis."

The fact that he was going to be all right finally penetrated, and a joy so poignant it hurt swept through her. Suddenly she wanted to touch him, hold him, feel his lips on hers more than anything in the world.

He grimaced. "Do I look that bad?"

"You look wonderful."

"Then why are you standing there like I have leprosy? This rail does move out of the way. I'd put it down myself, but I'm afraid of falling out of the bed."

She let the rail down and perched gingerly beside him, as if he were a crystalline formation that might shatter if she were to jiggle him too roughly. He smelled like the capsule room—oranges and spice.

She couldn't speak, her emotions suddenly so tangled, so powerful, they washed her mind blank. She could only sit and stare and try not to burst into tears.

His hand closed over hers. "It's all right, Callie. We've made it."

"I thought I'd lost you," she whispered.

She touched his brow, his cheek, his lips, slid her fingers through the beard and into the strange long hair, and he pulled her down into his arms and kissed her. Suddenly she was drowning in him, intoxicated by his touch, the musky scent of *him* beneath the orange, the tickle of his beard, the hard muscles of his chest and arms, the heat of his hands sliding over her skin—

When they broke apart, he held her away from him, wide-eyed with surprise.

She fingered the new scar where the quarrel had pierced his chest. "I thought you said you were tired and weak."

"I am. And a good thing, too." He straightened the folds of her dress over one shoulder. "You never know when someone's going to walk in around here, and anyway I intend to—" He stopped and let his hand fall away, averting his gaze.

"What?"

"Never mind." He rubbed his face, then covered a yawn. "So what about the others? How many did we lose?"

She sat back, her emotions cooling reluctantly. "Well, Evvi had a fractured skull. Anna had some kind of brain injury. Karl and Jesse were hurt pretty badly, too, but seeing what our hosts have done for you, I expect everyone is okay."

When she said no more, he looked up. "That's it?"

"Isn't that enough?"

"I thought it would be more. It seemed like we were in that cavern forever. I kept hearing people screaming, moaning." He frowned. "Arguing?"

With a grimace she told him how they couldn't find the gate, how Ian had wanted to surrender, and John was going to go out and search for another opening, and Brody meant to kill himself before they got him. "We were pretty pathetic."

"But we made it."

She sighed and toyed with the hair along his temple. "I thought it would be simpler than this. They shoot at us—we shoot at them. I didn't think I'd have to fight myself so much." She let her hand fall back to her side.

Pierce covered another huge yawn and shook his head. "Wow. They said I'd be sleepy, but I didn't figure it would be this soon. Seems like I just came out of the tank."

"I should go."

"It's not that bad. Tell me what it's like out there. Is it all as beautiful as this?" He gestured at the flower-trimmed lawn outside his window, already streaked with afternoon shadow.

"From what I've seen, yes. I haven't paid much attention, actually. You were in pretty bad shape, you know."

"Yeah. They told me." He covered another yawn. "The rocks blew right after I'd sent you off, and I thought—" His voice broke. He swallowed and his eyes slid away. "That's when the quarrel hit me. . . ."

Silence stretched between them. Then she roused herself and

changed the subject, telling him about her room, and her calm joy on the edge of the cliff. "I think it's the link," she said. "It's so strong here. I can't see how I ever ignored it."

"Maybe we're closer to the source here." He yawned again. "Or maybe there's not so much interference."

She rubbed the back of his hand with her thumb. "I saw a plain from my room. That's the Inner Realm, isn't it?"

He read her thought and smiled. "Don't borrow trouble, Cal. We'll get there when we get there. Besides, we're doing well." He covered yet another yawn. "Very few witnesses get as far as we have. The last group was something like seven years ago. Apparently we've acquired quite a following."

"A following?"

"Of Aggillon." He smiled and his eyelids drooped, fluttered open, drooped again.

Callie pulled her hand free of his feeble grasp and patted his hand. "I'd better go."

"Sorry, Cal," he murmured, "but I . . . feel like I'm gonna . . . pass out."

His eyes closed and soon his breathing deepened. Despite her words, Callie didn't leave. She was content to sit and watch him, delighting in the healthy flush of his skin, the peace in his expression.

"Miss Hayes?" She turned to find Jaalel standing in the doorway. "They'll be serving dinner in about half an hour. I wasn't sure if you knew."

"I didn't. Thank you."

The Aggillon's gaze went to Pierce. "He'll be out for the night at least now, ma'am. His body is still in accelerated recovery."

When she said nothing, he started to leave. She called him back. "I have a question for you." He waited, watching her. The perfection of his features was heartrending. "The bodies we saw in the Devil's Cauldron," she said. "The ones the Trogs had—"

He guessed her concern before she voiced it. "Not everyone comes to the Inner Realm through Elhanu's Gate, Miss Hayes."

*That's right. There was Mander's elevator. And the route the slave traders used through the Canyon of the Damned. Probably other ways as well.*

"Their Unchanged bodies can't pass through our collection gates without disintegrating."

"So the Trogs collect them instead of you."

"Yes."

"Which means . . . when they die, they're dead. I mean really dead. They don't go back to Earth."

"I'm afraid not."

She paused to consider his answer. Then one more question pressed, one that had been bouncing around the back of her mind ever since she'd awakened.

"One other thing."

A blond brow arched.

"Our friend, Mr. C. You called him 'my lord' last night. Why?"

"Because that is who he is, ma'am."

Callie's pulse accelerated. It was obvious, from the deference the others showed him and the difference in his uniform, that he was set apart. But could it really mean what she thought it might? She hesitated, not sure she wanted to know.

"So he's not just any Aggillon, then."

Jaalel's blue eyes pierced to her heart. "He is our king, ma'am. Elhanu."

# CHAPTER

## 25

Callie found the others waiting outside the dining room, in considerably better shape than when she'd last seen them. The women wore gowns like her own, the men loose, long-sleeved jackets belted over trousers in various colors. Brody, Dell, and Jesse all appeared completely on the mend, betraying evidence of their exposure to the healing gel in their freshly cut hair and the new, tidily clipped beard on Brody's face. Unnoticed, Callie watched them from the periphery, marveling at what had been accomplished: that they had survived mutiny, disaster, and a climb over perilous mountain cliffs; that they had crossed two hundred miles of trackless wilderness and actually found the entrance to the promised Safehaven; that six had walked into a camp of hundreds and lived to reach that entrance, rescuing sixteen others in the process. It boggled her mind, and she knew they couldn't have done it without Elhanu.

Elhanu. Mr. C. She still struggled to get her mind around the notion of their being the same person. It made sense in the big picture, for there'd been indications. But she had always imagined Elhanu as someone removed—a powerful, untouchable, incomprehensible being. Mr. C was more open and approachable than anyone she'd ever known. Images spun off the spindle of memory: his grin, his assurances atop the rappelling cliff, his conversations with Pierce and Tuck before the evening lectures, his unflagging support of Pierce's leadership, the way he'd opened Callie's eyes to the possibility of love. He was a friend, a confidant, a surrogate father. Now he was Elhanu, as well.

Whit finally spotted her and hurried over, John and LaTeisha trailing after him.

"He's going to make it," Callie said in answer to their unspoken question. "Has already been on his feet once today."

"With a broken pelvis?" LaTeisha exclaimed.

Callie explained about the tank of super-healing gel, and Whit nodded. "Karl and Jess had the same treatment, and they're well on the road to recovery, too. Must be pretty effective." He wore midnight blue sparked with silver threads and a new eye patch. Clean, rested, and shaven, he was a new man, right down to the unexpected white hairs threading his mustache.

"What about Evvi?" Callie asked.

LaTeisha frowned. "Don't know. Anna died before they got her to surgery, though."

"I don't get it," John mused. "If we can be resuscitated and sent back to Earth, why not just put us back into the game and let us try again?"

No one knew, but the question reminded Callie of her talk with Jaalel. Whit must've seen a change in her expression because he cocked a questioning brow.

She looked around at them, wondering how to tell them. "I saw Mr. C last night," she finally said.

"He made it?" John cried.

"Not exactly. He didn't go through the Cauldron."

John's blond brows drew together.

"What are you saying?" Whit asked.

"That he's Aggillon?" LaTeisha suggested, wryly.

"Elhanu himself."

Shocked disbelief froze their faces.

After a long minute, LaTeisha shook her head. "Someone's putting you on, girl."

"Jaalel? I doubt it. Besides, it fits, doesn't it? I mean, it's hard to believe, and yet . . . it's not."

Silence followed as each of them pondered Callie's revelation, their expressions turning blank and flat. No further protest followed, but they seemed as disoriented by the notion as Callie had been.

Then the dining room doors swung open and it was time to eat. Inside, a linen-covered sideboard held dishes of every color, temperature, and texture, from kiwi-exotic to mashed-potato-plain. Delicate radish roses, turnip irises, and cucumber fans garnished platters set among elegant flower arrangements and ice carvings of a dolphin and a swooping hawk. A table lined with high-backed chairs stood at room center. Twenty place settings of silver and crystal gleamed against white linen. Crisp-uniformed Aggillon stood ready to assist, pulling back chairs, pouring drinks, carrying away emptied plates, while one played quiet melodies on the baby grand piano in the corner.

"What a spread!" LaTeisha exclaimed as Callie settled beside her at the table. "And not a hair in the lot of it."

"None of it burned, either," Callie said dryly.

They laughed, then sobered as they realized their comrade could well be gone.

"As maddening as she was," LaTeisha said, "she had her good points. I never knew anyone as unrelentingly optimistic."

"Or as devoted to the manual," Callie added, finding herself more concerned about Evvi's recovery than she would have expected.

They talked and ate and marveled, and afterward lingered over truffles and coffee, ribbing the former Morgan-supporters for their poor judgment. Hope, it turned out, was no simple rest stop. A veritable resort, it boasted two Olympic-sized swimming pools, three spas, tennis and racquetball courts, Ping-Pong and pool tables, weight rooms, a movie theater, a well-stocked library, and a network of trails that wound through acres of gardens, ranging from tropical paradises to the stark beauty of wind-sculpted rock.

"The ultimate getaway!" LaTeisha pronounced.

"Rowena would die, wouldn't she?" John said. He was slouched back in his chair across the table from Callie, arms folded across his chest. "To find Pierce proven right—and in spades! Ooh!"

"Why *is* she so down on Pierce?" Callie asked, stroking the handle of her coffee cup. "She's not even rational about it anymore."

"I figure they were lovers once," said Tuck, popping a truffle into his mouth.

"Nah," LaTeisha said. "Pierce is a regular Victorian. No sex outside of marriage. Not her type at all."

"That was the problem," John said. "He was the only man she went after and couldn't get."

"Get out!" LaTeisha scoffed. "She never went after Pierce."

"She did, Teish. Big time. He turned her down." John brushed at the crumbs on the tablecloth before him. "After she recovered, he became a sort of hero to her. To Garth, too. Remember when we first knew them? Pierce could do no wrong—he was the man everyone wanted to be with in a pinch. But after the Trogs had him, it was different. He wasn't a hero anymore. He was just a man, and it was much too obvious."

They fell silent, mulling over his words. Callie stirred cream and sugar into her freshened coffee and admitted to herself that John's explanation made sense. She remembered her own disappointment on first seeing Pierce's weakness, even though she'd understood better than most how debilitating—and humiliating—panic attacks could be.

"Well," she said, "he's sure back to hero status as far as I'm concerned."

"Amen to that," Whit murmured.

Beside her LaTeisha exhaled. "I wonder if any of them made it back."

John raised a brow at her. "To the road, you mean?"

"It'd be a miracle if they did," Gerry drawled.

Tuck waved another truffle dismissively. "They made their choices."

"But they were our friends," Callie murmured.

Tuck snorted. "Some friends. Did you know Rowena stole the map just before they ran out that night by the lake?" Everyone turned to stare at him.

"No," Whit said softly. "How is it you do?"

Tuck popped the last truffle into his mouth and glanced down the table at Brody, sitting on the end.

Brody's face reddened. "Hey, at the time I thought she was right."

"You were going to leave us in the middle of nowhere without a map?" LaTeisha squeaked.

"We were desperate."

"We would've made you a copy," Callie said.

"There wasn't time. And no one thought Pierce would go for it."

"He would've called you fools," Callie agreed, "but he wouldn't have stopped you."

She recalled how nervous Meg had been that last night. The desperate ring in her voice. Had she known Rowena was taking the map? She must have.

Movement at the edge of her vision distracted her from her bitter musings. Mr. C—Elhanu—stood in the doorway. He was still the same white-bearded, white-haired, medium-framed man, but now a tingle washed through her as she met his gaze. Slowly she stood, chair whispering across the carpet. Other chairs thumped and squeaked as Whit, LaTeisha, and John followed her lead. The rest of them watched in consternation, and then rose to their feet as well.

The Aggillon leader strode to the chair at the head of the table opposite Brody and gestured toward them. "Please, sit down." And sat himself.

They settled back into their places, but no one spoke, the air suddenly thick with tension.

Finally Whit said, "It's good to see you again, sir."

Elhanu grinned—the old twinkly-eyed expression that was pure Mr. C. "And you're wondering why in the world I played this little game, aren't you?"

They glanced at one another uncertainly.

The Aggillon leader sobered. "It's not a game. You need to trust me. This"—he gestured at himself—"seems to help."

Again his words met silence. Then Whit shook his head. "But that isn't really you, is it, sir? I mean, you look like somebody's father, when you're anything but."

"Here, I *am* your father," Elhanu said quietly. "In more ways than you know. And there is nothing false in this image I present to you."

"Except that it isn't real."

Elhanu smiled. "It may not be all that I am, but it is very real. And certainly it is the most comfortable for you right now."

"Will we ever see you as you really are, sir?" Callie asked.

"Eventually."

"What *are* you guys talking about?" Brody erupted testily. "And what is all this 'sir' stuff?"

He wasn't the only one who didn't know the truth about Mr. C, but as Callie looked down the table at him, she realized he would have the most trouble accepting it. He'd never liked the older man, thought him a liability who never should've been allowed to leave Rimlight.

"Mr. C is Elhanu, Brody," she explained, when no one else did.

Brody blinked. Jaws fell open around him, glazed eyes turning to the older man. No one spoke for a long, long moment. Then Brody drove to his feet. "You're the one who did all this? Kidnapped me, ruined everything for your silly little game?" His fury blazed, bright and shocking.

Elhanu regarded him with utter calm. "If not for this, you would be dead, Brody Jamarillo. Remember? Your chute didn't open."

Brody's flush drained to dead white. He stood trembling, then sagged into his chair. "I hit the ground," he whispered, staring at the table. "I remember now. . . ." Slowly his gaze climbed back to Elhanu's bearded face. "When I go back—"

"You will recover completely. They'll call it a miracle."

As Brody stared up at him, something changed in his swarthy face. It was as if a wall crumbled away and something like . . . awe? . . . took the place of his bitterness. Blushing, he dropped his gaze to his hands.

John broke the ensuing silence. "So, Mr.—er, Elhanu, sir. Do you really forbid the Tohvani to appear in their true form, as they say?"

Callie's gaze flicked to him in surprise. She hadn't told John about her encounter.

Elhanu's lips quirked. "Actually the Tohvani *are* in their true form. It's just their bodies you're not seeing."

"Huh?"

"Oh, come now, think about it. The real you is not this outward flesh; it's the part that thinks and feels and remembers and decides. Your soul resides in your body as your body resides in your clothes—

that is your true self. I have merely stipulated that the Tohvani must appear naked in your presence."

"Why?" Callie asked.

Elhanu turned gentle eyes upon her. "You would find them mind-bogglingly beautiful. They'd have you bedazzled before you knew it. I thought it better you should see them for what they really are. It is not so great a handicap for them. They've found ways around it."

Jaalel entered and spoke in Elhanu's ear. Watching him, Callie appreciated anew how beautiful he was, how even with their deferent manner, he and his kind inspired feelings of worship. If the Tohvani looked like them . . .

Jaalel stepped back, and Elhanu addressed them. "My servants have prepared a ballad in honor of your arrival."

His announcement elicited low exclamations of approval. Exquisitely executed, breathtakingly beautiful, and invariably illuminating, Aggillon performances were always a treat. Now three of them entered and stood before the empty sideboard. One carried a small, triangular stringed instrument, which seemed to float before him as his fingers played an intricate introduction.

The vocalists had sung only a few lines before the hairs on Callie's neck stood up. They were singing about Pierce. And Morgan. And all the rest of it—the doubts, the desertion, the battle by the lake, the mountain trek, the freeing of the prisoners . . .

The music rose and fell in sympathy with the events, shifting from major to minor key and back. It covered the gamut of emotion—the melody often so stirring it made them sound like heroes. Callie wasn't the only one to shift in restless embarrassment. Finally the singers moved into a tenderly peaceful passage only to break off mid-measure, leaving their listeners blinking in surprise. The lead singer, the dark-featured Nahmel, explained with a smile. "I'm afraid we don't know the end of this one yet."

They bowed and exited, leaving their bewildered audience to grapple with disappointment, and then understanding. A few of them even laughed, for they should have seen it coming.

"Is it true what they sang about the others?" LaTeisha asked. "Reaching the road, I mean?"

"Of course," Elhanu replied.

"Can you tell us who?" Callie asked.

"Meg is still with us," he assured her with a small smile. "And Rowena. And Morgan, as well, although"—his smile faded—"not for long."

"Is there any way we can help?" Callie asked.

"They are more than a hundred miles away—even further in their souls. Whatever help you might offer, they would refuse." He sighed, his regret palpable. "I have given them as much as they will accept. But I cannot—I will not—override their volition."

He changed the subject then, asking about their accommodations—if they were satisfied, if there was anything they needed. Of course there wasn't, so he advised them to enjoy themselves, then stood to take his leave. Pausing behind his chair, he looked down at them, a half smile curving his lips. "You've done very well, people. I know it's been hard, but you've stuck with it. That has pleased me more than you know." He met each person's gaze, and when it was Callie's turn she felt the link pulse, flooding her with affection and an approval so strong, so warm and tender, so incredibly intimate, it brought her to tears. Even after he left, the glow remained, metamorphosing into the most profoundly satisfying sense of accomplishment she had ever known.

No one spoke for some minutes after his departure. Then Whit expressed it for them all. "Wow!"

And John murmured, "Aggillon or not, I'd follow that man anywhere."

# CHAPTER

## 26

Pierce was vastly improved the next day, so much so that by the time Callie went to his room, he'd already been to an early rehab session, met with Elhanu, and retired to seclusion, asking not to be disturbed until evening. Disappointed, she spent the day swimming, gabbing, and looking forward to dinner.

She'd just gone through the buffet line when he walked in, using a cane. He was still too thin, but he'd gotten his hair cut, as promised, and had lost the beard. Everyone applauded his arrival, and Brody publicly apologized for doubting him. After that, Pierce passed through the buffet line four times, consuming an amazing amount of food. It was another side effect of the gel, and the others had a great time teasing him about his appetite. There was much laughing, joking, and tale telling, but though it was fun, Callie found herself growing impatient.

Not until the meal was well over were the two of them able to slip away. They took a short walk into the garden, where Callie learned he'd been feeling as frustrated as she, and the physical chemistry she'd once declared nonexistent once again made itself known with knee-jellying intensity.

Pierce was the one who broke it off, stepping away and taking a couple of deep breaths before he spoke. "Do you mind if we walk around?"

Callie regarded him wordlessly, partly relieved, and partly absurdly hurt. They were both committed to limiting physical intimacy outside of marriage, yet here she was, wanting to throw herself on him anyway.

A crease formed between his brows. "Did I say something wrong?"

"No." She blushed furiously. "Walking is a good idea."

The main buildings of the compound stood at one end of the plateau. Below them lay the gardens, where gravel paths wound through a wonderland of trees and sculpted shrubbery, sparkling with twinkle lights. Low foot lamps illuminated the path, and a rainbow of decorative spotlights provided variety, turning a fountain green, a pond blue, and a waterfall amber. Night had drained the flowers of their color and substituted a mingling of sweet fragrances, and the friendly silence was broken only by the crickets, the fountains chuckling, and every now and then, a burst of laughter ringing down from the main courtyard.

They walked side by side, not speaking at first, but gradually moving into easy surface talk—the compound's amenities, the Aggillon's delight in serving them, the incredible shock of learning Mr. C's true identity. Pierce described his exit from the capsule and, from the way he talked, seemed not to know she'd been to see him. She was content to leave it at that.

"So what's with all the frantic studying?" she asked finally.

"Frantic studying?"

"Well, you've hardly recovered, and here you spend the day sequestered. Jaalel said you were studying."

"I was thinking mostly. I spoke with Elhanu this morning."

"Ah. He has a way of making one think, I must admit."

He flashed her a sly grin. "I understand you've had your own talks with him. Not so private as mine, either."

"He told you!" she said, rounding on him.

"Hey, I was the one in my birthday suit."

"You were the one who was almost dead." She turned and continued up the path. "At the time, that was all I was thinking about."

"Sorry." He hurried to catch up with her, and they walked on in silence.

Then she asked, "So what did you talk about?"

"Everything. Him. Me. My many failures. They don't surprise him at all, you know. I sometimes wonder if anything does." He drew a deep breath, let it out as if discharging the subject with the used air. "Anyway, he left me with much to consider. I didn't want to shut you out, but to be honest, you were one of the things I had to think about."

"Me?" Her chest clenched. Was he going to tell her it was over? That he didn't really care about her? That they had to break things off because they had no time for a proper relationship, or because it would be too distracting for him?

They stopped beside a pool, its glassy surface mirroring the lights in the trees. Hidden in the fanlike foliage on the far bank, a bird ruffled its feathers. Pierce hung his cane on the railing and leaned on his forearms. "I thought a lot about going home," he said.

Callie stroked the rail with her palm. "Sometimes I'm not sure I even *want* to go home," she said. "It won't be the same."

"No."

"*We're* not the same."

"No."

At their feet a fish kissed the pond's surface with a faint popping. Pierce stared across the water, hands steepled before him. "You'll probably think I'm nuts. Maybe I shouldn't even say anything, but . . ."

*Here it comes*, she thought, feeling light-headed.

He seemed to nerve himself and pressed on. "But we've known each other for almost a year. We've worked together side by side, faced every problem you can imagine, and we've certainly seen each other at our worst. I don't think we'd be going into it blind."

Everything stood still: her heart, her breath, the birds, the fish. "Going into what, Pierce?"

He looked over his shoulder at her, surprised. "Marriage. Didn't I say that? I'm hoping when we get back you'll marry me."

Her heart was beating so hard and fast she could barely hear him, and her head felt like Styrofoam. "Marry you?"

He turned to face her. "I know you're skittish about it. I know you don't want to repeat your parents' mistakes, and I remember your lecture about being reasonable and rational, so I don't expect you to give me an answer now. I just want you to think about it. And I want you to know how I feel." He stroked her hair. "I love you, and I want to share my life with you. Wherever that may be."

She swallowed on a dry throat. "You'll—" She stopped and tried again. "It'll be different back home. There'll be other girls—"

His fingers touched her lips, silencing her. "I know what I want. I've known for a long time."

She was in his arms again, and he was kissing her lips, her throat, her neck, her shoulders. She clung to him, wanting him with an unbearable ache, wanting all of him—his body, his soul, his life—so there was only one answer she could give him, and no point trying to be rational and reasonable.

He drew back to stare at her wide-eyed.

"Yes," she said, laughing and caressing the side of his face. "I'll marry you, Pierce. I'll marry you here or back home or anywhere you wish."

———

The next day Pierce began to teach. They had three weeks to prepare for the final leg of their journey, which would take them through the Inner Realm by way of the city-states of Zelos, Morres, and Splagnos. It would be no picnic. The plain was an inhospitable waste, its air fouled past breathing by the toxic residuals of perpetual warfare. People dwelt in terrarium cities, traveling outside only in sealed cars or by way of an elaborate underground rail system. No one traveled the open plain if they could avoid it, and all the soldiers wore life-support suits.

Thanks to the Change worked by their passage through Elhanu's Gate, participants were immune to the poisons and therefore enjoyed significantly greater mobility than their adversaries. Their biggest problem would be crossing the crevasses that scored the plain, because all the active bridges were tightly controlled, often by warring factions. There were, however, a number of ruins—abandoned, toxin-reeking casualties of war—that housed the remnants of old bridges. Augmented by secret Aggillon-placed passpoints, these routes would provide safe passage. The travelers would have to keep their belts operational to find the activation ports, but if they got that far, that discipline would be old hat.

The belts themselves—and the armor they controlled—would be upgraded. Thin and lightweight, they would require no hand switch to activate them. Finding and accessing the link was enough. Instead of a spongy breastplate, fibers woven into the fabric of their clothing would provide the energy matrix to support the belt's protective field, and a single golden circlet worn round the head would suffice for a helmet. As before, the devices provided shielding and the vision enhancement necessary to find both the passpoint ports and the randomly appearing Auxiliary Supply Boxes that would provide logistical needs and instructions.

This time there would be no predetermined route. They would be directed as they went, so if they missed an ASB or a passpoint, they'd be in trouble. The key to success was their link with Elhanu, the strength of which depended solely upon their trust in him. That, in essence, was what would resolve this otherworldly trial. By trusting Elhanu, they allowed him to prove himself the better master. There was no spoken testimony, no verbal deposition, no swearing upon holy books, for words alone could lie. Decision and action, repeated over time, did not.

"He forged a link with us when he changed us back at the Gate," Pierce told them, "and so far we've made poor use of it at best. No more. From here on that link must be more real to us than anything our eyes and ears tell us. Only then will we have the wit and strength of will to choose the right path and resist our enemies' lies. We must see everything from Elhanu's perspective, never lose sight of the reason we were brought here, and never give up, no matter how bad things get. And they will get bad. So far the Tohvani haven't taken us very seriously. From now on, they will."

---

As Callie's relationship with Elhanu grew and clarified, her relationship with Pierce grew equally strong. In some inexplicable way the two bonds were intertwined. The more she got to know Pierce, the better she understood Elhanu, and the deeper became her regard for him. Conversely, the more she understood Elhanu and the greater her affection for him, the more she appreciated Pierce's devotion to his cause.

As a teacher, Pierce held nothing back. He spoke plainly, forcefully, bluntly. Sometimes the power of the link blazed through him, lighting his face, vibrating in his voice, its energy leaping through the air to link with the power in Callie's own soul until her skin tingled with it. He inspired them, drove them, challenged them. And Callie wasn't the only one who loved him.

She was, however, the only one he intended to marry, and he'd made no bones about it. He'd even produced a ring for her—compliments of the Aggillon—so they could be officially engaged. He refused to marry her here, though, despite everyone's contention that he should get Elhanu to perform the ceremony. "I want it to be right and proper on Earth," he told her.

Every night after dinner, they strolled the gardens, never running out of things to discuss. Past, present, future—they covered it all, though most often they talked of the future. It had acquired a new luster now that they saw themselves together in it.

"I suppose we'd live in Colorado?" Callie asked him one night.

He looked down at her with cocked brow. "Only if we agreed. I do have work there—the ranch and all. It's a beautiful spot. You could paint to your heart's content."

"You wouldn't want me to go to work?"

"I'd consider that your work." He grinned. "I've seen what you can do."

Another time she asked him, "What about kids?"

And he said, brows arched, "What about kids?"

"Do you want any?"

"Yeah. Do you?"

"Maybe one. Or two."

"What a thought!" he murmured with a grin and slid a hand around her waist to pull her against him, ending conversation for a while.

They talked of furniture and finances and families—the one they hoped to create and the ones they already had. Callie delighted in anticipating the reaction of her mother and sister when she introduced them to her *fiancé*. How shocked they'd be to find she'd picked a cowboy— shocked she'd picked anyone at all. Or perhaps that anyone would have her. It was a joyful, golden time, and of course it couldn't last. On the eve of their departure from Hope, the expanding bubble of anticipation burst.

Pierce was unusually preoccupied at dinner, and afterward, as they strolled the Wilderness of Rock at the far end of the plateau, he grew even more so. They walked silently, hand in hand, past a succession of fantastic formations—huge slabs balanced mushroomlike on slender pillars, or stacked like pancakes, or combined to form whimsical animal figures. Callie barely noticed them, so keyed was she on Pierce, while he seemed barely to notice her.

They climbed past a dark pool sprinkled with stars to a stone pavilion on the hilltop. Marking the farthest point of the loop trail, it offered a breathtaking view of the plain, and, as they stood surveying the dark expanse with a balmy breeze sighing around them, it felt as if they were the only two people in the world. She glanced at him occasionally, standing like a statue at her side, the breeze ruffling the short locks of his hair, newly shorn in preparation for their departure.

The silence stretched out, long and taut as she waited for him to tell her what was wrong, and she finally could stand it no longer. "You've changed your mind, haven't you?"

When at first he didn't answer, she nearly died.

Then he started and turned toward her, frowning. "What did you say?"

She repeated the question, and his expression turned to horror. "Changed my mind? Heavens, no! I love you more now than ever—so much I can hardly bear it."

"Then what's wrong?"

The stone mask slid back into place. "I'm not sure it's something I should tell you."

"Better to tell me the truth than let me stew in my imagination!"

"Perhaps." Still, he hesitated. Then, "If we die out there"—he nodded at the plain—"we aren't going to remember."

She brushed dancing tendrils of hair from her face. "Remember what?"

"Anything." His hands clutched the stone ledge. "When they resuscitate someone, there's a significant amount of memory loss, encompassing most of the individual's recent past—which would be all the time spent in the Arena and possibly some period prior to it. That's why they can't put us back into the game. We'd have to start all over again.''

It took her a few moments to process what he was saying, and then she sagged against the stone, feeling sick and shivery. "You're saying if we die here, we won't remember each other once we get back?''

"For most participants it's a blessing, since they leave without understanding most of what's going on anyway—and their memories are often anything but good. It makes it easier to slide back into their old lives.''

"But that's not how it is for us. We do understand. Surely—''

"I suppose it depends on how one dies." In the shadow his eyes were as dark and deep as Elhanu's. "The nature of the injury, how long it takes them to collect you . . .'' He was reaching for something positive, and they both knew it.

Callie bit her lip. "How could we go through all this, learn everything we learned, and not remember anything? Not remember him? Each other? Just go back to what we were before? There'd be no point.''

"Not that we can see anyway." He wrapped an arm around her and she pressed her face into his chest.

"They'd put you back in Colorado," she said, "and me in Tucson. There's no way we'd meet by chance.''

He sighed. "You're jumping to conclusions. We probably won't both die. One of us might make it through the portal.''

"But if the other one doesn't remember—''

He stroked the back of her head, fingers sliding through her long hair. "You think I wouldn't fall in love with you all over again?''

"But how would you meet me?" She pushed away to look at him.

He smiled. "Durango's not that far from Tucson. You could find me.''

"And do what? Tell you I'm a lost love you can't remember? Hire on as a cowhand?''

"Ask my folks to let you visit for a week so you can paint the mountains. They'd go for that. Especially my mom.''

"They'd think I was nuts. And so would you.''

"After a week of being with you, I'd be totally smitten. The last time it only took a day. Some things are just right, just meant to be."

*And some things aren't*, she thought. *Oh, I knew this was too good to be true.* Suddenly the dreadful conviction that she was going to lose him dropped over her. Her thoughts began to bolt like frightened mice, seeking shelter anywhere they could find it—they could stay here, or go back to Rimlight, or, or—

Pierce took her face in both hands and looked into her eyes. "Callie, we have to trust him, remember? That's the whole point. He's promised us reward when we return to Earth, but what reward could be worth losing each other? I don't think he'll do that to us. He brought us together in the first place. He knows how we feel, how right we are for each other. Our happiness is important to him. We have to believe that."

She looked up into his sober face, into those wonderful eyes, so like Elhanu's. The link pulsed, and she remembered the quiet understanding, the steadfast care, the warm blessing of approval—and knew the truth of Pierce's words.

"If we can't trust him here and now," he said, "we've lost already. You know that."

"Of course," she whispered. "Of course, I do."

He regarded her gravely, then bent and kissed her with such exquisite tenderness she cried.

## RAISED UP

"IF GOD IS FOR US, WHO IS AGAINST US?
FOR THIS VERY PURPOSE I RAISED YOU UP,
TO DEMONSTRATE MY POWER ... AND THAT
MY NAME MIGHT BE PROCLAIMED...."

ROMANS 8:31; 9:17

# CHAPTER

# 27

Firing in bursts at the low, crumbling wall behind which the first of the Morresian patrol had taken cover, Callie and the others retreated up the rubble-strewn street of Old Morres. They'd hoped the patrol would not follow them into this ruined city, but the number of Watchers clinging to the walls and balconies around them predicted otherwise. As two more armored giants dashed for cover behind the wall, the blue beams of Callie's SI–42 stitched small explosions around the doorway through which they had emerged. Her companions' fire followed suit and they stopped the advance. For now.

The four Morresians at the wall opened fire, forcing her to dive behind a fallen wrought-iron balcony, their pursuing beams sizzling off the metal. A scent of ozone mingled with the dust and the sour-dishrag stench of the ruins. Wiping the sweat from her brow, she rose and fired again, aware of Brody crouched behind a fallen pillar across the street. With the rest of the squad they covered Dell and Tuck, now rushing past them to the rear.

Callie's last burst flickered and turned pink as she withdrew behind the metal, popping out the spent cube and slapping in a new one. Another burst sizzled along the ruined balcony, and she jumped up, firing again. An answering lance zinged off her shoulder, disrupting her aim and sending tingling numbness down her back and arms. Improved though their shielding was, the weapons of the Nine Cities matched it.

Successive hits would produce temporary paralysis—and sometimes a disastrous loss of mental composure.

The bridge into Splagnos lay at their backs, not far now, but they'd been counting on the Morresians' fear of the ruin to discourage pursuit. Old Morres had not lain abandoned sixty years without reason. When the Splagnosians had penetrated the city's protective dome and slaughtered its inhabitants years ago, they had left it drenched with poisonous residues. To this day, nothing lived here, except mites and a vine that fed off the toxins themselves.

Pierce's voice crackled over the receiver in her ear, "Okay, Two. Go."

The others were in position now and firing. Callie caught Brody's eye, and together they sprinted another leg. Something exploded behind her, black smoke roiling past her feet. Shouts followed, then the rapid *zip-zip-zip* of SIs, then another explosion, and the stench of ozone. The Morresians must have lobbed some stink bombs, in hopes the sedating gas would slow them. She skidded behind a wide stone stairway and resumed firing while the others ran by in their turns. Sweat dribbled down her sides. She wiped her brow again, drying her fingers on the leg of her khaki jumpsuit. The bandana she'd tied around her forehead was already soaked, useless until she could wring it out.

Ten Morresians now held the end of the long street, with more coming in behind them. If the bridge passpoint wasn't there . . .

*It'll be there*, she told herself as she picked a target and fired. She hit once, then twice, but missed the third shot that would have brought the Morresian down before he dove for cover.

By then her friends were past, the whole group leapfrogging down the street, until it was again Callie and Brody's turn.

"All the way to the bridge, Cal," Pierce said in her ear. She gave him a thumbs-up and sprinted down the road, her pack bouncing against her back. Careening around a black hulk of building, she raced into a crater-pocked plaza. On its far side stood the stone-and-iron wall that lined the river chasm bisecting Old Morres.

Two nights ago an ASB had given them a map of the ruins and a six-inch blood crystal. The map showed a long-destroyed bridge where there would likely be a passpoint for the crystal to activate. There'd been no direct instruction, as usual, but since the main bridge was under guard by both Morresian and Splagnosian troops, the passpoint seemed the perfect solution to the problem of crossing into Splagnos.

Now Callie sprinted across the plaza, dodging car-sized blocks and leaping runners of the oily-leaved toxvine. Impressive in its time, the bridge gateway had been reduced to a jungle of toppled stones and twisted, thigh-thick rails. Brody's rapid footsteps slapped the pavement behind her as she climbed the pile to peer over the top. Blue-black walls plunged a hundred feet to the frothy, emerald-hued Black River. Debris cluttered its narrow banks: stone blocks, wood beams, hunks of iron tangled with the detritus of vegetation carried through on high water. On the far wall all that remained of the opposing gatehouse was a gaping hole framed by dangling tendrils of iron. On the near side just to her right, a pair of supports arched thirty feet over the river before shearing off into nothing. There was maybe fifty feet between them and the other side.

And more of the obnoxious Watchers.

Brody climbed up beside her, panting. Behind him, the rear guard was firing from the point where the road curved.

"You look for a port up here," Callie told him. "Try the gate pillars. I'll check the rail tunnel under us."

Brody dropped back to do as she suggested while she slipped off her pack and slung her SI across her back, then eased down the far side of the wall. A breeze that was almost cool rushed up around her. About ten feet above the level where the bridge supports extended from the cliff wall, she was forced to stop. She could see the gap between the sheered-off bridge and far bank clearly now. If they couldn't find the activation port, maybe they could use their grappling hooks to swing over and rig a cable crossing. Their armor could withstand a good number of hits before the paralysis set in, and the Morresians hadn't proved to be especially good marksmen. It might work.

Tuck peered down at her from the top of the wall. "Brody's come up empty."

She glanced over the edge of her rocky perch. The ledge lay just below. "I'm almost there," she called as she turned onto her belly and wriggled over the meeting of two stones.

"Need a rope?" Tuck asked.

"No." Her toes reached the bottom of the block, then nothing. She risked another glance down. Cliffs and river spun up at her, dark rock, white foam, green ribbon. She shut her eyes and swallowed hard, willing the dizziness away. At least she had confirmed that the ledge extended out from her present position. An easy jump.

Touching the link for reassurance, she slipped off the rock, landed lightly, and immediately dropped forward onto knees and hands. For a moment she held the position, struggling to regain her breath and bring her heart rate back down, as new zips of SI fire above reminded her that time was short. The tunnel cut back into the rock before her, its single rail twisted and raised from its bed, the end standing about a yard above the ground. Shifting, hissing movement and frequent glimmers of light reflecting off undulating carapaces—along with a sharp acidic smell—told her the tunnel was crawling with mites.

Grimacing, she stood and began inspecting the walls.

The Tohvani's pale figure appeared even as its words formed in her mind. *You actually like this, don't you?* It stood five yards into the tunnel, swallowed in shadow, its scaly "skin" softly luminescent. *It's exciting, challenging, and you're good at it. Even if you won't admit it.*

She ignored the thing, studying the walls around it.

*It won't be like this at home, you know. Your overbearing mother, your matchmaking sister, your dead-end job.*

Annoyance rose in her. She cut it off.

*You're not going to have* him *there, either. We'll see to that.*

Callie's earpiece crackled, and Pierce's voice came through, calm and clear. "Find anything?"

She pressed the patch at her throat and spoke. "An old tunnel, dust, a zillion mites, and—yes! There it is."

High on the wall to the Tohvani's left, three blue circles glowed in the shadow. She'd seen red, gold, and silver ports before, but this was the first blue one.

"Great. I'll send Gerry down with the crystal." As the group's best marksman, Pierce would stay topside to cover their escape.

*You don't have to go home,* the Tohvani persisted. *We treat our own very well.*

"I can see that." She glanced sourly at the rubble around her. "Wonderful city you've provided here."

*Witnesses like you caused the destruction of this city. We tried to stop it.*

"Right." *Why are you talking to this thing, Callie?*

She turned from the Watcher as a pair of legs dangled past the overhang in a shower of dirt and pebbles. Gerry dropped onto the ledge, his pack, a rope with a grappling hook, and his SI strapped to his back. Immediately the earth began to shake, releasing a cloud of dust. Together they backed warily toward the precipice, eyeing the ten-ton blocks jittering above their heads. Earthquakes were common in the Inner Realm, and those rocks had been up there a long time. No reason to think they'd come down now, right?

Before a minute had passed, the trembling faded. Sneezing on the dust, Gerry handed her a rectangular prism of clear crimson flecked with gold, the finest blood crystal she'd ever seen; it would've brought a fortune in the Outer Realm. She took it to the insignia, then hesitated, made uneasy by the Watcher's brief appearance and struck again by the device's blue color. A false box would destroy the crystal and the person inserting it. Still, the configuration was right. . . .

She aligned the crystal with the central dot, feeling inexplicably tense, as if she might be shocked on contact. Yet, there was no reason—

"Hold up, there, Cal!"

She recoiled from the wall.

"Here's another one."

Gerry stood at the tunnel's mouth. A second circle-and-dot device glowed on the wall outside. Her nape hairs crawled. Distracted by the Tohvani, she hadn't seen it. Like the first, it, too, was blue.

She told Gerry about the Watcher. "I thought it was trying to distract me from that one," she said, gesturing to the first device, "but it must have been yours it didn't want me to see."

His brown eyes narrowed. "Or else that's what it *wants* us to think."

Callie inspected the second insignia. "You mean draw our attention to the right one in hopes we'll think it's wrong?"

Blue beams shot overhead in quick succession, startling them both.

Then Callie heard shouting and falling rock, the zip of the SIs. The ground trembled again in aftershock, and Pierce's voice rattled in her earpiece. "We can't hold them off much longer, love. You got something or not?"

She could almost hear the Tohvani's laughter.

*Think!* She told herself. And immediately sought the link. Though she could feel Elhanu's comforting presence, he never spoke to her directly through it, at least not in words. But that aversion she'd felt toward inserting the crystal into the first insignia—surely that was from him. Which meant the outer one was the real one.

Without hesitation, she stepped to the wall and pressed the crystal's end to the device. It stuck with a click and she jerked her hand back as a current zinged through it. The crystal vanished into the rock with a high-pitched whine, and the ground trembled a third time. Then a shaft of red light shot out from the ledge, arcing over the gorge to the rock on the far side.

"Outstanding!" Gerry cried, slapping her back. Grinning with relief, Callie pressed her transmission patch. "We've got activation. Come on down."

The last word had barely left her mouth before three packs dropped onto the ledge—one was her own—and Tuck and Dell slithered over the rocks after them. As they turned to the bridge, Tuck exclaimed in horror, "It has no side rails."

He was right. It was not a bridge so much as a walkway of light, with nothing to hang on to.

"But it's a good yard across," Dell pointed out. "If it were on flat ground we wouldn't think twice."

LaTeisha landed beside them, saw the bridge, and made the same observation as Tuck.

"Well," Gerry said finally, "the longer we stand here, the worse it'll git."

He stepped onto the red span and started rapidly across it. As he topped the central rise, Callie took a deep breath and followed, fixing her gaze on the point where the bridge met the rock on the far side.

The Morresians spread out along the cliff behind them, yelling and firing wildly. They hit few of their targets, and everyone reached the far bank. Then Pierce shot out the activation port and the bridge dissolved—just as a couple of Morresians were climbing down to it.

Leaving their enraged howls behind, Pierce led the way into the Splagnosian side of the city. Tall, soot-stained buildings sagged around them, walls pocked by the acid rains which daily leaked through the crumbling dome overhead. Dark green toxvine snaked across the rubble in a glistening carpet pierced by six-inch thorns. Foot-long mites the same color as the vine scuttled beneath it, providing a hissing, rustling accompaniment to their passage. The sour-dishrag stench, carried on air that was hotter and steamier than ever, became nauseating.

Twenty minutes later Pierce called a break, and the group settled on the stairs of a once-dignified building relatively free of the noxious vine. Callie sat just below him and pulled out her second water bottle—the first one long emptied—and a vacuum-sealed packet of cheese and crackers. John and Whit broke out their own food just below her, and Brody, Gerry, Tuck, and Dell scattered in a ragged half circle around them. Evvi and LaTeisha chose a higher spot, away from the others.

The two had formed an unexpected friendship in the weeks since they'd left Hope. Evvi had sobered greatly since her brush with death, and though it seemed she had made peace with the fact she'd never have Pierce, her manner toward Callie remained cool. The one constant was her devotion to Elhanu—and surprisingly, to Pierce, for all he'd disappointed her. Callie couldn't help but admire her for it.

LaTeisha, on the other hand, worried her. Two weeks ago Pierce had shot Ian in the act of betrayal, then left him for his Morresian cohorts to care for. LaTeisha was appalled by this lack of compassion, particularly in light of Pierce's own past failures. She'd called him a hypocritical tyrant, though it was his own failures that had given him the insight—and resolve—to do what he'd done. It wasn't Ian's first slip, after all. He'd been tasting fire curtains and flirting with the enemy for weeks. Whit insisted Pierce had let it go too long as it was.

LaTeisha remained unmollified, her outrage festering into a resentment that was becoming dangerous to them all. Ironically, Evvi was the only one Teish would listen to anymore. If Evvi didn't get her squared away soon, they were likely to find themselves with yet another casualty of war.

"Hey, people," John said, lounging back on the step in front of Callie. "We're in Splagnos! Congratulations!" He lifted his water bottle in salute.

A low chorus of *all-right*s and *whoo-hoo*s followed.

"Don't get cocky," Pierce admonished them. "We're not done yet."

They'd left Hope over six weeks ago, crossing corners of Orgais and Fobehho, all of the width of Zelos and Morres, and, just now, the border into Splagnos. They had sneaked through cities disguised as soldiers, smuggled themselves past checkpoints in the secret compartments of traders' carts, and once even pulled off a direct confrontation. They'd been trailed and trapped and ambushed and nearly apprehended, and though they'd lost people along the way, a good third of them remained. Just when they needed it, they had found an ASB with a cache of ammunition or a hidden passage—or important information like when the guard would change, or how to bypass the main gate, or when the rail tunnels were empty. The one time they'd been caught, the opposition was so intoxicated by their own success they had become careless, and the group had easily escaped.

After that they gained a reputation—and a price on their heads. The city that captured them would win prestige, bragging rights, and the favor of the "gods." Starting halfway across the state of Morres, they'd been pursued by a continual relay of patrols. Splagnos would be no better.

Surprisingly, the prospect no longer scared her. In fact, the Tohvani was right when it accused her of liking this. Every success increased her confidence—not only in Elhanu's ability to keep his promises, but also in her own ability to follow his lead and survive. Despite Pierce's admonition, it was hard not to be cocky.

The others were talking in twos and threes now, and behind her, Pierce said quietly, "That was pretty terrific what you did back there, Cal. Climbing down to find the port."

She shrugged, watching Whit fire stones at the mites as they tried to make their way up the steps. His praise embarrassed her. "Anyone else would've done the same. I just happened to think of it first."

He tugged on her braid. "Don't make it less than it is. You did good. And walking over that bridge even unnerved me. You've come a long way, my love."

"We all have," she said, twisting around to grin up at him.

He wore the days-old grizzle that had been almost perpetual since they'd left Hope, and his hair, cut so very short in anticipation of these weeks in the field, now curled in sweat-drenched waves over his ears and neck. Like the rest of them, he'd tied a bandana around his head to soak up the sweat. The thin gold circlet that served as his upgraded helmet peeked out beneath it.

He also wore a stitched-leather bandoleer, its pockets filled with turquoise E-cubes. It was a gift from a sympathetic Zelosian trader who had nursed the desire, but not the courage, to make his own run for the exit portal. The bandoleer had once belonged to a Splagnosian captain, and it had pleased the Zelosian to see Pierce wear it.

It pleased Callie as well. In fact, everything about Pierce pleased her. Not a day went by that she didn't warm with admiration and affection for him—and thank Elhanu for bringing them together. Not a day went by that she didn't have to shove down the still-simmering fear of losing him.

Pierce smiled, reading her feelings. He brushed her cheek with his knuckles. "We're gonna make it," he murmured. "He'll see us through."

Of course he would. She really did believe the promise. When the doubts came, she had only to bring up an image of Elhanu's twinkly-eyed grin and gentle voice, or the goats that had helped them cross the mountain, or the Aggillon who had served them so willingly in Hope and had serenaded them with their wonderful ballad that still lacked a proper ending. To say nothing of all the remarkable "coincidences" that had brought them to these steps.

"Six days!" John crowed, lifting his bottle to the skies. "Six days and we're home! Whoo-eee!"

"Six days is a long time," Whit rumbled beside him, beaning another mite with one of his stones.

"That was just a guesstimate, anyway," Pierce said. "We could be weeks yet."

John twisted to look at him, his face greasy with sweat and grime.

"Not if the rail tunnels really *do* go all the way to Splagnos."

Their map of Old Morres showed an abandoned hub in the Nine Cities' monorail system not far from their location. John wanted to use the old tunnels to cross *under* the plain to Splagnos.

"Let's find the tunnel first," Pierce advised. He bit into a ration bar, then squinted up the street. Callie followed the direction of his gaze to the dome arching overhead—a dilapidated framework of holes and gray, cracked panels. Beyond it lay the great Splagnosian plain, where rocky expanses offered no cover and little usable water. Plagued with earthquakes and violent windstorms, it was pocked with sulfurous steam vents, as well as bottomless mud flats, scalding pools under thin rock shells, and unexpected pockets of lava. With such natural defenses, one would think the Splagnosians would rest easy. Not so. Swarms of surveillance drones searched out the first sign of intruders, marking their location for the regular manned patrols, the number of which had undoubtedly increased in honor of their arrival.

The next few days were sure to be interesting.

Shortly after resuming their trek, they came to what had once been a vast plaza, but was now transformed into a dish-shaped field of tox-vine. Craters alternated with the rubble of toppled buildings, giving the plaza an undulating, hilly appearance. At the center, a sagging rotunda housed the deteriorating poles of a fire curtain—one snapped off about five feet from the ground, the other listing at a forty-five-degree angle.

Early in their crossing Tuck discovered a stairway leading to the very hub they sought. Unfortunately, it had caved in long ago and was crawling with mites. Passing it by, they had just climbed a tumble of stone blocks on the plaza's far side when Whit, on point, signaled an alert. In the ensuing silence, they heard muted voices up ahead accompanied by the thump of footfalls and the clatter of dislodged rock. At Pierce's silent signal, the group fanned out in opposite directions, taking cover in the buildings, the foliage, and behind the rocks.

No sooner were they hidden than, one by one, six strangers descended over the rubble into the pocket before them. Helmeted, goggled, and gloved, they wore clear plastic respirators and oxygen packs. Heavy leather armor of Zelosian make protected their upper bodies, and all carried short-barreled, thick-bodied Zelosian riot guns. Four of them eyed the surrounding buildings with weapons at the ready while the middle two poked around in the foliage. One came within feet of where Whit was lying. They were too small and poorly equipped to be Splagnosians, but with the respirators and bulky armor Callie didn't peg them for fellow witnesses, either. And careful inspection revealed the dark-threaded aura of fire-curtain addicts.

As the strangers crossed the flat and climbed the pile of stone Callie and her friends had just descended, her eye caught on the woman bringing up the rear. Considerably smaller than her companions, her over-large armor, helmet, and respirator did a good job of obscuring her identity. Nonetheless she looked familiar. As she climbed after her fellows, Callie leaned over the window ledge, dislodging a stream of gravel that caused the stranger to whirl back, weapon leveled.

Callie recognized her with a jolt. Meg! Before she could gather her wits to speak, however, the woman turned and hurried after her companions, clearly spooked. Callie scrambled through the window in pursuit, calling after her to wait. Meg turned and fired so quickly she could not have seen what she was shooting at, and still the bolt struck Callie squarely, staggering her backward with a grunt of surprise, green fire sizzling across her protective shield. When she didn't go down, Meg stood there, staring stupidly.

Recovering her breath, Callie moved toward her friend again. "Don't shoot, Meg! It's Callie!" Which should have been obvious, since, unlike Meg, Callie wore neither goggles nor respirator.

Meg kept the weapon trained on her, but did not fire, her mouth gaping behind the respirator.

Callie stopped at the base of the pile, four feet below her, nostrils curling at a fetid odor.

Finally, Meg's weapon sagged to her side. "Callie?" Her voice sounded small and hollow through the plastic.

Rustles and crunchings from behind told Callie her friends were emerging. Meg looked at them, then back at Callie. "Your belt worked," she said. "And you're not wearing a respirator."

"No."

Meg looked at the others again. "John? Tuck?" Her mouth sagged. "Brody?"

Brody stopped at Callie's side. "Hi, Meg. Guess you made it."

"Yeah." Meg seemed overwhelmed. She turned to Callie again and a smile bloomed on her face. "He did it," she murmured. "He actually did it."

At that moment Meg's companions reappeared atop the rubble, and she twisted back to hail them. "Hold off, Row! It's Callie and Brody and the others."

Warily the newcomers clambered down to meet them. Only one was female, so that had to be Rowena, bigger and bustier than Callie remembered. She wore a molded breastplate and carbon-streaked thigh guards. The sleeves of her shirt, which might have been red once, were rolled up over grimy arms marred with oozing boils. Her eyes hid behind tinted goggles, but her mouth hung slack-jawed behind the respirator. For a moment she stood staring, as Meg had, then jumped down to face Callie on even ground. "Bloody harries! It really is you." They eyed each other, and then she said, "We figured the Trogs had gotten you."

"You figured wrong," Callie said.

Meg descended to stand shoulder to shoulder with Callie as she turned back to face Rowena. She smelled terrible.

Rowena held herself stiffly. "How'd you guys get down the mountain? Don't tell me you followed us?"

Brody cradled his SI in one arm. "We found Pierce's Safehaven."

"No kidding?" She glanced at the bearded, heavy-browed man who'd shadowed her down the hill—not anyone Callie recognized. "I left the rim with these people."

"More gaters, eh?"

Row snorted and scratched under her respirator strap.

"It was just like he described it," Brody added.

"Too bad he never got to see it for himself," said Rowena.

"Who says I didn't?" Pierce's voice drew their attention to the mat of vines from which he, Whit, and Evvi were now emerging.

If Rowena had been surprised before, now she nearly dropped her rifle. She swayed and stared at him openmouthed. Her skin paled, and when she finally spoke, her voice was flat. "Pierce. You're alive."

"Sorry to disappoint you."

"I'm not disappointed." Her voice remained creepily expressionless.

"So where's Morgan?" Whit asked.

Rowena turned from Pierce. "Killed six weeks ago. Trogs took out more than half our people." She paused. "I can't believe you guys made it this far with no armor. What do you do? Dodge energy beams?"

John said, "We have our belts, Row."

Rowena flicked a dismissive hand. "Those worthless things? We threw ours away weeks ago. You guys must not have seen much action."

"So what are *you* doing here?" Pierce asked.

"Heading for Splagnos, of course."

"Shouldn't you be going in the opposite direction?"

Rowena cradled her weapon loosely in her arms as she scanned the buildings behind them. "There's an old hub under this plaza. Used to be part of the rail system linking the Nine Cities." She finally met his gaze, tilting her head back slightly. "That's the way we're going in. Soon as we find the opening."

"It's back there." Pierce nodded across the plaza. "Under that twisted railing."

She straightened to rigidity. "You found it?"

"It's not gonna—"

"Show me!"

He glanced at Whit, who arched the brow over his good eye.

Pierce only shrugged. "Okay."

As the combined groups followed him, Meg leaned against Callie and whispered, "When you go, can I come with you?"

"Go?"

"You don't want to stay with these people. They're all crazy. Especially the General."

"Who's the General?"

"Our leader. But he's completely whacked out. Too much fire curtain. He'll think you're here to accompany him to Splagnos. If you refuse, he'll accuse you of being Splagnosian spies. It's happened before."

"Why are you still with him?"

"I had no choice. You have no idea how glad I am to see you." She patted Callie's shoulder. "But you have to go—soon. I'll be ready. Just say the word. It is all right, isn't it? If I go with you?"

"Of course, but . . ." She hesitated. "Meg, what if this passage is for real?"

Meg had no response to that.

Once Rowena had confirmed the hub's location, she was ecstatic. While she radioed the good news to the rest of her group, Callie relayed Meg's message about the General to Pierce and the others.

"Leave?" John cried when she finished. "Are you kidding? If Row knows the way, it's got to be the reason we were sent here."

"We could always come back later after they're gone," Callie suggested, glancing at Pierce. He was watching Rowena, hunched over the radio, the three larger men clustered around her.

"No," Tuck said, pulling off his bandana and wringing it out. "Once they come through in Splagnos, the route'll surely be found and closed."

Behind him Gerry and Dell nodded.

"They probably already know about it," Pierce said.

Whit looked at him sharply. "You think it's a trap?"

"It'd be a good one."

"True," Tuck agreed, retying the cloth around his head.

"Then why're we here?" John demanded.

"Maybe to rescue Meg," said Callie.

The way Pierce looked at her, she surmised it wasn't a bad guess. He only said, "These people stink of fire curtain. No way we're to stay with them."

"So what do we do?" John asked.

"Take Meg's advice."

Pierce turned to Rowena as she rejoined them.

"Well, that got his attention," she said. "You say you already checked it out?" She indicated the opening.

"It's in bad shape," Pierce told her. "The way the ground shakes around here, I wouldn't risk using it."

Rowena waved off the concern. "Those shivers relieve the pressure so there won't *be* a big one. And the General says the tunnel's clear all the way."

"How can he know that?"

"He knows." She took off her helmet and scratched at one of several oozing sores on her barren, bristling scalp. Tufts of longer hair stood out here and there, but most of it had been hacked close, presumably in an attempt to tend the sores. Part of one of her ears was missing, as well, the remainder swollen and distorted.

"So who is this general, anyway?" John asked. "And how'd you hook up with him?"

Rowena got a funny expression on her face. "We'd be dead if not for him. Muties had us hemmed in and outnumbered three to one when the General and his men drove 'em off."

"How many men does he have?" Callie asked.

"About a hundred then. Not so many now." She scratched the nub of her ear and settled the helmet back into place. "So how were you all planning on getting into Splagnos?"

"Cross the plain and slip through the gates," Pierce said.

Rowena gaped. "Don't you know *anything*? No one crosses the plain. It's a good thing you found us."

Pierce looked amused. "I think we'll take our chances topside. Good luck with the tunnel, though."

"What?"

He turned away.

"You can't leave." She hurried to block his path. "We should work together. It makes sense. We'd be a bigger force. And we are on the same side."

He held her gaze levelly. "I don't think so, Row. But thanks anyway."

As he started past she seized his arm. "You can't go. Not until you meet the General."

"Why?"

"Because—because you have to!"

"No, I don't." He slipped from her grasp and started across the plaza toward the Splagnosian plain. The rest of his group followed, Meg scampering childlike to Callie's side. They'd only gone a few yards when seven men appeared over the rubble twenty feet to their right.

Big men all, they were uniformly armored and more heavily armed than the others. Their leader was solid, broad-shouldered, and tallest by a head. His dark goggles and clear respirator covered a bearded, strong-featured face, and long black hair flowed from under a horned Zelosian helmet.

Callie recognized him instantly.

CHAPTER

28

Garth expressed his own recognition with a curse and turned to Rowena. "*This* was your surprise?"

She smiled.

"You told me he was dead."

"I thought he was."

Garth crossed the remaining ten feet that separated them. His dark goggles glittered like spider's eyes, and the closer he got, the more suffocating his presence became. His face was hard and haggard. Black threads cavorted about him and the exposed portions of his face flickered iridescent yellow—both indications of regular fire-curtain exposure. And Pierce was right about the smell, almost sweet, with a tinge of decay.

He stopped in front of them, standing a good foot and a half taller than when they had parted. Pierce met his stony regard unflinchingly, but Callie fought to hold her ground. The psychic force of Garth's personality was even more daunting than his size, and his close proximity generated the same tooth-gritting sensation as a fire curtain.

Pierce spoke quietly. "Hello, Garth. I guess you made it up the canyon all right."

"Sure did, buddy. Thor and Lokai with me." He half turned, indicating two of the men who had accompanied him. Thor's hair had grown out in a mane of red that billowed around his helmet. He was almost as big as Garth. Lokai, by contrast, was all bones and teeth.

"It was one rockin' hot fight," Garth went on, "but we made it. Without any help, either." He spat off to the side. "Matter of fact, we've come all this way without kissing up to one stinking alien. Did it all on our own."

*What about the weapons you carry?* Callie thought. *And the armor you're wearing?*

He grinned at Pierce, his chest swelling. "Told you it could be done."

*And the fire curtain. You can't deny that's alien made.*

"We're gonna go all the way, too. Straight through Splagnos to the portal."

"Are you?" Pierce said mildly.

"Hey, if it wasn't for us, these fool gaters'd all be dead. You should've seen those muties run when we came up. We've got a reputation, you know. No one tangles with Hell's Horsemen. That's what they call us—Hell's Horsemen."

Rowena handed him a water bottle. He spat again, then drained the vessel in huge, sloppy gulps, liquid spilling down his beard and chest. Done, he handed it back to her, wiping his mouth with the back of his hand, goggle eyes fixed on Pierce. "You come through Zelos, too?"

"Of course."

Garth shook his head. "I am truly amazed. You are one lucky sucker!" He turned to Rowena. "You check the subway yet?"

"Earl and Grandy are now."

Garth motioned for Thor and Lokai to go below, as well.

Pierce started forward again, continuing in the direction he'd been heading when the newcomers arrived.

"Did I say you could go anywhere?" Garth asked.

Pierce eyed him sidelong.

At the stairway's mouth, Thor and Lokai paused.

"We've got a lot of catching up to do," Garth said.

"And we have a lot of city to cross before dark," Pierce countered. He brought the SI up, bracing the butt on his hip.

Garth laughed. "You know, I thought you just said you were gonna cross this city before dark. Isn't that crazy?"

Pierce walked on.

"You're gonna get those people killed," Garth yelled.

Pierce ignored him as Callie and the others followed.

Garth erupted in an explosion of curses. "You're not gonna do this to me again."

Pierce kept walking.

"NO!"

The back of Callie's neck crawled. Then a wave of rage slammed into her, washing through her like liquid fire. Red tinged her vision, violence swelled within her—and changed, instantly, to paralyzing terror.

*He's doing this*, she thought. *Find the link and you can turn it off.*

Feeling as if she was drowning, she fought through the emotion, seeking the connection with Elhanu. Warmth bloomed within her as his reassuring touch drove away the dark passions. Exhaling deeply, she walked on. An instant later green fire slammed into her back, hurling her forward into the rubble. She smelled ozone, but when it faded she was unhurt. Pierce helped her up and they kept going.

"You stop now, Pierce," Garth roared, "or I'll set my men on you. You know we'll win."

They'd almost reached the first rise of blocks when a fountain of rocks erupted to the left, and then one of the fallen pillars danced upright to fall at Pierce's feet, a yard from crushing him. Dust billowed up as another psychic wave assaulted them, sluicing by Callie like water around a rock.

As it died Pierce wheeled, SI leveled. "Back off, Garth."

Growling, the bigger man lifted a meaty hand, the motion sharp and jerky. Pierce's weapon leapt from his grasp as if on a string and sailed through the air, clattering to the ground at Garth's feet. Callie stared, struggling to accept what she'd seen. She knew there were Trogs who could do this, mutants in the wilds, but Garth was not—

Understanding made her sick and cold. His size, the edge in his voice, the growths on his arms—she had seen it all before.

Suddenly a wall of bodies hurtled toward her from the right, armored giants that took at least three hits to drop—the rest of Garth's men, she realized, hiding out of sight until needed. She shot three of them before she was bowled over.

Shortly she and her friends were disarmed, relieved of their belts and headbands, and lined up at gunpoint before the substation opening. Garth strutted up and down before them, the dark goggles still obscuring his eyes. He stopped in front of Pierce.

"When you left," he said, "you might as well have taken the rest of the group. Those that didn't desert worried about everything, doubted my every word. In the end, it got them killed. And left the rest of us fighting for our lives. I lost an eye, Thor lost his hand, and Lokai'll never be the same. You're *not* running out on me again."

He turned to his followers. "We'll let them lead the way. If those rumors of poison gas pockets are true, they'll be the first to know."

"General, sir—?" One of his men slipped through the ranks, panting. "Splagnosians just entered the city."

Garth gave passionate and profane vent to his annoyance, then ordered everyone into the hole. "The drones'll come first, so make it fast, people."

They hurried into the substation, herding their prisoners before them. A wide stair descended through successive curtains of age-stiffened vinyl slats to a vast shadow-swathed rotunda. Hand-lamp beams revealed lines of sagging wooden partitions and crumbling walls extending toward them from beneath the great fall of debris where the ceiling's center had collapsed. Massive iron beams rusted with age, angled amid boulders and dark veins of earth. To the right of the entrance, railed passenger aisles gleamed dully before a pair of featureless sliding doors in the curved outer wall. Several Watchers clung to that wall, their eyes reflecting the light in eerie yellow-green disks.

Callie followed Pierce down the stair, sneezing in the dust, her nose burning from the acidic stench of mites. In the darkness she could hear them chittering and rasping. At least it was cooler here.

The prisoners were prodded into the ruins of a three-sided vendor's stall, stone walls crumbling at waist height. Relieved of their boots, they were left under guard as the rest of the men began assembling what appeared to be a pair of generating poles.

"Are they making what I think they're making?" Callie asked Pierce in alarm.

He nodded grimly. "They've got some injuries to heal, and if they're planning a run on Splagnos they'll want to be as strong as possible. There won't be time for this later."

"When they come through, though," she whispered, "won't they want to eat and . . ." She trailed off uneasily.

Pierce's jaw muscles rippled beneath the grizzle of his beard. "The eat part for sure." He directed her attention to where several of the Horsemen were emptying their absconded packs, tossing aside clothes and equipment, but piling up any food or E-cubes they found.

Rowena came over to gloat. She wore one of their stolen belts and had removed her goggles and helmet, leaving only the respirator. "You thought you were so smart," she sneered at Pierce. "That you were the only one who could get us out, the only one who could really understand the precious manual." Her face twisted. "What a worthless waste of paper *that* turned out to be. All those glowing promises, the armor, the invincible belts—not much good to you now, are they?"

"It's not the equipment that matters, Rowena. It's the source."

"Your alien master, you mean? Wonderful Elhanu, who's promised to deliver us all? Well, where is he? Where was he when the Trogs attacked? When forty-seven of our friends were slaughtered on the road from Rimlight? Where was he, Pierce?" She advanced on him till she was shouting in his face.

Her voice faded into silence. Everyone was watching them. After a long moment, Pierce said quietly, "I think you know."

She slapped him. He stood like a stone, holding her gaze.

Her face fluoresced yellow-green. "You are so arrogant! So absolutely convinced you're right. Even now, even here, you still believe he's going to bail you out!"

"Only if it suits his purpose."

She shook her head. "What's happened to you, Pierce? You used to be a man."

"Rowena!" Garth's rough voice echoed through the chamber. "Knock it off. I need you over here."

She eyed Pierce a moment more, then stalked away.

"She hates you," Meg said, standing at Callie's shoulder. "Ever since we split, everything was always your fault."

"It's not me she hates," Pierce said, settling against one of the walls. "It's Elhanu."

"Or herself," said Callie, watching Rowena squat beside Garth as the two bent over some kind of box.

Meg was hovering too close again, as if she took comfort in the nearness. Puzzled, Callie looked at her. They'd taken her helmet along with those of the other prisoners, and like Rowena, her hair had been hacked away. A seven-inch gash lay open and suppurating on the side of her head.

"Oh, Meg," Callie murmured. "What happened?"

Meg probed the swollen skin around it with hesitant fingers, tears glittering in her eyes. "No one would sew it up. And we don't carry antibiotics. Garth says we don't need them as long as we have the curtain."

"Which you aren't using." She'd known that from the beginning. Meg lacked the curtain aura.

"I didn't like what it did to me. I didn't like what it did to them. I guess maybe I saw—well, anyway, I only used it a couple times." Her eyes watched Garth's men, setting up their generator. "It's getting better, though. I think it's going to heal, given enough time."

"The scar will be horrendous."

Meg smiled bitterly. "As if that matters."

"Of course it matters. The Aggillon may be able to resuscitate us, but they might not be able to do anything about scars. Teish, do you have some of that miracle salve?"

"Not anymore."

"I've got some," John said, handing over a small plastic vial.

Callie took it and sat Meg on a tilted block.

Her friend eyed the vial. "Miracle salve?"

"We got it in a harries' nest. More than that, you don't want to know. But it works wonders."

"You were in a harries' nest?"

Callie nodded. "They ignored us. I guess they only get aggressive outside their nests." She frowned at the wound. "I oughta wash this first."

She got up and asked Lokai, who was their guard, for some water. He met her gaze sullenly, dark eyes blank in his gaunt face. After a few seconds, he looked away. "She chose to let it fester, she can suffer with it."

"Don't be a jerk, Lokai. Give me the water."

He shifted uncomfortably, and then Garth joined them. "There a problem here?"

Like the others, he had removed his goggles. One of his eyes rested blindly askew in a horribly scarred socket. Now he grinned at Callie with a familiar leer, and she fought to keep from walking away.

"I want some water," she said.

Garth stroked her face. "You still look good enough to eat, babe."

She slapped his fingers and he grabbed her hand, jerking her close. "Don't get feisty, girl. I can have anything I want from you, anytime I choose."

"Except my respect."

His eyes flashed and his teeth bared. Then he smiled. "Maybe I only want your body."

She glared at him. "Can I have the water?"

Working his jaw, he released her and motioned for Lokai to get it. But he stood grinning while the man complied, and when she turned away, bottle in hand, he pinched her bottom. She flinched, swallowed her cry of outrage, and hurried on, his laughter burning in her ears.

Pierce stood twenty feet away, fists clenched. Whit blocked his path, one hand on his chest, the other on his arm. John had the other arm.

"You know he's nuts," Callie murmured as she drew even with them. "It's not worth making trouble over."

Pierce didn't acknowledge her comments, his gaze fixed on Garth. She exchanged glances with Whit, then returned to her patient.

Meg hissed at Callie's first touch but held still after that. Presently she said, "You know him? The General, I mean?"

"Remember Garth?"

"The one who abandoned you on the trail?" Meg turned wide eyes upon her. "That's *him?*"

"He's bigger now. And uglier." Callie set the rag aside, fingered oily salve from the vial, and daubed it onto the wound. Meg hissed again and ground her teeth until she was finished. The stuff stung fiercely— Callie knew from experience.

As Callie recapped the container, Meg sobbed. "Oh, Cal, I've been such a fool. And I'm so sorry I said all those things to you."

Callie sat back on her heels, wiping her fingers on her pants. "Well, I deserved most of it. And you were right about me and Pierce." She smiled. "I am in love with him."

Meg's eyes rounded. "Does he know?"

Callie nodded.

Her friend glanced over her shoulder at him, sitting now with Whit and John, their backs braced against the tottering masonry. "Does he . . . care?"

Callie held up the hand with the ring on it. "You might say that."

Meg's eyes widened further. She seized Callie's hand and pulled it close to inspect the ring, a single blood crystal on a band of gold. "He gave this to you?" She looked up. "You're going to *marry* him?"

Callie nodded, enjoying Meg's shock. "When we get back."

She expected Meg to squeal and giggle hysterically. Instead, after a minute of stunned silence, her friend burst into tears and threw her arms around her. As Meg bawled into her shoulder, Callie patted her back, completely bewildered.

"I'm sorry," Meg blubbered. "It's just—from the night I left you at the lake it's been one awful thing after another. Coming down that road was a nightmare. We had to leave the injured, and they begged us to kill them so the Trogs wouldn't get them. There was no place to hide, no place to rest. We didn't sleep for days. And then the harries came. And the fear—you have no idea. Constant terror, never knowing what was going to happen. I thought I'd go crazy. When the General saved us, we were so happy. But then he—"

Her face twitched and she looked away, wiping the tears from her cheeks. Her eyes fastened on Garth as he supervised the construction of the fire curtain, the poles extending eight feet high now. Hatred hardened her face, and, given what Callie knew of Garth's sexual appetite before his exposure to the fire curtain, she guessed what must've happened.

"Oh, Meg," she murmured.

"The second night after he rescued us," Meg said bitterly. "And any time he's wanted it since. It doesn't matter where we are. Or who's around to see." Her face crumpled and she started crying again.

Callie held her, swaying with nausea and fury and a hot regret for having told her about Pierce. Meg's nightmare made her own good fortune seem hideously unfair and sent an irrational knife of guilt twisting into her heart.

It took Meg a while to stop weeping. Then they sat in silence, holding each other until Meg asked, "What's going to happen now?"

"I don't know. But something will turn up. You can count on that."

Meg raised hopeful eyes. "You honestly believe that? Even now?"

"Especially now. This is the way Elhanu works. You'll see."

The ground began to shake, and everyone froze, all eyes darting to the darkness above. Dirt and small rocks rained briefly upon them, then the tremor faded. Gradually activity started up again.

The grit of a footstep and the sense of someone nearby drew their eyes to Brody, standing beside them, his eyes on Meg, his expression hesitant. "You okay?"

Meg wiped her face again, smearing dirt across her freckles. "Better than I've been in a while."

Brody squatted beside her, and suddenly Callie felt like a third wheel. Murmuring an excuse she knew neither of them heard, she went to join Pierce. Whit idly tossed a palm-sized rock in one hand as the others watched their captors put the final touches on the curtain.

"How is she?" Pierce asked as she settled beside him.

"About as gutted as this substation." She watched Garth gesticulating at his cronies. "I hope he does make it to the portal. And that I'm there to see him fry when he tries to go through it."

Pierce said nothing. But after a moment his hand slid over the back of her neck, fingers massaging away the gathered tension. She leaned into the pressure, grateful for the comfort of his touch, wishing there was some way to offer similar comfort to her friend.

Meg and Brody were talking quietly now, keeping their distance, their body language still strained. Their trials had forged them into different people—there was a brokenness in Meg, a humility and soberness Callie had never seen before, and in Brody, a compassion and a gentleness that reminded her of Mr. C.

"I don't get it," John muttered. "What're they doing here?" He gestured toward Garth and the others. "Why were they allowed to make it up that canyon?"

"For the same reason Mander was allowed to bring Jacki and Brian to the top of the cliff," Pierce said. "Volition. The cliffs aren't there to keep people out of the Inner Realm so much as to discourage them from seeking the Exit before they've been Changed. They make it harder to do the wrong thing, rather than removing the opportunity altogether. But those who are determined to go their own way, no matter how difficult, will ultimately be allowed to do so."

"And in the end reap the consequences of their decisions," Whit said, still tossing the stone in his hand.

"Yes," Pierce said softly. To Callie's ear, sensitive as it was to the subtle tones of his voice, he sounded almost sad.

Garth's voice rose abruptly over the murmur of conversation. "No, you moron! If they're all battered, they'll only hold us back." He said something more in a lower voice, and then more loudly, "We'll do this fast and get out, understand? Now turn it on."

Someone flipped a switch and a high-pitched hum accompanied the leap of energy from one pole to the other. Neon shades of green and blue oozed between slowly shifting globs of black, the light reflecting in a greenish arc that betrayed an ominous gathering of Watchers in the shadows around them.

The curtain had long ceased to entice Callie. Now its whine only triggered an annoying vibration in her teeth.

The first man stepped through, his bloodied right arm hanging limp at his side. The membrane jerked him off the ground, pulling out both arms like a marionette. He cried out as white flashes swarmed along his injured limb like fireflies. For three seconds he hung there, moaning and twitching. It released him abruptly and he staggered through, his arm no longer limp. Immediately he fell upon the food packets.

A man with a ruined leg was shoved through next. The curtain caught him mid-stumble, and he spasmed upright with a cry of pleasure, just like the other man. Again he hung spread-eagled, shivering and shaking as the healing sparks crackled up and down his leg. It reminded Callie of the Aggillon's regenerating gel, only more aggressive.

They ran several more through, then Garth called for Pierce and Callie. He sat in a field chair about thirty feet from the curtain. This close its energy field sent unpleasant chills across Callie's skin and set her teeth on edge.

Garth stood and walked around Pierce, looking him up and down. "You've tasted it before, haven't you?" he said at length.

Pierce eyed him calmly. "So what if I have?"

Garth sat down again. "Figured as much. It was the only way you could've survived with them as long as you did. Is that why you lived and Tom didn't?"

Pierce did not answer.

"You're feeling the pull, aren't you?" Garth asked with a grin. "The need, the shaking want of it."

As far as Callie could see, Pierce was calm and solid as a rock.

Garth tilted his head back. "How long's it been, huh? A week? Two? I can see the craving in your eyes."

There was nothing of the kind in Pierce's eyes. He couldn't have been more deadpan. Besides, with the link so consistently open and active within him, Callie had long ago stopped worrying about his vulnerability to the curtain's allure. Right now she suspected he was as revolted as she was, and Garth was simply projecting his own desires.

"You can have it now," Garth said, motioning for the guard to free him. Pierce didn't move. "If you don't, you'll die before the day is over."

Pierce cocked a brow. "I thought you didn't hold with accepting alien help."

Garth laughed. "I don't see any aliens helping us."

"What do you call that?" Pierce gestured at the fire curtain.

"It may be an alien device, but *I* stole it for *my* purposes." He looked at the thing with an expression of warm pride. "That little baby's given us the edge we need to make it to the Exit."

Pierce shook his head sadly. "It's not making it to the Exit that sets us free, Garth. If you're not Changed first, you'll only die trying to walk through it. And if you die in this Arena Unchanged, that's it for you. You'll never see Earth again. There'll be no more second chances."

For a moment it seemed he had captured Garth's attention, that somehow the respect the man had carried for him all those years they were together pushed itself to the fore and made him listen where he wouldn't have listened to anyone else. Callie saw it in his face—the sudden uncertainty, even alarm, with which he considered the possibility his old friend was right. But then it was swallowed up by the passions he'd so completely surrendered to of late, and he rejected it with a forceful vulgarity.

Even then Pierce didn't give up. "Come on, Garth. You must see our bodies aren't like yours anymore. How else can we walk this realm unprotected and suffer no ill effects? How else can we can touch the toxvine, go unaffected by mite venom, and breathe the poisoned air?"

"I can breathe the air fine." Garth yanked off his respirator, glaring. "See?"

"Then why were you wearing that thing?"

Garth lurched out of his chair and seized Pierce by the throat. "Don't mock me, you miserable Trog licker! I could kill you in a heartbeat!"

Pierce's face turned red. He began to gasp and pry at the fingers gripping his throat. Laughing, Garth lifted him off his feet, holding him one-handed. Callie threw herself at them but was knocked away as if she were a fly. She slammed into the ground, and blinding agony speared her side. At first she could only twitch and gasp, dizzy and nauseated by the pain. When she came back to herself, Garth loomed over her, Pierce still in hand.

"Please," she said, her voice coming out high-pitched and infuriat-ingly meek.

He grinned. "Oh, that's nice. Beg some more, woman. I like it."

"Don't hurt him." She sat up, gathering her feet beneath her, trying to think of something aggressive and useful to do.

Garth's black eye glittered. "What will you give me in return, babe? Obedience?"

"Yes." She noticed Rowena behind him, watching avidly, the pur-loined belt sagging at her waist.

"Respect?" Garth demanded.

Callie swallowed. Nodded. The belt was fastened only by its Velcro tabs—Rowena hadn't snugged it down, nor had she fed the end into its finishing slot.

"Will you give me your love?"

"Garth, please."

"Love?" Rowena grabbed his arm. "What do you mean by—"

Callie charged, driving her shoulder into the woman's side and carrying them both into Garth. He staggered, losing his hold on Pierce, as with a bellow, he flung both women off. By then Callie had her hands on the belt, swinging Rowena around to make her fall first. One yank on the Velcro, and the object was hers, though no one noticed because Pierce and Garth were now grappling with each other on the ground. Fastening the belt around her waist, Callie sprang for the fire curtain, whirling inches from the undulating membrane. Garth had Pierce pinned on his back, a knee in his belly, hands once more on his throat.

"Let him go!" Callie screamed. "Or I'll blow this thing out of exis-tence."

She sought the link and power flooded through it, igniting the field in her clothes. Behind her the curtain flickered and crackled with its interference.

Garth's face peered over his shoulder, blazing yellow-green. "Do it, and I'll kill him."

Coldness clenched her middle, but she hung on to the connection. "Don't you get it, Garth? You can't kill him. You can only send him home."

"Fine, then. I'll send him home!"

But during the distraction Callie had provided, Pierce had grabbed a rock with his free hand and now slammed it into Garth's ear. He reeled backward, shook his bloodied head, and then lurched at Pierce with a roar. But something flew out of the prisoner's stall—Whit's rock?—to hit Garth square in the forehead, toppling him like a felled tree. Simultaneously Callie was tackled by one of the others, crushed into the ground by his weight. Rocks dug into her side, and pain flashed outward in nauseating waves. She couldn't breathe. Dirt filled her mouth. Then the weight lifted. Light flared, and twisted currents zapped between the fire curtain's poles.

"Get him!"

"Aiee! I can't see."

"He's got a gun."

She forced herself up and crawled toward the shadows, pain wracking her body with every breath. She must've cracked a rib.

One of the curtain's poles popped like a Fourth of July sparkler, fountaining a plume of blinding sparks and white smoke. Dark figures scrambled about, shielding their eyes and yelling for weapons. She heard a *zip-zip-zip* and crawled faster, flinching under recurring showers of sparks. The tang of ozone burned her nose.

She was certain she was crawling undetected, but at the margin of shadow someone grabbed her arm, hauling her over a low wall. As she recognized Pierce, she stopped struggling and collapsed against him. They hid there in the shadows a few minutes, catching their breath, then set off for the interior. He had one of the short-barreled riot guns, and she bent down to pick up a good-sized rock, wincing at the pain in her side. Together they stole around a partition into deeper shadow.

Garth's people had their weapons out and were clustered into groups, one backed around their fallen leader, another guarding the fire curtain and the two men repairing it. A third group blocked the stairway leading topside, their hand-lamp beams stabbing wildly through the darkness. Apparently all their prisoners had escaped.

Callie crawled after Pierce as they inched toward the hub's center, but they'd not gone twenty yards when a commotion erupted on the stair, and new, more powerful lights speared the darkness. Then the rapid, high-pitched zips of weaponry overlaid the sputtering fire curtain. Someone screamed. Someone else started shouting, but the words were lost in a thunder of footfalls.

"Splagnosians!" Pierce muttered. "Come on."

A glance back showed Garth's men running, their wounded slung over their shoulders like sacks of grain. The Splagnosians clattered after them, shouting and firing, as Pierce and Callie picked their way through the darkness in the opposite direction, moving as fast as they could with bare feet. They soon met up with Whit, LaTeisha, and John, and shortly thereafter the rest of the group joined them. Between them they had two weapons, no boots, and one belt.

"We'll find a place to hide," Pierce said. "If Garth was right about his reputation, they should be satisfied with him."

The chamber's center was a maze of thick, slanting beams, half buried in mounds of earth and stone. They found a series of pockets—crawling with mites, but better that than Splagnosians—and portioned the group into three of them, Callie cramming with Pierce, John, and Tuck into one five-foot-long cavity. Pierce took the belt and sat on the outside with the riot gun, staring into the darkness. Callie huddled beside him, her rib aching dully. She was not at all worried. This was like on the mountain when the goats had distracted their mutant pursuers, only now it was Garth who would provide the distraction. They might have to wait a while, but she was confident they had weathered the storm.

In the darkness she could see nothing, but she could hear Pierce's heart beating under her ear. He smelled of sweat and dirt, the odor strong but not unpleasant, because it was his. Around them the mites chittered and began to move again. She flinched as one crawled over her foot, clenching her teeth to keep from squirming. The shouts, thumps, and zaps faded to silence as the mite, leg-tips pricking through her trousers, explored her hip. She wanted to brush it aside but had nothing to do it with, so she shifted slightly, hoping to discourage it from further exploration.

Pierce's arm tightened about her, and he whispered, so faintly she could hardly hear him, "Something's out there." In an instant her confidence evaporated. What was it? Some monster of the dark? They had no weapons, no boots. How would they fight it off? And if they did, wouldn't that draw down the Splagnosians?

She pushed away the fears and touched the link, feeling calmness return.

Suddenly voices and footfalls erupted in the darkness, stunningly close. Light pierced their burrow, sending renewed alarm firing through her. It was only reflected light from a lamp they couldn't see, but it seemed bright as day. Pierce held her tightly, and beneath her palm, his heart raced. Why had the Splagnosians come back when they had Garth to chase?

From somewhere close a deep voice said, "We've got the exits covered. Must we come in after you, or will you do this the easy way?"

No one said a word.

Low voices conferred. Then the original speaker said, "You will not be harmed if you cooperate. If you resist, however, I can make no promises."

*How can we resist with two riot guns and no boots?*

Pierce's chest rose and fell with a resigned sigh. Then he crawled out of the hole. Reluctantly she followed. Whit, Gerry and the others were already emerging from their respective hiding places. One by one they stepped into the light, and when Pierce stood up, squinting before their visored, armored captors, a visible start went through them.

"That's *him!*" one of them hissed.

Soft laughter followed. "We've got him," the one who appeared to be the leader said, apparently into some communications link. "Looks like we've got his whole bunch."

There was a pause. Then, "No. We'll get them at the other end. These are the ones we came for anyway." He turned to someone standing in the shadows behind him. "Rest assured, you'll be well compensated." As his men surrounded their captives, light played across the figure's face—Rowena.

With a satisfied smirk, she turned away, escorted into the darkness by one of the Splagnosians.

# CHAPTER

## 29

By the time their captors prodded them into an armored transport and chained them to the bulkhead, Callie had stopped reeling from the shock of betrayal and capture and had come to terms with the fact that they wouldn't be sneaking into Splagnos after all. Elhanu had arranged a different way to get them in—one commensurate with his sense of humor.

When they were in Hope, the Aggillon had sung a ballad about a Guide and three witnesses from a sister compound of Rimlight's whom the Zelosians caught. Resisting the torture and attempted brainwashing, the trio was put to work on the lowest level of a blood-crystal mine near the Splagnosian border. They had been there a year when the Splagnosians bombed the mine. Too deep to suffer the devastation that rocked the upper levels, the witnesses escaped in the ensuing chaos and used a military caravan to smuggle themselves into Splagnos. When the caravan dropped them at the door of the palace, it was a simple matter to find the portal.

Callie encouraged herself with that story now, certain she and her friends were right where Elhanu wanted them.

---

A day of bone-crunching travel brought them to Splagnos City where they were separated by sex, then stripped, dunked in several foul-smelling pools, and finally bathed in clear, warm water. After that, plastic locator devices were fused around their ankles, and they were dressed in knee-length tunics and sandals. Though their captors took everything else, they left Callie her engagement ring. She had no doubt the "oversight" was deliberate.

"Guess they're gonna try cajoling first," Evvi said as they came together in the changing room. A guard barked at her to be silent, so Callie only raised her brows in agreement.

They were then introduced to their counselors. Callie's was a gorgeous redheaded giantess named Mira, whose friendly smile and honeyed voice could not have contrasted more with the soldiers' sullen brusqueness. Bright, sympathetic, and cheerful, she escorted Callie to a spacious three-room suite where a meal of lemon-herbed chicken, buttered new potatoes, and tender asparagus awaited. Though the food was delicious, the utensils were annoyingly overlarge. Callie needed two hands to hold the glass, and with her feet dangling above the floor, she felt like a child, a sensation aggravated by Mira's size and chirpy manner.

During the meal, the woman gushed over how exceptional Callie and her friends were. Most travelers never reached Splagnos, waylaid instead by the brutes in the neighboring cities who thought only of war and blood crystal. "And sex, of course," Mira added. "They're absolute perverts there. That's why there are hardly any women in Zelos. But who wants to talk about them? You're safe in Splagnos now."

"I'd rather walk through the portal," Callie said.

Mira smiled. "Eat your lunch, dear. When you're finished I'll give you a tour."

"I don't need a tour. I have no intention of joining you."

"That's what everyone says." Mira patted her hand. "You'll change your mind now that you're no longer bound."

"No longer bound?"

"Can't you feel it?" She regarded Callie with Watcherlike intensity—of which, come to think of it, Callie had seen not one since they'd been picked up. There were none to watch them herded into the transport, none to watch them get out, none in the bathing chamber or reception rooms. . . .

Mira still stared at her.

*No longer bound? What does she mean by—*

Suddenly Callie realized she could not sense her link with Elhanu. Even after she squelched the instant reaction of fear and shock and *knew* she was doing nothing to quench it, no amount of mental groping could find it.

Mira smiled at her bewilderment. "Our energy shields keep him out. You're free to think for yourself again."

*No*, Callie thought. *They couldn't block it if—*

Then she remembered Pierce teaching, weeks ago, that they wouldn't feel the link once they entered Splagnos proper. It was a concession Elhanu made to Cephelus's demand for fairness. The link would still function in terms of protection and direction of thought, they just wouldn't feel it. Experientially they'd be on their own, them and their volition and whatever they truly believed. But knowing that would happen was not the same as experiencing it. She wasn't at all prepared for this dismaying sense of vulnerability.

After lunch Mira showed her around Splagnos. Tucked beneath its bubble on the steep slopes of the towering Iron Crown, it was built of black basalt, the buildings polished to a mirrorlike sheen. Pale, spongy paths wound throughout, accented with colorful flower beds and a surprising amount of water—streams, fountains, and ponds shimmered everywhere. There was even a public bathhouse.

The Splagnosians themselves were no less disconcerting. Beautiful, graceful giants in muted robes, all made a point to welcome Callie graciously. Looming over her, they treated her as if she were Mira's little girl, a role Mira actively encouraged. She took Callie to the palatial Halls of Government—seat of Splagnos's dictator, the Partas Guivas—and then to the city square, the open market, and finally the art museum, which was hosting a reception for a new exhibit.

The museum was a lovely vaulted building with clean white walls and two hundred pieces of Splagnosian art. Most of it was too confrontational for Callie's tastes, though Mira babbled on about innovation and passion of line and color. They strolled the garden, sipping fruited mineral water and nibbling butter cookies. In a tree-shaded courtyard, Mira settled on a basalt bench and pulled Callie up beside her. Across the way a trio of musicians plucked an atonal composition while two women clad only in strips of gold veil contorted before them. Unable to watch without squirming, Callie focused on the bed of purple iris beside her.

"So," Mira said, patting her leg. "Not what you expected, is it?"

"I knew it would be nice."

"This nice?" She waved around the courtyard. "You'd have the freedom to pursue your art and a guaranteed audience. No more worries about making ends meet. And the weather is wonderful."

"Where are the children?"

Mira shifted uncomfortably, eyes flicking away from Callie's gaze. Then she smiled and patted Callie's hand. "*You* are our children. As you grow and learn our ways, we nurture you as if you were our blood born."

"There are no old people, either."

Now Mira was confident. "Nor will there ever be. We do not age. In Splagnos you can truly have eternal life."

"You never die?"

"No."

Callie glanced at the other patrons. "Well, then . . . how do you control your population?"

The Splagnosian woman blinked.

"If everyone lives forever," Callie went on, "with no disease or star-vation or death, why is Splagnos so small? I'd think it would wrap clear around this mountain."

Mira was frowning now. "Well . . . there are the wars, of course. The other cities are always attacking. They want what we have, and so we are forced to defend against them."

"With everyone obligated to take his turn of service."

Mira lifted her chin. "It is an honor to serve. Splagnos has the finest soldiers in the Inner Realm."

"But there must be casualties."

"A few."

Callie eyed the patchwork of tinted panes in the dome overhead, their mismatched colors and transparencies betraying decades of ongoing repair. "And living on the flanks of a volcano must bring its problems. An earthquake would cause considerable damage, might even crack the dome. To say nothing of an eruption."

"The volcano is dormant," Mira said tightly. "And we have lava channels and underground shelters."

"An earthquake could damage those, too."

"Very well, yes. We have occasional disasters. And people die." The Splagnosian woman stood, clearly annoyed. "Come. We have much to see."

It took the rest of the afternoon to tour all the museum's exhibits, the most intriguing of which was a series of idyllic landscapes said to depict the Inner Realm "before Elhanu destroyed it." During that time Callie tried to see if she could slip away from Mira even momentarily—without success. There were surveillance devices everywhere, and with the locator strap on her ankle, escape wasn't likely.

They ate dinner in one of the fern-decorated, city-run restaurants—another fabulous meal—and afterward attended an elaborately costumed but incomprehensible opera at the Partas's own Crown Theater. The plot seemed to concern a man falling in love with a shovel, and the four hours it consumed were among the most boring Callie had ever endured. She dozed through a good deal of it.

When they returned to her suite, she learned she would not leave Mira's side even to sleep—twin beds awaited in the bedroom. Since both doors and windows were sealed, guaranteeing she wouldn't escape, she assumed Mira's continual presence was part of a brainwashing attempt. Well, they wouldn't get far tonight. Except for the nap in the opera, Callie had hardly slept for many days. She'd barely laid her head on the pillow before she was out.

She dreamed of Pierce—a dream so vivid, so intense, she awakened panting in sweat-soaked sheets. Frustration sharpened the pleasure she had felt, but the memory embarrassed her deeply. To distract herself she concentrated on the sensations around her—the morning sun filtering through the blinds, the soft sheets, the rhythmic clipping of the gardener outside her window. When she rolled over, Mira was sitting on the other bed, fully clothed, watching her with a self-satisfied smirk.

At once the smirk broadened into a cheery smile. "Hello, sleepyhead. Breakfast's waiting, and we've got a full schedule."

They spent the morning at a hydroponics installation viewing giant corn and cabbages produced by adapting the "curtains of life" to agricultural use. Afterward they visited a clinic, whose technicians assured Callie that the worst side effect of the Splagnosians' carefully calibrated, state-of-the-art Sigma-Alpha Wave Generators were some occasional lesions, easily removed. In exchange, one received excellent health, vibrant beauty, the instant healing of any injuries, and various other "enhancements." Their final stop was the music hall and a concert by the Splagnosian civic orchestra. It was better than the opera.

That night Callie was again tormented by vivid dreams of Pierce. When she awoke in the morning and again found Mira watching her, she began to suspect the dreams were not of her own making. Pierce had warned of the Splagnosians' telepathic abilities. Planting dream images was likely one of the simpler skills. The next night Callie made a point of acknowledging her fears and frustrations and concentrating on Elhanu as she drifted into sleep. The disturbing dreams ended, and Mira did not look pleased the next morning. Nevertheless, she forced a smile and bubbled on about the day's plans as Callie dressed.

Except for the dreams, and the fact that Mira never let her out of her sight, Callie really couldn't complain about how she was being treated—the woman's main purpose seemed to be to show her a good time. They toured the transportation system, the zoo, the city garden, and the library. To her credit, Mira was an excellent conversationalist, relating interesting stories and drawing out Callie's opinions without being judgmental. It turned out, not surprisingly, that they shared much common ground. Mira's parents had divorced, too, her mother even more domineering than Callie's. And Mira was also an artist.

They went on several sketching expeditions, and even spent a day painting in Mira's wonderful light-filled studio. The time they spent together made it difficult for Callie to think of the woman as the enemy—which, she kept reminding herself, was entirely the point.

Finally, late on the sixth day, the Partas himself summoned Callie to dine with him, an invitation that clearly shocked and dismayed Mira, though she tried to hide it with her usual exuberance. "How wonderful!

We must find you something to wear!"

They didn't have to search long. A dress and matching jewelry arrived shortly after the summons. The dark green satin gown fell in a floor-length drape from a low-cut neckline trimmed with emeralds and pearls. It had thin shoulder straps, no back, and was slit up one side to the hip. Callie took one look and refused to wear it, which distressed Mira even more than the initial invitation. Nearly in tears, she said that Callie absolutely must not offend the Partas. She insisted that this was a great honor and the dress was much preferable to the alternative. Chilled by Mira's words, Callie relented, unhappily allowing the woman to pin her long red hair into a pile of ridiculous curls atop her head, then thread the pearl earrings through her earlobes.

Babbling nervously about what an enormous privilege the invitation was, Mira delivered her to the palace on the hill above the Halls of Government, where a white-tunicked giant brought her through a maze of gleaming corridors to the Partas's private sitting room.

The sitting room, a vaulted L-shaped chamber, was furnished in a dark European style of massive scale. Potted palms and marble statuary, lit by recessed lamps, stood at strategic points, and large paintings decorated the walls. Some depicted the Old Inner Realm, and others were more contemporary, with strident colors and grotesque imagery. Windows on the far wall overlooked the city, its lights glowing red-orange against the dark buildings.

In front of them, the Partas reclined on a couch—waist high from Callie's perspective—and was attended by two scantily clad women. He was huge, extremely well muscled, and wore only a short skirt of red leather and a wide gold belt. Light gleamed off his bared torso and the thick auburn hair flowing over his shoulders. Even from a distance Callie felt a jolt of the same animal magnetism she'd once sensed in Garth, though this at ten times the power.

The Partas waved her over while his attendants, so small she figured they must be new acquisitions, rubbed his shoulders and back with spice-scented oil.

Callie stopped ten feet away and, as he looked her over, was finally forced to confront the reason for Mira's distress—this visit clearly would entail more than dinner.

"You may go," he said to his women.

Wordlessly, they picked up their flagons and slipped away. It was then that she recognized the taller one—pale skinned, narrow waisted, big busted, with silver blond hair cropped to fuzz on her skull. The oozing sores had healed, but one ear was still a lump. Rowena—slave girl to the Partas. This was the Splagnosians' idea of "well compensated"?

"She's happy with it."

The Partas's smooth voice drew Callie's gaze. His eyes were clear green beneath level brows, his face Aggillon-gorgeous, a perfect match for his splendid body. Except for something in the eyes, she might have been totally enamored.

Those eyes moved over her now, head to toe and back again. He was so clearly stripping away the satin, she wanted to cover herself, and it took an act of will not to turn away.

"You *are* lovely," he breathed. "No wonder my ward is smitten."

Ward? Of the Partas? Surely he didn't mean Pierce.

His focus shifted to something behind her, his lips twitching with amusement. She turned and found herself reflected in a gilt-framed mirror, her naked back—bared to several inches below the waist—gleaming in the soft light. Heat flared into her face, and again she fought the compulsion to run.

"Don't worry, little gazelle. I'm just looking." Her gaze snapped back to him.

He grinned, a dazzling little-boy expression that, in spite of everything she sensed about him, stole her breath and sent shivers across her skin. Aghast, she tore her eyes away and looked out the window behind him onto the glowing, fulminating city.

He chuckled, then waved toward the adjoining couch. "Please. Sit down."

When she did not move, he sighed. "Miss Hayes, I only want to talk."

They had provided a step stool so she didn't have to climb onto the couch like a child. She settled onto the velvet upholstery, tucking her feet under her so they wouldn't dangle over the edge.

The Partas gestured to the goblets and food tray on the table between them. "Have some wine. It will relax you."

"Maybe I don't want to relax."

He chuckled again, plucking blue plum-sized grapes from the cluster beside the goblets and popping them into his mouth. The grace of his action, the play of light upon his face and on the grapes themselves, drew her eyes like a moth to flame. He was mind-numbingly attractive. Even the way he ate the grapes—slowly, deliberately, savoring every nuance—was arousing.

"I trust your rooms are comfortable?" His voice broke the spell, and she forced her gaze away from him, onto the tray between them. Some flatbread and a wedge of white cheese accompanied the fruit. He sliced off a piece of cheese and laid it on a piece of flatbread. "We've gone to great lengths to see that you are happy."

"It's difficult to be happy when one is a prisoner."

The Partas snared her gaze again. "Well, your state has not changed from the day you set foot in the Arena, now, has it?" He bit into the cheese and bread and chewed. "You should try some of this." He ate the rest. She did not move.

"Your lover is quite entertaining," he said when he'd finished. "A worthy antagonist—and soon to be a friend, I hope. If he joins us, he will be well compensated."

She thought wryly of Rowena's compensation. "He'll never join you."

"Mmm." The Partas sliced more cheese, laid it on another piece of bread, and handed it to her. Reluctantly she took it.

"So," he said, fixing another for himself, "what did you think of our opera company's opus?"

"I thought it an ingenious form of torture."

He threw back his head and laughed. "Oh, Miss Hayes, you are indeed a cool breeze on a hot day. I could get used to you!"

She nibbled her cheese and cracker. It was quite good.

"And our fine-arts exhibit?"

"Some of it was nice."

"And some of it should have gone to the recyclers." He shook his head. "The price we pay for freedom. Artists must be allowed to create as they see fit or the muse is stifled. They aren't all so atrocious."

"Are there a lot of artists in Splagnos, then?"

"A good number, yes."

He poured wine into his emptied goblet, then handed her hers, so far untouched. Using both hands to hold it, she sipped under his watchful eye.

"Well?"

"It's good." And it was, though she wasn't fond of wine. She sipped some more, then set down the goblet and tried a grape.

Though she felt like the fly in the spider's parlor, the Partas Guivas was undeniably a charming host. Gracious, witty, easygoing—a smoother talker she had never met. And she could not keep her eyes off him. The way the light played off his musculature and highlighted the even planes of his face was fascinating. Time and again she found herself wanting to touch those sculpted muscles, and, as with Garth, she became disconcertingly aware of her sexuality. But she was also aware that he knew exactly how he was affecting her, was probably even enhancing the effect with his telepathic abilities. She was sure he was deliberately striking poses, glancing at the mirror as he flowed from one position to the next, holding each just long enough to pique her artist's eye.

They had finished the flatbread and cheese and he was topping off her goblet when the building began to shake. The curtains swayed, the tray rattled, the statuary jittered briefly in place, and the tremor faded. Though Callie clutched the couch, Guivas weathered it unconcerned.

"Don't you worry the volcano will erupt?" she asked finally.

"It can't unless I let it." The Partas handed her the newly filled goblet and smiled. A shadow flicked across his face, and Callie glanced around, thinking someone had entered the room. But they were alone. His lips curved as he watched her, waited for her . . .

To understand. He was Tohvani. Or rather—

Her confusion must have shown, for his brow arched. "You thought we could only appear in that humiliating nakedness? Not at all."

Elhanu *had* said they'd found a way around his prohibition, but surely he didn't mean because his own power had failed. Besides, this man was as solid as she was. She'd seen the slave women rubbing oil into him.

Then she remembered something else Pierce had taught them—extended exposure to the fire curtain eroded the barriers between human and alien, allowing the Tohvani to enter and inhabit human bodies. The man with whom she spoke was not the one who owned this body. Or at least, not the one who had originally owned it.

The realization had the same effect on her as suddenly discovering he had leprosy.

The Partas smiled. "I assure you we're both very happy with this arrangement. He invited me, after all. I wouldn't be here otherwise."

"Why don't you let him tell me that?"

He picked up the goblet, watching her in the mirror. "So suspicious. So sure everything we do is bad. So sure you're right." He sipped his wine, closing his eyes as he held it in his mouth, savoring the taste. Finally he swallowed and looked at her. "You won't even talk to us. How can you know our side of the matter? Where is the proof that we're wrong and Elhanu's right? Where is the proof you can even walk through the portal should you find it?" He shook his head. "There is none. You're operating solely on faith."

Callie fingered the plastic band around her ankle. "I'd have to operate on faith regardless. And anyway, it's not faith that's the issue, it's the object of faith." She met his gaze. "And while I haven't walked through the portal yet, and don't know anyone who has, I *do* know Elhanu."

"And of course you could not be deceived. Especially not with that mind-control switch he put in your brain, hmm?"

"If it was a mind-control switch, shouldn't it be disabled now that I'm 'free' in Splagnos?"

He scowled. "Why must you be so stubborn? Look what we're offering you!"

"Slavery and deception?" She snorted. "I know your fire curtain is no secret to eternal life. No matter how finely calibrated your devices are, long-term exposure still leads eventually to madness and deformity. That's why every city on the plain has a termination policy for those who cease to conform to the acknowledged standards."

He laughed again. "How could you know—"

"It's in the manual."

"Just because your manual—"

"It hasn't been wrong yet. And I've seen the Zelosian execution booths in action. Beyond that, it's the only explanation for how you've been able to keep your population of alleged immortals small enough to live within the dome."

He swirled the wine left in his glass, sniffed its bouquet, his nostrils flaring, then sipped and savored. "You'll die on Earth eventually, too," he said at last.

She felt a thrill of triumph. "Better there than here."

"Why? What is so *bad* about here? Even if the curtain is addictive, how is that any worse than the normal aging you'll go through on Earth?"

She looked at the two of them in the mirror. "Maybe it's not. But I'd rather do it Elhanu's way. Your kind care nothing for us. You're just using us to gain your own end."

"And he isn't?"

"His care is genuine, proven when he took us into himself to free us. You only pretend. Everything you do proves that fact. You just want to win your master's appeal—and who cares what you destroy in the process?" She turned to look at him directly. "You claim to offer eternal life, yet your neighbors hate you, the outside air is poisoned, and the plain is littered with the ruins of past 'heavens.' And I've had a gardener clipping the same plant outside my window for days now. What kind of eternal life is that? Clipping the same plant day after day?"

The Partas Guivas lay propped on his elbow, probing her with his eyes. Silence closed around them. A sulfur-tainted breeze drifted in the window. Somewhere a fountain gurgled.

Finally he sighed. "I'm sorry you feel this way, Callie, because you're not going home. Not for a very long time, anyway." He set the goblet on the table and sat up. "You're right. People do die here, but not so many as you think, for Splagnos is bigger than it looks. It has many levels below ground, you see, all lined with isolation cells."

His eyes held her, pouring images and sensations into her mind— the sour smell, the cold hard floor, the distant screams, the eternal blackness, the unending, mind-wrenching loneliness. She shuddered with horror but tried not to show it.

"You'll spend the rest of your life there," he murmured, so softly she barely heard him. "We'll take very good care of you. But since all your friends are just as caught as you, you'll never see them again. Any of them . . ."

Callie tore her eyes from his, and stared at her hands. Pierce's promise ring gleamed on her left third finger.

"Your life is ours, dear girl," he whispered. "Your only choice now is whether to live down there, alone, or to live up here, with the man you love."

Callie studied the ring, the stone's red facets flaring white as they caught the light. Her fingers trembled, and she clenched them tightly.

"Is Elhanu worth your life?" Guivas murmured.

Nausea swirled under her heart.

"Callie. Answer me."

She refused to look at him, seeking desperately for some touch of reassurance through the link. Something. Anything.

But her insides remained as cold and dead as ever. No warmth, no pulse of strength, just empty, silent deadness.

And then, a single thought: *It's not trust unless it looks really bad.*

Her heart leaped. *It looks really bad, all right. And it must have looked bad for those Zelosian prisoners, too. But he delivered them.*

The Partas interrupted her thoughts. "We'll hold your trial tomorrow. You may give me your answer then."

She lifted her gaze, suddenly angry. "You can have it now. The very choice shows what kind of master you serve. And that's what this is all about, isn't it? Who is the better master? Well, as far as I'm concerned, it's no contest. Elhanu *can* deliver us if that's what he wishes. I don't believe your master's power or that of any of your creepy friends can hold a candle to his."

The Partas Guivas stared at her long and hard, his eyes dark, his face suffused with blood. Finally he said, "You want to play hardball? Fine. But know this—I serve no master but myself. And my power is more than you know."

Callie gaped at him, rocked by the impact of his words. *"I serve no master but . . ."* Was this Cephelus himself?

"Yes, you ought to shiver. I could kill you with my little finger." The whites of his eyes had disappeared, swallowed by solid black orbs. "And you're right—I don't care about you. You're only a weapon, a pawn—one I intend to use to the fullest. We'll see how loyal you are when things start to hurt. Both of you."

He glanced at the mirror again. "A better master, is he? Well, what good is he if he can't save you from me?"

He stood and left the room. A few minutes later his giant came to bring Callie back to Mira.

# CHAPTER

## 30

Callie awakened the next morning to a shaking bed and rattling windows—ominous portents of the day to come. As the seismic shivers faded, the gardener outside her window began clipping again. She stared at the ceiling, wishing she didn't have to get out of bed.

Sleep had been long in coming last night, held at bay by churning afterthoughts of her interview with the Partas. That it was Cephelus himself she'd faced gave her satisfaction, for he wouldn't waste his time with her if she wasn't close to success. But the way he'd kept eyeing the mirror had nagged at her. Perhaps he wasn't admiring her—or himself—after all. Perhaps he was looking at someone behind the glass. Like Pierce. However Cephelus threatened Callie, Pierce would know he could stop it.

A rustle from the doorway preceded Mira's voice. "It's time."

Callie shut her eyes and breathed deeply, trying to slow the wild acceleration of her pulse. She clung to her memories, reminding herself of what Elhanu had done and what he was and what he'd promised. *It's not trust unless it looks really bad.* And it must've looked really bad for those Zelosian prisoners when they were put down into the mine.

It must've looked bad when they were tortured, too. The knot in her stomach twisted.

*Don't think about that.*

"Callie."

"I heard you."

She got up, put on her tunic, and braided her hair. In the kitchen, Mira had prepared oatmeal and fresh peaches, but Callie's stomach was too tight to eat them. The two women sat at the table in silence as the news played on the table screen. A picture of Pierce appeared, the announcer reporting that the captives would be given their final chance for absolution at today's trial. After a week of kind and gracious treatment, it was expected that all would see the light and join the Splagnosians in new life. After the first few words, Callie recognized the report as another attempt to sway her, and turned her gaze to the window, willing herself to tune it out.

Time ticked slowly by until suddenly Mira stood and snatched the bowl from Callie's place, her lips tight, her eyes bright with moisture. She cast their utensils in the cleanser, yanked open the kitchen door, gestured Callie outside, and escorted her wordlessly through the city to a side door in one of the larger government buildings. A guard in a short leather skirt brought her to the other holdouts, who were waiting in a dimly lit corridor—Whit, Evvi, John, Brody, and Meg. The sight of them was deeply heartening. That Pierce wasn't among them didn't worry her. She knew if he had turned, she would have heard of it, and being the Partas's ward—and "a worthy antagonist"—he would certainly have a special place in all this.

They shuffled down the hall to a vast chamber packed with spectators, where mammoth pillars marched in tandem down a central aisle as long as a football field. A strip of gold-flecked black marble gleamed between facing lines of red-roped silver stanchions, set up to restrain the jostling crowd. Armed and armored giants stood the length of both ropes, and gray Tohvani bodies covered the pillars and vaulted ceiling.

Silence greeted the prisoners as they entered, the rustle of their clothing and the slap-thump of their bare feet echoing loudly around them. Callie stared at John's back, feeling the Splagnosians' hostility, and wondering if there were familiar faces in that crowd. She couldn't bring herself to look, though, and by the time they reached the gauntlet's end, her chest was tight and her hands sweat slicked and icy.

A circular dais arose at the head of the hall, surrounded by an expanse of shining black marble across which the opposing lines of guards angled away from each other to encircle the stage. The Partas Guivas sat upon it in a great white chair, bracketed by guards in gold gilt and high-ranking government ministers. Above it all, a domed ceiling glowed sky blue.

A man stood on the dais at Guivas's immediate right, wearing the gold-banded garment of citizenship, and Callie's heart seized the instant she saw him. His blue eyes flicked once over the prisoners, then fixed on a point above them, his teeth clenched. He looked ravaged—thin, haggard, almost as gray as a Watcher, with deep circles under his eyes. Even from the distance she could see him shiver and twitch. He probably hadn't slept in days.

The prisoners were directed into a line along the dais's base, and the Partas Guivas let his green-eyed gaze slip over them one by one. Callie refused to meet it when it reached her, lifting her chin and staring at a spot midway up the blue dome. His attention moved on, and her glance caught Pierce's. A current leapt through her at the contact, but at the same time she saw a terror that shook her to the core.

"For six days you have enjoyed our hospitality," the Partas Guivas said finally. "Your counselors have freely answered all your questions and tried hard to persuade you against throwing away your lives. But you have spurned them. And if you will not join us, we must consider you our enemies. I give you one last chance. Declare allegiance to Splagnos and join with us in the baptism of fire or become slaves of the state."

No one moved or spoke.

He glanced at Pierce and said something Callie could not hear. When Pierce did not respond, Guivas waved a hand at one of the guards. "Begin with the redhead."

He stood and walked to a wooden box standing at the side of the dais beside the last pillar. A small gate permitted him egress and closed behind him as the box rose six feet alongside the pillar and stopped. Simultaneously the throne sank into the floor and a panel slid over it. At Callie's back, a motor whined and whirred, and as the guards herded the prisoners to one side, she saw two thick bronze poles spearing out of the floor toward the roof and beyond them a stone table rising into view. When the poles reached their full extension, the whirring stopped. A succession of clicks and thumps followed, and then men hastened forward to activate the device. As the membrane of blue fire leaped between the poles, several gaunt Splagnosians in loincloths emerged from a side door.

"You can stop this whenever you wish," Guivas said to Pierce. And to one of the guards, he ordered, "Bring him closer, where he can feel it."

Pierce was brought to within arm's reach of the pulsating energy. Another guard dragged Callie to the table. Four sets of shackles told her what they intended—she was to be chained onto the stone to serve the needs of those who came through the curtain.

The guard lifted her onto the table, and at first it all seemed so unreal, she didn't even struggle. He snapped the bracelet around her left wrist, his hands rough and heavy, and she drew a low hiccupping breath—part cry, part sob. The stone was icy beneath her thin shift, and as he moved to her left ankle, she struggled for calm, reaching as never before for the invisible, untouchable link. No matter what they did to her body, they couldn't touch her soul. And if they killed her, they would only send her home.

She was breathing rapidly now, a selfish, craven part of her hoping fiercely that Pierce would give in and save her. Cold metal pressed unpleasantly against her anklebone as the latch snicked shut, and terror—so violent, so oppressive she could hardly breathe—pounded at the doors of her soul.

"No!" The cry rang sharply, tinged with desperation.

The guard froze. Callie turned her head to see Pierce launch himself into the curtain, his body seized in midair, spread-eagled, jittering with blue-green-gold incandescence. Despite Mira's assurance that this was a pleasant experience, he screamed, the sound mingling with Callie's own shriek of denial.

It held him for an exceedingly long time. Sparks flew along his limbs and up the poles. The curtain flickered as the blue and green drained into his body. He shuddered and twitched and screamed until only blackness swirled around him. Then, in a blinding flare, he was hurled out, staggering for balance as the crowd erupted in a savage cheer. Horrified, Callie watched him veer drunkenly into the line of guards—

And drop all pretense of incapacitation as he slammed into the nearest giant, shoulder to belly, the two of them falling in a tangle of legs and arms. Seconds later blue fire flared from the pile. The short triple bursts found their marks with deadly accuracy. The guards to either side of him dropped like empty garments. Then he was up on one knee, his SI pointing toward the box where the Partas stood openmouthed with astonishment. Three blue lances cut the air, and Guivas crashed forward to the floor, a gray vapor trailing briefly behind him and vanishing.

By then Pierce had taken out the guards closest to the other prisoners and was running for Callie, the guards beyond her diving for cover. Behind him their fellows had recovered their wits and began firing on him as the spectators scrambled to escape. Callie could see the lances of light striking his body, but this soon after exposure they didn't faze him. He loomed over her, his face awful. Sweeping the SI from side to side as he continued to fire, he gripped the ankle shackle that held her, wrenched it out of the stone, then did the same with the wrist restraint. As she scrambled down, he upended the whole table, pulling it from its moorings in a display of superhuman strength that left her awestruck. Pushing her behind it and using his own body to shield her further, he fired at the crowd. Civilians and soldiers alike fled in panic.

New firing broke out from the side of the stage, aimed at the soldiers shooting at Pierce. Whit and the others had commandeered their dead guards' weapons and had taken cover behind the fire curtain's control box, which was now raining plumes of sparks and smoke. Pierce stood over Callie, taking hit after hit, and firing as if nothing was happening. But he was bleeding now. The wounds closed quickly enough, but clearly his invulnerability was fading.

Then his weapon's beam turned purplish pink. Paled. Sputtered. He looked down, surprised, then dove behind the table as his enemies quickly took advantage. Blue fire danced off the stone, filling the air with a fine vibration. And stopped.

Crouching with Pierce behind the table, Callie looked into the gun barrels of four huge guards. The nearest guard reached for her, then staggered back as the floor lurched. She heard a low rumble as the other guards looked around in alarm and people started screaming. Down the hall toward the open doorway, she saw the floor undulate like an oily black sea, and the rocking intensified, bouncing her hard against the tile. The fire curtain's poles whipped back and forth, spewing sparks as plaster chunks rained from the ceiling. To the right a pillar cracked with a boom, half of it peeling away to fall on screaming, fleeing Splagnosians. Thinking she needed to get under a doorway, Callie pushed herself to her feet, only to be thrown back into Pierce. He pulled her close as rocks pelted them, and another pillar gave way, thundering down the length of the hall. She clung to him as the ground churned and the dust thickened and the ceiling came down around them. It seemed the awful roar would never stop, that the floor would never stop rocking, that surely they would be crushed at any moment.

But they were not. And gradually the tumult slowed, the screaming stopped, and the world fell back to stillness. When Callie finally dared open her eyes, she found a slab of ceiling angling inches above her, one end propped on the overturned table.

She and Pierce sat up together, coughing in the settling dust and looking around, astonished to be alive. Voices at the chamber's far end drew their attention to their friends, staggering up from the rubble. Aside from them, though, and a few residual trickles of plaster, nothing moved. Chills crawling from scalp to heels, Callie realized they alone had survived.

Beside her Pierce was surveying the wreckage with a horror that had nothing to do with the carnage. When he finally looked at her, his face was dead, his eyes bright with tears.

"Oh, Callie," he whispered, "what have I done?"

And for the first time it dawned on her that going through the fire curtain had killed his chances of using the exit portal anytime soon.

"Why didn't I wait?" He stared at the floor, layered with dust and rock. "Why didn't I trust him?"

Battling her own horror and dread and rising anger, Callie had no words of comfort. He closed his eyes and speared his fingers through his dusty hair, shaking his head. She wanted to hit him, scream at him, and fall sobbing into his arms all at once.

The others congregated silently near the crushed fire curtain, looking around in bewilderment until John's voice broke the spell. "Hey, look! Is that a passage beyond that crack?'' He gestured toward the only patch of sky-painted backdrop remaining at the rear of the curve, rent now by a yard-high crack. Evvi investigated and confirmed there was indeed a passage, and one by one they disappeared into it.

Callie stood. "Are you coming?" she asked Pierce.

He swallowed, opened his eyes without looking at her, and got up.

The crack led into a corridor lit by a glowing white line in the floor. They stood in silence, puzzling over it, and then Evvi said, "Hey! I can feel the link again."

The others looked at her, first in surprise, then in blankness as they sought their own connections and found them.

Callie hesitated, still entangled in the riot of emotion that gripped her. Beside her, Pierce sagged against the wall and closed his eyes. To her surprise, the tightness of his jaw immediately loosened, and the anguish between his brows softened as pain gave way to peace and renewed purpose. His gaze caught her own, and she could almost feel the warmth of the link through it. Elhanu had forgiven him. Again.

She turned away, chagrined by the sudden memory of her own wish that Pierce do exactly as he'd done—go through the curtain and save her, no matter the cost. She had trusted no more than he.

Chastised, she took her own failure to the link and found the wondrous warmth she craved. He wasn't even surprised. It was as if he had known all along. . . .

And knowing, he'd be able to make it all work out. Wouldn't he?

Footfalls and shouting sounded outside. Even in the midst of disaster the surviving Splagnosians weren't going to let them go without a fight. She wondered if Cephelus had already found a new body.

Together they hurried up the serpentine path through a honeycomb of intersecting corridors. Without the lighted line they would have been hopelessly lost, and Callie gave thanks that the Splagnosians apparently couldn't see it. Behind them, the shouts and footfalls waxed and waned erratically, but never actually caught up. It wasn't long, however, before she realized Pierce was failing. Stopping to face him, she saw blood wreathing a walnut-sized hole in his thigh and numerous stains marring his tunic. He was disturbingly pale, and the pain in his face was now purely physical.

"You're hurting," she said. "We'd better stop."

"I'm fine. It's just taking longer to heal."

"You're not fine."

"The longer we wait, the worse I'll get."

She pressed her lips together and did not argue with him, but his pace continued to slow. Finally, when they stepped into a grotto from which several corridors opened, she insisted he rest, and he let her push him onto a rock, still protesting his wounds were not serious.

"Don't lie to me," she said, pulling up his tunic to examine him. "You haven't a clue how bad they are."

He pulled the tunic back down before she could see anything. "It doesn't matter, Callie."

She frowned at him.

Then Whit and John entered the chamber, the others right behind. "Someone's following us," Whit said. "Not Splagnosian—at least he's not wearing armor. And he's sneaking, like he doesn't want us to know he's there."

"Just one?" Pierce asked.

"Sounds like it."

"Maybe he can't see the guide light," Evvi said.

"A lot of good it'll do him to find the portal, then," Pierce said, standing up.

"NO!" The rough bellow echoed off the stone walls as a wild-haired man lurched through the doorway behind them. He wore blood-stained leathers and held a Zelosian riot gun low across his body. His one good eye was ringed with white and was full of madness.

Screaming invectives, he insisted they couldn't be here. "I'm the one who worked for this. Not you."

"Garth, we can both go," Pierce said, reaching for his weapon.

"You're not going anywhere, you traitorous bone sucker! None of you are!"

Callie's eye flicked to the firing lever of the riot gun, saw it was on automatic, and understood—Garth meant to shoot them all. In that instant everything seemed to slow down and clarify. She saw the tendons in his arm ripple, contracting his trigger finger as she dove for the floor, seemingly miles away. Whit was bringing his weapon slowly around as Pierce launched himself at Garth. Two green beams slid out of the riot gun, penetrating Pierce's chest one after the other as he hung in space. Then momentum carried him into his target, and both men fell, the gun clattering aside. Callie scrambled for it, but Garth rolled free and recovered it first.

Whit's weapon finally discharged, its blue lance burrowing into Garth's shoulder, hurling him back against the wall. He pushed off, gazed about wildly, and fled a blaze of pursuing fire.

Callie rushed to Pierce, who was now struggling to rise. Bright blood soaked the front of his tunic in a huge, spreading stain, but again he refused her attentions. "I'm not gonna make it anyway, and you've got to reach the portal."

"I'll carry you," Whit suggested.

"No. Garth won't know which way to go if there's another fork. He'll wait for you—try to take you out once he knows the way."

"Ah, Pierce, why would he do that?"

"Because we prove everything he believes to be a lie. Because he's whacked out from too much fire curtain. Because he's being driven by something other than his own passions."

For a moment, no one spoke. They stood panting, looking at one another in surprise.

Then Whit said gravely, "You mean a Tohvani?"

"I mean Cephelus himself. He had to go somewhere after I killed the Partas."

"*Cephelus* was in the Partas?" John asked, wide-eyed.

"We can't just leave you," Whit persisted.

"You don't have a choice, my friend. Please. *Go!*"

The black man regarded him unhappily but finally turned away. As he and the others disappeared up the dark corridor, Callie turned to Pierce. "I'm *not* leaving, so don't even suggest it."

"Callie, one of us has to make it."

"You said yourself it's close now. Just get up and let's go."

"I can't." His body trembled under her touch, and his skin felt cold. His breathing was coming fast and shallow. It was like reliving the nightmare in the Cauldron cave all over again. "Everything's getting numb and fuzzy," he murmured.

She grabbed his tunic, strange little whimperings issuing from her throat. "Please, Pierce. Don't do this. You have to go on."

His eyes were starting to glaze. "Look at me, Cal." He slid his hands through the blood on his chest. "I'm all shot up. And you know I can't go through the portal this soon."

She struggled to breathe. "We could wait. Hide out until you're better. Even go back. They could heal you. We could live here—"

He pressed a hand to her mouth. "Go home. You know that's the right thing to do. Splagnos is a ruin. And even if it wasn't, you don't want their lies."

"Oh, Pierce, I can't do this."

"You have to."

"It's not fair. If not for you, the rest of us would never have made it. You don't deserve an ending like this."

He smiled ruefully. "Yes, I do. I took the bait . . . tried to do it myself when I very well knew better. More than anyone else . . . I knew. This is exactly what I deserve."

Her throat was tight and hot. Tears blurred her vision. "Oh, Pierce . . ."

He stroked her cheek. "It won't be as bad as you think. Trust him, Cal."

"I love you."

He smoothed her hair, then cupped the back of her head with his palm and drew her down to him, kissing her gently. Even in the kiss she felt him slipping away, and when they drew apart, he was gray.

He touched her tears. "Find me. On the other side."

# CHAPTER

## 31

He was gone.

She sat blankly, shivering, her hands touching him, then pulling away. She kept expecting him to open his eyes, for it all to be a dream or a joke—anything but reality. But the stillness in him was utter, and it was the stillness that finally got to her. She backed away on her knees. "No!" she murmured. "You weren't supposed to leave me. We were supposed to go through together. How can I do this? I can't. I can't!"

She stood up, wanting to run or scream or do something, but she could only shake her hands helplessly.

Peripheral movement drew her eye as two Aggillon emerged from a lighted opening in the rock, a gurney floating behind them. Chilled, she watched them place Pierce's body gently on the table. As they left one of them looked into her eyes, jolting her as nothing else had.

He wasn't totally lost to her. Not yet. But if she didn't reach that portal, he would be.

Seizing his SI, she fled up the corridor. The passage undulated, angling increasingly upward, and soon the steepness slowed her to a walk as she struggled to control the noisy rasp of her breath. She wanted to hear whatever might lie ahead—and at the same time, not give her own approach away. She rounded a bend and stopped in surprise at finding two more Aggillon with another body—Meg's this time. Numbly she watched them bear her friend away and close the door behind them. It was splattered with blood. So was the floor.

Garth must have caught them here.

She continued cautiously as the Splagnosians' distant shouts echoed behind her. From ahead she heard nothing, but the blood was fresh, and there was lots of it.

Suddenly a Watcher stood in her path, laughing at her. *You'll never make it without him. You're too weak and stupid. You have no friends to help. You'll never do it.*

Rage swelled in her, fueling a desire to hurt this creature as she'd never wanted to hurt anything in her life. But the only way to really hurt it was to get through the portal, so she walked straight ahead. The Tohvani vanished before she reached it, but still her heart pounded with the anger it had triggered. Her thoughts roiled with vengeance and *I'll-show-you*s until she realized she was still letting her emotion distract her. Her priority was to get up this corridor alive, and she'd best concentrate solely on that if she wished to succeed.

She rounded another bend and stopped in the doorway of yet another grotto, much larger than those she'd encountered earlier. Great mounds of blackened bones piled the floor to either side of her, gleaming in the light of the center stripe. Forty feet ahead, the piles ended and the ground sheered off into a moatlike chasm spanned by a narrow footbridge. The stripe ran straight up to and over the bridge, ending at a man-sized doorway cut into the far wall and covered with what appeared to be clear plastic wrap.

Callie stared in disbelief. Was this the end?

Then she saw the Watchers—thousands of them clinging to the walls and ceiling. Sudden suspicion sent her gaze back around the chamber, and now she saw a figure sprawled among the bones—tall, dark-skinned, wearing a bloodied white tunic—Whit. She also spotted Evvi and John and Brody, the latter's chest stained with blood. John had something wrong with his leg. Evvi, nearest of the three, worked her way across the bones toward a jutting wall of rock, her weapon clamped under one arm as she pulled herself along with the other. There was no sign of Garth.

Callie hesitated in the doorway, SI leveled, ready to fire. But there was nothing. Maybe he'd gone through.

Except, he couldn't go through. Had he fallen into the pit?

She started toward Evvi, and the woman finally saw her. "Callie, no! He's waiting—"

Callie whirled a second too late as the gun was slapped from her hands and she was hurled to the ground. The wind driven from her lungs, she shuddered as hard hands groped her through the linen shift. Bright sparkles danced across her vision, but she recognized the black beard and coal-bright eyes of her attacker.

"I told you I wasn't done with you," he said. Holding both her hands above her head in one of his, he used the other to scrunch her shift up toward her hips.

"The Splagnosians are coming," she gasped. "Don't you want to go through the portal?"

"This won't take long—"

She slammed her knee between his legs, loosening his grip enough to twist a hand free. Trying to shove him away with her upraised knee, she watched his eyes turn black as the Tohvani within him asserted itself. Its psychic power crushed her like a rock. Gasping and whimpering, she clung to the link for dear life and kept on shoving and hitting. It did no good.

He yanked her arm up, and she felt his full weight upon her, driving the air from her lungs. With her free hand she boxed his ears and poked his eyes until he caught it. His breath rushed hot and sour on her neck and the side of her face.

Once more transferring her wrists to one hand, he reared back and slapped her so hard the stars returned. "Now, hold still," he grated.

Blue fire came out of nowhere, searing the stars and flinging him off her. Rolling blindly in the opposite direction, Callie tried to crawl away. A lance of green light glanced off the side of her head, spearing pain down her neck as he grabbed her heel and dragged her back, kicking and struggling.

The chamber flared again, and again she was released. She scrambled toward Evvi and happened, as she did so, upon her own weapon. She pushed up to bring it around—

Only to be tackled from behind. Garth's laugh rasped in her ear as he flipped her onto her back and caught her wrists again. Desperately, she turned her head and bit his arm. Howling outrage, he released her wrists and gripped her throat. Within seconds lights flared around her field of vision, and her lungs screamed for air. But though she fought wildly, she could do nothing to free herself. Her strength ebbing, she finally sought the link again, and its power flowed into her, even as her hand fell aside onto something familiar—Garth's riot gun. Awkwardly, weakly, she managed to drag it up and over her thigh. With no idea where the thing was even pointed, she found the trigger and squeezed.

He toppled away, releasing her throat to life-giving air. At first all she could do was lie there and gasp, wondering why he didn't come back and disarm her. Only when she'd regained her breath enough to sit up did she see that he lay motionless on his back beside her, one arm flung wide, the other limp across his ruined belly.

Nauseated, she stumbled over the bones to where Evvi lay drenched in blood. She was still alive, but the Aggillon were taking Brody.

"Where are you hurt?" she asked Evvi.

"My arm's broken."

"But all this blood on you—"

"Most of it's Meg's. How's Whit?"

Callie looked up the pile. At the chasm's edge, Whit had begun to moan and stir. "Alive."

"And Garth?" Evvi glanced toward his body.

"I shot his guts out." Callie shuddered.

"Head shot's the only sure kill, Cal."

"He doesn't have an abdomen anymore. I'll check on Whit and John, then I'll see about him."

Whit sat up as she approached. A red crease angled along his temple, but beyond that he seemed fine. John was not so fine. Garth had jumped them, shot Brody point-blank, and threw John across the chamber into the wall. His leg was broken, the white tibia jutting through the skin below his knee. He was in a lot of pain, but they had nothing to give him. His only relief lay in crossing the bridge and walking through the portal—which he had to do on his own power.

She and Whit lashed two femurs into a shaky makeshift crutch, then Callie picked her way back to Evvi. As she bent to help the woman up, a shadow erupted from where Garth had lain. Incredibly, he stood erect in the light, his abdomen a bloody mess, his eyes still Tohvani black, piercing her heart like arrows of malevolence. Never had she sensed such hatred, such pure incandescent rage. Around her the Watchers shifted on the walls, chittering eagerly.

Without the slightest warning, he flew at her. She almost didn't fire in time—her beam caught him in the shoulder a mere five feet away. It flung him back onto the bones, but he got up screeching blasphemies. She braced for another attack, but instead, he whirled and raced across the bridge into the portal. It flung him out with a high-pitched scream. Like a blazing effigy, his remains sailed across the chamber and bounced off the wall, falling onto the bone pile, a smoking, stinking nightmare that would never rise again.

Choking down bile, Callie sank weakly to the ground.

Evvi sat down beside her. They eyed the gleaming portal, and Evvi swallowed. "Well, now we know where these bones came from."

Laughter echoed around them, overlying the rustling Tohvani on the walls. *Do you believe me now? It's all a lie.* Cephelus now stood, gray and naked, over Garth's skeleton. His eyepits were deeper, darker, more mesmerizing than those of other Tohvani, and he was considerably bigger. But beyond that, Callie saw little difference between him and the creatures who served him.

*No one escapes from here*, he said in her mind. *No one.*

Callie snorted. *No one can go through the Exit without being Changed. Of course he was flung out. My question is why you let him try. A last-ditch effort to trick us? Or merely a fit of pique because you've lost?*

Turning her back on the Tohvani leader, she stood and said, "Who wants to go first?"

The others were still staring at Cephelus. Now they refocused on Callie. Whit grinned. "You do, I think."

*NO!* Cephelus shrieked.

Her friends stood beside her and she sensed them focusing on the link as she was, using it as a shield against the sudden cacophony of protests in their brains. Callie faced the portal, then glanced back at Evvi. "You know . . . about Pierce. I never meant you to be hurt. I just didn't realize—"

"It's all right." Evvi smiled. "I'm over it. You go home and find him."

Around them the Tohvani skittered across the walls, screaming furious abuse. As Callie stepped toward the bridge, Cephelus flew to block her path, radiating all the violent menace he could muster. She hesitated but then, at the link's urging, walked through him. His obscenities, no doubt shrieked at full volume, sounded small and tinny in her ears. She mounted the bridge. Black depths plummeted on either side, but she hardly noticed as the portal blazed to life. A visible version of the link within, it reached out and enfolded her.

Enraged Tohvani flung themselves upon her as she moved forward. Their bodies shredded impotently against her flesh. The portal loomed ahead, its light spilling over the walls, filling up the darkness, enfolding her in glory. She could see figures within it now, silhouettes cloaked in familiarity—Aggillon waiting to welcome her. Eagerness quickened her steps, and she crossed over the threshold, out of the Arena and into a world of cheers and smiling faces and that wondrous soul-deep sense of approval.

# EPILOGUE

The ringing telephone jarred Callie awake. She rolled onto her back and blinked at the room. Memories of cheering crowds, a crystalline amphitheater, and a massive golden throne hung in her mind. She had stood before that throne. . . . Elhanu had commended her . . . And then she'd been swimming in a light-filled river of pure joy. She hadn't wanted to leave.

Daylight flooded around the miniblinds, casting horizontal lines across the rumpled bedclothes. An overgrown spider plant hung in front of it. From another room, a cockatiel called.

The phone rang again.

*I'm home!* She sat up, snatching the receiver on the third ring.

It was Lisa. "Callie, where were you last night?"

"Huh?"

"Are you hung over? You were supposed to come to my birthday party."

"Birthday? What day is this?"

"Sunday, the twenty-fifth. Are you all right?"

She had been in the Arena almost thirteen months. Could the time have translated into exactly a year here or—?

"Which birthday, Lisa?"

"Which birthday? What's the matter with you?"

"I'm sorry. I'm a little foggy. How old are you?"

"You're trying to get me off track. What you did last night was low. At least you could've called."

"How old are you, Lisa?" Desperation sharpened Callie's voice, stopping the tide of her sister's anger.

"You're being very weird, Callie."

"I need to know. "

"You're scaring me. Maybe I should come over. You're clearly disoriented."

"Lisa. Please. How old are you?"

"I'm thirty-three. Did something happen last night?"

*Thirty-three?* Callie thought, reeling. Thirty-three. The same age she was last year. Except there was no last year. Thirteen months in the Arena had consumed less than a day in this world. Was that possible?

Unless it hadn't happened.

Maybe she *had* hit her head, and it was all a dream—like in *The Wizard of Oz*. She closed her eyes and rubbed her temples, vaguely aware of Lisa blathering in her ear. *No, it can't have been a dream. It was too real, too involved.*

"Lisa, I'm sorry I didn't call," she cut in, "but there wasn't a phone."

"Where were you?"

"I'll be by later with your gift."

"But you—"

Callie hung up and stood by the phone, shivering. *It can't have been a dream.*

Yet here in this familiar room with the peeling plaster, the books cluttering the end table, the faded sheets, the root-bound plant—suddenly the adventure seemed impossibly fantastic. Carried away by aliens and forced to find her way home?

*I have to find Meg.*

The phone rang again. She jerked her hand away from it. That was either Lisa, trying again, or her mother.

It was a short bike ride to Meg's. At first Callie thought her friend was not there, for the blinds were drawn and no one answered the bell. She was turning to leave when the thump of footfalls drew her back, and Meg opened the door, wearing her bathrobe. Her hair, grown out to her usual chin-length style, was tousled from sleep.

"Cal, what are you doing here so early?"

"It's almost lunchtime, Meg," Callie said, stepping inside.

"But we didn't go to bed till dawn." She shut the door behind them.

Callie sat on the couch. Light filtered through the cracks around the shade, illuminating the gloom. "What did we do last night?"

Meg dropped onto the beanbag chair across from her, frowning. "You don't remember?"

"Do you?"

"We went out after the experiment. The lab techs threw a party." Meg brushed her long top hair out of her eyes. "Alex was there, and . . . some others." She laughed uneasily. "The punch must've been spiked. And I know I ate too many chili nachos because I've had the weirdest dreams."

Nachos and spiked punch?

*She's remembering snatches of the celebration before we came back to Earth,* Callie thought. Which was what they said would happen. *"It makes it easier for most to re-enter their old lives,"* Elhanu had told her. And Meg's hair would have grown out in the rejuvenation tank.

Callie swallowed. "What about the experiment itself?"

"You don't even remember that? The pegs in the boards? The ink blots? The virtual-reality stuff?"

"Virtual-reality stuff?"

"Yeah, there was this little car. And a white road . . ."

"What happened with Alex?"

Meg blushed. "To be honest, I can't remember. And somehow I don't even care. I hope I didn't make a fool of myself. At least we got the fifty dollars out of it."

"We did?"

"They gave it to us at the end." She picked up an envelope lying on the end table. "I know you got one, too. I saw you put it in your purse."

"Oh." She'd have to check when she got home.

Meg's eyes had focused on something in Callie's lap and now widened. "Is that an *engagement* ring?"

Callie looked down at her hands. Her right hand was nervously turning the ring on the third finger of her left—a gold ring, inset with a glittering blood crystal. Her heart leapt. It *had* happened!

Meg frowned. "Is there something you want to tell me?"

"No. Uh . . ." Callie pulled the ring off her left hand and put it on her right. "I was trying to discourage this guy, so I told him I was engaged. Don't you remember?"

Meg appeared unconvinced but accepted the story and moved on, wondering aloud what Jack would think if she called.

Callie tuned her out. Meg's memories—what few were left—were being distorted by the need to make them fit her old reality. Beyond that her mind had been washed. Just as Pierce's would be. The thought made Callie reel again. She stood in the middle of Meg's sentence. "I have to go."

Meg gaped at her, but Callie couldn't explain. She just had to find him.

When she got home, the phone was ringing again. After it stopped, she picked up the receiver, dialed information, and got the numbers for six Andrewses in Durango. She called them all. One was a secretary. One had died. One invited her via answering machine to leave a message. One's phone was disconnected. The other two did not answer.

She called local feed stores next, and hit pay dirt on the second try with a friendly and garrulous clerk. Of *course* she knew Andy Andrews, and wasn't it awful about his son gone missing?

"The sheriff's just called off the search yesterday," the woman said, "and why not? After eight days of looking and no sign, what else could he do? Poor boy's been gone over two weeks now, and is probably hurt besides. He's a tough kid, but the odds are against him in this. I hear Andy and Helen are taking it hard."

"I'm sorry to hear that," Callie said, her voice trembling. "Their son . . . would be Pierce?"

"Of course." The woman hesitated. "You don't know them well, then?"

"Not the parents, no."

Another silence. "Where'd you say you're calling from?"

"Tucson."

"*Arizona?*" Suspicion rang sharply in the woman's voice now. Again she paused, apparently to marshal her thoughts. "Look, I don't mean to be rude, miss, but do you know something about this situation that the Andrewses ought to hear?"

"I might. You wouldn't happen to have their phone number, would you?"

The clerk was reluctant to give it over, but she did. Unfortunately it was one Callie had already called, and again, no one answered. Probably out searching, she realized—but she was bitterly disappointed nonetheless. Of course, if she kept calling, someone was bound to answer eventually. But then what would she say? The feed store clerk's suspicion had made it clear how untenable her position was, and since she couldn't really tell anyone where Pierce had been, and since he himself wouldn't even remember her . . . well, hopefully she'd think of something. At least she had a number now.

But already the horrible suspicion that she wasn't supposed to find him had begun to gnaw at her.

Again the phone rang. It was her mother.

Callie hung up half an hour later, surprised at how easily she'd taken control of the conversation. Mom hadn't known what to make of her assertiveness, had hardly known what to say when Callie had refused to let her go on and on and deftly redirected the discussion. She had even managed to end the call in a relatively short time without being ugly.

She sat there a moment, feeling unexpectedly pleased.

*Find yourself*, the flyer had promised. Maybe she had. In more ways than one.

She surveyed her small living room with its bricks-and-boards bookshelf, and the drawing table littered with paint box, water jars, and brushes. Her books, sketches, and supply bins lay scattered across the floor where she'd left them Friday night. Her current project—a watercolor of desert wild flowers—stood taped to its board in a corner for viewing. It wasn't done. She had left it in that awkward stage where it looked awful and hopeless.

Except that it didn't anymore. In fact, she saw just what she needed to do.

At nine that evening, she set the finished painting, matted and framed, on the couch and surveyed it critically. Late afternoon shadows streaked across an adobe wall. The stems were a little awkward, but the values worked. And it was evocative, conjuring memories of her early-morning walks down the alley out back—

Her thought halted and excitement flushed her. Maybe there *was* a way to keep the fading memories alive, a way to hold on, if only in part.

She pulled her sketchpad from the cabinet and began blocking in the planes of a man's face. Miraculously, the image took shape before her, and her heart began to pound. Seeing his face made her exquisitely aware of how much he'd meant to her. She would go to Durango herself.

On Monday she quit her job to make the trip, withdrawing her meager savings and going into debt with Lisa. But in Durango, she learned Pierce had been found the day she'd first called, walking out of the woods with no memory of what had befallen him. His parents had immediately taken him to be evaluated at a hospital in Denver and hadn't been home since. She followed them there, but nothing worked out as she hoped. Neither hospitals nor doctors were willing to give out information to non-family members, and she didn't want to lie for fear of alienating her quarry once she finally caught up with them. They were sure to be just as suspicious and put off as the people she'd questioned in Durango, and, having no reasonable explanation for her interest to offer them, she knew lying would only make things worse.

In the end it didn't matter. With both funds and options depleted, she was finally forced to face the fact that she wasn't going to find him. Not without help, anyway. *"Trust Elhanu,"* he'd said. It seemed she had no other recourse.

———

Back in Tucson, she decided that rather than find a new job she would take the plunge as a full-time artist. Her mother had a fit, but Callie ignored her doomsaying and set to work gathering a body of paintings and approaching galleries. Within a month she had representation for her traditional watercolors.

Summer turned to fall. Her career took off. Three months after that fateful weekend, her work was selling briskly. In October, the fantasy paintings of her memories found a market. She won two national awards that winter, received a commission for a book cover the following spring, and had collectors in New York, Denver, and L.A. buying her work by the next summer. She bought a car and moved into a house on the eastside with horse property. She even bought a piano and began taking lessons. She knew she would never be a professional pianist—as Pierce might have been—but she practiced diligently, and it fed her soul.

Everyone marveled at the way everything suddenly came together for her, but Callie knew it for Elhanu's promised reward.

Her desperate need for Pierce waned. It helped that she had never known him in this life. She had only the ring and the painting in her bedroom to remind her. It was an oil of him standing on that hillside above Rimlight. She supposed she ought to take it down—and forget— but somehow she never got around to it.

Meg had also experienced the reward of prosperity. Shortly after the weekend in June she married Jack. He had made her deliriously happy. And before long, pregnant, as well.

---

The next June Lisa threw another party—a black-tie affair at the *Westin La Paloma*. Jack was out of town, so Callie dragged Meg along for moral support. Parties didn't intimidate her as they once had, but she still disliked them, and once again, Lisa had some guy for her to meet. His name was Alan, and Tom had met him on the plane.

"You'll like this one, Callie," Lisa had assured her. "And remember, it's black tie, so gussy up a little."

Reluctantly Callie obeyed. At least now she had something to gussy up in—a white chiffon dress she'd bought for the reception in New York. Hitting just above the knee, it had a Grecian style neckline and a figure-flattering drape. She put her hair up in a soft chignon, threw on a string of pearls, and even condescended to wear a pair of low heels. That was as gussy as she would go, however. If Lisa didn't like it, too bad.

"And we're not staying long," she told Meg as they drove across town. "We'll just eat and run."

"Just like old times, huh?" Meg asked with a smile. Her baby was due in a little over a month, and she was showing substantially. "Have you ever considered that this might be to your benefit? You might meet a client or potential client—"

"Of course I thought of that. Why else do you think I'm going willingly?"

"You might even like this Alan character."

"He's a stockbroker, Meg."

It was dusk as they parked and entered the resort. Heading for the Canyon Four Ballroom, they passed a dimpled blond youth manning the sign-up table for a seminar on Life Management, and Callie did a double take. The crowd around the table made it hard to see him, and she finally decided she didn't know him. But he was young enough, and handsome enough—he *could* have been Aggillon.

She couldn't see an ad for a seminar now without wondering—were they recruiting again? "Life Management" would certainly fit the bill. And the young preppies bent over the table wouldn't be there if they weren't searching for something. Maybe this time they'd find it.

"What?" Meg asked, noting the direction of her gaze. "You interested in that seminar?"

Callie laughed. "No. My life's doing just fine, thanks."

The hall and balcony outside the ballroom had been roped off, and a young hostess stood at the opening to take their invitations. As they stepped into the company of the glitterati—Lisa's parties always included state senators, city council members, bigwig business types, and local celebrities—a waiter passed with an empty hors d'oeuvre tray. The name on his badge brought Callie up short: Angelo. Before she could get a good look at him, though, he had disappeared into the crowd.

Meg was eyeing her again. "What is it now?"

Callie shook her head. "An attack of déjà vu. Come on. Let's find Lisa, and get Alan out of the way."

She had to admit the meetings with Lisa's prospects had not been so bad lately. Maybe it was because of her increased self-confidence, or maybe she had previously perceived negativity where there had been none. At least Alan was supposed to be interested in art.

The ballroom was decorated with potted palms and white twinkle lights. White-linened tables ringed a wooden dance floor, and a band played in the far corner. To the left, servers were restocking the buffet table. Callie spotted her sister talking to a group of gowned and tuxedoed movers and shakers near the gift table. Tom stood between her and a slender man in a tan, western-cut suit with wavy brown hair and eyes so brilliantly blue Callie could see their color from across the room.

Her knees went weak, and her breath left as if the wind had been knocked out of her. She managed to duck around a knot of people, then sagged against the wall. Meg was immediately at her side. "What's the matter? Are you sick?"

"I'm fine." She drew a deep breath. *It was just coincidence*, she thought. *It wasn't him. It was just someone who looked like him.* She drew herself together and stepped out for another glance.

It wasn't coincidence. And it wasn't hallucination. It was him. He looked up and met her eyes from across the room, but there was no sign of recognition. Just the brief glance, and then he was speaking to one of Lisa's friends.

She was shaking violently, aware of Meg frowning at her, but there was no way she could walk up to that group and speak to anyone normally. Abruptly she turned and headed out of the room.

Meg waddled after her. "Callie, where are you going?"

The restroom was clogged with women attending to their makeup and fixing their hair. Callie collapsed into a chair in the outer salon and stared at the wall. He didn't know her. He didn't know her at all. But what was he doing in Tucson? At her sister's birthday party?

Meg pulled up a chair. "All right, what gives?"

Callie looked at her. How could she ever explain?

"Did you forget to eat again today?" her friend asked with narrowed eyes.

"No."

Meg raised a skeptical brow. "What did you have for lunch?"

"I had a . . . I don't remember."

Meg stood and hauled her to her feet. "Come on. Let's get you some food."

Halfway to the buffet Lisa pounced, hugging Callie, admiring her dress and hair, then urging her to "Come say hello to Alan."

"Oh, Lisa . . ." How could she even be civil to Alan when Pierce was in the room, maybe even standing beside him? She wouldn't be able to think, much less talk.

"I think you'll like this one."

"A stockbroker Tom met on an airplane?"

"He's not just a stockbroker. He's a pianist and a student, and he used to be a cowboy. He's also quite good-looking."

Callie felt the blood drain from her face. *Cowboy?* No, that made no sense. Why would he call himself Alan?

Lisa's smile turned to a frown. "Are you all right?"

"She's only about to pass out from low blood sugar," Meg said.

Lisa's frown deepened. "Did you forget to eat again?"

"I'll get something at the buffet," Callie said, "then I'll come over, okay?"

The frown was disapproving but uncertain. "Okay, but don't wait too long. You've got competition, you know. He's rich as well as handsome."

*Rich?* Pierce hadn't been rich. His father's ranch had been in trouble. . . . But then, his financial situation had likely changed as dramatically as her own this last year. . . .

Could it really be him? The pieces were falling into place, and suddenly she was panic-stricken. What if she did the wrong thing, said the wrong thing? What if she turned him off?

The buffet was only lightly attended. She strolled alongside it, but nothing seemed appealing. Her stomach was too knotted to even think about eating. Someone came up beside her as she stared at the offerings.

"The taquitos are pretty good." His voice thrummed through her like a clarion call.

"Are they?" She made herself look up at him. Mercy! When had he gotten so handsome?

He cocked a brow, still not showing the slightest hint of recognition. "Are you all right?"

"I'm fine, thank you." She tore her eyes away and put a piece of parsley on her plate.

"Maybe you should sit down or something."

"No, I just need to eat. I get caught up in my work and forget to."

What was she going to do with this parsley?

He was regarding her curiously. "You're Lisa's sister, aren't you? The artist."

"Yes." With trembling fingers she picked up the tongs and fumbled two taquitos onto her plate.

"I'm a big fan of your work."

She gaped at him.

He grinned and she nearly died. "The Henley Gallery's practically next door to my office in Denver."

"That's my fantasy work."

"Yes. Your traditional work is excellent, too. I saw some over at Tom and Lisa's. But the fantasy pieces are so evocative I could swear I'm standing right there. Are they based on any particular place?"

She stared at him intently, knowing she was being weird, unable to help herself. Was he remembering something? "I . . . uh . . . well, not on any specific earthly place, no." She added a cheese enchilada to her taquitos. *Hurry! Small talk—anything.* "So, uh, how do you know my sister?"

"Actually, I know your brother-in-law. We've worked together over the Net. He suggested I vacation in Tucson, but it was pure coincidence we ended up on the same plane."

Callie's nape hairs stood upright. "I assume you're in stocks, too, then?"

He nodded.

"You're not Alan, are you?"

He smiled his wonderful smile. "Lisa told you about me?"

"A little." She hesitated, wondering how to ask this without it sounding strange. "She said you were a cowboy before you were a stockbroker."

"I grew up on a ranch. We sold out last year. I'd been researching investments and decided to risk some of the proceeds. It's worked out well enough for my folks to buy a smaller place outside Denver."

"And you live with them?"

"I have a place in the city, though I have to admit, I prefer country living."

"With computers and faxes and teleconferences, I'd think you could."

"Yes, but I'm also going to school—finishing up my degree."

"In business?"

"History. With a minor in language."

She shook her head, marveling. Always some new facet to surprise her.

"I never planned to be a broker forever, and I've done well enough that it seems I won't have to."

"So what language are you studying?"

"Greek."

Now she was dumbfounded. "Greek? Whatever would you—"

Before she could finish, Lisa swooped down upon them. "I see you've met. Great! Did Alan tell you he's a fan of your work?"

"Actually, he did."

Lisa beamed at them as if she expected them to fall into each other's arms on the spot. They stared back, and her smile broadened. "I'll leave you two to get acquainted."

After she left, Pierce said, "Do I detect a bit of matchmaking here?"

Callie blushed hotly. "She's always doing this. I'm sorry."

"Well, I'm not." He smiled. "Though she must not be very successful if she's always doing it."

"Hope springs eternal."

"Ah."

When they reached the end of the food line, Callie remembered Meg, still trailing behind, listening intently. When she introduced them, Meg smiled and bobbed her head and immediately made her exit. "I see your mom over there," she said. "It's been ages since we've visited."

Grinning slyly, she waddled off. Callie rolled her eyes and followed Pierce to a table on the fringes.

"I wouldn't have pegged you for an Alan," she said, picking up a taquito.

"No? What would you have pegged me for?"

"Something unusual."

"Like Poindexter or Cuthbert?"

She laughed. "Not that unusual."

"Well, Alan's my middle name. I've been Pierce most of my life."

"Why the change?"

"There's a firm in Denver called Lane, Simpson, Andrews, and Pierce. I wanted to avoid the confusion when I put my own shingle out. And Alan Andrews has a kind of ring."

"Pierce suits you better, though."

"That's what my mother says."

Callie flushed and concentrated on her taquito. If her heart beat any faster, it would go into ventricular fibrillation. And she was coming on way too strong.

Gradually, though, she relaxed. He was still easy to talk to, even if he didn't remember her. Artful questioning confirmed what she had learned last summer—how he had wandered out of the mountains after two weeks of allegedly being lost, remembering nothing. Since his horse had returned earlier, it was assumed he'd fallen and hit his head. His parents had taken him to a round of specialists in Denver and had been forced to sell the ranch to pay the bills, but nothing had helped. He still couldn't remember.

After dinner Lisa opened her gifts, then cut the cake. Pierce volunteered to get some for both of them, and as soon as he walked off, Meg collapsed into his chair, clasping her hands on the table and leaning toward Callie. "He looks *just* like the guy in that picture in your bedroom! The one you made up. Did you notice?"

*Did I notice?* Callie looked from Pierce to Meg and fought to keep a straight face. "You think so?"

"The likeness is uncanny."

"You're exaggerating." Her eyes returned to Pierce, lean and fit in the tan suit. "This guy's *much* better looking."

Meg gaped at her. "You're taken with him!"

"Maybe."

"We've known each other too long for 'maybe.' And if I'm any judge, he's not exactly bored."

"You think so?"

Meg rolled her eyes. "Are jalapeños hot? Oh, he's coming back. I gotta say hello to Tom." She stood. "And you didn't believe in love at first sight."

As Pierce settled at her side, a white-haired waiter reached over her shoulder to fill her coffee cup. She glanced up as he turned away, and a jolt went up her spine. But he disappeared behind a knot of people without turning, and she decided she must have imagined the likeness.

Before long the band started up, and of course, Pierce asked her to dance, and of course, she said yes, even knowing Lisa would gloat for months. Stepping into his arms was just like the first time—she was nervous, jittery, aware of all those little sparks from his touch. They danced two fast numbers and a slow one, and by then she was hopelessly in love with him all over again.

"You know," he murmured alongside her ear, "this is going to sound weird, but I keep wondering—have we met before?"

She drew back to look at him. "Why do you ask?"

A crease furrowed his brow. "Because I have the strangest feeling I already know you."

She could not keep the shock from her face, and he grimaced. "Coming on a little strong, am I? Sorry."

"It's not that," she assured him. "You just surprised me."

He gazed blindly at the crowd behind her. "The blank spot from last summer haunts me. I keep trying to remember, and sometimes something will trigger the feeling that, if I can just turn this corner in my mind, it will all come back." He paused, dropped his eyes to her face. "You're sure you weren't in Colorado last June?"

"Positive. Are you sure you were?"

He gave her a funny look, and she trained her gaze over his shoulder again, wondering why she had asked *that*. Now he'd think she was making fun of him. But to try to explain—

And then she saw the white-haired waiter again, the one who had poured her coffee, the one who looked startlingly like Elhanu. He stood near the table, watching them, and as her gaze met his, he smiled, his dark eyes twinkling.

*He understood too much to lose it all.* The words sounded in her mind as clearly as if he had spoken in her ear.

*You mean eventually he'll remember me?* Callie asked silently.

*You and all the rest of it. Quite rapidly now, I expect. Let him find it on his own, though. Rushing things will only distress you both unnecessarily.*

*But I thought the rejuvenation process removed—*

*Normally, it does. However, his mind was just so saturated with under-standing that much of it is still there. Finding you will finally allow him to access it.* He paused. *But don't concern yourself overly with the past, Callie. The future is what matters.*

He gave her a small nod, then set down his coffeepot and pushed through the swinging door to the kitchen beyond.

She wanted to run after him but knew she wouldn't find him. Not there anyway.

"You know, that's the weirdest thing about it," Pierce said softly in her ear. "For the longest time I've felt I wasn't in Colorado. That I was somewhere else, and that I was there for longer than two weeks. But that doesn't make sense, does it? Because where else could I have been?"

# The Future of Fiction Is *Thrilling!*

## Sci-Fi the Way It's Supposed to be Written

At the heart of Kathy Tyers's FIREBIRD trilogy rests an examination of faith, courage, and love, as well as an intriguing portrait of a woman determined to live by her newfound faith. Compelling plots, distant worlds, and the epic battle between good and evil combine in three exciting books you'll rank among the best of classic science-fiction.

*"A science-fiction stunner, wonderfully plotted, and it anticipates the coming Messiah. A must read for people of science and people of faith."*
—Bob Briner, author of *The Leadership Lessons of Jesus*

*Firebird* • *Fusion Fire* • *Crown of Fire* by Kathy Tyers

## "Buckle in, take a deep breath, and get ready for a fantastic ride." —Moody Magazine

Taut and exciting, *Oxygen*, a futuristic thriller from Christy Award-winner Randall Ingermanson and John Olson, is a blend of suspense, romance, and emotion that's impossible to find in Christian fiction. It will have you holding your breath as the intricate plot unwinds and as four astronauts on a doomed mission to Mars come to realize the importance of faith and the reality of something bigger than even the universe.

*Oxygen* by Randall Ingermanson and John Olson

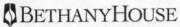

## ❖ BETHANYHOUSE

11400 Hampshire Ave. S., Minneapolis, MN 55438
1-800-328-6109   www.bethanyhouse.com